Praise for

JENNIFER McMAHON

THE DROWNING KIND

"*The Drowning Kind* is satisfying on every level: marvelously chilling, elegantly written, a true page-turner. I couldn't wait to get to the end; I also wanted to savor every page. Jennifer McMahon is a master of mood."
— Janelle Brown, *New York Times* bestselling author of *Pretty Things* and *Watch Me Disappear*

"The details are so juicy and the revelations of how the past has led to the present so deftly done that you can't help being terrified."
— *The New York Times Book Review*

"McMahon has a gift for creating creepy atmosphere and letting spooky suggestions linger in the mind. She's also adept at weaving legends and stories into the fabric of what feels like real life, because her characters are so believably vulnerable. For best results, read it on a dark and stormy night—in a well-lit room, far away from the water."
— *Kirkus Reviews* (starred review)

"Two sisters, a cursed Vermont house, and a spring-fed pool with a mind of its own. An otherworldly treat."
— *People*

"*The Drowning Kind* is both a haunting exploration of grief and a tale that will make the hairs on the back of your neck stand up. You'll stay up late reading, but take my advice: Whatever you do, don't go in the water."
— Simone St. James, *New York Times* bestselling author of *The Sun Down Motel*

"Lush, dark, and relentlessly eerie—a fast-paced tug-of-war between suspicion and the supernatural."

—Sue Rainsford, author of *Follow Me to Ground*

THE INVITED

"Jennifer McMahon's latest premise is utterly chilling: Imagine you don't stumble upon a haunted house; you build one. *The Invited* deserves a special spot in the canon of great ghost stories and will remind McMahon's readers why she is such a worthy literary descendant of Shirley Jackson."

—Chris Bohjalian, bestselling author of *The Flight Attendant*

"A dream home becomes one of nightmares for a husband and wife attempting to start a new life in the woods of Vermont. Board by board, stone by stone, tragic events of the past creep toward the light in this delicious slow burn of a haunted tale."

—J. D. Barker, bestselling author of *The Fourth Monkey* and *Dracul*

THE WINTER PEOPLE

"Jennifer McMahon is a writer of exceptional talent, and *The Winter People* is a hypnotic, gripping, and deeply moving thriller. With her beautifully drawn characters and complex, layered, and painfully suspenseful story, McMahon has woven a dream from which I didn't want to wake—and couldn't have even if I wanted to."

—Lisa Unger, author of *In the Blood*

"This is not a book that will sit unread on anyone's bedside table for very long. Open the first few pages and you are swept into a swift, dark current of unfolding events that will hold you enthralled. Much more than a spooky mystery of murder and mayhem, *The Winter People* blends the anguish of loss and the yearning for connection into one great story, well told."

—Kate Alcott, author of *The Dressmaker*

Also by Jennifer McMahon

Jennifer McMahon

THE DROWNING KIND

POCKET BOOKS

New York   London   Toronto   Sydney   New Delhi

Pocket Books
An Imprint of Simon & Schuster, Inc.
1230 Avenue of the Americas
New York, NY 10020

This Pocket Books paperback edition June 2022

POCKET and colophon are registered trademarks of Simon & Schuster, Inc.

For information about special discounts for bulk purchases, please contact Simon & Schuster Special Sales at 1-866-506-1949 or business@simonandschuster.com.

The Simon & Schuster Speakers Bureau can bring authors to your live event. For more information or to book an event, contact the Simon & Schuster Speakers Bureau at 1-866-248-3049 or visit our website at www.simonspeakers.com.

Interior design by Davina Mock-Maniscalco

Manufactured in the United States of America

10 9 8 7 6 5 4 3 2 1

ISBN 978-1-9821-7919-9
ISBN 978-1-9821-5394-6 (ebook)

For everyone out there who has the good sense to be a little afraid when swimming in deep, dark water. You tell yourself there's nothing down there, but there is. There always is.

In the water, dark and deep
where she waits, fast asleep

All alone, pale and cold,
don't wake her up, or she'll catch hold

Her soothing voice, so soft and low
is the last thing you'll ever know

Four simple words whispered in your ear,
a gentle wind only you can hear:
Come swimming with me

—Rhyme recited by children in Brandenburg, Vermont,
  circa 1900

THE
DROWNING
KIND

prologue

July 18, 2000

"The dead have nothing to fear," Lexie said.

The two of us treaded water, lips blue, teeth chattering.

My sister wore her new light-blue bikini, the color of the sky, and I had on one of her hand-me-downs, the fabric so worn that it was sheer in places.

"So when we play the Dead Game, we keep our eyes open, no matter what." Her face was as serious as serious got. "Swear it? Swear you'll keep them open?"

I nodded.

"Even if you see Rita?" she asked.

"Shut up, Lex."

"She's down there, you know. She's waiting for us."

"Shut up!" I swam away from her, closer to the edge of the pool.

She laughed, shook her head. "Don't be such a chicken." Then she seemed to feel bad, to take pity on me maybe; to remember I was only nine. She put out her hand, pointer finger extended. "Come on," she called. I swam back to her, reached out, crossed her finger with my own. "The X girls," she said.

"Now and forever," I finished. Then we hooked our fingers together, squeezed, and let go.

"If she comes for one of us, she'll have to take us both," Lexie said.

"Lex!"

"On three," she said. "One. Two. Keep your eyes open, Jax. I'll know if you cheat."

I took the deepest breath I could.

"Three!"

We put our faces under and floated, suspended in the dark water like twins in the womb.

Our grandmother's pool was twenty by forty-five feet and surrounded by carved granite. Moss grew in the cracks between the damp, gray stones; the sides were stained green with algae. Because it was spring fed, there was no pump, only an outlet at the far end that drained into a stone-lined canal that made its way across the yard and down to the brook below, which led, eventually, to the river. Weeds grew along the edges, clinging to the stone, floating with Lexie and me. When they got too thick, Gram would scoop them out; for a time, she kept a trout, saying the fish helped keep the water clean and free of insects. My sister loved the pool. I hated it; the water was black—so dark that you couldn't see your feet when you treaded water. It stank of rot and sulphur, tasted like burnt matches and rust, and was colder than the ice bath my mother plunged me in once when my fever got too high. It sucked the breath out of you; numbed your limbs, left your skin red and your lips blue. Each time we came out of the water, we really did look like the dead girls we were pretending to be.

Lexie and I spent every summer at Sparrow Crest with Gram, in the tiny village of Brandenburg, Vermont. It was a three-hour drive (yet felt worlds away) from our dull ranch house in the suburbs of Massachusetts, part of a huge grid of equally dull houses with postage-stamp yards and a garage if you were lucky. Sparrow Crest was a dark, damp, sprawling place, made of stone and huge hand-hewn beams, covered in decades of ivy. There was a half-round window in the front like an eye. Behind the house were two immense hills, thick with trees. Mom and Ted would stay with us for a long weekend here and there, but mostly it was the three of us. Gram looked forward to our visits all year. She was "lonely in her big old house all by herself." That's what Mom said.

So our summer lives centered around visiting our grandmother—and the pool. Gram had a lot of rules about swimming: We couldn't go in the pool unless she was home. We were never to go in alone. We had to take breaks and warm up after half an hour at most. And we were never, ever to swim at night. "Too dangerous," she pronounced. As if she'd needed to warn us—the knowledge of what had happened to our aunt Rita, our mother's baby sister, who drowned when she was only seven years old, should have been enough.

I let myself picture it as I held my breath beside my sister playing the Dead Game: a little girl floating, hair fanned around her, tangled with weeds. A girl who would never grow up. I knew Rita was the reason we could never let Gram see us playing the Dead Game. The one time she'd caught us floating facedown together, she'd ordered us out of the water, shaking, terrified. Lexie explained it was a breath-holding game, but Gram announced a new pool rule: We must never, ever do such a morbid thing again, or she'd ban us from the water altogether.

We knew we shouldn't play it, but it was Lexie's favorite, and she always won. We only played the game when we knew Gram was in the living room watching her afternoon programs and wouldn't catch us. But still, the idea that she might, made it seem extra dangerous. Gram didn't get mad often, but when she did it was like one of those summer thunderstorms that shook the house to its very foundation, that had you hiding under the covers, praying for it to pass.

Gram had grown up at Sparrow Crest. She'd been married here, under a big canopy set up in the backyard. She had her babies here, three healthy girls born in the upstairs bedroom with a local midwife attending. She swam in the pool every day, even did cold plunges in the winter, chopping the ice until she had a hole wide enough to slip into. She'd strip off her parka and ski pants to reveal her polka-dot bathing suit, then lower herself feetfirst until only her head popped out like a seal. She claimed it kept her young, that it rejuvenated her. Gram seemed strong and brave to me, but Lexie once told me she had a sickness called agoraphobia.

"She doesn't seem sick," I'd argued. The only part I understood was "gore," which meant blood and guts and things in R-rated movies I wasn't allowed to see.

"It's not a sickness you can see, dummy," Lexie shot back. "Aunt Diane told me."

Lexie was right: Gram almost never left the house, had never learned to drive, had all her groceries delivered. She was tough enough to chop a hole in the ice and swim in January, so it was hard to think of her being trapped by her own mind.

———

Facedown, we floated. Lexie timed us with a fancy diving watch she'd gotten for her birthday: My record for staying under the water was one minute, twelve seconds. Lexie had gone up to two minutes. She was like a fish, my sister. Sometimes, I was sure she had secret gills no one could see. But I was a creature of land, and my heart did funny things when I was in the water and not moving to stay warm. I lost all sense of time.

I had no idea how long we'd been under now, and it took every ounce of willpower not to swim furiously to the edge and pull myself out of the pool. I kept my eyes open, scanning the darkness, searching for a glimpse of Rita: a flash of her white nightgown, a pale hand reaching up from the depths.

I knew from old photos that Rita was tiny, a girl with dark hair, bright blue eyes, that she was never a camera hog like her two older sisters. And I knew she had loved to read. Lexie and I found books she'd written her name in: *Charlotte's Web*, *Little House on the Prairie*, the Ramona books, *Charlie and the Chocolate Factory*. Our favorite board game in the house was Snakes and Ladders because it had Rita's name in big block letters on the inside of the box, along with a drawing of a snake and a little girl in a dress—Rita's imaginary friend Martha. Whenever we found something with her name on it, we'd talk about why Rita had gone to the pool in the middle of the night; whether it was Mom, Gram, or Aunt Diane who found her floating the next morning. And my sister loved to torment me with made-up stories about Rita. "She's still here, you know. She lives in the pool. Haven't you seen her down there? When you open your eyes underwater? She *lives* in the pool, but she comes out sometimes."

I pictured it, pale little Rita with her dark hair dripping wet, pulling herself up out of the pool, eyes on the house where other children were playing with her toys, reading her books.

"Listen," Lexie would whisper late at night when she snuck into my room, crawled under the covers with me. "Don't you hear that? That squish, squish, squish of footsteps? She's coming for you. Coming for us both."

———————

My fingers and toes were numb. My lungs were crying out for air. My heart was banging inside my chest, but I held still, kept my eyes wide open.

We floated, my sister and I.

Two dead girls, side by side, bodies bumping against each other.

Alone, but together.

chapter one

June 14, 2019

"How are things going at school, Declan?" I asked. Declan was hunched over a drawing he'd been working on for the past twenty minutes, showing no sign of having heard me.

He was my last appointment of the day. The client before him had been a fourteen-year-old girl with PTSD—listening to her detail her abuse was always gut-wrenching. I usually made sure she was my last appointment, because after an hour of helping her navigate trauma and work on coping mechanisms, I was drained, sick-feeling and headachy. But it was an extra-busy week—too many kids and too little time—so I'd scheduled Declan at the end of the day. Things had been going so well with him lately that I'd actually been looking forward to our session.

I'd been seeing Declan for nearly eight months. For the first three, he had sat drawing, giving monosyllabic answers to all my questions. But then, in the fourth month, we'd made a breakthrough. He'd started talking. He'd drawn a picture of a bird's nest and in it, three blue eggs. Resting in with them was a smaller, speckled brown egg.

"Robin's eggs?" I asked, pointing at the blue ones. He nodded.

"But what's this brown one?"

"Cowbird egg," he said. "Cowbirds don't make nests of their own. The females lay eggs in other birds' nests."

"For real?" I asked. "What happens when they hatch?"

"The mother robin or blue jay takes care of it, treats it like the others. But it's *not* like the others."

This led to a discussion about what it might feel like to be the odd one out, to not belong. Declan loved animals and had an encyclopedic knowledge of animal facts, and I learned to use them as a springboard for our discussions—I even added nature books and field guides to the shelves in my office for us to look through together. Soon, he was opening up about his father's abandonment, and how his mother continued to lie to him about it—to say he'd be back any day, or that he'd called to check in on Declan and had told her how much he missed his son. "It's all a bunch of stupid lies," Declan told me. "She's always telling these crazy stories that I know aren't true. She thinks she's protecting me, but really she's just lying."

Declan had come to trust me, to share things that he wasn't able to share with anyone else. But today, it seemed we were back to square one.

I tried to relax my shoulders, put aside my fierce headache, and focus on figuring out what was going on right now with this little boy who sat at the small table in my office, studiously ignoring me. The drawing paper was crumpled in places, damp from his sweaty hand; he was grinding the blue crayon into angry, cyclonic swirls. I studied his face, his body language. His dark hair was tousled. His breathing was quick and shallow. The crayon broke in two. He picked up both halves, clenched them in his fist, and continued to scribble hard.

"Did something happen at school?" I asked. "Or at home? Anything you want to tell me about?" I felt like I had a spike going through my left eye. Even my teeth ached. I'd been getting migraines since I was twelve, and had learned there wasn't much that helped them other than holing up in a dark, quiet place, which wasn't an option right now.

Declan was nine years old. He'd been to three schools in the last year, but we'd finally found one that seemed to be a perfect fit—small, alternative, and with a nature-based curriculum that he loved. His mother and I had pushed hard to get him accepted, meeting with the principal and the behavioral special-ist, convincing them to take a chance. Declan seemed to be thriving. He was doing well with academics and fitting in socially. Students spent half the day outside; there was a community nature center, gardens, and a pond. They'd been raising their own trout from eggs— Declan gave me weekly trout updates during our ses-sions. They were nearly big enough to release, and the whole school was going to have a big party on the last day and release the fish into the pond. Declan had been so excited: Little fish he'd watched hatch were ready to leave the tank.

"How are the trout doing?" I tried.

He scribbled harder, keeping his eyes on the paper. "I had a dream about them. A bad dream."

"Yeah?" I leaned in. "Can you tell me about it?"

He frowned, stared down at the furious swirls. "They weren't who they said they were."

I took in a breath. Rubbed at my left eye, which had started to water. "Who weren't? The trout?"

He nodded. "They were something else. They'd *turned* into something else."

"What did they turn into?"

He didn't answer, just pursed his lips tighter.

"Dreams can be scary," I said at last. "But they're only dreams, Declan. They can't follow you into real life."

He looked up at me. "Promise?"

"Promise," I said. "The fish in your class, they're still the same beautiful trout they always were, right?"

He looked up and gave me a half smile. "Right," he said. "They are."

"And you're going to let them go in the pond next week, right?"

He nodded, started putting all the crayons away. He took the drawing, crumpled it up, put it in the trash.

"Are you feeling sad about letting them go? Worried, maybe?"

He thought a minute. "No. It's time. They're meant to be free, not live in a tank."

"And you'll still be able to see them," I said. "They'll be in the pond. You can go visit them anytime you want."

He nodded. "Ms. Evans says we can even catch them in nets if we want, but I don't think it'll be that easy, do you? If I was one of those fish, I wouldn't let anyone catch me ever again."

He spent the rest of the session talking excitedly about all the activities planned for the final week of school: the trout release, a picnic, a field trip to the science museum. When he left, his mom and I confirmed his appointment for next Friday.

"Have a great last week of school," I told him.

As I was closing up my office for the night, I pulled the picture out of the trash. I opened up the paper and smoothed it out. He'd drawn what appeared to be a turbulent sea with big, dark fish. His nightmare trout? They had black eyes, open mouths with jagged teeth. Some had long tentacles. And there was a little stick figure in with them, sinking, being pulled down by the tentacles, drowning. Himself?

I looked closer. No. This was not a little boy with dark hair and eyes. This was a woman with long black hair, a white shirt, and gray pants.

It was me.

———————

I unlocked the door to my studio apartment, shouldering my way in, my laptop bag bulging with my work computer and notes. I set it down on the floor and attended to the first order of business: pouring myself a very large glass of wine and taking three ibuprofen. I took my first fortifying sip, then went over to the bed, stripped off my social worker outfit, and put on sweats and a They Might Be Giants T-shirt. My ex-boyfriend, Phil, had bought the shirt for me. Phil enjoyed outings of all sorts—concerts, plays, basketball games. I was more of a stay-at-home-and-watch-Netflix kind of gal, but Phil insisted that going out on proper dates was something normal couples did, so I went along with it. Phil was long gone, but the T-shirt was still going strong.

As I settled in on the couch and put my head back, I thought of Declan's words: *They weren't who they said they were.* And his drawing. I made a mental note to call the school on Monday to check in with his teacher, Ms. Evans, and see if she'd noticed any changes in his demeanor.

My job could be stressful as shit, but it had its good days, too. And on the good days—the breakthrough days when a cowbird was not just a cowbird or when a girl came into my office grinning, saying she'd used the techniques we'd been working on to get through a panic attack at school—it was all worth it. Even though I'd been in private practice for a little less than a year, my schedule was always full, and I had a waiting list of clients. Sadly, there was no shortage of messed-up kids. I gravitated toward the tough cases— the kids everyone else had given up on. My undergrad was in psychology, and I worked in community mental health out of college for several years before deciding to go back to school for my master's in social work. I did it while working full time, taking night classes, filling my weekends with reading and writing. My area of focus was always kids.

It didn't take a genius to figure out why I'd gotten into this line of work. And it was something my own therapist, Barbara, was fond of pointing out: "You've never gotten over the fact that you couldn't fix your sister when she got sick. You couldn't save her, so you're trying to save all these other kids." I'd been seeing Barbara since my undergrad days and was pretty sure she knew me far better than I knew myself—not that hard, since I rarely pointed my carefully honed skills of observation and insight at myself, figuring it was far more productive to save it for my clients.

I opened my eyes, took a sip of wine, and noticed the digital answering machine was blinking. Nine new messages. My stomach knotted.

I knew exactly who it was without needing to push play: Lexie. And if she'd called this many times, she was, no doubt, off her meds again. When she was off her meds, she forgot that we didn't talk anymore. That we were now properly estranged.

As if on cue, the phone rang again—call number ten. I reached for it—following some deeply ingrained instinct, the need to connect with my sister—then stopped myself.

"Jax? Jax!" she shouted into the machine. "The measurements don't lie. It's science! The fucking scientific method. Construct a hypothesis. Test your hypothesis."

I could go months without hearing from her, then all at once, I'd get a burst of Lexie. It was like all of a sudden, she remembered: *Hey,* I've got a sister. *Maybe I should give her a call and say something really fucking cryptic.*

And the truth was, we'd barely spoken at all over the past year or so. Since Gram died—a heart attack while in Arizona, the one vacation she'd ever taken—and left most of her savings to Lexie, as well as her huge house, Sparrow Crest, the place we'd loved so much when we were kids and dreamed of one day living in together. Aunt Diane got a small chunk of the money, though she was doing fine financially and didn't need it. Me, ass-deep in student loan debt, driving a fifteen-year-old car and living in a shoebox apartment on the other side of the country: I got my grandfather's old coin collection and some first-edition books. None of it turned out to be worth a thing. It was petty, feeling furious and scorned for being left out of the will; my sister had always been everyone's favorite. I knew it but couldn't help it. I was pissed off and tired of pretending that I wasn't. I stopped calling to check in on Lexie. I made excuses for not visiting the house that was now *her* house. I relied on our aunt Diane to keep me informed on Lexie's life back in Brandenburg. Barbara encouraged me to set boundaries, to distance myself from my sister. She told me that distancing myself from my sister was the healthiest choice I'd made in years, one that both Lexie and I were sure to benefit from. "Lexie needs to learn to take better care of herself, and you jumping in to help her all the time isn't helping her. And you, Jackie, need to focus on your own life and well-being. You need to learn who you are outside your sister's orbit."

It still didn't feel right, not picking up the phone. Part of me longed to answer, to reconnect with my sister, to apologize for being such a shit over this past year; to tell her I'd made a terrible mistake.

"Over fifty meters!" Lex was shouting, fast and furious, as I sat sipping my wine.

"Seven yesterday, over fifty today," Lex said, nearly breathless with frenzy. "Oh, Jax, you've gotta call me. No, better yet, you've gotta get on a plane. You've gotta come see this. Please, Jax! You're the only one who would understand this!"

She clicked off. Less than a minute later, the phone rang again.

Lexie didn't have my cell number. I told her, via Aunt Diane, that I'd given up my cell phone, that the bills were too high, and I was going to be one of those old-school landline people who used an answering machine.

"Jax?" Lexie said into the machine. "I know you're there. I can feel you listening."

I turned the volume all the way down. There was no way to mute it, but I could lower it to a dull murmur. Guilt gnawed away at my stomach as I walked away from my sister's disembodied voice, poured myself the hottest bath I could coax from the old water heater in the basement, complete with a handful of calming salts. I shut the door, tuned the radio to jazz, and did my best to forget all about my sister. I watched the faucet drip into the tub, saw the rust stains years of leaks had left in the old porcelain. I leaned back, closed my eyes, and went under, trying to still my mind, the water filling my ears and nose, muffling the world around me.

———————

Hours later, the bottle of wine was long gone; I'd had a dinner of cheese, crackers, and olives and passed out on the couch watching *The Body Snatcher*. My sister had stopped calling around eleven.

The dull ring of the phone woke me a little before one. I was still stretched out on the couch, but Boris Karloff was gone and there was an exercise infomercial on. My mouth tasted like wine, and my stomach churned unpleasantly. My head still ached.

"Jax?" Lexie cooed into the machine. Even though I'd turned it down as low as it would go, I still heard her. "This is important. The biggest thing that has ever happened to me. Or to anyone. This changes everything."

I stumbled off the couch, reached for the phone. By the time I picked it up, my sister was gone.

———————

The next morning, after half a pot of coffee and three Advil, I sucked it up and called my sister. She didn't answer. I left a message, apologizing for not getting back to her sooner. I lied and said I'd been away overnight and had just gotten home. I had a cover story figured out—a conference in Seattle on mood disorders. I probably wouldn't need it—Lexie didn't ask questions about my life, especially not when she was manic; she was too caught up in her own drama.

"Call me back when you get this," I said. "I'd love to catch up."

I let myself imagine it: How easy it would be to fall into the familiar patter of conversation with her; how comforting to slip back in like there had never been a rift.

But it wouldn't be like that, not really. Lexie was off her meds, and I'd be thrust into the role of coaxing her to get back on them, to go see her doctor, to seek help. I could already hear Barbara's advice: "Boundaries, Jackie. Remember your boundaries."

I went through my usual Saturday routine: the gym, grocery shopping, a trip to the dry cleaners. I called her again before lunch. Then in the afternoon. I imagined her at Sparrow Crest, looking at the ringing phone, too wrapped up in her own mania to answer. Or, maybe she was being petty. *You don't pick up for me, I don't pick up for you.*

Touché.

"It's me again," I said to voice mail. "If you're mad at me, I get it, but do me a favor and call me back anyway, okay?" My words were clipped, annoyance coming through loud and clear. Around three, I was actually worried enough, or maybe I was just pissed off enough, to call Aunt Diane.

"Lexie is off her meds again," I said instead of hello.

"Is she? I haven't heard a peep from her. Not a single message."

Odd. When my sister had a manic episode, she called everyone, starting with my father and Diane. "I guess that makes me the lucky one," I said. "She's left me over a dozen, none making sense. And now she's not answering her phone."

"Do you want me to go check on her? I'm heading out that way this evening. There's a poetry reading in Hanover."

"Poetry reading?"

"I'm not getting all hoity-toity intellectual. Are you imagining me all beatnik with a black turtleneck and beret? I'm actually in hot pursuit of a woman—a poetry lover."

"Really?" I snorted into the phone. Our fifty-six-year-old aunt had divorced our uncle Ralph ten years ago, come out of the closet, and now seemed to be with a new woman each week, "making up for lost time." Diane usually called me at least once a week to check in, but it had been over two weeks since I'd heard from her. I figured either she was super busy at work or caught up in one of her brief, feverish flings.

"Nothing like wine, a bookstore, and a little poetry to open one up to the powers of love."

"I'm not sure how much love has to do with it," I said.

"'What's love got to do with it?'" she sang, doing her best Tina Turner. Then she stopped, chuckled. "Are you calling it a secondhand emotion? Speaking of which—" She paused, seemed to hesitate, then plunged ahead. "Have you heard anything from Phil?"

I blew out an exasperated breath. "Phil and I have been officially over for nearly a year now."

I closed my eyes, saw his face when I'd told him it was finally over. His normally ruddy cheeks went pale, his lips turned blue like he'd forgotten to breathe. We were in the grocery store, of all places, and he had been pointing out for the millionth time how much easier it would be if we moved in together, so we wouldn't need to buy things like separate toothpaste and bags of coffee and toilet bowl cleaner. We were in the toothpaste aisle when I told him that I couldn't ever be the person he was asking me to be, the person who would share everything with him.

"I know," Diane said. "But you said he was still calling. I thought maybe . . ."

"Maybe what?"

"You'd decide to give him a second chance, Jax. You're far too young to be playing old maid. He was a good one."

This was too much.

"You never even met him!"

"And whose fault is that?" she asked. "You two were together what, like three years on and off, and you never once brought him home."

I stiffened. This was one of the many ongoing arguments I'd had with Phil before I finally had the sense to break things off. I wouldn't let him meet my family. I was too closed off. Not willing to commit or make myself emotionally vulnerable.

I wouldn't even let him come with me to Gram's funeral.

"Don't you think that's more than a little fucked up, Jackie?" he'd asked. "How are we supposed to move forward with this relationship with all these careful walls you build around parts of your life? Jesus, you know everything about my family, and I know next to nothing about yours."

But these were learned behaviors, as Barbara aptly pointed out in our weekly sessions. Defense mechanisms after a lifetime with Lexie, when I had no room in my life for friends or boyfriends. I learned at a young age not to bring anyone home because she might lash out, do something awful, or tell them an unbearable secret or an out-and-out lie. When I was in fifth grade, I made the mistake of having a slumber party and inviting four girls from school. Lexie took over the evening and ended up confiding in the guests—quietly thanking them for coming. "You must be real friends to risk your own health for her," she said. The poor girls, including my then best friend, Zoey Landover, sat wide-eyed while Lexie told them about some horrible, incurable, possibly contagious disease I had. She threw out a bunch of medical-sounding terms, and implied that it was something embarrassing that affected private parts. I tried to argue, to tell them it was all a lie, and Lex gave me a look of pity and said, "If they're your real friends, shouldn't they know the truth?" All four girls were calling for rides home before it even got dark.

"How can you be so mean?" I asked Lexie later, when it was just the two of us alone in the little bedroom we shared.

She smiled sweetly, stroked my hair. "I did you a favor, Jax. It was a test. To see who was really a true friend. And not one of them passed."

Lexie always made me choose between my friends and her, and in the end, I'd always chosen Lexie.

Even after moving all the way across the country to try to distance myself, to focus on my own life; even after years of therapy and the boundaries I'd worked so hard to develop, Lexie still had that strong of a hold over me.

"I'm happy on my own, thank you very much," I

told Diane. "Besides, work is crazy. I don't have time for romance. I can barely keep my plants alive, much less a relationship."

"Sure. Keep telling yourself that. All work and no play makes Jax a dull girl."

"Anyway, back to Lexie . . ." I said.

"I was just at Sparrow Crest two weeks ago. Your sister seemed fine. Happy."

"Have you spoken to her since?" I asked.

"No," Diane admitted with what may have been a tinge of guilt in her voice. "I've been crazy busy with work. And like I said, she was doing really well when I last saw her."

"Well, something has changed, so a visit today would not be a bad idea if you have the time."

"She seemed really together, honestly . . . she made me lemonade with fresh mint she'd picked. All the family albums were out. She had lots of questions about your grandmother, your mother, and Rita. She's doing research, working on a family tree. Maybe that's what she was calling you about?"

I was not going to debate Lexie's mental state with Diane. "Just talk her into getting back on the meds again. If she gives you any shit, remind her how much she hates hospitals and that going down this no-meds path always lands her in one."

"Will do."

After we said our goodbyes, I pulled out my laptop to get caught up on my client notes for the week. I couldn't focus. I kept thinking about Lexie learning the butterfly when she was ten years old and already an exquisite swimmer. That was what Gram said: *Alexia, you are an exquisite swimmer.*

When we were kids, Lexie was one of those people

who excelled at whatever she tried. She made every-thing look easy: math, science, knitting, any sport or game she tried. She'd cook something, and it would turn out perfectly and our family would ooh and ahh and say how delicious it was even though she hadn't followed the recipe at all. "You're a natural," our father would say, and my stomach would clench into a hard knot because Lexie was a natural at every-thing, while I struggled just to get by, to get passing grades, just to get noticed. My sister was everyone's favorite: teachers, our parents, Gram, even our friend Ryan, who made no attempt to hide the fact that he'd been totally in love with her since he was eight years old. It was easy to love Lexie. To be caught up in her radiance.

Lexie mastered the butterfly like she mastered every-thing: by throwing herself into it and closing everything else off. She was in the pool, windmilling her arms, dunking her face, coming up for a breath, then going back down again. Gram had given her a Speedo swim-ming cap because that's what swimmers in the Olym-pics wore, and Lexie claimed it made her faster. She had blue-tinted goggles on, too. I sat perched on the edge of the pool, watching. When she was in the water, she wasn't like my sister at all. The Lexie on land was like a real butterfly, flitting from one thing to the next, staying focused only long enough to briefly excel, then growing bored and moving on. But when she swam, she was pure grace and focus. She'd lost track of time and had been in way over Gram's thirty-minute limit. She didn't seem to feel the cold. She didn't seem to get tired.

My legs turned to pins and needles, but I sat with my eyes on my sister, transfixed.

Her face, arms, and chest rose out of the water, her legs working in perfect dolphin kicks. Her body moved like a wave, undulating. And I thought, watching her, that my sister wasn't moving through the water, but that she was a part of it. And I was terrified—that she could slip away so easily, choosing the water instead of me, never looking back.

———————

The phone rang a little after five o'clock.

"Hello?"

"Jackie?" It was Aunt Diane, and her voice sounded shaky.

I already knew it was about Lexie. She must have done something really stupid. When she was in college, she'd gone off her meds and then lined her dorm room with plastic and piped in water from the girls' shower with a garden hose, doing twenty-thousand dollars' worth of damage. Then, there was the time she went missing for three weeks and called from Albuquerque—

"Lexie's gone."

"Oh shit, did she leave any clues about where? Remember the time she—"

"Jackie . . . she's dead." Diane's voice broke. "Lexie is dead."

I'd misheard. That was it. Some wires in my brain got crossed and delivered the wrong message. I leaned back against the kitchen wall.

"I found her in the swimming pool." Diane was sobbing, the words barely understandable. "I pulled her out, called 911. Terri and Ryan just got here."

Terri was one of Diane's oldest friends. Her mother,

Shirley, had been Gram's best friend. And Terri's son, Ryan, was the only kid Lexie and I played with during our summers at Sparrow Crest. He was my first crush. I thought he was living down in South Carolina.

The room came in and out of focus. I felt like I was going to be sick.

"Can you come, Jackie?" Diane asked. "Right away?" More crying. "She was so cold. Naked. Her lips were blue. The paramedics couldn't do anything. They said it looked like she'd been dead for hours. It was just like all those years ago with Rita. Oh, Jackie. Oh God!" she wailed.

I made my living hearing terrible things and always knew what to say, what needed to happen next. But now the floor seemed to ripple like water, and I slid down the wall, my legs giving out beneath me.

I closed my eyes and was back at the pool, watching Lexie practice the butterfly in her blue goggles and cap, watching her become her very own wave, the dark water swallowing her up.

I hung up, hands shaking, and ran for the toilet, throwing up until there was nothing left, then sank to the cold tiled bathroom floor and curled up, sobbing.

Behind me, the bathtub dripped, slowly and methodically, its own rusty metronome.

I tried to steady my breathing, control the short, jagged breaths.

Lexie couldn't be dead. She just couldn't.

Denial. Kübler-Ross's first stage of grief.

I took in a breath, stood up, and looked in the mirror. My face was patchy, my eyes red and puffy. "Lexie is dead," I said, trying to make the words seem more real. The tears came, blurring my reflection until my nine-year-old face looked back at me, reflected in the dark mirror of the pool.

What now? I asked Lexie.

Gram says the pool will give you wishes.

It was well past midnight, and she'd woken me up, dragged me down to the pool, breaking Gram's rule. The night air was cool. I got goose bumps under my thin nightgown. The water was black as ever, chilling the air, smelling vaguely poisonous.

When did she tell you that? I scoffed, even as I imagined little Rita sneaking down to this same pool at night years ago.

Tonight, when she was having sherry. You were in the bath.

Gram was always sharing secrets with Lexie. Telling her things she would never tell me. Adults were often confiding in her—like Aunt Diane telling her about Gram's agoraphobia. Treating her like she was so much older than she was. And Ryan loved to whisper secrets to her, too. I'd even caught him handing her little notes. Notes she just stuck in her pocket and never even read. It wasn't fair.

Lexie put her face right against the water and started whispering. Her words were fast, determined, and sure. It sounded like she was chanting; repeating the same phrase over and over. I had no doubt that whatever she was asking for, she'd get it, because that's how things always worked with Lexie.

I leaned down, too, so close that my breath left ripples on my reflection. I whispered: *I wish that Lexie wasn't always the special one. That she wasn't the best at everything. That things were hard for her instead of always being so easy. I wish something bad would happen to her.*

I blinked, and my adult face appeared again in the mirror. And there, just behind me, I was sure I saw my sister, her eyes sad and furious.

How could you?

And I understood, in those blurry seconds, that there are no secrets from the dead.

chapter two

Ethel O'Shay Monroe
June 8, 1929
Lanesborough, New Hampshire

I have a sparrow egg tucked against my breast, softly resting there, a strange secret.

I am a great keeper of secrets, have been since I was a little girl. Oh, the secrets I kept then! The things I dreamed! I was a princess in a fairy tale. I was Sleeping Beauty waiting for the prince to come and wake me with a glorious kiss.

There were other secrets I kept. Terrible things I saw in the dark but knew better than to speak of. Sometimes, to make them go away, I'd scratch myself with a pin. Seeing the little red line, the tiny drops of blood, was a way to ward off evil. The scratches on my skin, hidden under dresses, they were secrets, too.

"You hold things close to your chest," my friend Myrtle says. "It makes you a fine card player. But at times, a difficult friend."

Myrtle's a good deal older than me, and the person I am closest to here in town, the person I share the most with besides Will.

My darling Will. I watch him walk around the Lanesborough town picnic. It's a picture-perfect day. The children are just out of school for the year, and summer has begun; summer, with all its promise and possibility. Everyone has gathered on the green in the center of town: a colorful patchwork of blankets and quilts laid out across the grass, scattered with baskets full of sandwiches, fried chicken, jars of lemonade and sweet tea. Over in the corner, the brass band is setting up to play on the bandstand, as they will do each Saturday night until September. The whole town comes out to picnic, listen to the music, and dance until midnight. Bootleg rum gets passed around, along with Chester Miller's hard cider and bottles of beer snuck down from Canada.

I watch Will, and my heart aches a little. He is organizing all the children in a three-legged race, putting them in pairs, binding their legs together, and he has them all giggling. He's making silly faces, pretending he's forgotten how to tie a knot, pretending he's going to tie his own two legs together. The children love him. "Hello, darling wife!" he shouts. I wave back. The children coo and plead for his attention; "Dr. Monroe, Dr. Monroe," they call, pulling at the untucked tail of his shirt, and he pretends to trip and fall. Children pile on top of him in fits of laughter.

I turn away and nearly run into Jane Parsons, whom I play bridge with each Thursday. "I was looking for Anna, but I see she's in good hands," Jane says, nodding at the pile of children tickling Will, her daughter Anna on top. "He's simply marvelous with them." And I'm sure I catch the question in her eyes: *When will you give him a child?*

"Yes, he is," I agree. "Excuse me, I must check on the raffle."

I walk away, carefully pulling out the little pin I have hidden in the folds of my dress, just below the waistband. I hold the head between two fingers like a magician palming a coin and make a fist, pricking myself once, twice, three times.

I have been married for a little over a year. I was thirty-six, an old maid, when we married, and Will was thirty-nine.

"Some flowers bloom late," Myrtle says with a wink, "but the late ones, they always smell the sweetest."

I am the oldest of four girls, and our mother died young. It fell on me to make a good home for my sisters and father, and I did not mind one bit. I took to the role quite well, donning Mother's apron to cook dinners each night, mending clothes, getting them to school on time. I have always loved to be busy. After my sisters—first Bernice, then Mary, and finally our willful baby sister, Constance—got married and went off to start families of their own, it was only Father I was caring for. He was perfectly capable, but his responsibility as the town doctor made it hard for him to find the time to keep house, cook meals. And I didn't mind. I helped him in his office, too, keeping track of his appointments, organizing his books. I have always been good at math; working columns of numbers calms my mind.

Father introduced me to Will. They'd met at a medical symposium in Boston. Will soon became a regular visitor at our home, talking medicine with Father and playing cards with me. We'd play hearts for hours in our little parlor, sipping coffee and eating spice cake or molasses cookies. Every week I'd bake something new for him. He had his own medical practice in Lanesborough. He'd never married. Too busy, he'd said. Will's own father had died, leaving him a great sum of money made in the railroads, and Will had a lovely house, a new car, crisply tailored clothes. My father encouraged our courtship, was overjoyed when we got engaged. I suggested a small, simple wedding, but Father and Will would hear none of it and enlisted my sisters' help in planning an enormous, elaborate affair. My father gave me away and said it was the proudest moment of his life and that he only wished my mother were there to share in our joy. Sadly, he died in his sleep soon after. His heart. I blamed myself for his death, which is silly, I know, but I couldn't help thinking that if I had still been there, things might have turned out differently. I still have the scar on the inside of my left thigh from the night he died; usually, I am more careful—but that night, I drew the blade too deep. It was one of my father's razor blades, taken from his medicine cabinet. I have it still, tucked in a little tin at the bottom of my sewing basket.

My own heart is thumping hard, beating against the little egg inside the lacy front of my brassiere, as I slip the pin back into my dress and walk over to the table set up in front of the Methodist Church where the quilt made by several of the ladies—myself included—is being raffled. It's the latest fund-raiser for the Ladies Auxiliary. The money we raise will go to help the needy in our community. I stare at the squares of the nine-patch quilt: Its vivid summer colors seem too bright, too cheerful. "How are ticket sales?" I ask Catherine Delaney, our secretary.

"Excellent," she tells me.

I've already bought a dozen, but I buy a dozen more, checking my palm as I reach into my patent leather clutch purse to retrieve the money. No blood, just three little red dots. Three is a magic number. Ruth Edsell approaches with her daughter Hannah, who must be around sixteen now. She's the perfect image of her mother. Ruth is a dressmaker and tailor, and Hannah has learned the trade from her. They're both members of the ladies' sewing circle I attend on Mondays; I keep busy here in my new life in Lanesborough. There are always fund-raisers and food drives, finding speakers for our monthly lecture series—last month we had an expert talk about growing roses.

"Lovely to see you, Mrs. Monroe," Hannah says. Such a polite girl. Rosy cheeked, always smiling. She and her mother are so alike, so close. They walk the same way, hold their heads at the same angle, even their smiles match.

"You ladies have outdone yourselves with this quilt," Ruth says. "It's positively divine!"

I turn, see that the three-legged race has begun, and Will is wildly cheering the children on. When it's over, he gives them each a sweet as a prize and pats them on the head, job well done, then bounds over to me as though I'm the biggest prize of all. He takes my hand, kissing each of my knuckles, then leads me over to where we've set up our picnic blanket. We settle in, and I open the wicker basket, pull out the plates and cups and all the food I've prepared: little sandwiches, pickled beet salad (Will's favorite), cold lemonade in mason jars, lemon chiffon pie. He leans over and kisses me. "You have outdone yourself, darling wife," he says. His face is sweaty, his shirt grass-stained. He runs his hand over his oiled hair, brushing it back into place. I watch the way his eyes wander back to the children, and my stomach goes hard and cold.

We've talked about it, of course. Our child. We've stayed up late into the night discussing names, playfully arguing over silly ones.

"I think we should call her Brunhilda," Will suggested.

"Barnabus Rex, if it's a boy," I said.

"That's a perfectly respectable name," Will said. "I had an Uncle Barnabus."

"You did not!"

"You're right. Sadly, no Uncle Barnabus."

We've talked about which of us our child would look like, what color we would paint the nursery, who they might grow up to be (a doctor like Daddy, a seamstress and cook like Mommy, the president of the United States, perhaps). We'd lie awake in bed at night imagining our child; this human being that he and I would make together, would love so perfectly.

But there is no child yet, and I am beginning to wonder if something is wrong with me. I haven't confessed this fear to Will, but I think he sees it in my eyes. I am thirty-seven years old. Soon it will be too late. I have secretly tried things, desperate things, recommended by my sisters and other well-meaning women: bitter tinctures, lying with hips elevated for hours after intercourse. And the sparrow egg tucked against my breast, of course.

Mrs. Tuttle, who plays the organ at church, told me of the folk remedy. She said that a woman who wishes to be with child should steal a tiny egg from a sparrow's nest and keep it tucked against her body for three days, then bury it in the ground. I spent weeks following sparrows, searching for a nest. How silly I felt climbing the tree, stealing that egg, carefully wrapping it in a silk handkerchief, carrying it around tucked into my clothes! I have not told Will about the egg.

Tomorrow, I shall bury it in our yard.

Will finishes his sandwich, leans back on the picnic blanket, and looks up at the clouds.

"I see a bear," he says. "I think his name is Oscar."

"Oh yes, I see him, too. Definitely an Oscar. It looks like he's walking to that castle."

"Castle? It looks more like a boat."

"Perhaps it is," I say. "Perhaps he's a pirate bear? Oscar, King of the Pirate Bears! He'll sail over to that island in the west, bury all his bear treasure."

We laugh. Will takes my hand, kisses my nose. I feel giddy and light. I tell myself that our love is enough. That it is selfish to want more.

"I have a surprise for you, darling wife," he says, grinning in his boyish way. "Have you heard of the Brandenburg Springs?"

"No," I say.

"Well, people have been traveling to them for years. There are four underground springs that bubble up to fill a pool. The minerals are supposed to be quite healing. I have patients who swear that a soak in the springs will cure anything from gout to consumption. They say it's very restorative. And," he adds, raising one eyebrow in a wonderfully devilish way, "there are spooky stories about the place."

Will knows I love an odd, spooky story. He speaks in a low, creepy voice. "Some say the springs are cursed. Haunted, even. Some people go and never return."

"Oh?" I say, suppressing a little shiver, imagining what it might be like to disappear forever.

"Absolute bunk, of course," he says. "The truth is, the most beautiful hotel in Vermont has opened there. It's supposed to be very grand, indeed." He reaches into his pants pocket and pulls out a folded brochure, which he opens and holds out to me.

There is a picture of a lovely white hotel with two green hills beyond it. It looks quite large, three and a half stories, with an enormous porch around the whole bottom floor and little balconies in front. Sumptuous gardens surround a large fountain.

"Oh! It looks lovely," I say. "Positively swanky!" I lean in and read the words beneath the picture:

We invite you to the Brandenburg Springs Hotel and Resort—Vermont's newest elite destination for the most discerning clientele tucked away in the idyllic Green Mountains. Come take the waters and experience the legendary restorative healing powers of our natural springs! Vermont's own Fountain of Youth and Vitality! Our luxury hotel features 35 private rooms, each piped with water from the famous Brandenburg Springs. Dining room with world-class chef, sunroom, tennis courts, immaculate gardens. Open May through November. Do not delay! Book your room today!

"It looks like something from a storybook," I say.

Behind us, the children laugh and race in circles. Catherine is announcing "Last call!" for the raffle tickets. "Last chance, folks! You do not want to miss out on this opportunity!" The band has started to play "Bye Bye Blackbird." The air is sweet with the scent of apple blossoms and freshly cut grass.

"What would you say to going next weekend?" Will asks, voice slightly raised so I can hear him above the music. "Are you keen?"

"Of course! But what's the occasion?"

"Does there need to be an occasion to take my wife for a romantic weekend out in the country?"

"I don't suppose there does," I tell him, kissing his cheek. He smells of hair tonic and shaving cream. "It sounds like an absolute dream," I say, lying back on the blanket, my fingers brushing the fabric of my dress just above where the egg lies, waiting.

chapter three

June 16, 2019

My flight was leaving Seattle at seven thirty.

I'd asked my neighbor Lucy to come water my plants and bring in my mail. I'd called all my clients for the week and canceled, referring them to Karen Hurst, the therapist I shared office space with, who was happy to cover for me if anything came up that couldn't wait. I'd even steeled up the courage to call my father, whom I hadn't spoken to in weeks, but he didn't pick up. "Ted," I said to his voice mail. "It's Jackie. Call me, okay? Call me as soon as you get this."

And I'd called Barbara and told her what had happened.

"I didn't pick up the phone," I said, feeling another sob building in my chest.

"You can't blame yourself, Jackie."

"I know," I said. "Logically, I know that."

Barbara told me to call anytime if I needed her, to take things slow and give myself permission to feel whatever feelings came up. "Grief is a monster," she said. It sounded exactly like something my sister would say.

Now, I sat with all the lights on, drinking the last of the pot of coffee I'd brewed a couple of hours ago. My bags were waiting by the door. I was showered and in clean clothes. I was thinking of Lexie, of the silly rhyming songs she'd make up when we were kids. "Jax, Jax, you are so lax, please do not fall into the cracks, or else you might just meet the Zax."

"What's a Zax?" I asked, interrupting. "Is it like . . . a monster or something?"

"The worst sort, Jax." She nodded, grinning. "The absolute worst. You meet one and you're never the same. There's no going back." Then she'd start to sing again, at the top of her lungs. "Zax, Zax, you've met the Zax, nothing can save you, not a gun or an ax, you better run, better make tracks! Jax, Jax, he's breathing tacks, can't you feel him? He's behind our backs!"

I shook the memory away, went to the sink and rinsed out my coffee cup, then turned quickly, half expecting . . . what? Lexie? A Zax? *Can't you feel him? He's behind our backs!*

Grief is a monster.

There was still one last thing I needed to do before I got in the car to drive to the airport—the thing I'd been putting off all night. I went to the answering machine, reached to turn up the volume, and pressed play. The room filled with the sound of her voice. It slammed into me, filled my ears, my lungs and chest. I sat frozen, crying, as I listened to all fourteen messages from my sister. There were no funny rhyming songs. No made-up words or creatures. Only her frantic voice, words tangled and knotted. Mostly, she was reciting letters, numbers, distances, as if it was all some kind of code. *I know it seems impossible*, she said. *But the numbers don't lie.* In another, she was practically shouting: *H9, six meters! H9, over fifty meters! How do you explain that, Jax? It's the scientific method, for fuck's sake!*

The messages got more desperate, more angry. *Why the fuck don't you pick up the phone? I know you're there! Don't you dare fucking ignore me! What kind of a fucking social worker are you, Jax?*

Then, the final message. Lexie sounded worn out. Hoarse. She spoke in a whisper. She was crying. I had to move close, put my ear right against the machine to hear her. *She's here, Jax. Oh my God, she's here.*

chapter four

We found the town of Brandenburg without any problem by following the map: I navigated while Will drove, coaxing our Franklin touring car over the hills and around the bends, the backseat full of suitcases and hatboxes. I traced our route along the map with my finger—the road twisting and turning like a great black snake as it made its way through the mountains. It was a lovely day, and we drove with the top down. I wore my new black wool cloche hat to keep my hair from getting too mussed. We passed more cows and sheep than people on the four-hour journey from our home to Brandenburg through fields and woods, with a few villages scattered along the way—tiny places with just a scattering of homes, a church, and a general store. The sun beat down on the hills we wound our way through, lighting up a thousand different shades of green. We caught sight of train tracks running perpendicular to the road at times.

The town of Brandenburg was quite quaint: a small fire department, two churches (Methodist and Presbyterian), a post office, and a general store where Will and I stopped in for sodas and directions. The store had uneven old wooden floors that creaked. There was a moose head on the wall with an enormous rack of antlers. I elbowed Will, nodded in the poor creature's direction, whispered, "What do you suppose his name was?"

"Looks like a Stanley to me," Will whispered back.

"Poor Stan," I said.

There was a woman in a battered-looking wide-brimmed straw hat filling a basket with eggs, milk, and flour. The place seemed to sell everything: molasses, hats, fishing reels, tobacco, buttons and thread, large blocks of ice. Next to the cash register was a wooden crate of jelly jars full of water. A hand-lettered sign said: Genuine Brandenburg Springs Water, 5¢, SURE TO CURE WHAT AILS YOU!

"That's the real stuff. Got it right from the springs. Has a funny taste, but it brings good luck and good health," said the old man behind the counter when he saw me looking at them. "Cured my wife's gout. I burned my hand real bad, back when I was young and foolish—the skin turned black, and the wound wept something awful. I soaked my hand in the springs every day, and it was healed in a week." He held up his hand for inspection. "I don't even have a scar."

Will leaned in to study his hand. "Incredible," he said. "Do you know the mineral content of the waters?"

The man shook his head, held out a jar of water. "Don't know what's in it, but I swear it works. People have been traveling to the springs to take the waters since before the town was founded. World famous, it is. Would you like one? Cost you just a nickel."

"No, thank you," I said, giving him my best smile. "We're actually on our way to the Brandenburg Springs

Hotel. We have a reservation for the weekend, so we'll be enjoying plenty of the water soon enough."

"You have to be a paying guest to get to the springs these days." He scowled, accentuating the lines in his face.

"How do you get these jars to sell, then?" Will asked.

"I got my ways," he said. He clenched his jaw. "That Benson Harding can put up fences, but that water, it don't belong to him. You can't own the springs."

"No, you can't," said the woman in the hat, who'd come up behind us and was looking at sweets kept in jars on the counter: lemon drops, puffed peppermints, horehound drops, licorice. Beside them was a box of Teaberry gum. "Last man who called the springs his own paid a terrible price."

"What's that?" I asked. "Who?"

"That'd be Nelson DeWitt," said the shopkeeper. "He owned the land before Mr. Harding. A bit of an odd man. He ran a boardinghouse and bottled the water, had it taken by the trainload into New York City and Boston. 'DeWitt's Elixir,' he called it."

"So what happened to DeWitt?" Will asked.

"Drowned." The man shook his head. "Like I said, you can't own the springs. That's not what they're there for."

"Those springs are a dark place," the woman said. "You'd do best to keep away from them."

"Oh, Harriet, come on now—"

"It's true and you know it," she said, flashing him a don't-you-dare-contradict-me look. The shopkeeper looked like he was going to say something more but thought better of it.

"There's a fine hotel out on the lake, the Pine Point Inn. You can swim, boat, fish," Harriet went on. "There's a dance hall! You're better off heading there for the weekend."

"Thank you for the recommendation, but I think we'll stick to our original plan," Will said as he dropped a dime on the counter for our sodas. "Could you tell us how to get to the Brandenburg Springs Hotel?"

The shopkeeper nodded. "Make a left out of here and bear right at the fork. That road will take you all the way to the hotel. You'll probably pass the carriage on the way—they drive down every day at five to pick guests up from the train."

The woman in the hat, Harriet, shook her head in disappointment. As we left, she said in a low voice, "At least I warned them."

———————

"Well that was a bit odd, wasn't it?" Will said once we were back in the car. We each held a bottle of ice-cold Coca-Cola. "Did you see his hand? Not a trace of a scar. If it's true that he burned it as badly as he said, that's amazing." He turned the Coke bottle in his hand. "There's got to be a mineral in there with antiseptic properties. Or perhaps it's the combination of minerals? I wonder if the water has ever been tested to discover its true contents." He looked into the soda bottle as if it had the answers.

"What did you make of Harriet and her warning?"

"That the long winters here are good for storytelling," he said. "I told you, there are lots of foolish stories about the springs."

A *dark place*, I thought as we followed the dirt

road from the center of town up into the hills. There were no houses up here—only trees and rocks, low stone walls that had toppled in places. The air got cooler as the trees grew thicker, seemed to almost overtake the road. The whole time we were traveling, we thought we must be lost—that there couldn't possibly be a luxurious hotel out here. The dirt road grew narrower and narrower, more and more rutted and muddy from spring floods. The wheels caught in the ruts, making it sway this way and that; it felt as if the road itself was pulling our car along. I was afraid we'd sink too deep and get stuck. We did not pass another motorist, or the coach from the hotel, which was good because the road was far too narrow for two cars.

"Maybe we should turn back," I suggested, but just then we saw a hand-painted white board nailed along the roadside telling us the hotel was just ahead. We crept along at a snail's pace, the trees thickening, the forest seeming to swallow us deeper and deeper. We passed another white sign. I began to wonder if it was some sort of trick, if we were being drawn to our demise. Silly, really, but my fear was getting the better of me.

"Maybe this isn't right," I said.

"It must be right. We're following the signs," Will said, gripping the wheel too tightly. "Besides, the road's too narrow. There's no way to turn around."

But then, the trees thinned, and the building appeared like a vision from a dream; it actually took my breath away. I squealed like a schoolgirl, clutched Will's hand in excitement. And he squeezed back, seeming as excited as I was. The hotel was in a clearing completely surrounded by forest. There were two large hills looming behind it, so green against a sky so blue that it all looked like the backdrop to a play. The building was as grand as the brochure had promised—three floors, painted pure white with a lovely wrap-around porch. It seemed to glow against the backdrop of lawn and trees, like a moon in the night sky. Directly in front of the building was a fountain surrounded by luscious flower gardens. Off to the right was the rose garden, set in concentric circles with a gazebo at the center walled with trellised roses. And the best part—peacocks roamed the grounds! They strutted to and fro, crying out and flashing their spectacular tail feathers.

Will pulled the car up the circular drive of crushed stone. The bellboy took our luggage, and we made our way to the front desk to check in. The lobby was beautiful! Polished wooden floors and counter, landscape paintings on the walls, and a gorgeous cut-glass crystal chandelier. The curtains were of heavy red velvet. The desk clerk helpfully pointed out the tennis court, the walking paths, the arboretum, and the springs on a drawn map of the grounds.

"Can we go to the water right away?" I asked Will. The map showed the springs behind the hotel at the edge of the woods.

The clerk shook his head. "I'm sorry, but the springs close every day at five for the safety of our guests." He looked away, seeming suddenly nervous, almost frightened. Then he seemed to recompose himself. He turned back and smiled right at me. "They'll reopen tomorrow morning at eight."

Will seemed almost more disappointed than I was to hear this bit of news. "Oh, that's too bad. Is the water piped into the hotel truly from the springs?"

"Oh yes, sir. You'll be drinking it and bathing in it the entire time you're here."

The first thing we did when we got up to our room was pour two glasses of spring water.

"Cheers," Will said, clinking his glass against mine.

The water was clear and cold and tasted slightly metallic. The rusty tang lingered at the back of my throat like blood.

"What do you think?" he asked. "Do you feel any different yet?"

I laughed. "I don't think it works like that."

He frowned, finished the water in his glass. "Tastes a bit like nails."

Our room was on the second floor, at the front. There was floral wallpaper, an enormous canopy bed, and a private bath with a claw-foot tub. We had a balcony overlooking the fountain and gardens. As Will led me out onto the balcony, I had the oddest sensation. Not déjà vu, exactly, but something akin to it. The feeling brought with it a sense of vertigo. I swayed slightly, and Will steadied me with an arm around my waist.

"Easy there," he said. "That was water we drank. You can't be tipsy."

"It's this place!" I said. "It's like something out of a storybook! I feel like . . . like I *know* this place."

Below us, a peacock cried out. The sweet, heady scent of the rose garden drifted its way up.

He kissed my head. "You've been studying the brochure for days."

"Not the way it *looks*," I struggled to explain. "The way it *feels*. Like we're meant to be here. Like coming home when you've been away a long time."

Will gave me an odd look. "You have the most fanciful thoughts sometimes." He kissed me again, on the lips. I kissed him back, let myself melt into him, his arms around me solid and sure, holding me tight while the world seemed to spin around us.

chapter five

June 16, 2019

I told the funeral home we were thinking of a short service there, Wednesday. "Do you think that's too soon?" Aunt Diane asked, clawing at the steering wheel. She looked stylish as ever: coppery red hair in a neat bob, beige purse matching her heels. Navy dress pants and a silk blouse. Even her manicure looked perfect.

"No," I said, not having any idea whether that was too soon or not. I tried to imagine myself being ready for Lexie's memorial service in just a few days, and it felt impossible. But even if we waited weeks, I knew I'd never be ready for it.

My head ached and my stomach was queasy. In the past twenty-four hours, I hadn't had anything to eat or drink but coffee and the little bag of free pretzels on the plane. I'd offered to rent a car, but Diane had insisted on coming to get me in her black Lincoln Navigator. It was nearly a two-hour drive from the airport to Sparrow Crest, an hour on highways, the rest along back roads. I remembered the long three-hour drives from our house in Massachusetts to Brandenburg each June, the trunk loaded with bulging suitcases, stuffed animals, our bikes on the roof rack. Our father would be driving, fiddling with the radio, always looking for just the right road-trip music—anything to help him forget where he was going. And Mom would sit quietly, watching the scenery, her face getting and more tense the closer we got to Sparrow Crest. I knew once we arrived, Gram would invite them in for dinner, but our parents would make excuses, talk about bad traffic, an early morning, anything to get out as quickly as possible. They never stayed, just dropped and ran with lots of *I love yous, have a good a summer, behave for your grandmother*. My parents both hated Sparrow Crest. More than hating it, they seemed wary of it. Our mother said it made her cold, held too many bad memories. Our father said it was obviously haunted and creepy as hell. "Have a good summer in Dracula's castle," he'd whisper as he kissed us goodbye. "Watch out for the bats."

Lexie and I spent the long drive from home to Sparrow Crest in the backseat playing the License Plate Game or Twenty Questions, but then, as we got closer to Gram's and the landscape turned more green and mountainous, we'd start making plans—trips to the store for candy and root beer, who was going to jump in the pool first, if Ryan would be there at Sparrow Crest waiting for us or if we'd have to ride down to the bakery to find him.

Diane followed the exit ramp off the highway, and I remembered the little jolt I felt at the beginning of each summer when we got off at the same exit: the promise of great adventures to come. This time, instead of the happy rush, a weight in my chest sank deep down into my stomach.

Air-conditioning blasted out of the vents, turning the car into an icebox. A stack of business cards in the console read: *Diane Harkness Real Estate*.

"I spoke to your father," Diane said as she put on

the left-turn signal and checked for oncoming traffic. Her large-framed sunglasses and light application of bronzing powder couldn't hide the fact that she was exhausted.

We turned onto the little two-lane road that would take us past farmhouses, fields, long stretches of woods, and the occasional gas station. "He'll be here Tuesday morning. I'll send a car to pick him up."

I nodded. Diane and Ted had an interesting relationship. They'd always been close and remained in touch. But Diane made it clear, both to him and to the rest of the world, that she felt like he'd failed our mother and Lexie and me; like he should have tried harder, should have been a better father.

"Thank you," I said, "for dealing with that. How did Ted sound?"

Our father had never been "Dad." Jax started calling him Ted when she learned to talk, parroting what she heard our mother call him. When I came along, I copied Lexie, calling our parents Mom and Ted. Maybe calling him Ted was a way we both had of setting him apart, distancing him somehow because we both understood, on some subconscious level, that he wasn't going to be part of our little family forever.

"He was sober enough to be making sense. I can't promise he'll be that way when he gets off the plane, though."

Growing up, my dad was one of those guys who always had a beer in his hand. Sometimes he drank to bring himself up, and sometimes to bring himself down.

It wasn't until my first psychology class at the University of Washington that I realized my father drank to self-medicate. That was also when I began to believe he was bipolar (though he'd never been officially diagnosed, and he's always denied it). His mood swings aren't nearly as bad as Lexie's, but he gets himself into some serious funks and some serious periods of what he calls "creative energy": no sleep for days, drawing and painting, playing music. His manic periods were fun to be around when we were kids—he'd take us out for late-night ice cream, or roller-skating, or out to the mall to watch two movies in a row, then fill a cart with art supplies. One time, we went into the music store and he bought us all ukuleles.

The last time I'd seen my father was a little over a year ago, when we moved Lexie into Sparrow Crest. The two of them were laughing, feeding off each other's mania. They were drawing ridiculous pictures on the boxes instead of labeling them, overloading the rented hand truck and dancing around with it so that all the mislabeled boxes fell off. I took on the role of the taskmaster, made lists and tried to keep things somewhat organized so we could get it done quickly and I could go back home. I was exhausted from seething with resentment and pretending not to be.

My father and I called each other every month for obligatory check-ins—how's work, how's the weather, what's new? It was like a careful dance we did, keeping everything easy and surface level, never prodding too deep. Unlike my relationship with Lexie, I had no problem establishing clear boundaries with my father.

"We'll all have to make some decisions, of course." Diane's voice faltered. "About what we think Lexie would have wanted."

"I know she didn't want to be buried," I said, remembering Lexie's horror when we were picking a casket out for Mom three years ago. "Stuck in a box for all eternity?" she'd said as we walked along the display row at the funeral home, the tops so shiny we could see our own distorted reflections in them. "No thanks."

I shivered at the memory. Diane reached over and turned down the AC.

"Cremation it is, then." Gram had been cremated and had her ashes buried in the rose garden at Sparrow Crest.

"Maybe we can bring the ashes out to Lake Wilmore," I suggested, remembering all the hours we'd spent swimming there as kids. The lake water felt downright warm compared with the ice water in Gram's pool, and we spent many summer days going back and forth between the two. The lake was on the other side of town, a fifteen-minute bike ride away. Lake Wilmore was lined with summer houses and cabins, and there was a big public swimming beach with a snack bar that served fried fish and clams. Often Ryan would tag along on his bike, the basket stuffed full of rolls and muffins his mother, Terri, had made; she and her husband, Randy, owned the Blue Heron Bakery. She did all the baking, and Ryan's dad handled the business side: the orders, the books, hiring and firing employees.

Sometimes Lexie and I would bring our blue-and-yellow inflatable raft down to the lake. Lexie called it the *Titanic II*. I'd accompany her on cross-lake swims—paddling along beside her in case she got tired, but she never did. I never attempted to swim across the lake with her; I knew I didn't have the stamina and could never keep up with Lexie's speed. Even when I tried my hardest, I wasn't half the swimmer my sister was.

She never spoke to me or acknowledged my presence during those cross-lake swims. It was just her and the water.

Those summers in Brandenburg had started Lexie's love affair with swimming; it was the one thing that would quiet her mind, drown out everything else. When we weren't at the lake, she'd practice in the pool at Sparrow Crest, doing endless laps, learning new strokes. My sister, restless and ill at ease on land, was quick and graceful in the water.

"I reserved the Lily Room for the service; it's the largest one," Aunt Diane continued. "It should hold everyone."

As far as family, only myself, Diane, and my father remained. Everyone else was gone. I pictured us, Terri and Ryan maybe. But who else might come? "You really think that many people will show up?" I asked.

"Your sister had *a lot* of friends in town."

I had a hard time picturing it. In my experience, she could be the life of the party but had few real friendships. She was just too difficult. She'd pull people to her one minute and do all she could to push them away the next. We were in Brandenburg now, driving past the fire station, Four Corners Store, bakery, and the Methodist Church, which had hung a big sign: PICNIC AFTER SERVICES TODAY! I nodded and looked out the window at the people gathered on the church lawn, spread out on blankets with their sandwiches and bottles of soda. "A service at the funeral home sounds good. Lexie hated churches."

She was suspicious of all religions, though she'd tried her fair share of them. She was a Buddhist for a few weeks, spent a summer at an ashram in upstate New York, went to silent meetings with the Quakers.

She'd been searching for something, for the missing piece that might make her feel whole.

"Do you believe in God?" she'd asked me last summer.

"No," I'd told her, and Lexie had said: "I believe in a thousand little gods."

I thought of Lexie's thousand little gods as we pulled up the long, circular driveway to Sparrow Crest, my grandmother's ivy-covered stone house looming like a small mountain. And behind it, the two hills forming a perfect tree-lined backdrop: Lord's Hill on the left, the slightly taller Devil's Hill to the right. The story went that the earliest settlers named it Devil's Hill because of the rough, rocky terrain. One of the first families to settle in town built their house at the base of the other hill, and their last name was Lord. Growing up, this explanation seemed far too boring, so Lexie and I would make up crazy stories about God and the devil battling it out in the woods behind Sparrow Crest. Lexie would point at the woods and say, "You see which hill is bigger, don't you? The devil wins every time, Jax."

Between the hills was a small valley that the stream ran through, all the way down to the river on the other side.

"What's up with all the no-trespassing signs?" I asked, noticing them nailed to trees all along the driveway.

"Lexie put them up," Diane said, lips tightening.

This didn't fit with the image she was trying to sell me of Lexie being the most popular woman in town. I bit my tongue to keep from saying, *Why, so she could keep all her good friends out?*

And there, at the house's foot, was my dead sister's yellow Mustang. A ridiculous car for Vermont. Impossible to drive during the long winters. But it was utterly hers, and seeing it brought the tears again.

Aunt Diane put her hand on mine. "Are you ready?" she asked, looking from me to the house.

She'd already warned me that she hadn't cleaned up anything. That the house was in a horrible state.

"Ready or not," I said.

The summer I was ten and Lexie was thirteen, things truly began to change. She'd spent the winter sick with mononucleosis—holed up in her room with sketchpads and books and an old TV our father had dragged up there, hibernating. And when she emerged in the spring, she wasn't the same. It wasn't just that she was thinner and more hollowed-out looking. She had a hard time focusing on conversations. She was quick to anger and swore all the time. Mom let it slide and Ted was amused, especially when Lex starting using his own colorful curses: *Cock-sucking pigs* was a favorite. Mom said I should ignore my sister's freak-outs. "It's hormones," she said. "Your sister is going through big changes."

I thought the "big changes" meant Lex had gotten her period. I saw the wrappers from pads and tampons in the bathroom. Mom fussed over her. Bought her new clothes, special face masks, hair ties, and pills for cramps. Lexie was restless, couldn't seem to hold still. On her sleepless nights, she'd stay with our father in his garage art studio, the two of them grooving out to classic rock and making sculptures out of wire, clothespins, and playing cards. Once, they stayed up all night making a working pinball machine out of an old card table, mousetraps, pieces of hose, rusted pulleys, and a lot of rubber bands.

That summer, when we went to Sparrow Crest, Lexie wanted to share her every secret with me—she kept me up until dawn some nights, talking and talking, telling stories, braiding my hair, painting my nails with fancy nail polish Mom had bought for her. Some days she wouldn't leave her room. One night, I woke up to pee and saw the light on in her room. I went in, but she wasn't there. She wasn't downstairs, or anywhere in the house, even though it was two in the morning. I opened the front door and went out to the pool. It was pitch-dark, so dark I could barely make out her shape. She was crouched, whispering to the water. I moved closer, creeping along the side of the house, wanting to know what she wished for.

"Hello? Are you there?" She seemed to listen for a minute, then stood and tugged her nightgown off over her head and slipped naked into the dark water. I held my breath, watching, waiting, making sure she was okay. Fifteen minutes later, she was back in her clothes and on her way into the house.

I asked her about it the next day. "Where were you last night? I woke up and you weren't in your room. Where'd you go?"

She looked at me like I was crazy. "You must have been dreaming, Jax."

Now, as I stepped through the heavy wooden door of Sparrow Crest and surveyed the wreckage, I wished I was dreaming. "What the hell happened in here?"

"I know," Aunt Diane said. "It's bad. Worse than

bad. Poor Lexie. I was here two weeks ago, and she seemed *fine*. All wrapped up in her genealogy project."

I nodded, looked around at the family photos carelessly strewn all over the front hall. "Right," I said. This was quintessential Lexie. At the beginning of a manic phase, she'd take on projects and seem like she had a handle on them. Then things quickly spun out of control.

Diane's face tensed and she said in a low voice, more to herself than to me, "I should have checked in on her again. I should have at least called."

I took her hand and gave it a squeeze. "You can't blame yourself."

"I know," she said, pulling away from me, making her way into the living room. She walked slowly, hesitantly, like she was a little afraid of what she might find there.

I left my roller bag by the front door and moved down the hall, plowing my way through paper, envelopes, drawings, mail, a rusty bucket, batteries. The old slate floor had large puddles of water on it. The little side table on the left was overturned. Cherished pictures—the sketch of Sparrow Crest by my great-grandfather, a wedding photo of my grandmother and grandfather, a yellow cross-stitch done by my grandmother when she was a little girl that read *To err is human, to forgive, divine*—were off the wall and on the floor, the glass smashed. I picked up a tangled nest of rope.

My aunt's phone rang, and she answered it. "Hi. Yup. She's here. Yeah. Uh-huh. We're at Sparrow Crest." She turned from me, listened a minute, laughed.

I took out my own phone and looked at it. I'd had

the ringer off. There were two new calls, one voice mail. I listened to the message. It was my client, Declan Shipee. All of my clients had my cell number to use in case of emergency. Declan had never called me before.

"You were wrong, Jackie," he said, voice small and faraway sounding. "The things in dreams, they *can* follow you into real life. Call me back, please. It's important."

I blew out a breath. I'd have to call Declan later, when I was alone and feeling a little less frazzled.

"Yeah, I know," my aunt was saying into her phone. "Thanks. Talk later." She hung up. "Terri wanted to make sure you made it safe and sound."

"Well, I made it. I'm not so sure about the 'safe and sound' part."

I navigated my way into the living room, past a diving mask and snorkel, a shop lamp attached to a long, heavy-duty extension cord. Every surface was covered with loose-leaf notebook paper full of scribbles and sketches, old photos pulled from albums, photocopied documents covered in notes, half-full cups of tea, plates of fossilized leftovers. Pieces of clothing— a sweater, running shorts, a bathing suit, a terry cloth robe—were scattered and draped. There was a near-empty bottle of Ketel One Vodka on the edge of the coffee table.

"I didn't think Lexie drank," I said, picking up the bottle. Lexie didn't like the way alcohol slowed down her thinking, said it was like putting on a thick, fuzzy bear suit that was hot and uncomfortable and made the world seem muffled. She claimed that marijuana leveled her out, helped slow her racing thoughts so the rest of her could catch up. I noticed a pack of rolling papers on the coffee table, a few spent joints at the bottom of drinking glasses.

Aunt Diane looked at the bottle in my hand now. "I've never known Lexic to drink either. She always hated the stuff."

Sooner or later, I'd get used to Lexie being referred to in the past tense.

"Now this, on the other hand," Diane said, picking up a baggie half-full of weed, "was totally her thing."

I watched in total disbelief as my aunt began to expertly roll a joint. "What are you doing?"

"Baking a pie, Jax. What does it look like I'm doing?"

"I didn't know you smoked."

"You know me: full of surprises." She licked the edge of the paper and smoothed it down.

"What on earth is this?" I asked, heading over to the antique sideboard that ran half the length of the room. It was where our grandmother had kept the silverware, the place mats and napkins, and all the fancy serving dishes and bowls we used on holidays. Now there were about thirty glasses and jars resting on top of it. The finished maple was stained with ghostly watermarks. Each glass was resting on a scrap of paper with numbers written on it. 6/1, 6/6, 6/11. I picked up a glass. The water—if it was water—was slightly cloudy but had no odor.

"Heaven knows," Aunt Diane said, pushing aside a pile of papers so she could sit on the couch with her newly rolled joint tucked between her lips. "I was here two weeks ago. The place was a little messy, but nothing like this." She reached forward, grabbed a lighter on the table. I set the glass down and picked up a sheet of loose-leaf notebook paper:

F9: 6/11 6 a.m.—7.2 meters
F9: 6/11 1 p.m.—7.2 meters
F9: 6/11 10:20 p.m.—over 50 meters!!!
*** *Must get more rope tomorrow*

There were other papers—backs of envelopes, Post-it Notes, torn bits from brown paper grocery bags—but most were loose-leaf, lined with three holes for keeping in a binder. Lexie had kept a journal this way for years. A haphazard combination of diary, shopping and to-do lists, and a place to capture random thoughts and ideas. I once bought her a fancy leather-bound notebook, but she never used it, saying she was intimidated by how permanent the pages seemed. "With my journal, I can go back through and remove anything I don't like later on. Or restructure things," she'd said. Like she could keep her life in some sort of order by rearranging a journal. Many were covered with similar codes, dates, times, and measurements: *J2*; *A7*; *D10*. It reminded me of Battleship: calling out coordinates, sinking each other's submarines. *Damn you, Jax! You sank my destroyer!*

I picked up one of Lexie's journal entries:

May 13
    Deduction.
    Reduction.
    Redaction.
    How much has been redacted from the carefully curated version of our story?
    The story of we. The story of us. The story of THIS PLACE! The story of THE SPRINGS!
    GRAM KNEW! Gram knew the truth and said nothing.

Another paper held all the details Lexie had been able to find out about Rita's drowning.

Facts I know about Rita's death:

Rita was 7 years old.
Mom was 10. Diane was 13.
Gram found Rita FLOATING facedown in the pool that morning. Rita was wearing her nightgown.
Gram, Mom, Diane and Rita and Great-Grandma were all at home. They'd had dinner the night before—beef stew, had watched some TV and gone to bed. No one heard or saw anything. At some point in the night or early morning, Rita must have gotten out of bed and gone down to the pool. Gram's screams woke Mom and Diane the next morning. They ran down to see what was the matter. There was Gram with Rita in her arms, pulled from the pool, soaking wet.
I found the death certificate.
Cause of death: ACCIDENTAL DROWNING.
Like it was really that simple.
Like that was really what happened.

I let the papers fall back to the floor as I sank down onto the couch beside my aunt. She held out the joint to me, and I shook my head; pot was the last thing I needed. She took another hit, held the breath, then let it out slowly. "Two weeks ago she seemed *fine*."

"How do you think it happened?" I asked. "She was the best swimmer I know. How did she drown? I mean, do you think . . ."

"That it was a suicide? That she drowned herself on purpose?" Diane's shoulders hunched. "I guess we'll never know. Maybe she just did too many laps, got tired, got a cramp, thought she was a fish. We'll never know. We'll never know what led Lexie out to the pool that night, or what was going through her head in her final days. Trying to figure it out, guessing . . . it's a fool's errand."

My sister the whirling dervish, I thought as I looked around the trashed room. The cyclone leaving ruin in her wake. She'd go on massive shopping sprees, start a renovation by sledgehammer, or decide she wanted to delve into her Scottish roots by taking up the bagpipe—then she would decide everything was complete shit. She'd call me sobbing, despondent, and suicidal. I'd spent a good part of my life helping Lexie clean up her messes, coaxing her back on her meds.

I glanced at the floor, saw an old photo of Lexie and me as kids. We were standing in front of the pool she had just drowned in. Lexie looked to be about twelve, which would make me nine. We were wearing bright bikinis, arms around each other, squinting into the camera. Behind us, the dark water shimmered obsidian, our reflections watching to see what we might do next.

Closing my eyes, I sank back into the cushions.

The smell of the pot reminded me of Lexie and, with my eyes closed, I could let myself imagine, for a half a second, that it was her beside me, not Diane.

I could almost hear her: *Hey, Jax. Long time no see.*

Something brushed against my left calf, a tentative touch at first, then firmer, more sure.

My eyes flew open, and I screamed.

Diane jumped, dropped the joint.

"What the hell was that?" I asked as a small black blur raced across the living room floor.

"Pig," Diane said. She sounded relieved.

"What? That was so not a pig," I said. But it occurred to me that at this point, I wouldn't be too shocked if Lexie did have a pig living in the house.

"It's Lexie's cat," Diane explained.

"Lexie had a cat? Since when?"

"A couple of months now. He was a stray who just kept coming around, and she kept feeding him. They kind of adopted each other, I guess."

I shook my head in disbelief. A cat. Lexie had a cat.

"She called him Pig," Diane said.

I stood up, looking for the cat. He had hidden underneath the antique sideboard in the dining room.

"Who names a cat Pig?" I asked, getting down on my knees, peering at the little black cat. His golden eyes glared back at me. I'd clearly scared him as much as he'd scared me—he was up against the wall, flat on his belly, ears back. "Come on out, big guy," I coaxed.

He hissed.

We were off to a great start.

"We'll have to catch him and get him to the shelter," Diane said.

"Can't you keep him?" I asked.

She shook her head. "I'm allergic."

"Well, don't you know anyone who might want him?"

She frowned. "I can ask around. You know lesbians and cats—it's one of those stereotypes that I've actually found to be true."

"Let's try to find a good home for him rather than drop him off at the shelter. In the meantime, I'll take care of him." I'd never had a cat, or any pet at all for that matter, but how hard could it be?

Why didn't you pick up the phone, Jax? my sister whispered in my ear.

Then she had her hand around my wrist and was pulling me down, down under the brackish water of the pool. It was dark and deathly cold as I struggled against her. But Lexie was stronger. Lexie was winning. Water filled my nose, my mouth, my lungs, and Declan's nightmare fish creatures were there: black with sharp teeth in open mouths, long tentacles reaching out, wrapping around me, helping my sister pull me down.

I sat up, gasping for breath.

A dream. A guilt-fed, grief-driven dream.

Forcing myself to take deep breaths, I saw that I was in my summer childhood twin brass bed where I'd fallen asleep exhausted hours before, intending to rest a few minutes, then get started on picking up the mess.

I rubbed at my wrist, sure I could still feel the tight grip of Lexie's fingers wrapped around it like a manacle.

"You can't stay here," Aunt Diane had said, spreading her arms, gesturing to the chaos, her bracelets jingling. "It's not fit for human habitation. Come to my place. I insist."

"I want to stay here. This place was a second home to me growing up." I swallowed my next thought: that I'd always thought it *would* be my home one day. Until my sister got it all. And now she was gone. "I can start cleaning. I need to be here," I'd assured Diane. "It was Lexie's home. If I'm miserable, I can switch to your place tomorrow. Besides, I won't be alone. I've got Pig. We can look after each other." I'd finally lured the cat out by leaving an open can of tuna on the floor. He gulped it down, eyeing me suspiciously between bites.

"There's no way I'm leaving you here on your own," Diane said, looking almost panicked.

"Please," I said. "It'll help me start to process everything. It's what I need to do."

Diane had relented at last, insisting that I call her if I changed my mind. "Or just get in Lexie's car and drive over, anytime, even if it's the middle of the night."

Now here I was, deeply regretting my decision. The moonlight cast a dim blue glow over the room—the small pine dresser with a mirror above it, the shelves once lined with Nancy Drew books and the treasures Lexie and I found in the woods behind Sparrow Crest: a cut-glass doorknob, a silver fork, broken china, pieces of blue ceramic tile with a flower pattern, a porcelain faucet handle with COLD printed on it. We knew that years ago, before Gram was even born, an old hotel had stood in the very spot where Sparrow Crest now was: the Brandenburg Springs Hotel and Resort. People came from all over by train and car to stay in our little valley, to take in the healing powers of the water at the springs. I found it weird to think about—that something else had existed on the same land before Sparrow Crest, before our family. Gram didn't like to talk about it, and whenever we asked her about the hotel, she'd shake her head and say, "That's ancient history." I remembered showing Gram our treasures, excitedly telling her that they were from the hotel.

"You shouldn't play back there," Gram warned. "You don't want to cut yourself on old metal and end up with lockjaw."

The bookshelves were empty now. I sat up, listening. The house seemed to be holding its breath. Lexie's was the room next to mine, our beds pressed against the same wall. We'd go to sleep tapping out goodnight codes, knocking again in the morning to say we were up. Lexie wanted to build a trapdoor in the wall. "Like what priests have for confessing. A secret door for whispering the things we'd never tell anyone else. Not even each other in the light of day."

I tapped lightly on the wall and listened.

Nothing. No one.

What had I expected?

Falling asleep again felt impossible. It was odd—being all alone in that big house. I missed my mother fiercely and wished she were still here. She'd been the rock in my life, the picture of clear thinking and sanity. I missed Gram and the way she'd always called us Jacqueline and Alexia; the afternoons we'd spent with her working in the rose garden while she told us the name of each variety: Snow Queen, Old Blush, Apothecary, Queen of Denmark.

And my sister. I missed my sister most of all.

I lay in the dark, listening to the house tick and hum around me. A sink dripped; the sound amplified as it traveled the still house. Outside, something made a high-pitched screech, then banged—once, twice, three times. My heart jackhammered. The sound broke out again. An eerie screech, then a bang. Moving as if underwater, I forced myself out of bed to investigate.

I flipped the light switch. No light. I slowly made my way out of the room, shuffling along with bare feet, my body knowing the way by heart. I felt for the hall switch and flipped it. Again, nothing. I stood at the top of the stairs, holding still in the dark, listening, willing my eyes to adjust. Was the power out? Had Lexie forgotten to pay the bill?

There it was again: *squeal, thump; squeal, thump; squeal, thump.*

Maybe it's a banshee, Lexie whispered, trying to scare me. Always insisting ghosts were real.

No, not *actual* Lexie, the memory of her.

Being back at Sparrow Crest was blurring the lines, bringing the past to life.

What's the difference, I wondered, *between a ghost and a memory?*

I reached for the banister, made my way carefully down the curved wooden steps. At the bottom of the stairs, my feet got wet. The puddles I'd noticed when we first entered the slate-floored hall hours ago. But . . . was there more water here now?

A smell, a terrible, damp, rotting smell filled the hall.

I fought the urge to run back up the stairs, crawl into bed, and pull the covers over my head just as I'd done as a child.

Don't you hear that? That squish, squish, squish of footsteps? She's coming for you. Coming for us both.

But I wasn't a little girl anymore. I was a grown woman. A social worker, for Christ's sake. I took in a breath, steadied myself.

My eyes adjusted enough to see the cat standing in the hall, back arched and fur raised.

"Hey, Pig," I said, the sound of my own voice calming me.

The cat looked past me, golden eyes focused on the front door. He let out a hiss.

I kicked at the papers, clothes, the overturned table. Tried the front hall lights, but they were out, too. "Shit." I stumbled in the dark.

I made my way to the front door, shuffling through the debris to keep from tripping, and looked out the tiny square window: the driveway was empty except for Lexie's yellow Mustang, which seemed to glow, casting its own pool of light. The yard around it was dark. The only movement was off to the right. The door in the white wooden fence that surrounded the pool was open, swinging in the breeze, the hinge squeaking as it banged against the fence. I let go of the breath I hadn't realized I'd been holding. It was only the gate.

"Nothing out there," I said to the cat in my most comforting voice. "It's just the gate."

He hissed once more, then turned and ran, unconvinced.

"Wuss," I called after him.

I let myself out the front door, walked the paved steps to the gate and closed it, sliding the metal latch into the place, keeping my eyes averted from the pool. I was not ready to acknowledge the pool. But I felt it there, waiting for me, taunting me in the dark.

"Not tonight," I said, and went back in the house, closed and locked the heavy front door, and clicked the dead bolt into place.

chapter six

June 15, 1929
Brandenburg, Vermont

Last night, after unpacking and settling in, we dined on brook trout and baby potatoes in an ornate dining room with cream-colored walls and lush velvet curtains. A man played low, moody music on the piano. Will produced a small flask of apple brandy from back home and tipped a little into my glass. I wore a new silver satin dress, and under the lights of crystal chandeliers it sparkled like fish scales.

Mr. Benson Harding, the owner of the hotel, visited each table with his wife, greeting his guests personally. He was a tall man with dark hair, a carefully trimmed mustache, and piercing blue eyes that seemed to be watching everything in the room at once. He shook Will's hand and introduced us to his wife, Eliza, a stunning woman with bobbed black hair and eyes just as dark. She had a small raised scar under her left eye, which somehow made her face more beautiful. Her lips were painted red, her eyelashes heavy with mascara. Her dress was black but covered in sequins that shimmered under the lights. They looked so perfect and happy together, arm in arm in their fine clothes. "And are you enjoying your stay so far, Mrs. Monroe?"

"It's delightful," I assured her. "Like something from a dream!"

She smiled, leaned in so that her lips were just inches from my ear, her breath warm on my neck, and said in a low voice meant only for me, "Isn't it just?"

———————

As the evening wore on, the music turned lively and the piano player was joined by a drummer, bass player, and a man with a horn. He sang "Everybody Loves My Baby," and some couples got up to dance. Will took my hand and led me to the small dance floor, and we spun until I was sure I would fall. The room was buzzing with music and people talking and laughing. Will whispered something in my ear, but I couldn't make out what it was. "I'm afraid I've had too much brandy," I admitted.

"No such thing," he said, and suggested we get some air. His eyes looked impossibly green. I leaned against him, said, "Aren't we just the luckiest people on earth? To have found each other?" He smiled and kissed me.

We took an evening stroll around the grounds, our arms linked. Crickets and katydids sang from the grass. The peacocks were tucked away somewhere for the night. We headed toward the springs, taking a stone-lined path, but they were roped off with DANGER and CLOSED signs. I could hear running water. There was a sharp, mineral tang in the air. Someone had clearly already disobeyed the signs, because I heard a splash and a giggle. I couldn't see anything but the dark shadows of the trees that lined the pool area. "Maybe they're skinny-dipping?" I said. I suggested that we sneak in, too.

"Scandalous, Mrs. Monroe," he said, and raised his eyebrows, blushing slightly. "If there is a couple in there already, I'm sure they'd like their privacy."

That night, I had the strangest dream. The sparrow's egg was resting against my chest again. I picked it up and it cracked open, and water began to flow out of it. The water took shape, and a small child, about five or six years old, stepped out from beneath the stream of water. It was a little girl with dark hair and eyes, a narrow face, elvish features. She looked at me and smiled, and my heart banged hard in my chest as I smiled back. I recognized her dark, almond-shaped eyes as my own. She was me and yet not me. I knew at once that this was my child. My daughter.

"I've been waiting for you," the child said.

I took her in my arms and wept, burying my face in her hair. She smelled like wind and summer rain, the forgotten afternoons of childhood. As I breathed her in, my chest ached with longing. I woke up crying, my arms empty. Moonlight filtered in through the windows, giving the room a pale blue glow, as if we were underwater. Will was asleep on his back beside me, his face slack and peaceful. I padded into the bathroom, latching the door. I opened my case, took out a pin, sat on the toilet, and scratched three short lines just above my right ankle, concentrating on the pain until the aching feeling in my chest began to fade.

This morning, after a lovely breakfast of poached eggs, toast, and fresh fruit, we went back to our room and changed into bathing costumes covered up with the plush robes the hotel provided. We followed the stone path from the back door of the hotel to the springs. It took us to the edge of the yard, to a small pool lined in granite, perhaps ten feet by ten feet. What struck me first was the smell: a sharp, mineral tang tinged with the rotten egg stench of sulfur. Will wrinkled his nose. "Smells haunted," he joked. I gave him a reproachful glare. Birds chattered from the nearby trees. One of the peacocks came close and gave a screech, but there were no other bathers in the water—we had the pool to ourselves. The water was black! So dark that it seemed to take our reflections and pull them into the darkness, making us disappear. I was actually frightened to get into that obsidian water. Will must have sensed my apprehension, because he put his hand on my arm and said, "We don't have to do this."

Was I imagining the nervousness in his voice?

"Of course we're going in. That's why we're here!" I said, slipping off my robe and shoes. I got to the edge and lowered myself in. The water stung the fresh scratches on my ankle. The cold was a shock! So frigid it was painful. I gasped. "I can't feel the bottom," I told Will. I held my breath and went down, trying to touch it, but could not. I resurfaced, teeth chattering. The pain of the cold was replaced by numbness. I could not feel the tips of my fingers and toes.

Will slid into the water. "Good God!" he exclaimed.

We swam in quick circles, moving our arms and legs to keep warm, teeth chattering. "You're beautiful when you're freezing to death," Will told me.

The water had weight to it—Will said it was the minerals. As I swam, I felt as if fingers were touching my skin, wrapping themselves around my arms and legs, holding me up then trying to tug me down. After five minutes, we could take no more and got out. We were toweling off when I looked down at my ankle. I blinked in disbelief. The scratches I'd made last night were gone!

A funny little gasp escaped my lips as I rubbed at the unflawed skin.

"Are you all right?" Will asked.

"Ye-yess," I managed. "Just cold."

"Your lips are blue, darling wife," Will announced. His were, too. His skin looked shockingly pale. Suddenly, his eyes focused on the pool, and he asked, "Did you see that?"

"What?" I asked.

He stared down into the dark water, frowning. "Nothing," he said. "It was nothing. A trick of the light."

I was sitting in the rose garden beside the hotel when I was approached by Eliza Harding, who waved and smiled as she walked over, greeting me like an old friend she was overjoyed to see. She wore a cheerful blue dress and had her lips painted the perfect shade of red. "May I join you, Mrs. Monroe?" she asked.

I nodded and moved over to make room on the wrought iron bench. "Please call me Ethel," I said. She sat close by my side, our legs touching.

She pulled a silver cigarette case from her black leather purse and held it open to me. I shook my head. She took out a cigarette and lit it. "You mustn't tell Benson," she said. "He thinks it's vile for a lady to smoke. I love him dearly, but he's a bit of a wet blanket at times."

I smiled. "It's our secret." I had the same feeling I'd had when I stepped out onto the balcony: an instant sense of familiarity. Like Eliza and I were old friends. Kindred spirits.

"Other than the springs, this rose garden is my favorite place," she confessed, exhaling a thin blue stream of smoke. "I designed it myself."

"Really?"

"Oh yes. The beds form three concentric circles bisected by the four paths perfectly aligned by directions: the north/south path and the east/west path. It was all very carefully laid out—months and months of planning and sketching."

"All your work paid off beautifully," I told her. "It's simply stunning."

She smiled. "It's odd, really. Trying to impose order on nature. The garden is a living, breathing thing; sometimes I'm quite sure it's got a mind of its own."

She could name all the varieties of roses: Aurora, Snow Queen, Persian Yellow, Maiden's Blush.

"Such lovely names!" I said.

She nodded. "Aren't they, just? I've had some shipped over from England. It's how I survive the winters here," she confessed. "Planning, poring over flower catalogs."

She told me she grew up in Brandenburg, on the back side of the hill where the hotel stands. "My family is there still. It's lovely to be so close to them."

She shared such fanciful stories—stories about the springs and the miracles the waters brought. The lame and crippled being able to walk again, soldiers from the war coming home with all sorts of injuries and being cured by the springs. "A soldier, a local boy from town named Ethan, came home. He'd been shot in the head over in France. When he got back, he wasn't able to speak. Didn't seem to recognize his own mother and father. It was like everything that made him who he was had been erased by that bullet. But his parents, they put him in that water, and the very next day he woke up begging his mother to make him his favorite dinner—chicken and dumplings. He works over at the quarry now as a foreman."

I shook my head in disbelief.

"I've seen it myself, over and over again," Eliza told me. "My uncle Raymond, he lived down in St. Albans. He was left blind after an accident at the foundry there. He came back here, took a dip in the springs, and his sight was restored. I swear it."

"My husband, Will, he's a doctor. He thinks perhaps there must be antiseptic properties in the minerals."

She smiled. "Perhaps."

"I had some cuts—scratches, really—when I went into the water this morning. When I came out, they were healed."

She nodded knowingly. "There's no doubt that the water has healing powers. But there's more to it than that."

She took a puff from her cigarette and exhaled, watching the smoke drift up.

"There are very old stories about the springs. Some say it's a door between worlds."

"Is that what you believe?" I asked.

She stubbed out her cigarette.

"I believe the water holds more power and mystery than most people understand."

"I heard some believe the springs are cursed," I said. "Haunted, even."

She seemed to bristle, her whole body tensing. "People are frightened by the things they don't understand. Things that can't be explained with reason and logic and science. The water is not a puzzle to be solved." She spoke of the springs like a living creature, a dear friend she was defending. "And it doesn't just cure you. It can grant wishes."

"Do you truly believe that?" I asked.

She smiled and nodded. "I know it for a fact." She played with the cuff of her dress, worrying at a loose thread. "It was the springs that brought my husband to me," she said, voice low and tentative, as though she wasn't sure she should be sharing this with me.

I raised my eyebrows, leaned closer to her. Our faces were only inches apart. I felt like a schoolgirl again, hidden away in the center of the garden, sharing secrets.

"I went to the water and wished for the thing I wanted most—true love and a family of my own. Soon after, Benson Harding appeared in town." She paused, closed her eyes, remembering. "Oh, he was so handsome, just the cat's meow! The bluest eyes I'd ever seen. I knew the instant I saw him that he was *the one* for me. That the springs had brought him to me!" She reached up, ran her fingers over one of the roses, pulling it close to smell. "He bought the springs, of course, and began to build the hotel. Our courtship lasted less than a year before he asked me to be his wife."

She plucked the rose, a small white flower, and handed it to me.

"Did you tell him?" I asked, taking the flower, smelling its sweet, heady scent. "Tell him of your wish?"

"Oh yes," she said. "He didn't believe a word of it, of course."

She brought her finger to her lips, and I saw there was a little drop of blood there—a thorn from the rosebush had pricked her.

"I owe it all to the springs," she said. "I would have

none of this if I hadn't made that wish." She gestured with her arms at the garden, the lawn, and the hotel. "This hotel, my beautiful garden, a husband I adore, and a brand-new baby who is too perfect for words!"

"A new baby?" My stomach knotted. She truly did have everything. "I didn't realize. Congratulations." I carefully pushed my thumb down onto a thorn on the stem she'd handed me, felt it pierce the skin ever so slightly.

"An absolute cherub. As if an angel were plucked down from heaven and given to us. Do you have any children, Ethel?"

"No," I said. My chest felt heavy, and I looked away, embarrassed as my eyes glazed with tears.

"Oh, I'm sorry," she said, taking my hand, noticing the blood. "You've pricked yourself." She pulled a lace hankie out of her purse.

"It's nothing."

"I didn't mean to upset you," she said, wiping the blood away, staining the white lace. "I shouldn't have pried. I can be perfectly lousy sometimes. It's really none of my business—"

"Please," I said, "I'm the one who's sorry, for being so emotional!" I wiped at my eyes. Thought of the little girl I'd held in my dreams last night. "It's just that it's been over a year of trying . . . And, well, I'm starting to think something must be wrong with me." Even though I'd only just met her, I told her about the egg I carried against my breast and buried in the yard. I laughed at my own foolishness, but her face stayed quiet and serious. "Will says we have plenty of time. But I can't help feeling that I'm a disappointment to him. You should see him with children. He'd be the best father! I wish I could give him the thing he wants most." I paused, realized I'd been crushing the poor rosebud Eliza had given me. "I truly believe we're meant to have a child. I swear, I can feel her out there waiting for me, just as I am waiting for her."

"Go to the water and tell it." She smiled slyly. "Promise me you'll try?"

———————

I kept my promise. Will took an afternoon nap, and I went out to the springs on my own, sneaking my way along the path, heart pounding. I felt like a young girl again, believing in fanciful things, that the world was full of magic and miracles. The green hills, the lush grounds, the roaming peacocks; I felt like a princess. And isn't it true that in fairy tales, wishes are granted?

Once again, there was no one else at the pool as I approached. It was waiting just for me, shimmering and winking in the sun. I walked up hesitantly, wondering what I was doing, feeling suddenly foolish. But hadn't I done plenty of foolish things already? Was making a wish at a spring that much different than carrying a sparrow's egg for days? None of what'd I done so far had worked. Why should this be any different?

It pained me to think how desperate I'd become. It seemed unfair that I had to go to such lengths when it was so easy for other women to bear child after child. And what would Will say if he found me here now?

"Idiot," I said out loud, and turned to leave before someone caught me there.

But then I thought of my promise to Eliza. And I remembered the feel of my arms around the little girl in my dream—how real she had seemed!—and how empty and aching I'd been when I woke.

Maybe I was an idiot, a foolish and desperate woman,

but I ran back to the water's edge, leaned down, pushed my face right against the surface, and I spoke to my reflection, the words making the deep water ripple. "Please," I said, "I would do anything. Anything at all, anything to have a child." My reflection went in and out of focus, and then it wasn't me I was looking at, but the face of a little girl. The child from my dream with eyes so like my own. My not-yet daughter.

"Please," I said to the water, "please bring her to me." I had begun to cry. My tears fell into the pool, and I thought I saw something far beneath my own distorted reflection. A pale flash of movement, here and then gone.

chapter seven

I started to clean up the kitchen the next morning. In the bright light of day, my middle-of-the-night fears seemed silly—I shook my head as I remembered creeping around the dark house imagining banshees. The power wasn't out after all; the outlets in the kitchen worked fine and the fridge was humming. I made myself a cup of espresso. It was burnt tasting, bitter and thick. I tried the kitchen lights and, when they didn't come on, further inspection revealed missing bulbs. I checked the closet where our grandma had always kept the household supplies, but didn't find any. Pig stalked into the kitchen and let out an angry meow, so I dumped another can of tuna onto a plate. There was no sign of cat food anywhere.

It looked like it had been weeks since Lexie had done the dishes. She'd gone through all the everyday ones and had moved on to the good china. Our grandmother's delicate floral-rimmed plates were chipped and hosting broken crackers and shriveled bits of cheese. The kitchen smelled. I tried opening the Dutch door that led out to the patio, thinking fresh air and sunshine would be nice, but it wouldn't budge. Looking more closely, I saw that metal brackets had been screwed in, sealing the door to the frame.

"Why on earth would you do that?" I asked, half expecting Lexie to give me some cockamamie explanation involving feng shui.

To the left of the Dutch door was a black rotary phone that had been there my entire life. The one Lexie had no doubt been calling me from before she drowned: *Answer the fucking phone, Jax! I know you're there. I can feel you listening.*

Next to the phone was a wall calendar. I looked at June, then flipped back to May. Therapist and doctors' appointments, a car tune-up, dental cleaning, lunch with Diane, dinner with Ryan. My sister had been having dinner with Ryan, when I didn't even know he was back in town.

I remembered young Ryan with his halo of curly red hair, who'd show up at Sparrow Crest on his blue ten-speed, ready to follow Lexie on whatever adventure she had in store for us. One year, they spent the entire summer searching the woods for a peacock. Gram, Terri, Randy, Aunt Diane, Uncle Ralph, Ryan, and I had all been sitting on the patio by the pool. It was a hot day, but no one was swimming, just trying to stay cool by being near the water. The adults were having cocktails. I was playing Go Fish with Ryan. I always won when I played with him—he was so easy to read, I could tell what cards he had just by watching his face. Lexie came tearing in, sweaty and scratched up, saying she'd seen a peacock in the woods. She'd chased him to the top of Devil's Hill, then lost him in the thick brush up there. Her hair was wild, and she was talking fast and loud as she told us her story.

The adults had laughed. "What on earth would a peacock be doing way back there?" Aunt Diane asked.

"Maybe it was a grouse?" Uncle Ralph suggested. "Or a wild turkey?"

"It was a peacock," Lexie insisted. "He fanned his tail and everything."

"A male turkey can fan its tail, too," Ryan's dad said.

It was just like Lexie, I thought, to see an ugly old Tom turkey and turn it into something beautiful.

"I'm not an idiot," she said. "I know what a turkey looks like. What I saw was a peacock. And I'm going to catch him. I'll do it on my own if none of you believe me." She turned to walk away.

"I believe you," Ryan said, setting down his cards, forgetting all about our game. Lexie stopped, turned back, and smiled at him.

"I'll help you catch it," he said. And I hated him a little then.

———

Coffee finished, I realized I was starving. I went to the fridge, found a list taped to it:

> *milk*
> *coffee*
> *cheese*
> *long nails and screws*
> **Ask Bill about night vision camera—*
>   *motion activated? infrared?*

The fridge was nearly empty—a carton of spoiled milk, a lidless pot of congealed soup, an empty container of Ben and Jerry's Cherry Garcia, a few shriveled limes, and ancient condiments. I found half a box of stale graham crackers in one of the cupboards and nibbled on them as I picked up.

I couldn't shake the feeling that Lexie was in the house, that she was just upstairs and would come down at any minute, hair disheveled, pajamas wrinkled. She'd sit down at the table, look around at the kitchen, and say, "Spick and span, Jax."

I swept the floor, the broom pulling out another sheet of notebook paper from under the table. I bent down to grab it.

June 1
Something's in the water

I froze, heart thudding in my ears. Then, slowly, I turned and looked out the kitchen window at the pool. The surface was still and black, like a great piece of polished onyx. I pulled the curtain closed so I didn't have to look anymore and went back to sweeping.

Once the kitchen was in some semblance of order, I headed for the living room. Pig followed at a safe distance, watching with curiosity. A quick check confirmed that all the light bulbs in there had been removed, too. In fact, some of them were not removed but smashed, the metal socket still in place along with a ring of jagged broken glass. I picked up all the dishes and cups in the living room and brought them into the kitchen. Then I started on the papers and family photos pulled from old albums. They were scattered everywhere.

Hurricane Lexie.

I studied the odd code I had noticed yesterday. A date and time with coordinates of some kind, measurements. *F6: 6/9 11:05 p.m.—over 50 meters!* I began to stack the loose pages in a pile on the coffee table, glancing at words Lexie had scrawled: *6/10:*

They don't like the light. They won't come when the lights are on. Christ. Was she feeding animals? Or having out-and-out hallucinations? It wasn't unheard of when her mania was at its peak. I tried to put them in chronological order the best I could. Not every entry was dated, and some were hardly legible. One read: *Ask Diane about Rita's imaginary friend, Martha. Call Jax and ask if she remembers any stories Mom told about Rita (especially anything about Rita and Martha!).*

Lexie had never asked me. She would have been disappointed anyway—I didn't have any stories to share. Mom didn't speak about Rita. Not to me.

I reached for a paper dated June 12, five days ago:

I know what I saw. I am not crazy. This was no hallucination. I think it came out of the water.

I shook my head. Then I spotted a little square of pink paper stuck under the leg of the coffee table. I pulled it out: *She isn't who she says she is.* I held the paper, fingers trembling, remembering what Declan had told me about the fish: *They weren't who they said they were. They'd turned into something else.*

———

I added the paper to the stack I'd made on the coffee table and reached for the next bunch. I grabbed a scattering of photocopied pages: a survey of Sparrow Crest and the surrounding property; tax records; a drawing of Brandenburg from 1865, with each property lot carefully marked—the land and springs had belonged to a man named Nelson DeWitt. There was an old map and deed from 1929 showing the location of the Brandenburg Springs Hotel and Resort, owned by Mr. Benson Harding. I found an old tattered paperback book: *The History of Brandenburg, Vermont.*

My sister's research hadn't been just about our family, but our family home, land, and town as well. There were pages and pages of journal entries, and I knew I'd never get through picking up if I stopped to read each one, so I just put them all into a pile. Some of them had neat, careful cursive; some were written in messy, hurried, childish scrawl—the way Lexie wrote when she was sick. It seemed she'd been incredibly prolific over these last months: hundreds of pages of notes and journal entries, many about the springs, the pool, the hotel, our family.

One scrap of paper dated May 27 was just a list of names:

> *Nelson Dewitt*
> *Martha W.*
> *Eliza Harding*
> *Rita Harkness*

The last journal entry I picked up did not have a date.

> *I remember what Grandma always told people when they asked her why she didn't have the pool filled in after Rita drowned; how she could bear to watch her children, then grandchildren continue to swim in that water; how she could possibly still swim there herself. "Rita loved the pool," Gram would tell them. "It's where I feel closest to her. When I'm in the water, I feel like she's still with me."*

My eyes went over the last line again and again, until, with a trembling hand, I set the paper down on the pile I'd made on the coffee table. The papers stood in tall, messy stacks, but at least they were up off the floor. I'd go out and get some three-ring binders and do a better job at organizing them later.

I picked up the book of town history again. It was published in 1977 by the Town of Brandenburg Bicentennial Committee. The typesetting was terrible, the photographs grainy. It looked more like some kid's middle school project than an actual book. I opened it to the first chapter, where Lexie had left a pink sticky note as a bookmark and underlined a passage.

In 1792, when the first settlers, led by Reverend Thomas Alcott, arrived in what is now Brandenburg, they found it had been settled once before. The remains of a village long abandoned were clear— a small gathering of half a dozen cabins, pastures cleared for planting, overgrown gardens, and trash: broken bottles, clay jars, piles of bones from deer and small game. At the heart of this little village was the spring, a small bubbling pool of dark water. And there, at the edge of the spring, Thomas Alcott and his group found a rock, a broken piece of granite about the size of a man's arm. On it was carved: *prendre garde.*

One of the men in the party translated: *beware.*

I tossed the book down, stood up, and walked away, turning my back on it.

In the center of the living room, I stood, taking deep breaths, then looked out the window, past my own reflection. I knew what I had to do next. The thing I'd been avoiding since I arrived. I walked down the hall, out the front door, and into the yard. The grass looked like it hadn't been mown at all this year.

The air hummed with the low drone of buzzing insects. I followed the path of stone pavers to the side of the house, to the gate. I undid the latch; the door screeched open. I forced myself through.

The pool was there, waiting for me; the water dark as ink. A huge, unblinking pupil.

I imagined Lexie there, floating facedown and naked. My mind went to all sorts of places: Had she been close enough to the edge for Diane to pull her out without having to jump in? Where were her clothes? They were details that didn't matter, things I knew I would never ask Diane, but my mind was stuck on them, spinning in circles, trying to picture it, trying to make it feel more real.

When I'm in the water, I feel like she's still with me.

The water from the natural spring that fed the pool was colder than any water I've experienced, before or since. The carved granite stones along the edge were stained green, spotted with moss. I could hear the water flowing through the spillway, down the canal that ran across the yard, to the stream and river. Lexie said once, "Water from our pool flows all the way to the ocean—fish out in the Atlantic are tasting the water from our little spring!"

I stared at it now, the surface perfectly still; a black mirror. Our grandmother always told us it was bottomless.

"Could I swim to the other side of the world?" Lexie asked when she was nine.

"If you could hold your breath that long, then yes, I suppose you could, Alexia."

"You'd die if you held your breath that long," I warned.

That whole summer, and every summer after, my

sister practiced holding her breath and diving down into the darkest part of the water.

"It's stupid, you know," I told her. "You can't really swim to the other side of the world."

"How do you know?" she asked.

"Because I just know. And you should, too. You're the one who gets straight As in science."

"So?"

"So the earth has layers of rock and at the center there's a fiery core—even I know that."

She gave me this pitying look and dove back under.

She said sometimes, when she was deep, it was hard to tell which way was up. But she never managed to touch the bottom. And she never got to the other side of the world.

"Until now," I said to the pool.

My chest felt empty and hollow, my limbs impossibly heavy. If I were to fall into the water, I knew I would sink down, down, down. Tears blurred my vision, matching the rich, mineral smell to the damp air.

Before my great-grandfather built the house, Gram used to say, people used to come to the springs to bathe and drink, and claimed the water had healing, even magical properties. They came before the hotel was built, and then, once the hotel went up, they came by the trainful.

Some people said the magic was good, but some stories we heard in town, passed down over generations, warned that the springs were cursed: If you came to the water looking for a miracle, you had to be prepared to pay a price. When we asked Gram about these stories, she laughed and said they were nonsense, even gently boxed our ears and warned us not to listen to such tall tales.

"Maybe it was the curse that killed poor Aunt Rita," Lexie hypothesized when we were alone.

Cursed or not, people still believed that the water healed. A constant stream of visitors came to Sparrow Crest each summer: ladies Gram knew from church, old friends, neighbors, and acquaintances. They wanted a quick swim or to fill bottles, swearing the water helped their arthritis, their headaches, their gout. Sometimes, we'd hear the visitors whispering to the water, talking to it like it was a living thing. They'd leave little gifts, too. I'd seen an old man dumping brandy into the water, and Gram's friend Shirley leaving flower petals scattered over the surface.

It seemed silly to me, but Lexie really believed that the water might have some kind of power. She said we should each drink the water every day, just a few sips so our magical abilities could surface.

"How will we know if it's changing us?" I asked.

"Maybe we won't. The biggest changes happen so slowly you hardly notice them."

The water tasted like burnt matches and old rocks. Sometimes we'd find dead frogs floating, and I imagined that's what the water tasted like: the green skin of the ones who weren't able to get themselves back out. I looked around now but saw no frogs, thankfully. We'd snuck down to the pool at night to tell it our wishes, too. Lexie had wished to be a better swimmer, and me, I'd wished for a terrible thing.

I blinked away the memory, looked over the pool and across the yard where Lord's Hill and Devil's Hill loomed like sleeping giants, casting long shadows, the trees so dark green they looked black.

A yellow-and-blue inflatable raft drifted, unmoored, at the far end of the pool. Two wooden lounge chairs were on the stone patio. There was a wrought iron table full of glasses, some half-full. Other objects were scattered around the edge of the pool—a box of crackers, a plate with bread crusts, an ashtray with the remains of several joints, mason jars, a coil of rope, an empty wine bottle, a blue nylon bag that had held the inflatable raft. And a box of spilled crayons—the big, fat kind, like the ones I kept in my office and pulled out for the youngest children.

I soon saw what Lexie had been using the crayons for: The stones around the edge of the pool had markings on them, in multiple colors. Letters along the short edge of the pool (A through T), and numbers along the long edge (1 to 45), evenly spaced at about a foot apart and separated by short, roughly drawn lines. A grid. Lexie had been studying the pool.

I walked around to the other side to get a better look at the raft. There were plastic oars inside it, and a net. And a long coil of rope with markings on it. I looked closer—not rope. It was more like an oversized, super sturdy measuring tape, with meters and tenths of a meter marked in red and black, up to 50 meters. A small loop at one end had a metal weight tied to it, a bit bigger than a golf ball and teardrop-shaped.

Now Lexie's coded messages made sense: She was measuring the depth of the pool using the grid and weighted measuring rope. But why? I shook my head. Trying to explain Lexie's behaviors with logic was a losing battle. My phone rang, the sudden noise and vibration from my back pocket making me jump. I'd forgotten I'd tucked it back there. I pulled out my phone and looked at the screen. Karen Hurst, the social worker helping out with my clients while I was away.

"Hello?" I answered.

"Hi, Jackie. I'm so, so sorry to bother you at a time like this, but I've got a bit of a crisis here. Apparently, Declan Shipee went into school today and dumped a gallon of bleach into a fish tank full of trout? His teacher tried to stop him; he threw bleach on her, got some in her eyes."

"Oh Jesus, no," I said. "He called me yesterday and left a message. He sounded . . . off. But I've been so caught up in stuff here, I haven't had a chance to call him back. How's his teacher?"

"She's going to be okay. No permanent damage. Sounds like he's burned his bridges at the school, though—they've asked him not to return. Declan's mom came and got him. I spoke with her over the phone. She's furious and blaming the school for what happened."

"She's fiercely protective of Declan, to the point of denial sometimes."

"I'm seeing Declan first thing tomorrow," Karen said. "I've been going over your notes in his file to get a little background. Other than the heads-up about his mom, do you have any additional thoughts or advice?"

I thought of Declan's drawing again, his nightmare fish. *They weren't who they said they were.* "He's really into animals and nature; that's always been a door in. I've got a bunch of field guides and nature books in my office. But, Karen, he *loved* those fish. I saw him on Friday, and he told me he'd had a nightmare about them—but we talked through it and he seemed okay." Had I missed something? Had I been too cranky and headachy to deal with the situation as I should have? "Damn it," I said. "I should have called him back when I got his message yesterday."

I looked at the raft on the water and noticed a piece of paper next to it, drifting. It was a folded paper boat, like something a child would make.

The things in dreams, they can follow you into real life.

I walked toward the far end of the pool, where the little boat was floating.

"You've got enough to deal with there," she said. "Leave Declan to me."

"Call me after you see you him, okay?"

"I don't want to keep bothering you, Jackie," she said. "How are you holding up?"

Lexie and I made little paper boats like that and sent them down the canal that flowed to the stream. She'd write messages inside them, hoping they would get carried far away, be picked up by a stranger who would read: *I'm being held prisoner, send help, please! This is a note from the other side of the world. Everything is upside down here.*

"I'm doing okay, all things considered. And it's fine. I'd really appreciate an update tomorrow."

I ended the call as I crept up to the edge of the pool, got down on my knees on the damp stone, and reached to grab the paper boat. It was made from lined notebook paper with three holes along the edge—there were words visible through the damp page. I carefully unfolded it and saw the message scribbled in green crayon in what appeared to be my sister's handwriting: *Why didn't you pick up the phone?*

I dropped the paper, watched it flutter back down into the pool. And just at that moment, I was dead sure I caught a glimpse of something in the water—a shifting shadow, a trick of light—and for a half a second, I expected Lexie to come bursting out of the water, gasping for breath, saying she still hadn't touched bottom.

chapter eight

It doesn't seem real," I admitted, picking at my cuticle until it bled.

Myrtle had gotten very quiet as I spoke and was now poking at the strawberry tart on her plate, spreading the jam around with her fork.

Will and I had been back at home since Sunday evening, and I was having a difficult time getting back into the rhythm of real life. Our trip felt like something I'd imagined or dreamed. Since our return, I'd done my best to get back into my usual routines, but nothing feels quite right. I've cleaned the windows until I can see my own reflection as well as in a mirror. I sewed a new button on Will's good shirt. I helped him go over the books for his practice. I attended a luncheon with ladies from the Auxiliary to plan our fall foliage festival—I was appointed chairwoman! Yet still, I feel like a sleepwalker. As if I'm under a spell. The world seems off. Colors are dim and pale. The grass and trees don't seem as green, the sky isn't as blue. The beautiful silver dress I wore to dinner at the hotel that seemed to sparkle now looks faded and sad on its hanger. Tucked away in the back corner of our closet, in an old hat box, are the two jars of spring water Eliza sent me home with. Will does not know I snuck them into our suitcase.

"You know," Myrtle said at last, "I've been there."

This caught me by surprise. "What? To the hotel?"

"No, no. This was years ago, long before they built the hotel. When it was just the springs." She abandoned her half-eaten tart, the smeared jam looking like coagulated blood.

"My Felix, he returned from the war in a wheelchair. Did you know that?"

I thought of her husband, who ran the feed and tack shop in town. I'd seen him lifting great bales of hay, sacks of grain. He'd once been in a wheelchair?

"He was shot on the battlefield in France. Took two bullets in his hip, one right in his spine that the doctors weren't able to remove. They said he'd never walk again. We were resigned to it. And then, one of Felix's friends told him about the springs. Encouraged us to go."

Myrtle is one of the most matter-of-fact people I know. She doesn't seem the sort to believe in water with healing powers.

"We thought it was silly, of course." She chuffed out a meek laugh. "My husband had a bullet lodged in his spine. How was sitting in spring water going to help him? But . . . after bathing in the waters, Felix was able to feel his legs again." She shuffled her feet against the painted floorboards. Sunlight filtered in through the kitchen window, lit up the dust in the air around us, making it sparkle.

"So it worked!" I said. Her face was full of awe, but underneath, I detected a hint of fear.

"Yes, he walked out of that water on his own." She paused, rubbed her face. "And now, he dances with me on Saturday nights." She smiled, then the smile faded, her lips pursing together tightly. "I had no idea they'd built a hotel there," she said. She looked out the window, then back at me. "Did you drink the water? Bathe in the springs?" She sounded worried.

"Of course. Why wouldn't we? Your Felix was able to walk again—"

"The water gives miracles, yes, but I think it takes, too." Myrtle looked pale. "Whatever's in that water, maybe it should be left alone."

"Did something happen to you after you went? Something bad?" I have been sipping at the water Eliza gave me, a little each day, tasting the rusted metal and blood, and focusing all of my energy on the wish I made down at the pool.

We heard the front door open, Will calling, "Hello! I'm home!"

"Myrtle?" I whispered urgently. "Tell me."

Myrtle straightened up in her chair, looked in my direction—not at me, but through me, as though I weren't really there. Then she smiled a thin, nervous smile and reached for her tea, called out, "Hello, William! We're in the kitchen with Ethel's famous tarts!"

———————

Later that night, tucked under the covers, safe and warm in our bedroom with its clean white plaster walls, Will's arms around me, there's a moment between waking and sleeping when I found myself back at the springs. I was on my hands and knees, whispering my secret, watching my reflection, and feeling with deep certainty that there was something down in that water. Something listening, waiting, watching.

Something I'm sure I caught a glimpse of.

Something that I'm also sure caught a glimpse of me.

chapter nine

June 17, 2019

Just after lunch, Aunt Diane arrived in jeans and a T-shirt with two professional housecleaners. I gave her a tight hug.

"How'd you sleep last night?" she asked, studying my face with concern.

"Fine," I lied. "But it was a little difficult finding my way around in the dark. The light bulbs are all either missing or broken."

Diane frowned. "Well, that's odd. We'll do a grocery store run later, pick some up."

She donned a pair of pink rubber gloves. "Let's dive in," she said.

We opened all the windows to fill the place with fresh air. While the four of us worked inside, a landscaping crew came and cut the grass, trimmed the bushes. Terrified by the invasion, Pig took off into the hills behind the house.

Slowly, we made progress. We threw away six trash bags full of garbage, scrubbed spills and stains, rehung art and photos, dumped all the cups of water from the antique sideboard. We gathered the clothing scattered all over the house—swimming suits, running shorts, underwear, T-shirts. Threw out fossilized food and countless spent joints. I caught Diane lighting up one that still had a few good puffs left. "Really?" I asked.

"Don't be a stick in the mud, Jax. Lexie would want me to have it."

Her phone kept making an assortment of sounds: a locomotive, songs, crickets chirping, an old-fashioned car horn, a regular ringtone. She ignored them all.

"Do you have a different sound for each girlfriend?" I joked.

"Very funny," she said.

"How come you're not answering any of them?" I asked. Her phone chirped again.

She switched her phone to silent and stuck it in her back pocket. "Now where the hell did the broom go?" she asked, wandering off.

We picked up and put away flashlights, extension cords, kitchen knives, the diving mask and snorkel, a hammer. Every strange item we found got held up and stared at, wondered over like an archeological find. An unopened bag of previously frozen peas under the couch. An enormous pipe wrench on the kitchen table. An old Coleman camping lantern and some tent stakes in the bathtub. The board game Lex and I had played so many times in childhood—Snakes and Ladders. I took the lid off, and there, just as I'd remembered, was Rita's name along with the crayon drawing she'd made. A stick figure girl in a blue dress with pale yellow hair. Underneath, it read: *Martha W. 7 years old*.

Beside the game was a photo of Ryan, Lexie, me, Gram, Terri, Randy, Shirley, and Aunt Diane all sitting around the pool. I showed it to Aunt Diane.

"Ralph must have taken it."

"How is Ralph?" Although they'd been divorced for over a decade, they'd remained friends.

"He's well. Still with Emily. He's talking about early retirement. Moving down to Florida. He's done with the winters here."

I looked down at the photo—Lexie in faded cut-offs and a Nike T-shirt. Curly-haired Ryan squinting into the camera because he wasn't wearing his glasses. Lexie had teased him about them, so he rarely wore them when he was around her.

"Do you remember when Lexie thought she'd seen a peacock in the woods?" I asked, thinking this might be a photo from that very day.

"Yes!" Diane laughed. "She and Ryan made all those ridiculous traps trying to catch it! It's a wonder we didn't get sued by some poor hiker falling into a pit trap!"

"What's Ryan up to these days? Isn't he married? Kids?"

"Divorced now," Aunt Diane said. "No kids. He came up last summer to help his parents with the bakery when Terri got diagnosed with MS. It was supposed to be a temporary thing, but I think he's here to stay. He's pretty much running things now."

"I'll have to stop in and see him," I said.

"He'd like that. He and Terri would both love to see you, I'm sure."

Nodding, I gathered all the papers and photographs. "Should we try to organize any of it now?" I asked. "Like photos in one and journal pages in another? I thought I'd pick up some binders and arrange her journal entries as best I could by date." *Spick and span, Jax. Spick and span!*

She shook her head. "Let's just get it all into boxes and go through them later."

I flipped through Lexie's journal entries again, then stopped:

May 16:

I bet Mom could have been saved by the pool. I remember when she got sick, Gram encouraged her to come out and swim, or even just take a jar home. But Mom refused. Even though I think she knew it might actually help. She hated the pool that much. And she understood that if it did make her well, there would be a price to pay. As Gram always said, "The water gives and the water takes."

I held the journal entry in my hands, rereading it, my tears dripping down onto the page. Diane gently touched my arm.

"Don't go through that now, Jackie. Just box it all up. We can read through everything later."

———————

By nightfall, Diane and I collapsed exhausted on the couch, eating Chinese takeout and sharing a bottle of Malbec. Diane had suggested that we go out to dinner, leave Sparrow Crest, but I was too tired and filthy and couldn't face going out.

"You're coming back to my place tonight," she said. "No arguments."

I shook my head.

"A hotel, then," Diane insisted.

"I'm fine here, really."

"Jackie, I don't think—"

"And besides," I interrupted, "it's all cleaned up now. The place looks great."

Diane sank back in the couch, taking a long sip of wine and looking around at the cleared and scrubbed floors and furniture.

"This is how I remember it," I said. "It even smells the same—Gram's lemon wood polish."

"It's like Lex was never here. We've taken every sign of her and boxed it up, thrown it away. It's like we've erased her." She looked so devastated, so guilty. And was I imagining it or was that accusation in her eyes—like this was what I'd wanted all along?

Pig was curled up on the chair across the room, watching us warily. He'd wolfed down an entire can of the cat food Diane had brought, always keeping a cautious eye on us, never letting us get too close.

"Your father's flight arrives at eleven tomorrow in Manchester," Diane said. She stabbed a dumpling with a chopstick. "I can send a car to pick him up."

"No. I can go get him. I'll take Lexie's car. The drive will do me good."

"I know you and he have your difficulties. It's a long ride from the airport. Are you sure you want to put yourself through that right now?"

The truth was my father had no difficulties with me. "He's my father."

When I'd visited him in Key West two years ago, he took me to the sunset celebration, art galleries, the Hemingway house, and of course, his favorite bars. He introduced me to artists, cops, street performers, and fishermen. We were having a lovely time until I ruined it with my clumsy, yet determined, attempt at an intervention. I sat him down, explained that I believed he was drinking to self-medicate his bipolar disorder, that I was sure his life would really turn around if he'd get on meds, go to therapy, deal with his illness. I pulled out a list I'd made of local treatment centers and hospitals and offered to make some calls.

He was the one who ended up calling: First, he called to reserve me a room at a local motel, then he called a cab to take me there.

All my life I'd wanted him to change: to give up booze, seek help, be a better father. I wanted him to love me as much as he loved Lexie. But everything I ever did just pushed him further away.

As if reading my mind, Diane said, "He's never going to change."

I blew out a breath. "I know."

"Your mother knew it, too. She knew it and she fell in love with him anyway. And he loved her. He really did, in his own way. He's not a bad man. He is the way he is. "

I nodded.

"And he and Lexie," Diane said. "They were so close."

"I know," I said, pushing aside my plate but holding on to my wine. "I know."

"They both shared that . . . what did Ted used to call it? 'The artist's spirit'?"

I sank back on the couch. "Artist's soul."

"Yeah, that's it," she said, smiling.

———

Looking back, my social worker brain sees all the warning signs, but at the time none of us understood them for what they were. Lexie had always been a moody girl, ecstatically happy one minute, and then she'd lash out, in terrible, cruel ways. She knew everyone's soft spots—the places that would hurt most if she poked them.

"She has an artist's soul," our father would say, a red flag in and of itself. He blamed his own "artist's soul" for the behaviors that infuriated our mother and wreaked havoc on our family: He'd leave home for a week, saying he was "following the muse," going on a vision quest and returning after having drained their savings account or crashed the car; once, my mother had to get him out of jail for drunk and disorderly conduct down in Maryland.

The big warning came when Lexie turned sixteen. Lexie, always a straight-A student, started failing all her classes junior year. Gram bought her a car for her birthday. Not a shitty beater, but a brand-new Volvo. Our grandmother was an all-or-nothing kind of person.

Lexie was supposed to pick me up from school to drive to Sparrow Crest for the weekend. I'd brought an extra backpack to school full of clothes and some of our favorite road-trip snacks for the three-hour drive—Fritos, root beer, and M&Ms. But she didn't show. All the school buses had left. Half an hour passed. She was often late, but this was crazy. We'd promised Gram we'd be there by six thirty; she was making Lexie's favorite dinner, meatloaf. And now we were going to be late.

I stood out front, pacing around. Girls from the field hockey team were warming up out on the field. They watched me, snickering. "Someone forget you, Metcalf?" Zoey Landover called. She was captain of the team, my long-ago best friend who now thought I was a total freak. I did what I always did, my method of middle school survival: I ignored her. Pretended she was invisible. Pretended they all were.

I called home, knowing my dad was there. He was doing overnight shifts at the 7-Eleven and sleeping during the day. Lexie picked up. There was music blasting in the background—Joan Jett & the Blackhearts.

"Um, did you forget me?"

"Hello? Who is this?" she'd yelled into the phone.

"Don't be an asshole, Lex. Come get me."

The music got louder.

Joan Jett singing "Cherry Bomb."

"Who?"

"Jackie! The sister you totally left stranded in the school parking lot!"

"W-R-O-N-G spells wrong number," she'd said, laughing as she hung up.

I called back. She didn't answer, so I called Mom at work. Mom agreed to swing by and pick me up. "The high school called me," she said. "Apparently your sister took it upon herself to leave school after second period without permission."

I could tell from Mom's tone that Lexie was in big trouble. I was sure my sister would talk herself out of it—give Mom some plausible reason for ditching, and we'd pack our bags into the Volvo and be off to Sparrow Crest for the weekend. But that's not what happened.

Mom and I got home to an absolute disaster. We pulled into the driveway to see Ted's little Mercury parked neatly against the garage. My sister's Volvo was half in the driveway, half on our scraggly brown lawn. The front door to our little green ranch house was open, and we could hear the living room stereo blasting. I followed Mom up the cracked cement front steps and through the front door. The stereo and TV were on full blast, as was the radio in the kitchen. I looked to the left at the kitchen—the water in the sink was running and had overflowed onto the floor. In the living room, furniture was overturned, the cushions were off our ugly plaid couch. Lexie was pushing the vacuum cleaner frantically across the frayed living room carpet. Her movements seemed so jerky, puppet-like. The house smelled like bleach and lemons.

"Are you high?" Mom asked after she'd shut off the music. I'd turned off the kitchen faucet, my sneakers sloshing through the water on the floor.

My father came staggering out of the master bedroom in his boxer shorts and a rumpled T-shirt. "What's going on?"

Lexie laughed, a loud hyena laugh. "I'm cleaning! Cleaning, keening, keening and cleaning! Do you have any idea how filthy the average house is? We talked about it this morning in science. And about dust. Did you know that a huge percentage of dust is made up of human skin? There's probably sloughed-off skin cells from some dude who lived here fifty years ago hiding in the cracks in the floor. Just imagine it, Mama! When you're taking a bath or sitting down on the couch, you're wallowing in little pieces of other people!"

"Lexie," Mom said. "I don't think—"

"Spick and span!" Lexie had shouted at her, turning on the vacuum. "Spick and span! Spick and span!" she sang as she danced around with the vacuum.

"Did you take something, Lexie?"

"I took a bite out of crime," Lexie said, laughing. "I mean, grime! Get it? Take a bite out of grime?" Her face was red, sweaty. Her hair was wild.

My father started laughing, too. "I get it. Grime!"

"Lexie, put the vacuum down. Let's sit a minute," Mom said.

"Oh, Mama, we can't sit. Not when there's so much to do! Do, do, da do run run! Let's get our motors running. Grab a mop, Mom! Jax, you get the bucket. Ted, grab the broom and sweep along."

Our father smiled, grabbed the broom, started singing, "Sweep low, sweet chariot, coming for to carry me home."

"That's it," Lexie said. "Come on now, Mom and Jax! Spick and span!"

And what did we do? Did we put her in the car and get her to the ER to be evaluated and tested for drugs? Did we call Dr. Bradley, who'd been looking after Lexie and me since we'd been born?

No. We cleaned.

Ted, Mom, and I rolled up our sleeves and went to work beside Lexie. Although my father was oblivious, Mom and I were both scared. We knew something was wrong, really wrong—but we didn't know what to do.

When Mom and I went to bed at two in the morning, Lexie and Ted were up, still cleaning. When Lexie finally crashed, she didn't get out of bed for three days. Even then, Mom didn't call Dr. Bradley. She'd hoped it was a one-time thing, a fluke.

I heard Ted talking to her about it later: "She's fine. She's an original, you know that. Christ, Linda! Some of us aren't meant to lead cookie-cutter lives. The best thing we can do for Lex is to back the fuck off!"

In the end, Lexie's illness, in all its toothy ugliness, could no longer be ignored.

We were all staying with Grandma at Sparrow Crest for Christmas that year. We'd had our traditional dinner of lasagna washed down with eggnog and cookies. Around two a.m., there was a terrible crash from downstairs. I was thirteen, too old for Santa, so I knew it wasn't the fat man in the red suit. The hall lights came on—Gram, Mom, and Aunt Diane all came out of their rooms; my father was passed out from too much rum in his eggnog. In the living room, the tree had been tipped over—the colored lights were plugged in, and the ones that weren't broken were flickering in a fire-hazard kind of way. The presents had been ripped open. And there sat Lexie in the center of it all. "Alexia?" Gram said, her voice surprisingly level and calm. "What are you doing?"

"Inside-outing," Lexie said, eyes bright and cheeks red. "Everything we know and see, it's right side out, right?" She laughed. "Right, right?" She paused, looked at each of us. "The way our skin holds everything else inside. All the bones and muscles and tendons and the stuff that really makes us work. We can't see any of that. But what if we could? What if we could truly see everything, all the way through? What if we could take the whole world and turn it inside out?"

The room seemed to flicker in and out of focus. No one knew what to say.

"The presents," Lexie went on. "They're a metaphor. Don't you *get it*?" She shook her head, disgusted because our faces told her we were most certainly not getting it. "Inside-outing! We open everything up. The presents! The tree! The goddamn clock in the hall— all of it! That way nothing can hide. That way we see *everything*. But everything is *nothing*, right? Inside and outside. Backwards and forwards!" She swiveled her head at me then, eyes beady and frantic, pleading. "Jax understands. Don't you, Jax?"

I looked at the unwrapped gifts—gloves, slippers, a box of Whitman's chocolates with all the chocolates and their little paper cups strewn across the carpet. The iPod I'd wanted so badly sat five feet away from me in its shiny white box. I didn't want it anymore. Then I noticed Lexie's right arm. Blood. Aunt Diane saw it, too.

"Lexie," Aunt Diane said, stepping forward. "I need to see your arm, sweetie. I think you've hurt yourself." Diane pulled back the robe to expose a deep gash on her forearm.

Lexie touched it, smearing blood. "Inside out," she said. "Now you understand, right?"

She was hospitalized for a week and released on New Year's Eve with a diagnosis: schizoaffective disorder of the bipolar type.

After being discharged, we drove from Vermont back home to Massachusetts in a snowstorm, Lexie and I tucked into the backseat. She smelled like the hospital and spent the whole ride with her face pressed against the window, fogging it up with her breath, then wiping the fog away.

As soon as we got home, my parents turned on the TV so we could watch the ball drop in Times Square. There was champagne for my parents, Shirley Temples for Lex and me.

"Isn't it great to all be back home?" Ted said over and over. I looked around our dumpy little living room, at my sister's expressionless face, at the way my mom studied Lexie's every move, the way my father kept refilling his own glass.

After midnight, our parents retreated to their bedroom. Lex and I could hear them fighting. "I will not have her labeled like this," my father said.

"Christ Ted, it's a sickness, not a label. And you know what? It's genetic. She gets it from *your* genes! *You* passed it down to her!"

"That is such bullshit!" my father yelled. "You wanna talk about crazy genes? How about your mother? She can't even leave her fucking house, Linda!"

"Happy New Year," Lex said to me, dumping her

untouched Shirley Temple in a plant, then trudged off to bed.

Those first weeks and months after her diagnosis, while they tweaked meds, sent her to the hospital for weekly blood tests, to psychiatrist and therapy appointments, she became a strange one-dimensional form of who she'd once been, a paper doll version of herself.

My father lived with us for less than six months after Lexie's diagnosis. He battled with my mother and Lexie's doctors constantly, refusing any treatment plan. My mother came home one evening to find Ted flushing all of Lexie's medication down the toilet.

"What the hell are you doing, Ted?"

"She hates them!" Ted said. "They're turning her into a fucking zombie!"

"They're managing her symptoms, Ted." My mom salvaged what pills she could.

"Symptoms? You mean *emotions*? Since when is feeling things deeply an illness, Linda? It's what makes us human!"

He stormed off to his art studio in the garage, my mother at his heels. They were yelling so loud, Lexie and I could hear them in the kitchen.

Their argument ended with her throwing him out. It didn't seem like that big a deal at the time. She'd told him to leave before, but he'd always come back. This was different, though. This time he left and stayed gone. Our mother had gotten rid of him once and for all, and Lexie hated her for it. She loved our father fiercely and was devoted to him, no matter what.

Mom moved through the house like a woman on autopilot, a strange brokenhearted ghost. She knew she'd done the right thing, and that if there was any hope at all of Lexie getting a handle on her illness, it wouldn't happen with my father around.

Our father took an apartment above Al's Bar in town and moved his things little by little with a friend's van. It was a crappy one-bedroom place that basically became his live-in art studio. When Lexie and I spent nights there on weekends, we slept in sleeping bags and camping mattresses on the floor between unfinished paintings and sculptures. His drinking took a turn for the worse, and Lexie and I sometimes skipped our weekend visits with him because it just wasn't all that much fun to eat frozen dinners and watch him get shit-faced then pass out.

After Lexie went off to college, our father gave up his apartment and headed south. Eventually, he went as far south as you could go without hitting the ocean: Key West. We didn't see him a whole lot after that. A couple times a year, he'd drive up to New England, bags loaded with crappy presents, and regale us with tales of his life in Florida: a life full of artists, strippers, fishermen, and beach bums. He was drinking a lot but seemed tan and happy. He started painting landscapes and selling them to the tourists. For the first time in his life, he was actually making a living from his art.

I went away to college in Seattle, and my father never came to visit me. Not even for graduation.

My mother never dated another man. She confessed to me once, not long before her death, that my father had been the great love of her life, and once you've experienced that, everything else pales in comparison. "Your father," she'd said, "for all his complications, is the only person I ever felt whole with. Sometimes I think our brokenness held us together. But maybe, Jackie, maybe that's enough."

She died three years ago after a long struggle with breast cancer. We were all with her those last days in hospice: me, Lexie, and Ted. Ted had flown up from Florida and brought Key lime pie and a suitcase full of his old sketchbooks, dating back years. He fed Mom bites of pie and showed her his drawings from their lives together: Niagara Falls, where they'd had their honeymoon; my mother naked and pregnant, smiling up at him from the bed in their first apartment; baby Lexie sleeping in her crib; Lex and me on swings in the backyard; Lex and me in homemade Halloween costumes, both of us dressed as aliens from outer space; Mom sitting under a Christmas tree, laughing.

Together, they turned the pages and told stories that all started with "*Remember . . .*"

Mom died with our father holding her hand and Lexie telling her one of her fabulous stories that went on and on, one unbelievable turn after another.

I took a big sip of wine, turned to my aunt on the couch. "It's so strange, isn't it? That me and you and Ted, we're all that's left." I looked around. "Us and the house."

chapter ten

Ethel!" Will was shaking my shoulder.

I opened my eyes, sat up, heart racing, night-gown soaked with sweat.

"Another nightmare?" he asked, stroking my hair.

I nodded, sure that whoever had been chasing me in my dream had just been there in the bedroom; had somehow followed me into this world.

And they left a damp, rotting odor behind.

"Do you smell that?" I asked.

"Smell what?" his voice went up a bit.

"Nothing. It's just my silly dream." I forced out a little giggle, just to show how silly it was. The pale square of the window was just starting to lighten in the early dawn. "I'll go make breakfast."

Will gave my hand a squeeze. "They're just dreams, Ethel. Don't let them trouble you."

I pulled on my robe and made my way to the kitchen to get the coffee percolator going on the stove.

It wasn't just the strange dream and nightmares. There were the physical symptoms: feeling queasy, a fullness in my breasts, my dresses a bit too tight. Still, I dared not to hope. I told myself it was all the rich food I'd been craving: whipped cream cakes, butter scones, eggs fried in sweet butter.

Morning after morning I would wake up and make breakfast and try to distract myself with the world around me. I brought in the paper for Will and read the headlines each day: President Hoover celebrated his fifty-fifth birthday and Charles and Anne Lindbergh were among the guests, Babe Ruth hit his five hundredth home run, Winston Churchill gave a speech in Ottawa. How strange it all felt: this world spinning around me, the faces looking back up at me from the pages of the newspaper; people who had no idea who I was or that I even existed at all. "I am Mrs. Monroe from Lanesborough, New Hampshire," I would whisper to them.

Sometimes, when I felt too lost, felt like I was in danger of floating away, I would give myself a little prick with a pin.

———

Eliza Harding and I exchanged letters each week. I so looked forward to Eliza's letters, and the glimpses of the hotel and springs: the list of which roses were blooming, the peacock who ran away to a neighboring farm and now thought he was a chicken.

In July, a man was cured of his limp. At the beginning of August, a woman whose asthma was so bad she could hardly breathe, threw away her medicines and danced all night without a trace of a wheeze. And it wasn't just cures the pool gave to those who came to take the waters.

"Back in June," Eliza wrote, "just before you came to visit, we had a man stay, a musician from New York City. He asked the water for the thing he wanted most: fame. I won't tell you his name, but if you turn on the radio right now, I guarantee you'll soon hear his song. It's a big hit. Someone from Hollywood has been in touch about putting it in a movie!"

I wrote back with details of my life in Lanesborough, which seemed terribly dull compared with her world at the hotel. I shared details of Will's practice and how I helped with the books each week, writing out neat columns in the ledger documenting home and office visits (two dollars each), who'd paid and who still owed. "The life of a country doctor is not at all glamorous," I told her. "Will spends some time in his office, but the majority of it is house calls. The highlights of last week included draining an abscessed foot, and a farmer who lost his eye after being kicked by a draft horse." I told Eliza how my own flower garden was faring; it's been a terrible year for aphids. I described the ladies who are members of the sewing circle and what each is working on (quilts and frocks and lace curtains), and of course, I've shared every detail about the foliage festival and how busy the preparations are keeping me. I invited her to attend if she was able.

In her last letter to me, she wrote of a family who had come to stay at the hotel, the Woodcocks from Brooklyn, New York. "Mr. Woodcock is in finance. His wife was an actress when they met—she's been on Broadway! Little Charles Woodcock is four years old—a cherub, but has been unable to walk since birth. His legs seem small and shriveled, poor darling. And his sister, Martha, she's seven, and oh she is such a delight! She has taken a great interest in the roses and wants to learn all their names. They have booked a room for an entire month with the hopes that bathing in the springs will help poor Charles. I just know it will! Don't you agree, Ethel?" And I found myself nodding along.

I busied myself with planning the foliage festival: horse-drawn wagon rides, apple bobbing, a pie-eating contest, and a chicken pie supper. In the evening, there would be music at the bandstand and dancing. There would even be a Charleston contest!

I grew fuller.

I watched the calendar—my time of the month came and went in July, then again in August. When I was certain, I cooked Will his favorite supper: chicken and biscuits the way his mother used to make, with triple-layer chocolate cake for dessert. I lit candles. Flitted around the house like a silly bird trying to make everything perfect. When he arrived home, I greeted him with a glass of the special apple wine that Mr. Miller, who owns the orchard, makes each Christmas and led him to the table.

"What's all this?" he asked.

"We're celebrating," I said.

He raised his eyebrows as he sat down. "Celebrating what?"

"It's a birthday, of a sort."

"It's six months till my birthday. And yours was in May."

"A birthday yet to come," I said, smiling.

His eyes grew wide, and he jumped up from the table so fast that he bumped the edge and his wine spilled. "Mother," he said, wrapping his arms around me.

"Yes! A little girl."

"How do you know it's a girl?" He hugged me tighter. "Little Brunhilda," he chuckled.

"We'll paint the nursery pale yellow," I said.

"Like a buttercup?"

"Too vivid. More like lemon chiffon."

"I have an old cradle out in the barn, the one I slept in, if you can believe it. It could probably use a coat of paint, but it should still be in excellent shape."

———————

The day after I told Will, I wrote my sisters with the news. Then I paid a visit to Myrtle, practically skipping down the street to tell her. I felt so light and strange as I passed each familiar house. Like an actress playing a role. I said the words to myself as I walked: "I am Mrs. Monroe from Lanesborough, and I am going to have a baby."

The whistle blew at the woolen mill.

I passed the turnoff to South Main Street, which led into the heart of town, to the church and town green, and Will's office. Up here on Elm, it was just big houses, almost all of them painted white, each with a tidy garden in the front. Myrtle's house had trellised roses out front and a wide porch with a rocking chair where her husband, Felix, liked to smoke his pipe each evening.

Myrtle invited me in, and we settled at her kitchen table over tea, using her good china cups.

"Are you well, dear?" she asked. "You look feverish."

I told her my news. She sprang up from her chair and threw her arms around me. "I'm so happy for you!" To celebrate, she cut into the pound cake she'd been saving for dinner. "Does anyone else know?"

I shook my head. "I've written my sisters, but other than Will, you're the only one I've told."

"When is the baby due?"

"Will has calculated her due date—March fifth."

"Her?"

"It's a girl. I know it is! Will doesn't believe me, but I'm sure of it."

"There are some things a mother just knows." Myrtle nodded. She sank back in her chair. "A spring baby, how perfect. Born just as the leaves start to turn green and the first flowers are poking up through the snow."

Myrtle stirred sugar into her tea. I took a bite of pound cake so sweet it made my teeth ache.

"Can I tell you a secret?" I asked. Her eyes lit up and she leaned forward in her chair. "When we were at the hotel in Brandenburg, I went out to the springs one afternoon on my own. I made a wish."

Myrtle set down her spoon. "A wish?"

I forced out a little laugh. "I know, it's silly, isn't it? But I did. I wished for a child."

Myrtle made a little sound, as if to speak, but no words came.

"I felt so foolish. But now . . . now I wonder. I'm sure it's just a coincidence, right?"

Myrtle said nothing. She just sat there, frozen, as if she were unable to move. All the color had gone from her face. She was like a wax figure.

I picked at my dense, buttery cake.

I remembered Myrtle telling me about her trip to the springs with Felix. And what she'd said after: *The water gives miracles, yes, but I think it takes, too.*

At last, Myrtle smiled at me, said, "March fifth. That seems far off now, but it'll be here in no time. Think of the baby clothes we can sew! Little dresses and nightgowns. I'll crochet a blanket for her." She picked up her teacup, and I saw her hand was trembling.

chapter eleven

June 18, 2019

I filled a travel mug with coffee and set out for the airport in my sister's yellow Mustang. The driver's seat held the indentation of her small, muscular frame. An empty Diet Coke bottle rolled around on the passenger side floor. A hair scrunchie was wrapped around the gearshift. Swimming goggles were hung over the rearview mirror. The car even smelled like Lexie: warm and floral, with a sharp tang of the tea tree oil soap she used. Sitting in the driver's seat, I missed my sister so fiercely that the longing for her became a physical pain, a throbbing I felt in my whole body.

I remembered watching her swim out from the beach at Lake Wilmore, standing on the shore as she got farther and farther away until she was just a tiny dot. Then she'd turn around, swim back, and once she was out of the water, I'd hug her tightly. "Good swim," I'd say like I was proud, when actually I'd just been terrified she wouldn't come back.

I pulled the scrunchie off the gear shift. A piece of her blond hair was tangled up in it.

I had wasted a year barely talking to her, and now she was gone forever. I'd never get that time back. I'd never get the chance to tell her how sorry I was, that I'd made a terrible mistake.

Maybe moving so far away had been a mistake, too. After high school, all I could think of was how I didn't want to get trapped by Lexie. It was too easy to get caught up in her chaos, to come running every time she had a crisis, to jump in and try to fix her messes for her. I only applied to colleges on the West Coast, telling everyone I wanted a change of scenery. I'm sure Lexie knew the truth. She knew me better than I knew myself.

I sank back in the leather bucket seat and sobbed. I screamed and pounded the steering wheel, hating myself, hating life for being so fucked up and unfair, hating my sister for finally leaving me for good. When I was emptied out, my chest hollow, my body drained, my eyes swollen, I turned on the ignition. Music blasted out from the oldies station. I shut it off, adjusted the seat and mirrors, and pulled out of the driveway and through the tiny center of Brandenburg, passing the Blue Heron Bakery, the general store, and the post office. I drove by the turnoff for Meadow Road that led out to Lake Wilmore. I crossed the train tracks where Lexie and I used to place pennies, letting the old freight cars crush them, turning them into flattened bits of copper that we pretended were gold.

There was no GPS in the car, and no maps, but I knew the way. It all came back easily. My sister's car purred along, handling so much better than the crappy old Honda I was used to driving, as I followed the two-lane roads and passed farms, cows, houses set back from the road with peeling paint and angry-looking dogs in the yard. I opened the sunroof and the air smelled green and alive; fresh-cut grass and warm leaves reaching up to touch the sun.

I turned the radio back on and cranked the volume,

listening to the music I always teased my sister for loving: Buddy Holly, Little Richard, Fats Domino.

I drove the back roads until I came to a Sunoco gas station just before the highway on-ramp. I stopped to fill up the tank—Lexie was famous for running on fumes and rarely kept more than a quarter-tank of gas—then shifted to fifth gear and cruised along Interstate 93. In my peripheral vision, I was sure I caught a glimpse of her in the passenger seat. *Why don't you open her up and see what she can really do?*

The speedometer hit eighty-seven before I stopped myself, tapping the brakes. I felt my sister rolling her eyes beside me.

"Shut up," I said out loud.

Great. Now I was talking to ghosts.

On the radio, a song I didn't recognize came on, the artist cheerily promising, "Like a rubber ball, I'll come bouncing back to you."

I took the exit for the airport and followed the signs to arrivals. Immediately recognizable by his Greek fisherman's cap and gaudy Hawaiian shirt, my father was standing outside the terminal waiting for me, a small duffle bag slung over his shoulder.

I pulled up and got out of the car.

He looked older than he had the last time I'd seen him, and he'd gotten skinnier. His hair had been cut recently, and his beard was neatly trimmed.

"Jax," he said, enveloping me in a hug. Lexie had started calling me Jax back when we were kids, so our names would match. It'd never caught on with Mom and Gram, but my father took to it, called us "The X girls." "Oh Jesus, Jax." He squeezed me tighter. He smelled like gin and Aqua Velva, a combo that melted me in a deep, primal way, and brought me right back to piggyback rides and scratchy daddy kisses. "I can't believe she's gone."

"I know," I said, squeezing back, feeling like I was hugging a skeleton. Ted had always been a little on the thin side, but this was concerning. "Come on, let's get you to Sparrow Crest."

"Can we stop for a bite on the way?" he asked.

"Sure," I said. But when I pulled into a McDonald's drive-through ten minutes later, he shook his head.

"There's a Mexican place down there," he said, pointing to a giant neon margarita glass flashing in the window. His hands trembled slightly; it wasn't food he wanted. I hesitated, thought of what Diane said: *He's never going to change.* I could have tried to put off the inevitable by pulling into the drive-through and getting him a burger and fries, but he'd find a drink with or without my help. I resolved that, on this trip, I wasn't going to be the booze police. The last thing I wanted to do was pass judgment; I'd done that with my sister and look where it led me.

I pointed the Mustang toward the Mexican restaurant.

The place was nearly empty—it was only a little after eleven, too early for the lunch crowd—and decorated with piñatas, fake cactuses, walls made to look like adobe. Mexican music, heavy on the horns, played from speakers in the ceiling. We got a table in the back corner, and my father ordered us both house margaritas before I'd touched a menu.

If you can't beat 'em, join 'em, Jax, Lexie whispered in my ear.

"I've gotta drive," I reminded him.

The drinks came, and he took them both. I bit my tongue and said nothing. Still, he waved his hand, pooh-

poohing me. "These are mostly sugar water. I need for-tification before going to that god-awful house."

He hated Sparrow Crest, or as he called it, "Drac-ula's castle." He loathed it even though he and Mom had been married there, in the gardens. The story I heard later was that Ted wanted to elope, but Gram had insisted, so in the end, Dracula's castle it was.

"Imagine it, loves," he said, telling Lex and me the story when we were little. "The organ playing, sound-ing more like a funeral march than 'Here Comes the Bride,' the bats swooping down from the belfry."

"There were no bats, Ted," Mom corrected, shaking her head, laughing. "And Sparrow Crest doesn't have a belfry."

"Well, the attic, then. There were too bats, and they came swooping down from the attic, got all tangled up in your mother's wedding veil. They joined up with the spiders and the ghosts, and the vampires—never have there been such strange guests at a wedding. I won't even tell you what happened when it was time to cut the cake!"

I ordered loaded nachos for us to share. I wasn't hungry, but my father could use something to absorb all the booze. "Have you been sick?" I asked.

"You look great, too, Jax," he said.

"Seriously, Ted. You kind of look like hell. Are you okay?"

He leaned back in his bench seat. "One of my kids just died, Jax. And I've been on a cleanse. Macrobiotic. I've been dating a woman—Vanessa. She wants to pu-rify my body and soul." He leaned forward, elbows on the table, and dropped his voice. "So what do we know? What happened to Lexie?"

"She went off her meds . . ."

He took a long sip of the margarita, twirled the plastic straw, rattled ice cubes, ran his finger along the edge of the glass, picking up salt. "She shouldn't have been all alone in that place," he said. "That house . . ." He shook his head.

"Gram left it to her. And Lexie loved Sparrow Crest."

"She had a hard winter there, Jax," Ted said. He looked at me icily, his eyes saying, *Not that you would know.*

"Diane said she was doing well," I said, defensively.

"Diane saw what Lexie wanted her to see," Ted said. He stared at his drink, then looked up at me. "When was the last time you talked to her, Jax? Really talked to her?"

Guilt gnawed at my insides like an angry rat. I didn't answer.

"She called me," my father said now. He sounded hesitant. Like he wasn't sure he should be telling me. As if he was betraying some confidence, even now. He'd always been like this when talking about Lexie. He was protective of their relationship, of the secrets they shared.

"When?"

"Three nights ago. The night before she . . . before it happened, I guess." He settled back in his vinyl bench seat.

"How did she sound?"

"A little manic. Not bad. Not off the charts. I've heard her much worse."

Lexie had the kind of relationship with him that I never did. They understood each other. She called him when she was off her meds, he called her when he was in a three-days-with-no-sleep painting frenzy. And both of them always picked up the phone.

"What did she say?" I asked.

"She was asking about Rita. Anything I could tell her about Rita. But mostly, she wanted to know . . ." He paused, looked forlornly into his glass. "If it was possible that what happened with Rita wasn't an accident. She said she'd found something, something that made her believe Rita might have been murdered."

"Murdered?" The word came out too loud, too angry. I bit my tongue to keep from saying the next words that flew into my head: *You've gotta be fucking kidding.* I took in a slow breath to calm myself.

Be objective, I told myself. *Use your listening skills. Take everything in and gather all the information you can before forming any opinions.*

"Okay," I said, voice level. "What else did she say? Did she tell you what she'd found?"

He shook his head. "She was talking fast. Saying she was onto something. Something big."

I nodded. "And what did you say to her?"

He looked down at his hands on the table. "I told her the truth."

"Which is?" I steeled myself.

"That your mother knew Rita wasn't alone at the pool that night. That she'd met someone down there."

"*What?*" I'd certainly never heard this part of the story. I was used to Lexie and my father keeping secrets from me, but the idea that my mother had kept a secret like this was too much.

"The way Linda told it, she woke up, noticed Rita was gone. She went to the window. She couldn't see the pool because she was in the room you always slept in—her view was blocked—but she heard voices. Rita and someone else. Linda wondered if Rita was just playing with Martha."

I nodded. I'd heard a few stories about Rita and her imaginary friend, Martha. How Rita would insist Gram make an extra plate at dinner that Rita could bring outside for Martha. They'd all hear her talking to Martha, giving the imaginary girl a high, squeaky voice. I thought of the drawing inside the Snakes and Ladders game: *Martha W. 7 years old*.

My father continued. "But apparently, it didn't sound like Rita talking to herself, you know, doing her funny Martha voice. This was different. Linda wanted to see who Rita was with, but she didn't want to get in trouble or get Rita in trouble. So she went back to bed."

"And Rita drowned that night."

Ted nodded. "Your mother always blamed herself. And she never told anyone else what she'd heard. Not her mother or sister or the police when they came to ask questions. She was afraid they would blame her— ask her why she didn't get out of bed to go check on Rita, to bring her back inside. I'm the only one she ever told."

I tried to imagine it: My mother living with that kind of guilt. Always wondering if things might have turned out differently if she'd gone out to the pool that night. And the pool, of course, was a constant reminder not only of what happened to Rita, but of the fact that she might have been able to stop it. No wonder she hated Sparrow Crest. No wonder I never once saw her swim.

"But who was Rita out there with?" I asked. "Who could it have been?"

"Maybe no one." He shrugged. "We'll never know."

I blew out an exasperated breath. "And you told all of this to Lexie?" I couldn't believe it. It wasn't like Lexie needed help getting crazy ideas in her head.

"What choice did I have? We were always straight with each other. And you know how she was—she knew there was more to the story than she'd been told. And once she got hold of an idea and it built up in her mind into an obsession—there was no stopping her." He flagged down the waitress, signaling for another margarita.

chapter twelve

I feel her, swimming like a little tadpole, growing bigger and stronger each day. I eat spinach and liver and raw eggs to help her grow. I walk down to the river behind the church every day and sit on the grassy bank and talk to my child, my hand resting on my belly. I tap as I speak: *Knock, knock, are you home, little one? Do you hear my voice, my one and only?* Dragonflies flit around us like fairies with jewellike wings, the crickets sing their end-of-summer song. I kick off my too-tight T-strap shoes, push my toes through the tangle of warm grass. *You are my wish come true*, I tell the baby. My words mix with the soft burble of the current, and sometimes it seems I leave English behind and speak to her in another language: the language of water.

"I can feel her moving," I told Will. He said it's too early, but I do feel her, I swear, little flutterings, a moth beating its delicate wings inside me.

I dance around the kitchen, singing, "'Yes sir, that's my baby. No sir, I don't mean maybe'!" Will laughs, takes my hands, and dances with me.

Eliza wrote with wonderful news: Little Charles Woodcock is able to move his legs! He stood up for the first time and took his first stumbling steps. It is, she wrote, a true miracle! The family is delighted and will be staying on at the hotel for two more weeks so he can continue taking the waters.

———————

My sister Bernice sent us a quilt she made for the baby—a cheerful little thing covered in bright yellow stars. I sewed curtains for her nursery, sitting at the Singer, pumping the treadle, humming along with the machine as I worked. *I am Mrs. Monroe and I am sewing curtains for the nursery!* The curtains are a lovely cream color with yellow edges that will match the stars in the quilt my sister sent perfectly! Will painted the cradle white, and I have started filling the little dresser with tiny outfits: soft cotton gowns, rompers, knit hats and socks. The tiniest little white shoes I have ever seen—I hold them in my fingers and say, "Hello, shoes," and then make them dance a jig. I bought a colorful picture of a peacock that reminded me of the hotel and the springs. I've hung it just over her cradle so the bird can watch over her while she sleeps. Oh, what grand and colorful dreams she'll have, this little creature growing inside me!

I keep terribly busy with the foliage festival, which is less than a month away! I have endless lists and charts and timetables to help keep track of each detail. Will tells me I am like a general planning a battle! He cautions me to take it easy, to not tire myself. But it's good to have something to do. Something to keep me busy. It makes the time go by so much faster. And oh, the dreams I'd been having! I dream of the hotel and springs almost every night.

I dream that the springs are calling my name. *"Come*

swimming," they call. *"Come swimming, my sweet little thing."*

And I go to the water, slip into it, let it caress and rock me. The water whispers in my ear like a lover. Tells me secrets no one else can ever know. That it has a name. I ask what it is.

The water whispers, *"My name is the sound of water running deep underground. My name seeps through bedrock, erodes fossils, rusts iron. My name, my name, you could not speak it, even if you tried."*

I dreamed that I was in the water and lifted a baby out—my baby, born from the water, a gift from deep beneath the surface and not entirely of this earth. She had gills and fins. And I loved her, I love her, I love her as I've never loved anyone or anything.

"She is ours," the water whispers. *"Yours and mine."*

———————

September 9, 1929

A new letter from Eliza arrived today.

> *Dear Ethel,*
>
> *I write with terrible news. Little Martha Woodcock has drowned in the springs. Her brother, Charles, is walking now, his legs growing stronger each day. The family had so much to be thankful for. Then, yesterday, Martha wandered off from the dining room—she was like that, always flitting around, saying hello to all the guests, coming to find me in the garden. They found her in the springs. Her parents pulled her out, but it was too late. They are, as you can imagine, devastated, as are we all.*

*Benson has shut down the hotel. We will
reopen in a week with new safety precautions in
place: a sturdy fence surrounding the springs,
life buoys and ropes, and a lifeguard on duty
whenever guests are bathing.*

*It seems impossible that something so terrible
could have happened. I can still see little Martha's
bright face, feel her small hand in mine as we
walk through the rose garden. I am heartbroken.*

*I hear whispering from some of the people in
town, including members of my own family. They
say it is a tragedy, but no surprise. "The spring
does not give without taking," they say. Could
they be right? It is a chilling thought; one that
keeps me up late into the night.*

Yours,
Eliza Harding

I read the letter again and again, hands trembling.
I could not tell Will about the drowning. I tried. I
opened my mouth to speak, but the words dried up
on my tongue. I went into the bathroom and pricked
myself eight times with a pin, making a perfect circle
with the dots on my thigh, letting the blood bloom like
the tiniest flowers on my pale skin. Then I went back
out and joined Will at the dinner table, smiling and
nodding and chirping like a funny little bird. All the
while I told myself, *I am Mrs. Monroe. I am having a
fine dinner with my husband. We live in a lovely house.
We are expecting a baby. Everything is fine, fine, fine.*

The blood seeped through my stockings, leaving
little tattletale stains: *Liar, Liar, Liar!*

chapter thirteen

June 18, 2019

My father fell asleep in the car on the way back to Sparrow Crest. We'd stopped off at an office supplies place, and I'd picked up some three-ring binders, plastic sleeves, and folders to help me start organizing Lexie's journals and notes. I ran into the pet shop next door for more cat food, litter, treats, and even some little catnip-stuffed toy mice. I woke Ted up once we were back at Sparrow Crest. He opened his eyes. "Jesus," he said, looking up at the house and giving a dramatic shiver. "Dracula's castle."

Once we got inside, he said he needed a "power nap." I helped him get settled into the bedroom next to mine—Lexie's childhood room. The last year, she'd been using Gram's old room at the end of the hall, so all her stuff was still in there. We'd have to go through it—a task I couldn't imagine myself ever being ready to face. For now, I'd just shut the door, sure I'd heard Lexie chiding, *Outta sight, outta mind, huh?*

The cat wandered in, and my father called out, "Pig!" He brushed against my father's ankles, then disappeared under the bed.

Of course Ted knew about the cat.

I took in a breath, told myself to let go of the jealousy—the distance was my own doing. The healthy thing, my therapist brain told me, would be to acknowledge my feelings of resentment, then reframe and focus on the positive—wasn't it wonderful that Lexie and Ted had been so close, that my sister had someone to tell all about Pig?

"Ted," I said as I laid a quilt on top of the freshly made bed. "Thank you. For always being there for Lexie."

He gave me a puzzled look, shook his head, said, "I wasn't. But I did my best. That's all any of us do, isn't it?"

His words hit me like a cannonball in the chest.

———

Once Ted was tucked in, I set off to walk to town. I pulled out my phone to call my therapist but got her voice mail.

"Barbara, it's Jackie Metcalf. I was hoping we could schedule a time to talk by phone. Being here, it's . . . it's, uh, bringing up a lot of stuff. Old issues and new questions. Anyway, I could use a rational voice to help me out a little."

The walk to town seemed farther than when we were kids. But then again, Lexie and I had made the trip on bikes, singing, screaming, daring each other to ride faster. We'd go to the Four Corners Store for penny candy—licorice pipes, Squirrel Nut Zippers, Bit-O-Honeys, Mint Juleps, tiny wax bottles full of bright liquid sugar. Stuff they didn't sell at the corner store back home—hadn't really sold anywhere else for years. Lexie called it "old lady candy." We'd park our bikes out front, go into the store with its old creaking wooden floorboards, and load up paper bags and then get a couple of ice-cold Hires Root Beers to wash it all down.

Now, I followed our dirt road to Lower Road, which had been dirt when I was a kid but was now paved. Lower Road ran downhill to Main Street. So little had changed. It felt like there was a protective bubble over Brandenburg, keeping everything frozen in time—like the dome of a snow globe with the perfect little New England village trapped inside.

There was the Brandenburg Post Office, where Lexie and I sent postcards to our mom and Ted and friends back home. *Having a great time at Sparrow Crest. Swimming every day. Gram sends her love.* And the Blue Heron Bakery. When I was growing up people had been known to drive all the way from Burlington for the lemon-blueberry muffins Terri Mueller made. Ryan's dad, Randy, greeted nearly every customer by name and gave Lexie and me free hot chocolate with extra whipped cream whenever we went in.

We played with other kids in town, kids whose names I can no longer recall—a girl with white-blond hair, a boy with thick glasses. But Ryan was like family. His grandmother, Shirley, was Gram's best friend. They'd grown up together, Shirley's family just on the other side of the hill from Sparrow Crest. They liked to sit by the pool drinking gin and tonics and playing cards on summer afternoons.

I passed Lily's Bed and Breakfast—a quaint old farmhouse with a white picket fence and tidy flower beds. Lily had been running the place forever. In addition to the rooms in the house, she had riverside cabins out back and a large renovated barn where she hosted weddings, graduations, and local theater productions.

The Four Corners Store had a large wooden porch with benches for people to sit and enjoy the ice cream cones they scooped inside. A bulletin board out front held notices for yard sales, camp wood, a fly-fishing tournament, and a chicken-pie supper at the Methodist Church. I pushed open the heavy front door and crossed the creaking old floorboards to the beer cooler in the back. I grabbed a six-pack of a local IPA—something I thought my dad would like. If he was going to drink, I knew from experience that we were better off having him stick with beer. Besides, IPA sounded good to me, too. As I was closing the cooler, a memory came to me. Standing right in this spot, picking root beers from the cooler as two women we didn't know talked in the next aisle over.

"Lets those girls run around wild with the Mueller boy."

"What's she going to do? Keep them locked up in the house with her?" the other woman had said to her companion.

"Those girls shouldn't be staying up there in that house. Shouldn't be swimming in that pool. That pool should be filled in. I don't understand why Maggie didn't do it after she lost poor Rita. Nothing good ever came from that place. Cursed, that's what my mother always said."

They'd been talking about us. Us and Gram.

I shook off the memory and brought my beer up to the counter, where an older man rang me up. The store owner. I struggled to remember his name. Bob? Bill?

"That be all for you today?" he asked.

"Actually, I don't know if you'll remember me. I'm Jackie Metcalf, my sister, Lexie, and I used to spend summers up at Sparrow Crest with our grandmother, Maggie Harkness. Lexie recently . . ." I fumbled for the word. Died? Passed away? Went totally out of her mind and drowned herself in her own pool?

"Oh my gosh, Lexie's sister! Of course I remember you. I was sorry as hell to hear what happened. My son, Vern, he's in the VFD, he was one of the paramedics who got there first. Terrible thing."

A knot formed in my throat as I imagined this man's son standing over Lexie's naked body, knowing there was no reviving her. "Thank you," I managed. "We're having a memorial service tomorrow. You're welcome to come." I gave him the details.

"Me and the missus will be there. She was in here a lot and always so friendly. A good girl."

I wasn't sure what to say.

"Oh hell, I nearly forgot," he said. "I've got something for you."

"For me?"

"Something your sister placed a special order for. It's all paid for. I've got it out back, just a sec."

Lexie never shopped online. She didn't own a computer. Or a cell phone. She hated the idea that people could track everything you did online, every site you visited, everything you looked at or bought.

He went through a curtained door behind the register and came back with a sealed and taped cardboard box addressed to Lexie, care of the Four Corners Store. "Here you go."

"Thanks," I said, taking the box from him. It was long and narrow—about four feet by eight inches. It weighed very little. I thought about opening it, but I wanted to be alone when I saw whatever Lexie had ordered. "I know Lexie wasn't a fan of computers."

"It wasn't just the computer thing," he said. "She didn't trust the UPS guy. Didn't like strangers coming to the house. Didn't even get her mail there, rented a PO box in town. If she needed something, she'd come to us and we'd order it for her. All her swimming and diving stuff, things for the house, whatever she needed and couldn't buy locally."

"That was very kind of you," I said. "Thank you. For being so good to my sister." Tears filled my eyes. I bit my cheek. I did not want to start crying here. Not like this.

"We were glad to do it. You need anything while you're here, you come see me," he said.

I thanked him and left the store, six-pack of beer in one hand, the long package tucked under my arm. In search of comfort, I headed straight for the Blue Heron. The warm bakery smell was instantly reassuring. I made my way to the counter, where rows of pastries, muffins, and cookies sat in a glass case.

"Hi there! What can I get for you?" the man behind the glass asked. He was tall and red-haired, and his eyes were as green as ever. "Oh my God," he said. He had the same infectious grin as when he was a boy. "Jax? Is that really you?"

"Ry," I said. "It's good to see you."

"Shit, I'm so sorry about Lex." He came out from behind the counter and we hugged. "I can't believe it's real. I keep expecting her to come in for a muffin and cappuccino."

She was a regular at the bakery. Of course. The little things I didn't know about my sister worried at me like splinters under my skin. *Your own fault, Jax.* "I know," I said, feeling my eyes tear up. "At Sparrow Crest I catch myself thinking she's upstairs or in the next room. Somewhere just out of sight."

"I know what you mean. Can I get you a coffee? A muffin?"

"Absolutely," I said.

He poured two cups of coffee, grabbed a couple of muffins, and joined me at a table.

"How is your mom?"

"She's doing really well now. I got divorced last year and came back up to help her out. It seemed like the MS was progressing really rapidly, but now things have stabilized, even improved a bit. She's on a medication regime that seems to be helping, and she's taking care of herself—eating well, doing yoga."

"And how about your dad?" I asked, looking around, wondering if Randy might be in the back baking.

Ryan frowned. "I guess you haven't heard. They got divorced. Are getting divorced, more exactly. I don't think it's legally official yet."

"I'm so sorry. I had no idea." Terri and Randy had always seemed so happy together, joking with each other all day at the bakery.

"You're not the only one. Mom hasn't told most of our family yet. She didn't even tell me. Dad did. Poor guy. Totally shell-shocked. This came out of nowhere. Mom just woke up one morning a couple months ago and told him it was over; she wanted a divorce. He moved out of the house and is down in Connecticut with my uncle James now."

"Wow," I said.

"Yeah," he said. "She won't talk to me about it at all. I don't have a clue what's going on with her. I'm trying to be supportive and all, but she's making it pretty difficult." He took a sip of coffee. "Your aunt didn't mention anything about it to you?"

I shook my head. "No."

"I just don't get it. I mean, if my dad was an ass-hole or something—but they seemed happy together. There were no warning signs. And my mom, she's always been so open with me, but these days she's like a closed book. I don't know how I'm supposed to be there for her when she won't let me in." His face tensed with frustration.

"That sounds hard for all of you," I said, feeling my-self slip into counseling mode. "I think the best thing you can do to support your mom is just let her know you're here and you'll be here no matter what. But give her the space she needs to go through whatever she's going through. I'm sure she'll open up to you again when she's able to."

"I hope so." He gripped his coffee cup hard, looked down into it. "Anyway . . ." he said, seeming eager to change the subject.

"The bakery looks the same," I said.

"That's pretty much true of the whole town," he said. "Brandenburg: the town that time forgot." We laughed. "That's not entirely true, though. We've made a few changes to the bakery. And there are some new houses here and there around town. The old Miller farm burned down last winter. The library got rid of the old card catalogs and got computerized. But some things haven't changed a bit. At the Four Corners the floors still creak, and Bill Bisette still calls me Red."

I laughed. "Bill! I just saw him. It's so great that you're back, though, Ryan. But aren't you a fancy ar-chitect?"

"I wouldn't say 'fancy,' but yeah, that's what I do. I've been taking on freelance work up here to keep my feet wet. And I've done some work to the bakery—

opened up the wall between the kitchen and storage room so it's one big space with better flow, added those skylights." He pointed up. "Did you see the solar panels on the roof? Helping make the building more green. And we've got a heat pump."

"How great!" I said. "Being an architect was always your dream."

I thought back to the summer he tried to help Lexie catch the peacock: how he'd drawn designs for all of these elaborate peacock traps on paper—things involving springs and hinges and underground chambers, contraptions that they'd never be able to build.

"Lexie didn't tell me you were back in town," I said now. "But then again, we weren't talking all that much."

Ryan nodded. "She told me."

I sank back in my chair. "I was an asshole, Ry."

"I wouldn't say that," he said.

"No? I got resentful because my mentally ill sister inherited the house and I didn't? So pissed off I stopped talking to her. And that doesn't make me an asshole?"

He shrugged. "It makes you human."

"I did my best to justify it. I told myself that distance was a healthy thing for both Lexie and me. That I needed time and space to work on myself." I shook my head.

We were quiet for a minute, sipping our coffees. Grief and guilt settled in the pit of my stomach, and the coffee swirled and burned. I pushed the mug away.

"She hadn't given up on things between the two of you," he said. "She said she was going to invite you to visit this fall."

"Really?"

He nodded. "She was determined to find a way to get you to come, making all kinds of plans. She wanted to do some work on the house, get it all fixed up. She had me up there a couple of months ago to give her my professional opinion on some renovations she was considering."

"What kind of renovations?"

"Nothing major. Some built-in bookcases. New windows. Another dormer up in the attic to let in more light. She wanted to cut a hole in the wall between two bedrooms upstairs and put a little door there."

Tears filled my eyes. I let myself imagine it—the little door letting us whisper to each other. What would I tell her? *I'm sorry. Sorry for being a shitty sister.*

"I was worried about her up in that house all alone," he said. "That house . . . the history."

"What history? You mean what happened with Rita?"

He looked down, and just then, I remembered the last time Ryan swam in the pool. He and Lexie had been treading water, trying to stay warm. He didn't have an ounce of fat on him. You could count his ribs, see every bone in his body. His lips were blue and chattering.

"Are you ready, Rye Bread?" she'd said with a mocking smile. "'Cause I am so gonna beat your ass."

She was good at psyching people out. Making them feel like they'd lost before the game even started. But she didn't notice other stuff about people. She had no idea that Ryan's favorite color was blue, his favorite place was his grandpa's cottage on Cape Cod, his favorite meal was spaghetti and meatballs. She didn't know because she'd never asked him. I had.

Ryan shook his head. "Not this time."

He'd never won against her. Not once. Not yet. But

I wanted him to. I was wishing for it. Wishing for it with all my might. I was so tired of her always winning at everything, then gloating about it.

"Jax, you're timekeeper," Lexie ordered. "And Rye Bread," she'd said, voice low. "Be careful down there. You don't want to meet up with poor little Rita."

"Shut up, Lex," I said.

"She's down there," Lexie said. "It's true and you know it, Jax."

"On three," I said. "One . . ."

"If you're a scaredy-cat chickenshit, you can always keep your eyes closed," Lexie told him.

"Two," I said. Ryan had looked terrified. "Three!"

They both dove.

Unlike the Dead Game my sister and I played, the goal here was different. They'd swim down deep and see who could stay under longer, try to touch the bottom. Neither ever had.

Ryan was a strong swimmer. Not as strong as Lexie, but close.

I kept my eye on the second hand of Ryan's Timex. Thirty seconds.

I looked down into the water, saw no sign of them. No movement. A few air bubbles rising up, but nothing else.

I listened to the sound of the water trickling down the spillway, imagined it had a voice, that it was whispering something I couldn't quite make out.

Fifty seconds! Ryan had never made it past one minute. At one minute and four seconds, Lexie popped up and looked around. "You have to be shitting me!" she'd yelped.

"You lose!" I said, elated.

We waited five seconds. Ten.

"Where the hell is Ryan?" Lexie asked—she had sounded scared, and Lex was never scared. I felt panic bubbling up. She went back under. Ryan surfaced five seconds later, gasping and choking, slapping at the water, lunging for the edge. Lexie was right behind him.

"There's something down there!" he yelled. He'd flailed his way to the side of the pool, pulled himself up, and scuttled away from the edge as fast as he could. "Something grabbed me!"

"That was me, dumbass," Lexie said. "You'd been under too long."

"No! This was before! Something had me by the ankle. It was pulling me down!"

"There's nothing down there, Ryan," Lexie said, swimming to the edge. "I'm sorry about what I said. About Rita. I was just . . ."

"Look!" Ryan said, pointing to his ankle. There, on the pale gooseflesh skin above his right ankle, were three red scratch marks, blood coming to the surface.

"I gotta go," he said, throwing on his T-shirt and sneakers. "Creepy-ass pool!" He'd practically run home.

"You're such an asshole," I told my sister. She was taken aback. I never called her names like this. She looked at me like she wasn't sure who I even was. "What? Why?"

I took a step closer to her, my face only inches from hers. She smelled watery and metallic. "Did you grab him?" I'd demanded, a fierceness in my tone that I didn't recognize.

"No! I mean, I grabbed his wrist for a second— I was gonna pull him up, but he swam up on his own."

"Swear to God?"

"I swear! It wasn't me. I didn't touch your stupid little boyfriend."

I scowled at her, furious. I thought back to the wish I'd made to the pool once: for her not to be the special one, for things to be harder for her, for something bad to happen. I looked at the black water and was angry with it, too, for never granting my wish.

We stared at each other for a few seconds, me with all the anger I could muster, and her with a look of bemusement.

"So if you didn't grab him, what did that to his ankle?"

She shrugged. "He probably scraped it on the side of the pool. It's so dark. Being under for a long time, down deep, you get disoriented. You see stuff that isn't there. Imagine things."

And hadn't I imagined that I'd seen things down there? A flash of white that I'd thought for a split second was a pale hand—but it was only a reflection.

Lexie added, "There's nothing in that water except what we bring in with us."

It was a phrase I thought about every time I got in the dark water. And it came back to me now as Ryan said, "It's a huge house for one person. Way out there with no neighbors. You're not staying there, are you?"

"I am," I admitted. "But Ted's with me now."

He looked at me for a long time, like he was waiting for me to say that he was right, it was a creepy place and I shouldn't be staying there; no one should.

"You know," he said at last. "It's hard not to blame myself for what happened. She was in here every morning. She'd go for a run, then end up here. The last few times, something seemed off about her."

"Off in what way? Manic?"

He shook his head. "I'm not sure. She just seemed . . . jumpy. Off. But not off the wall, talking a mile a minute. This was a different Lexie." He paused, looking at me. "A scared Lexie."

The only time I'd ever seen my sister afraid of anything was the day when Ryan hadn't come up from underwater. Fear just wasn't typically part of her emotional repertoire.

"We had this stupid argument," he said.

"Argument? About what?"

He shook his head, looked away. "Nothing really. Like I said, it was stupid. But she went away in a dramatic huff—you know how she could get—then didn't come by for days. I should have checked in on her. But I didn't want to piss her off. When she first got here, she was into having visitors, letting people come and use the pool. Then she closed everything up. Put up all those no-trespassing signs."

"Do you know what changed?" I asked. "What made her shut herself away?"

"Can't help you with that one," he said, looking away. "I have no idea."

Even though he was a grown man now, I could still read him like I'd been able to when he was a little boy. I knew, without a doubt, that Ryan was lying. I just didn't know why.

We finished our coffee and said our goodbyes. "It's really good to see you again, Jax," he said as he pulled me into a tight hug.

"Same," I said, feeling myself stiffen, then relax and hug him back just as tightly, comforted by the sense of familiarity. Maybe he wasn't being totally upfront with me about what had been going on with Lexie, but if I played my cards right, I just might be able to get him to open up and tell me the truth.

"I'll see you at the service tomorrow. And in the

meantime, if you need anything, anything at all, call me day or night." He wrote his number down on a napkin and handed it to me.

I thanked him and gathered up the beer and package.

He frowned at the long rectangular box tucked under my arm. "What's in the box?"

"I'm not sure. Something Lexie ordered."

"Take care of yourself, Jax. If staying up at Sparrow Crest turns out to be too much, call me anytime. I've got a spare room, and my door's always open."

chapter fourteen

September 16, 1929
Lanesborough, New Hampshire

W ork on the foliage festival has reached a frenzy: I am out of the house every day arranging things and making preparations. Today, we scoured the kitchen in the church basement and took stock of all the kitchen implements, making a list of the additional things we'd have to bring in to cook and serve the chicken-pie supper.

Will says I have become the Queen of Lists.

It does me good, hearing the scratch of pencil on paper. Writing down what needs to be done, then doing it and crossing it off the list. It makes me feel like I have a sense of control.

I have no control over my own body anymore. It's growing in new ways. I've had to let out my dresses. My stomach turns at the thought of food that isn't porridge, bread, or applesauce. Even my hair seems to have a will of its own, sticking up at funny angles and refusing to be held by pins.

Will says I look beautiful, that pregnancy has given me a healthy glow.

I feel more out of my body than ever before. Like I am floating outside it, watching the bloated and swollen Mrs. Monroe scratch things off her list, kiss her husband's cheek, let out her dresses and loosen her shoes. *You have no control over anything*, I want to tell her.

———————

Today, I arrived home to find that a new letter arrived from Eliza.

Dearest Ethel,

Since poor Martha's death, I have been very busy indeed. I have been engaged in secret research. I have not told Benson or anyone else what I have learned. You are the first.

I have contacted everyone I've been able to who has experienced a "miracle" at the springs. And what I've learned is very troubling indeed.

The musician I told you about who became an overnight sensation—his oldest son was hit by a streetcar and killed three weeks after his record hit the top of the charts. The woman whose asthma was cured—her husband took ill with consumption. Little Charles Woodcock is now walking, while his sister has been laid to rest.

The old folks in town, they know the truth. They say the springs give miracles, but they always take something in return.

The springs exact a price equal to what was given.

Please tell me, my darling friend, did you get your wish?

Please don't think it horrible of me to admit that I pray you did not.

There is one more thing I must tell you, though I am sure you will think me quite mad.

I have seen little Martha. I went to the pool at

night, and she was there, waiting for me. "Come swimming with me," she said. And oh, Ethel, I ran from her then. I ran and have not been back, but I know she's there still, waiting.

Yours,
Eliza Harding

———————

The room swam around me and before I even realized what I was doing, I crumpled the letter and threw it into the fireplace, where it landed on the hot coals from this morning and immediately caught fire.

September 23, 1929

After hearing from Eliza, I wrote back right away, confessing that her letter troubled me deeply. "I do not think you mad," I assured her. "I believe you were shaken to the core by the death of poor little Martha," I told her. "Grief can do funny things to the mind." I went on to say that I thought it would do her a world of good to get away from the hotel and springs. I invited her to come to visit me, to be our houseguest. "Come right away," I wrote. "Please, Eliza, I insist. You don't even need to take the time to write me back. Just get in your car and come."

And I waited, like a foolish girl, ever hopeful. With each sound of a car engine on our street, I peered out the window hoping to see Eliza, imagining our embrace, how lovely it would be to have her in our house. We would drink tea every morning. I would tell her about my pregnancy, and she would offer advice, tell me stories of what her own pregnancy had been like. And surely, once she was away from the hotel, the springs would lose their strange hold over her—she would see that the stories she'd heard, the things she believed she'd seen, simply could not be possible. We'd even laugh over it, how foolish she'd been for believing such things. I pictured it all so clearly as I sat alone in my kitchen with my tea. I'd made a whole pot, set out an extra cup and saucer across from me, told myself Eliza could show up at any moment.

When she did not come, I dumped the extra tea down the drain, went into the bathroom, and poked my arm with a pin six times. *She is not here now but she is coming,* I told myself as I pressed the needle into my skin.

I am Mrs. Monroe and I am having a houseguest. A good friend. We will share our secrets and laugh over tea. I will make her some of my famous raspberry tarts, and she will never want to leave.

"I've invited Eliza Harding to come visit," I told Will when he came home to find me setting up the guest room with clean bedding. I'd told him nothing about the death of poor little Martha at the hotel or Eliza's consequent unraveling. He knew we exchanged letters often and told each other about our gardens and sewing projects and favorite recipes. Such simple creatures he must think we are!

Will gave me a strange look. "Are you sure that's a good idea? Having a houseguest now? You're so caught up in the foliage festival. I don't want you to overtax yourself in your condition."

"Nonsense," I replied. "A visit from Eliza is just what I need. And she can help with the festival. She's ever so organized. Just think of all the work she's put into that rose garden, everything she does to help keep things at the hotel running smoothly."

He nodded. "If it will make you happy," he said.

"Oh, it will," I said, throwing my arms around him, kissing his neck. "Ever so happy!"

———————

This afternoon, I finally received a letter from the hotel! But when I looked at the return address, I saw that it was not from Eliza, but from her husband, Mr. Benson Harding.

> *Dear Mrs. Monroe,*
>
> *I'm afraid I write with terrible news. I regret to inform you that my wife, Eliza, drowned last week on the grounds of the hotel. As you can imagine, I am at an absolute loss.*
>
> *I must also confess that she was not of her right mind in the weeks leading up to the accident. Please disregard anything she might have written to you in recent letters.*
>
> *Sincerely,*
> *Mr. Benson Harding*
> *The Brandenburg Springs Hotel*

Will came home and found me, face puffy and tearstained. I'd scorched the squash soup and burned two loaves of bread. The kitchen smelled like singed and ruined things. He asked me what on earth happened. "Is it the baby?"

I started to cry. I opened my mouth to tell him, but I could not. Perhaps saying the words would make them too real? No. I wanted to protect him. I didn't want him to know such a terrible thing had happened at a place so special to us; the place where our child was brought to life. "The baby's fine," I said. "I was just feeling a little sorry for myself for no reason. And dinner turned into a disaster. I'm so sorry, Will."

He wrapped me up in a tight hug. "You're overdoing things," he said. "Working day and night on this festival. And I know you haven't been sleeping well, you toss and turn. You need rest, Ethel."

He tucked me into bed, slipping a little white pill under my tongue. "This will help you relax."

I closed my eyes and dreamed I was back at the springs with my newborn baby. Eliza Harding came up from underwater. But not the Eliza I remembered— she was pale with a green cast to her skin. Her hair was full of weeds, her breath was sharp and metallic. Her lips were blue. And her eyes, they were two dark pools, as black as the water itself.

She reached out from the water, her arms impossibly long, tendril-white fingers that turned to claws, and snatched my little girl. Just before pulling her under, Eliza said to me, "Don't you understand? She belongs to the springs."

chapter fifteen

June 18, 2019

J ackie? I'm really concerned," Karen said. "Declan's showing some psychotic symptoms. He's talking nonstop about the fish not being who they said they were. About monsters who sometimes look like fish and sometimes people. His thoughts are all over the place. He made a vague threat toward you."

"Toward me? What did he say?" I panted out the words as I walked quickly up the hill back toward Sparrow Crest, the package under my left arm, the beer in my left hand and my phone in my right.

"That bad things are going to happen to you."

I stopped to catch my breath. "That doesn't sound like Declan at all."

"He said the fish told him. He heard them speaking. They're still speaking to him even now that they're dead."

"Oh God," I said. I felt a vise tighten around my head. Poor Declan. He'd been doing so well—one of my success stories. I quickly sifted back through our interactions, sure I hadn't seen even a glimmer that any of this might have been coming. What symptoms had I missed? "He's been antisocial and withdrawn in the past, but to my knowledge he's never experienced any hallucinations. Never had any breaks with reality."

"He needs to be hospitalized, Jackie. I made some phone calls and sent him over to the Central Valley ER with his mom. But his mom isn't understanding the seriousness of the situation, resisted bringing him. She said she's tired of her son being poked and medicated and put under a magnifying glass."

"But she must see that this is different. He's showing clear psychotic symptoms: disorganized thinking, delusions, hallucinations."

"I went over all of that with her, but I'm not sure any of it truly sank in."

I started walking again. I'd reached the end of the driveway, the big black mailbox with Gram's last name painted in big white letters: HARKNESS.

"Okay. I'll call Mrs. Shipee. Just to make sure she's got him over there and help her see it's the right move. Can you give me her number?"

I set down the package and beer, fumbled in my purse for a pen, and wrote the phone number on my forearm. Then I thanked Karen, hung up, and called Mrs. Shipee before even getting to the house. It went straight to voice mail.

I left a message and asked her to please call me when she got a chance, explaining that I'd had to come to Vermont for a family emergency, but I was very concerned about Declan. "I'm available anytime," I told her, and gave her both my cell number and the landline for Sparrow Crest.

Back at the house, I found Diane and my father in the kitchen, and—even though it was well before five— a bottle of rum and cans of Diet Coke out on the table.

"Rum and Coke?" Diane offered.

I reminded myself I was officially no longer the booze police and smiled as cheerfully as I could.

"No thanks, I've got beer," I said. I popped open one of the IPAs before sliding the rest in the fridge. It was citrusy and bitter and perfect.

"I saw Ryan," I said. "You didn't mention Terri and Randy are getting divorced."

Diane's jaw tightened a little. "Didn't I?"

"Wow," Ted said. "Are they really? I'm surprised. Those two were the real deal."

Diane's phone chirped. She glanced down at the screen and decided to ignore whoever it was. "Your father and I have been going over tomorrow," Diane said as she laid her phone down and took a sip of her drink. "The service starts at one. I figure we should get to the funeral home at twelve thirty. I've had some photos of Lexie blown up, so we'll put those on stands around the Lily Room. All the flowers have been ordered. I think we should keep things informal. Invite anyone who wants to say something to get up and speak. And, if we're able to, maybe the three of us could say a few words, too. I have a Mary Oliver poem I'd like to read—Lexie liked her stuff."

I nodded and took several long sips as I leaned against the counter, Lexie's package behind me. "I'll speak," I said. I wasn't sure what I'd say. *You could always tell the truth*, Lexie whispered in my ear. But what truth would that be? There were so many to choose from.

How, for so long, we were each other's missing piece? How part of me worshiped and stood in awe of her, but another part secretly hated her for the way she captured the spotlight? How her illness swallowed us both up with sharp, grinding teeth then spit us out in pieces? How I moved all the way across the fucking country to try to distance myself, to stop trying to save my sister, hoping I might save myself? Or how when we sat in the lawyer's office to hear Gram's will, a part of me cracked open like a fragile dam? All the old resentments came roaring in, washing away any of the good feelings I had left.

Last year, after we'd gotten her ensconced at Sparrow Crest, I was saying goodbye to her at the airport. "Move in. Live with me," she'd said. "Like we always planned. The Jax and Lex show, remember? We come as a pair. There is no me without us. The X girls," she said, holding up her pointer finger, waiting.

But I'd kept my hands clenched into fists at my sides.

"Gram left it to you, remember?" I said. "You were her favorite. You've always been everyone's favorite."

She stared in disbelief. "That's not fair! And it's not my fault."

"No. Nothing ever is," I said, looking at her, my heavy bag slung on my shoulder. "Nothing's ever fair. And nothing's ever your fault. That's the whole fucking problem, Lex."

That was the last time I'd seen my sister.

"And, Ted, you should speak, too. I know Lexie would want you to. They'll have her . . . *cremains* ready for us," Diane said, not waiting for his reply. "It sounds ridiculous, like crumbs left over at the bottom of a box of crullers, but that's what the funeral director called them."

"I like 'ashes' better," my father said.

"Agreed," I said.

"Well, regardless of what we're going to call them," Diane said, "what should we *do* with them? I'm fairly certain Lexie wouldn't want to spend time in a box or an urn."

"The ocean?" Ted suggested.

"Water's a good idea," I said. "She always seemed more at home in the water than on land. I vote for Lake Wilmore. Lexie loved it there."

"We could put her in the swimming pool," my father said.

Diane and I stared at him, neither of us quite believing he'd really said what he had.

"You're kidding, right?" I snapped.

"It's where she learned to swim; where she found herself as a swimmer, I mean. She learned more about swimming in that water than anywhere—"

"It's where she *died*, Ted," Diane said, like she was talking to a dim-witted child.

"It's where she lived, too!" he countered.

"We're not putting her in that pool," I said. "No way! God, I can't even believe we're even talking about this as a possibility."

"But we're not talking about it," he said. "That's the whole problem. You're doing exactly what you always did with Lexie, Jax. You're stopping a conversation before it even starts because you've already labeled the idea 'crazy,' which just means it's outside your comfort zone, which just about everything is."

I glared at my father. "If by my 'comfort zone,' you mean that I'm thinking rationally and soberly and unwilling to follow you on absurd drunken tangents, then—"

"I *think*," Diane interrupted, "that the lake makes the most sense. I've got a friend with a canoe. Val. She is always trying to get me to do outdoorsy things, which is definitely outside of *my* comfort zone. I end up all swollen, covered in poison ivy and bug bites."

She laughed awkwardly, rubbed at her arms like the idea of it made her itchy.

We stared at her, stone-faced.

"Anyway," Aunt Diane went on, "we can borrow Val's canoe, say a few words, and let her go there."

Let her go. I let the words tumble through me. As if it were that easy. One night, we'd sat on her bed, making shadows on the ceiling with a flashlight, speaking in hushed voices so Gram wouldn't know we were still awake. "Even though we're three years apart, we're like twins," she'd said. We were nothing alike. Not really. We didn't even look alike. I had my mother's dark hair and eyes, and Lexie was blond and blue-eyed like our dad. When I'd said as much, she said, "That's the thing about *real* twins, Jax. They're opposites. They're yin and yang; balance each other out. That's what me and you do." She'd held up her index finger and I'd crossed my own over it. "The X girls now and forever."

I took another swig of beer. "What about after the service?" I asked. "Should we host a gathering of some kind?"

"We can rent a space, invite people for food and drink once we leave the funeral home. I'm not set up for many people at my condo; get more than two people in my kitchen and it feels sardine-like. There's a back room at Casa Rosa that's nice."

"Let's do it here," I said.

"Here?" Diane said, looking around.

"Seriously, Jax?" my father said. "Dracula's castle?"

I nodded. "Yeah, seriously, Ted. This was Lexie's home—she loved it here. God knows there's plenty of space. And it's pretty cleaned up now. We'll just need to get some snacks."

My father frowned.

"Okay," Diane said as she picked up her phone, started typing notes into it. "I'll get plenty of everything. If we have leftovers, we can send food home with people."

Her phone dinged as she held it. "Sorry," she said, standing. "I've gotta take this." She went into the hallway, and I could hear her say in a low voice, "I'm so happy you called." She listened, then whispered something.

"Mind if I try one of the beers?" my father asked.

"Not at all."

He grabbed a beer, and out in the hall Diane laughed, then said in a flirtatious voice, "Is that what you think?"

"I'm sorry, Jax," he said after a moment of awkward silence. "For what I said. I know you didn't always shut Lexie down. I know you tried."

This was almost worse than being criticized. I shook my head. "Not hard enough," I said. "And I'm sorry, too. Being back here is messing with me, clouding my thinking. And losing Lexie . . . it's—" I struggled to finish the sentence.

"It's impossibly difficult," my father said.

"Look," Diane was saying out in the hall, "I've gotta go. But I'll call you soon. Promise." She came into the kitchen, face flushed.

"One of your lady friends?" I asked.

She didn't answer. Just picked up her glass and topped it off with Diet Coke.

"Are you still seeing the woman who works in the bookstore?"

"No," Diane said.

"Jane? Was that her name?"

"No, that's Sylvie," Diane corrected. "Jane was the tax lawyer. That was over ages ago."

"Oh yeah," I said. "I remember. Jane was the one with the Great Dane. Is there someone else, then?" I pressed, smiling. "The poetry lover you were chasing?"

My aunt looked uncharacteristically flustered. "What's in that package?" my father asked, and Diane flashed him a look of thanks for changing the subject.

"Something Lexie ordered. They had it at the general store. Apparently, she didn't like the UPS driver."

"Or the mailman," added Diane.

"You knew about that?"

"She thought they were spying on her. I suggested she get a PO box in town. It seemed like the easiest solution."

"Right," I said. You had to pick your battles.

"Should we open it?" my father asked, already pulling a jackknife from his pocket. He carefully cut along the taped seams. We all held our breath. It felt, in a strange way, like getting a message from her.

My father opened the box to find layers of Bubble Wrap. He unrolled it and whistled. It was a gun-like weapon. It reminded me of a ray gun from an old sci-fi movie.

"What the *hell* is that?" Diane asked, stepping back.

My father turned the gun in his hands. "It's a spear-gun. They're used for fishing," he said. "I have a buddy down in Key West who runs a charter—takes tourists spearfishing. They get grouper, marlin, hogfish, all kinds of stuff."

He took spears from the package. "You load it by pulling back this piece of rubber tubing—it's basically a grown-up version of slingshots kids make in grade school." He got the spear in place, sighted down the shaft of the gun.

"Put it down, Ted," Diane said. "Before you end up shooting an arrow through your foot."

"It's a spear, not an arrow," my father corrected her, laying the gun down on the counter. He looked back in the box. "She got extra spears and a reel and line," he said, clearly pleased. "That way you don't lose your catch."

I looked at the thick, ropelike yellow line in his hand, then back down to the gun. I asked the obvious question. "But why the hell would Lexie order a speargun?"

"God only knows," Diane said.

My father picked it up again, with the intent of installing the reel. "It's a hell of a weapon," he said, running his finger over the sharp metal tip of the spear.

I remembered what Ryan had said: *This was a different Lexie. A scared Lexie.*

chapter sixteen

The entire town came out for the fall foliage festival! People from surrounding towns, too! There
were so many automobiles that they had to start parking in Loomis's meadow. The weather was perfect: the
air cool and tinged with the scent of moldering leaves
and woodsmoke from chimneys. Bands played all day
at the bandstand, and there was a grassy area where
people danced the Charleston and the fox-trot. Some
ladies even took off their shoes and danced in stock-
inged feet! The older Sunday school children sold
lemonade for a nickel a glass. The town green was
full of games, and young and old took turns throwing
bean bags and trying to get rings around the necks of
bottles. The yard in front of the church was filled with
long rows of tables for the dinner.

The children were bobbing for apples, the adults
sipping hot cider laced with bootleg rum from hidden
flasks. Tom Flannagan, the town constable, pretended
not to notice and might have even had a nip or two
himself! Dwight Miller was pulling a hay wagon with
his old Ford tractor in careful loops across the meadow.
There was a small pen on the south side of the green
where Everett Jaquith was giving pony rides for the
children, walking them round and round in circles.

Catherine Delaney hurried past me carrying the leaf garland the Sunday school children made to decorate the tables with, all reds and oranges and yellows, the fiery colors of fall. "Quarter to five," she said, as if I weren't watching the time. Fifteen minutes before we started seating people for the chicken-pie supper, the first of three serving times, staggered forty-five minutes apart.

I was on my way into the kitchen in the basement of the church when Myrtle approached, face flushed, eyes wild. She had a newspaper pressed against her chest, cradled like a wounded bird.

"Myrtle," I said. When I'd seen her earlier, judging the pie-eating contest, she had seemed fine. "Whatever is the matter?"

She took me by the arm and led me into the alcove inside the back door of the church. "The Brandenburg Springs Hotel. It's gone. Destroyed." She pulled the newspaper away from her chest and held it out for me to read.

I froze, feeling my heart slam inside my breast. The baby turned inside me.

STRAFFORD DAILY NEWS

September 27, 1929

FIRE DESTROYS THE BRANDENBURG SPRINGS HOTEL, KILLS 15

A fire swept through the Brandenburg Springs Hotel and Resort in Brandenburg, Vermont, on Wednesday night, killing fifteen people. The fire was discovered by a bellboy at eleven thirty p.m. The Brandenburg Volunteer Fire Department arrived just before midnight to find the building fully engulfed. Water was pumped from the springs on the property to battle the blaze, but the flames, driven by wind gusts, could not be brought under control despite departments being called in to assist from Clearwater and Bainbridge. Two firemen were hospitalized.

It is believed the fire started in the suite of Mr. Benson Harding, the owner of the hotel. Mr. Harding lost his wife, Eliza, in a drowning accident on the property only two weeks before.

A photograph showed a large group of firemen standing among the wreckage, smoke still rising from the charred timbers on the ground. The fountain out front had survived, and was still running, which seemed wrong somehow.

The news took my breath away. I could almost smell the smoke, feel the heat from the embers making my face flushed and sweaty. I felt dizzy and sick.

"Didn't you say you and Eliza Harding exchanged letters? Did you know the poor thing drowned?" Myrtle asked, studying my face.

I looked away.

The springs exact a price equal to what was given.

Please tell me, my darling friend, did you get your wish?

I smoothed the folds of my dress over my belly, kept my hand there, as though trying to keep the baby from hearing what had happened, to protect her in some way.

"No," I lied. "It's too awful for words."

Hannah Edsell came toward us carrying a tray full of plates heaping with chicken pie, mashed potatoes, cranberry sauce, and green beans. "Food's ready!" she said.

I had the newspaper still in my hands. Ruth Edsell came up behind Hannah with an equally heavy tray. "Could you ring the bell, Ethel? Start getting people seated?"

————————

Will and I sat down for dinner with the third group, and Myrtle joined us and Mr. and Mrs. Miller at our long table.

"Did you tell Will the news?" she asked.

I'd been busying myself with the supper, not allowing myself even a moment to think about the fire. I'd put it in a little scaled-up box at the back of my mind.

He raised his eyebrows. "What news is this?"

"The Brandenburg Springs Hotel burned down," Myrtle said.

"Oh, I heard!" said Mr. Miller, who was sitting beside us at the long table. "So many killed."

"Fifteen guests," Myrtle confirmed. "The entire hotel was destroyed." Her face was pink and sweaty, as though feeling the heat from the fire.

"How terrible!" Will said. "We were just there back in June. Weren't we, Ethel?"

I nodded, my mouth as dry as ash. Dancing with Will in the dining room, walking out to the springs. The peacocks. The heady scent of Eliza's rose garden.

"And you've been expecting Mrs. Harding to come visit, haven't you?"

I opened my mouth to speak, but no words came. I opened and closed it, like a fish out of water gasping for breath.

"Dead, poor thing. Drowned in the pool two weeks ago," Myrtle said.

"My God," Will said, setting down his fork and turning to me. "Did you know about this?"

I shook my head, took in a deep breath, closed my eyes.

I am Mrs. Monroe. Chairwoman of the fall foliage committee. We are all sitting down to dinner. My husband is beside me. I am going to have a baby in the spring. A healthy baby girl.

I dug my nails into my palms, then opened my eyes, looked down at my untouched food. I picked up my fork, took a bite of chicken pie, the gravy thick and too salty. The biscuit turned to tasteless paste in my mouth. But still, I chewed and swallowed, moving my own body the way one controls a puppet.

"My aunt Irma lives in Brandenburg," Mrs. Miller said around a bite of cranberry sauce that stained her lips bright red. "People come from all over the country to visit those springs. And something terrible always happens."

I dropped my fork, and it clanged against my plate. "Something terrible?"

"Oh yes," Mrs. Miller went on. "The springs help a blind man see again, but two months later all his cows die. Or his brother is struck by lightning. There's always bad to go with the good."

Please tell me, my darling friend, did you get your wish?

I felt myself floating away again, drifting up away from my husband, friends, and neighbors.

"Absolute bunk," Will said, stabbing a fork full of green beans. "It's terrible." He shook his head. "Those poor people. It was such a special place. It's an awful bit of news—both the fire and the death of

Mrs. Harding—but bad things happen, and when they do, we have to let them go and move on. No sense in giving in to superstition."

I wanted to tell him how the springs and hotel and our baby are all connected, how the fire was a kind of sign, a bad omen.

But I said nothing. I just floated up and up until they were all little specks down on the ground, and me . . . I disappeared right into the clouds.

November 11, 1929

The stock market has collapsed, and banks are closing all over. I fear we're in for dire times. Will tells me not to worry, that we'll weather the storm, that everyone always needs a doctor and we've got plenty of savings. But still, it worries me to bring a baby into the world when things seem so grim.

I do my best. Try to stay calm and happy and always with a smile on my face.

I am Mrs. Monroe, I tell myself. *My husband and I will weather the storm.*

Closer to home, Myrtle's husband, Felix, has taken a turn for the worse. It began with a backache and progressed rapidly. He was soon unable to walk and is now in a wheelchair. Myrtle says he's in terrible pain.

Other than giving Felix laudanum for the pain, Will wasn't able to help. He found Felix's spine and hips profoundly damaged. "I'm amazed he's been able to walk at all considering the damage," he told me. "He's got a bullet still lodged in his spine. He should have been crippled for life."

Myrtle has confided in me that she is going to go back to the springs to get water for Felix. Her eyes are ringed with dark circles now and her face is thinner, more lined than when last I saw her. Her husband's illness is taking its toll.

I tried to talk her out of it. "There won't be anything there," I said. "Just ruins."

"The hotel may be gone, but the springs must still flow," she said.

"It might be dangerous," I told her, remembering the newspaper photo of the cellar hole, the still-smoking remains of the hotel.

"I have to try," she said. "It's the only hope for my poor Felix."

She left yesterday morning in the auto she barely knows how to drive.

I find myself staring out at the gray sky, the bare trees like angry stick figures trembling in the cold November wind, and worrying over her. Did she find her way to Brandenburg? What did she find there?

Despite being a churchgoing woman, I am not much for praying. Not in the traditional way, at least. Still, I lit a candle for Myrtle. "Please keep her safe," I whispered. Then I went into the bathroom, took out my pin, and scratched a little *M* just above my ankle.

November 12, 1929

Myrtle arrived on my doorstep bundled up in a heavy coat, a wool hat, and a thick scarf. I was so relieved that I threw my arms around her and kissed her cheek. She stood still as a statue and seemed to stiffen at my touch. I led her inside and we settled in the kitchen with a pot of tea and some fresh apple cake. The kitchen was cozy, but she kept her coat on. "I can't get warm," she insisted. She gave me a glass jar of water from the springs. It seemed to glow in the jar—only a trick of light, the way the gas light overhead hit the glass, but still, I felt I was holding a jar of stars. A little "Ooh!" of joy escaped my lips.

I had a thousand questions: Was any part of the hotel left? What about the gardens? The peacocks?

Then Myrtle told her story. "The pool was untouched by the fire. There was a fence around it still standing, and it was left locked, but someone had broken the chain. The front gate was open when I arrived," she said. She paused. "And there was someone there, in the water."

Her hand trembled as she held her teacup. "Ethel, if I tell you what I saw, you mustn't think me mad."

"Of course not," I said, laying a hand on her arm. I got a chill; cold was coming off her, as if she was her own north breeze.

"There was a woman in the water," Myrtle said, setting down her cup, the untouched tea spilling over. "She was naked. Splashing around like it was the height of summer. Like the cold did not bother her one little bit."

"A woman?"

She did not answer, and I was sure she'd decided against finishing her story. And part of me was glad! Some part of me did not want to hear.

I thought, of course, of Eliza's story of seeing little Martha in the water.

The kitchen, which moments ago felt bright and warm, was now full of shadow and damp.

"Yes. A woman in her thirties. Dark bobbed hair, dark eyes. She had a scar under her left eye," Myrtle said.

My body grew cold. My heart seemed to stop for

two seconds, then three. The baby moved inside me, a soft flutter.

I bit my tongue to keep from letting out a cry.

It wasn't possible! It couldn't be.

Myrtle's face had gone gray. "She helped me fill my jars with water."

I looked at the jar on the table, the water inside darker now.

"She encouraged me to join her in the pool," Myrtle said. "To take a dip myself. In fact, she was rather insistent." Her jaw tensed and her breathing quickened.

"I declined, saying I had to hurry back to Felix. And I thought . . . no, I was sure—that if I got into that water, I'd never come back out again. It wasn't just the cold. It was *her*.

"'Maybe next time,' the woman said. And then she smiled at me and went under."

I remembered being in that pool, how stunningly cold it was. How my whole body screamed with it. And that feeling, that feeling of fingers touching me, hands reaching out of the darkness to take hold of me.

"She went under and did not come back up again," Myrtle said. "There were no bubbles, no splashes. What person leaves no trace like that?" Myrtle's chin began to quiver. "I stayed and watched until it began to get dark. I told myself I should move, should go in after her or go tell someone. But I just sat, frozen there. The woman did not surface."

chapter seventeen

I sat beside my father in the front row on a plastic folding chair, holding his hand. I'd been a little girl the last time I'd held his hand. My father wore a worn black suit and tie. The same thing he'd worn to my mother's funeral and then my grandmother's.

"Lexie had the unique ability to pull people in, draw them to her." Diane dabbed at her eyes. "She found ways to push me outside my comfort zone again and again. Those of you who know me know I've got a pretty wide comfort zone, so this was no small feat!"

Laughter from the attendees.

"She had this unique ability to see through the bullshit. To know what was really going on in your head, in your heart." Diane's throat hitched. "Lexie touched so many lives. That's never been more evident to me than today, as I look around this room."

The funeral home had had to bring in extra chairs, and some late arrivals stood hovering at the back of the room. It seemed half the residents of Brandenburg had come to say goodbye to my sister. Some I recognized. Some I'd never seen before in my life.

Beside Diane, on a wooden pedestal, sat a tacky gray plastic urn that was supposed to resemble granite. The funeral director had put it there. Inside was a small plastic bag containing Lexie's ashes. I knew they were in a plastic bag because my father had taken the lid off before the service to look inside. "I want to see," he said, opening the jar as if Lexie were a genie who might come bursting out. The bag was secured with a metal band and a tag with Lexie's name. I'd looked at the small bag full of chunky white-gray ash, at my sister's name on the tag—proof that she was really gone—and let out a small, strangled-sounding sob. Diane put a hand on my arm. My father had run his fingers over that tag, saying only, "There's so little of her left."

As the afternoon crept on, I realized he was right in one sense, but wrong in another. It was true that what remained of her physical self didn't amount to much, yet Lexie's vast influence, her spirit, it was everywhere. It was palpable in the air.

My father spoke first. He said in a sure and soothing voice, "Lex broke the mold. You hear that expression, and you think, *sure, sure*, but with Lex, it was true." He looked over the room. "She was the person I was closest to in all the world. The one who always got me no matter what. Even as a little girl, she had things to teach me."

He told the story of Lexie learning to ride a bike—how she skipped training wheels altogether and learned by pushing herself downhill over and over, refusing anyone's help or advice. "She had more guts at six years old than most people show in their lifetime."

Diane read the Mary Oliver poem "When Death Comes." Everyone in the room was crying at the end. My own chest ached and heaved with shuddering sobs. When Diane invited me to come up and speak, I wiped my eyes and stood, making my way to the podium on shaking legs. My sister whispered in my ear. *Are you going to tell them how you cut me out of your life, didn't even pick up the phone when I called?*

I looked out at the sea of faces, all eyes on me. Some of them had to know what a selfish asshole I'd been. I hadn't come to visit for a whole year, missing Thanksgiving, then Christmas, then Easter. A thin, cool layer of sweat beaded on my forehead. I got the telltale throbbing behind my left eye that signaled a whopper of a migraine was coming on.

"I have so many amazing Lexie memories. I thought I'd share one of them with you today," I began. I took in a steadying breath and continued. "When my sister was nine and I was six, she decided to build a rocket ship."

People laughed; some people nodded. My father smiled.

"She got this old refrigerator box, covered it with aluminum foil. She cut windows out of the sides and on the top and covered them with plastic wrap. She dragged it into our bedroom and closed the door and pulled down all the shades. Then, she brought out this big metal flashlight we used for camping. She'd attached a tin can to the end of it, and over the end of the can was more aluminum foil with pinpricks in it. When she turned on the flashlight and angled it up at that ceiling, it was covered in stars."

I closed my eyes and let myself really remember, go back in time. "Almost countdown time, Jax," she'd said. "Hurry up. We don't want to be late."

I cleared my throat and continued my story. "We toured the galaxy that afternoon. We touched the rings of Jupiter, had a picnic on Pluto. Lexie made the stars spin until we were dizzy. I never wanted to come back down to earth," I told the group. "My sister was magic."

———————

We invited everyone to Sparrow Crest for a reception. Before we left, people told us what a moving memorial it had been. Diane introduced me to one person after another until they all blurred together; I knew I'd never remember all their names. Each person had a story about my sister. I learned that she went to the farmer's market every Wednesday afternoon and bought organic strawberries to make jam. I was asked if I'd ever tasted Lexie's jam, and I lied and said I had. I was told she had exhibited watercolors in the local craft fair.

"I didn't know my sister was a painter," I said, unable to hide my surprise.

Marcy Deegan, head of the local art guild, gave me a *how could you not?* look, then said, "She was *quite* talented. She sold every painting she exhibited. I bought one myself."

My migraine was coming on strong, and each new fact about my sister's life felt like a screw being driven into my eye. There was so, so much I'd missed. So much I didn't know about the person I'd once shared everything with.

"I'd love to see it," I said. As soon as she left, I found my father and demanded, "Did you know Lexie painted?"

"Watercolors," he said. "Did you find them when you were cleaning up?"

Of course he knew.

"No." Only pages of scribbled notes. We hadn't come across a single sketch or painting, or any painting supplies.

Ryan approached me with his grandmother, Shirley, Gram's closest friend. She gave me a surprisingly strong hug for a woman who was eighty-eight. "So lovely to see you, dear," she said. She smelled like hairspray and lilacs. I was reminded so much of my own grandmother it brought tears to my eyes. I glanced across the room and saw that Ryan's mother, Terri, was talking with Diane. Terri looked amazing; if not for the cane she was using, I would never have guessed she had any health problems. Nodding at something Diane had said, she looked brimming with energy. Ryan followed my gaze, glancing at his mother, then back to me.

"I'm taking Grandma back to Edgewood," Ryan said. "Then Mom and I will come out to Sparrow Crest." He turned to his grandmother, raising his voice slightly and speaking slowly. "I'm going to go get the car and pull up to the front. I'll be back for you in a jiffy." He kissed her powdery cheek and hurried off.

"I'm sorry I can't join you at the house," Shirley said.

"I understand." I took her hand. "I'm so happy you were able to come to the service."

She squeezed my hand back, hard. "It's tough to get old. It's like being a child again—the way they all talk to you like you can't hear or aren't able to listen. Telling you what you can and can't do, worried you're going to tire yourself out, telling you you're confused over simple matters that you understand perfectly well. Your grandmother, she was smart to get out when she did."

I nodded at her, unsure what to say. She made it sound as if my grandmother had had a choice in the matter—like dying of heart failure on vacation was intentional.

"And your sister, well, your sister meant the world to me," Shirley said, tears filling her rheumy dark brown eyes. She held my face the way Gram used to, got right up close to me, and said, "Lexie isn't really gone."

The last thing I was in the mood for was reassuring words about how Lexie was an angel now, but I nodded again, not wanting to argue with an elderly woman's spiritual beliefs. I was relieved to see Ryan come back in and head our way. "Ready, Grandma?" he asked.

"Go out to the pool," Shirley whispered in my ear. "That's where you'll find her."

My whole body tensed. Then I took a breath, reminding myself this was an old, kindly woman, apparently with dementia.

I smiled warmly at her. "Thank you again for coming." Ryan linked arms with his grandmother, said his goodbyes, and led her away.

My father was bartending in the dining room, expertly mixing toxically strong drinks for people from the huge array of bottles and mixers Diane had set up on the sideboard. He made a gin and tonic for Lily, who owned the bed-and-breakfast. She had come to the service with her daughter, Mindy, who looked to be in her early twenties. "She had a party up here, beginning of May," Mindy told me. "She had the house and pool all lit up with candles! Floating candles on the water. God, it was pretty! Everyone wanted to swim, of course."

I nodded, thinking the water must have been frigid in May. Who would want to dive in?

I did not get a chance to ask; I noticed that her mother, Lily, was flirting with my father. And he was flirting back.

"I can't believe she's gone," Mindy said. She seemed to concentrate on pulling herself together. "When I think of Lexie, I'll always think of that night. Of how she put a Fats Domino record on and danced and sang to 'I Hear You Knocking.' She loved those old records. Did you know what an amazing collection she had?" She hummed the tune, swayed slightly.

I shook my head.

Knock knock, Jax. Aren't you gonna let me in?

In addition to the catered platters Diane had arranged for, guests had arrived laden with food: cold-cut plates, baked goods, casseroles, Crock-Pots full of meatballs and chili. People brought cases of beer, bottles of wine. Patrick and Jamie Brewer, who ran an organic farm in town, brought a bottle of homemade elderberry liqueur. Ryan showed up with a bottle of Ketel One, and as I thanked him, I made a mental note to ask him if he was the one who'd brought the bottle we'd found.

I'd had two glasses of wine, and was now drinking a large, strong margarita Diane had put in my hand. I knew the hard liquor wasn't the best idea, but I was enjoying the numb, removed feeling the booze gave me. I'd taken three Advil, and even with that and the alcohol, my head was still hurting. I circled through the small crowd in the living room and kitchen, saying hello to people I half recognized, and being introduced to people who all seemed to know me. People who had stories to tell about my grandmother, my mother and aunts, and my sister.

"So good to see you again," they all said. "So sorry for your loss."

Gladys Bisette, who owned the general store with her husband, Bill, cornered me. She'd had too many of my father's tequila sunrises and had spilled something on her dark gray dress. "I remember you and your sister riding those bikes—streamers on the handlebars, dinging the little bells. You'd come in to buy penny candy and sodas."

"Yes, I remember. We always got Hires Root Beer. It was Lexie's favorite."

"Such good children," she said wistfully. She took my hand. "Dear, I understand it's soon, but do you have any idea what will happen to the pool? Bill, he's got that bad leg. He was in Vietnam, you know. Shot," she said. "Nerve damage."

"Oh, I had no idea," I said.

"Swimming in the pool keeps him limber. On his feet."

"Don't pester the poor girl, Gladys!" Bill said as he came up, face red and sweaty, whiskey in his hand. "To your sister," he said, raising his glass then slugging it down. I raised my own glass in unison, finishing off the last of my drink.

"I didn't realize my sister was interested in fishing," I said as Bill moved to stand beside me. I thought of the fish in Lake Wilmore when we were growing up—perch, trout, pumpkinseeds. Was she really going to go after such tiny, dainty fish with a harpoon?

"She was interested in all sorts of things, wasn't

she?" said Bill. There was something odd about his look. He seemed to be implying that he knew other things, strange things, that Lexie had been interested in. Or maybe it was a look to remind me that I'd been away for a long time?

"True enough," I said, excusing myself to go and make the rounds.

My head was swimming from the wine and tequila, and from all the things I didn't know about my sister. Watercolors. Mary Oliver. Strawberry jam.

She had had a good year here at Sparrow Crest. And I had missed it all.

And now Lexie was dead.

She was dead, and there was no bringing her back.

The phone in the kitchen started to ring, just as loud and jangling as I remembered. I moved through the living room, feeling as if I were underwater, listening to pieces of conversation: *Poor Lexie; can't believe she's gone; that's the sister, I hear she cut her off completely.* In the empty kitchen I picked up the heavy black handset. It was cool against my hand and ear. "Hello?"

The crackling static of old wires and a bad connection.

No. Not static. Water. It was the sound of running water.

"Hello? Is anyone there?" I heard the faintest whisper: *Sorry. Sorry. Sorry. Are you sorry?*

I slammed the phone back into the cradle. Shit, shit, shit. I tried to steady my body and thoughts. Surely, I'd imagined it. It was the tequila, my headache, and stress combined with a bad phone line. I looked out the window over the sink.

Diane was out by the pool with Terri.

I watched them kiss; not a friendly, chaste kiss, but a long, deep one.

Now I was sure I was seeing things. Diane and Terri? They'd been friends since they were little girls. My mind spun in slow, drunken circles. Shit, was Diane the reason Terri and Randy were getting divorced? And Ryan didn't know?

Terri pulled away, flustered. Diane said something, and Terri handed her a jar. Diane dipped the jar into the pool, filling it, then screwed on the lid and handed it back to Terri. *Bizarre*. While my grandmother touted the healing powers of the water, Diane was an adamant nonbeliever. She openly despised the pool. Did she believe, after all? Or was she just using the water for romantic leverage? Diane glanced back toward the house. She seemed to look right at me.

Embarrassed, I turned away. I poured myself a cup of coffee. I needed to sober up. Get my head together. When I looked back a moment later, Diane and Terri were nowhere to be seen. There was only the pool, the water so black it absorbed the reflection of the sun. It was like looking up at the night sky; I even saw the faint outline of stars there, stars that moved, making me feel off-balance and queasy. All those years ago, Lexie got me out of bed, dragged me down to the pool. *Gram says it will give you wishes!* I took another a sip of coffee, the cup shaking in my trembling hand.

The pool will give you wishes.

My head pounded. The pain behind my left eye was so bad that I felt tears streaming down.

Air. I needed air, but the kitchen door was still sealed shut. I left the kitchen, went down the hall and through the front door. The sun was blindingly bright. I shut my eyes.

When I opened them, I was on my knees beside the pool.

What was I doing here? I tried to remember coming through the gate, walking up to the edge, but my head hurt too badly. Between the headache and the tequila, my thoughts were running together, blurred and distorted like a chalk drawing in the rain.

The pool will give you wishes.

And what would I wish for, if I believed in such things? What did I want most in the world?

I looked at my wavering reflection in the dark pool, imagined my sister under the water, holding her breath.

I touched the water, putting a hand through my own reflection.

"I want her back," I whispered to the water. "Please. I just want Lexie back."

I thought, for half a second, that there was a second reflection there, along with mine; one overlapping the other. I held my breath, leaned closer. Almost said her name out loud.

Lexie?

Yes, Jax. I'm right here.

"You're not thinking of going for a swim, are you?"

I jumped. Ryan was behind me.

"Because that's what's going to happen if you get any closer." He eyed the water warily, like an old enemy he hadn't seen in a while. He reached out his hand to me, and I took it in mine, standing up, staggering a little. "What do you say to going for a little walk?" he asked.

His hand still in mine, we walked out the gate and turned toward the garden. It was even more breathtaking than I remembered. The path leading into it was lined with yellow and orange daylilies tucked behind an edge of perfectly symmetrical fist-sized white rocks. *Moon rocks*, Lexie had called them when we were kids. The garden itself was laid out in concentric circles, with paths and a small gazebo at the center walled with rose trellises. Lexie always said the shape of the garden reminded her of a spiderweb. The garden was overgrown: The roses needed pruning and dead-heading; weeds grew up along the edges of the path and in the flower beds. The green leaves and flowers were full of bug holes. But in spite of the neglect, the garden seemed to be flourishing. I remembered, as we walked, the afternoons Lexie and I spent out in the garden with our grandmother, how she'd rattle off the names of each rose: Aurora, Snow Queen, Maiden's Blush. "Most of these roses," she'd say, "are older than I am. They were planted back when the hotel first opened." And it seemed so strange and fascinating to me then, as a girl: rosebushes older than Gram, older than Sparrow Crest.

Ryan headed for the gazebo, and we sat down on benches opposite each other, the way we had when we were kids. The air was cool and sweet. I wanted to hide out there for the rest of the afternoon.

"How are you holding up?" Ryan asked, his face full of concern.

"It's surreal. I can't believe she's gone. And today I'm learning all these things about her that I had no idea about. My own sister."

Someone closed a car door and drove off.

"I fucked up, Ry. I cut her out of my life. I missed out on so many things. Even her strawberry jam." I started crying, which made the pain in my head more piercing. "She was doing so well for a year, and I missed it—"

"You have to stop being so hard on yourself. Lexie would have forgiven you," he said. "You know that, right?" I nodded. He was right. My sister wasn't big on grudges.

"It's weird as hell to be back in that house," he said.

"The last time you were here was the day you and Lexie had the contest to see who could hold their breath longer. And you said something grabbed you."

He started, as if being grabbed all over again.

"You never came back in the house after that," I said. "You'd come to the front door and wait for us outside."

Ryan was quiet. So quiet and still that I was sure he was holding his breath.

"Jackie?" Aunt Diane was calling from the front yard. "You out here?"

"In the garden," I called, jumping up. We met Diane on the path. She looked at me coolly, eyes reminding me that she'd caught me spying on her. Did she wonder if I'd been telling Ryan what I'd seen? "Marcy's here," she said. "She's looking for you."

"Marcy?" I said, the name not clicking.

"Marcy Deegan. She runs the art guild here in town."

I nodded. "I'll go see if I can find her."

"I should check on my mother," Ryan said. "See if she's getting tired."

"I think she's out by the pool," Diane said.

———————

I didn't have to look hard for Marcy. I found her in the front hall, right in front of the cross-stitch I'd rehung—*To err is human, to forgive, divine*—holding something wrapped in a white sheet.

"Hello," I said. "Thank you so much for coming." I touched her arm gently as she turned to face me. "We've got food in the kitchen, drinks in the dining room."

"I have the painting," she said, offering what she was holding to me. "I want you to have it. I think it belongs with you."

"I can't," I protested. "Though I would love to take a peek—"

"I insist you keep it," she said. "It's what Lexie would have wanted."

"This means so much to me," I said. Carefully, I peeled back the folds of the sheet. It was like lifting the edges of a ghost costume, wondering who or what might be hiding underneath.

My sister looked back at me. I was so startled I nearly dropped the gift.

It was a self-portrait of Lexie's own reflection in the water, about twelve by sixteen inches. Not just any water, but the pool. She had captured herself *perfectly*: her blond hair pulled back in a loose ponytail, the smattering of freckles over her nose, her eyes. I had no idea my sister could paint like this. She doodled elaborately when we were kids. In college she'd taken a painting class, but I'd never seen any of her work.

"I thought on my way here, perhaps this image might be . . . too much so soon?" Marcy said anxiously. "But this was my favorite. And they were all similar, part of a series. Of the pool. Sometimes with her reflection in it, sometimes someone else's."

"No, it's not too much. I love it. What other reflections did she paint?"

"Women and girls. One of them was your grandmother. Another, your mother."

Now that I would like to see.

"Sometimes people I didn't recognize."

"And where are those paintings now?"

"She gave them away. Or sold most of them. I know for a fact that each one in the craft fair sold. It's mesmerizing, isn't it?" she said, looking down at the watercolor in my hands.

"Do you know any of the buyers? I'd love to see more of her work."

"Not offhand. But I'll ask around and let you know what I find out."

Aunt Diane joined us. "Have you seen your father— oh my God," she said, looking down at the picture. "I've never seen this one. It's incredible!"

We looked at the painting together in silence, Lexie holding both of us in her gaze. I covered the painting back up and said to Marcy, "Thank you again for this. It means so much to me."

"It's my pleasure, dear. And I'll be sure to let you know if I find out what happened to any of her other paintings."

"Thank you," I said again.

I carried the painting upstairs to my room and laid it down on the bed for safekeeping. My eyes were fixed on Lexie's, so many questions filling my head. What was she doing out at the pool that last night? What were all the strange coded notes she'd left behind? What had led her to believe Rita's drowning all those years ago might not have been an accident? One question tumbled into another like a row of dominoes.

I thought of what Diane had said—that we'd never know what had led Lexie out to the pool or what was going through her head in her final days. But I knew that wasn't true. She'd left clues. Insights into her thinking. I turned and looked at the white cardboard boxes we'd stacked in the corner of my room, full pages of notes, strange codes, journals, and photographs she'd left behind. I couldn't have my sister back, but maybe if I looked through them, really looked through them, I'd get some insight into her last days. Maybe I'd find some of the answers I was looking for.

I was taking the lid off the first box when I heard a scream from outside. By the pool. I ran downstairs and toward the kitchen door, then remembered I couldn't get out that way. I glanced out the kitchen window and saw a small gathering at the edge of the pool, and at least one person flailing and splashing in the water.

I dashed out of the kitchen, through the living room, to the front door, nearly knocking over a few guests. I plowed through the front door, around the corner, and through the open gate.

My father was beside the pool, soaking wet and coughing. Ryan was next to him, on his knees and also soaked. He had his arm around my father; his eyes were focused on the pool. Diane was crouched beside them. "Someone get us some towels!" she ordered. Two women I didn't recognize hurried past me through the gate.

"Your father fell in," Diane said, seeing me. "Ryan pulled him out."

My father stopped coughing. "I'm fine. And I did not fall in!"

I saw the large bald spot on the back of his gray-haired head. His soaked clothes clung to his gaunt frame. He looked so sad and old, like a strange, broken bird. It frightened me to see him so vulnerable.

I looked at the water. There was something there, floating just along the edge. "What's that?" I asked.

Diane leaned down, scooped it up. It was a paper boat folded together from a sheet of lined notebook paper. Diane shook her head, crumpled it up. "A piece of trash," she said.

"Did you fall in trying to get that paper boat?" I asked my father.

"No! And like I keep saying, I *did not* fall in. I jumped."

"Why?" I asked.

"There was someone in there," he said. He lowered his voice. "It was Lexie."

chapter eighteen

December 12, 1929
Lanesborough, New Hampshire

The baby is doing well. Growing, tapping out codes inside my steadily swelling belly. She wakes me up in the middle of the night to say, *Hello, I am here, floating inside you.*

I have been staying busy. Church on Sunday. The sewing circle Monday. Auxiliary meeting on Wednesday. Bridge with the ladies on Thursday. Times are hard. The foundry closed down, and the paper mill cut its hours in half. A lot of Will's patients barter for his services these days, paying him with fresh milk, eggs, butter, homemade hard cider, snow shoveling. We aren't as hard-hit as some, but it seems everywhere I turn I see signs of trouble.

I have been keeping myself busy, but mostly, I wait. I sit by the fire and I wait for winter to be over and for spring to come. For our baby to be born.

Poor Myrtle has not been the same since her trip to the springs. Will has given her pills for her nerves, but I don't believe they're helping. She's lost more weight—her dresses hang on her like a scarecrow woman. She's fidgety, can't seem to sit still. She jumps at her own shadow. Felix has been doing better. He's out of the wheelchair (Will can't understand how it's possible!) and now he's the one caring for her. She continues to attend church and confessed to me that she has nightmares about the woman she believes she saw in the water that day. I told her that the best thing is to forget about it. "Put it out of your mind," I said. "Felix is well again. Concentrate on that!"

As for myself, I wish I was able to forget the story Myrtle told. I keep playing it over in my mind as the days grow shorter and colder, and the winter shadows play tricks on me. I am nearly as jumpy as poor Myrtle these days.

It's worse when I'm alone in the house. That's when I put a Bessie Smith album on the phonograph Will got me for my birthday last year, turn up the lights, and make myself busy. I bake loaves of bread, mend clothing, work on my quilt, cook savory stews and roasts. I sing a little song to myself: *I am Mrs. Monroe. I am going to have a baby. Everything is fine. I am happy, happy, happy.*

And I clean. I clean until I am exhausted and my hands are red and chapped. I scrub the walls and floors, polish the woodwork. I wax the wood floors. Our house has never been so spotless!

I keep myself busy, but all the while, as I knead the bread or dip my scrub brush into a pail of hot soapy water, some part of my brain is mulling over the question: Could Myrtle truly have seen Eliza Harding in that water?

The thought chills me more deeply than the winter winds that rattle at my windows and doors.

December 15, 1929

Today we had our first real storm of the season. I made cups of hot cocoa, and together Will and I watched the snow fall, piling up along the drive and path, blanketing the house in quiet.

"Will we be trapped?" I asked.

"Certainly not," he said.

"But what if we were? What if it snowed so hard and for so long that we could not open the doors?"

He laughed. "Then I suppose I'd have to jump out a window." He leaned forward, kissed my nose. "Don't worry so, Ethel."

I closed my eyes.

I am Mrs. Monroe, and it is snowing hard, but I shall not worry. I shall not worry. I shall not worry.

"What are you thinking, darling wife?"

I opened my eyes. "I am thinking about how very lucky I am."

We stoked up the fire and played Parcheesi, rolling the dice, moving our little pawns around the board. I had a pot roast in the oven and was suddenly ravenous; I have the strangest cravings lately: raw potatoes, chard, sauerkraut, mint jelly. The other day, I found myself eating the peel of an orange, the bitterness deeply satisfying. I went to the kitchen, took a bite of a raw turnip from the root cellar, tasting the dirt that still clung to it, wonderfully gritty on my tongue.

I am Mrs. Monroe. I have strange appetites.

Will settled in by the fireplace with his brandy and a book. I went into the pantry, climbed onto the step stool, and moved aside canned tomatoes from last summer's garden, onion relish, string beans. At the back, hidden away, I found it: the glass jar Myrtle had brought me, nearly empty now. I untwisted the lid, opened it up, and allowed myself to take the final sip, the one I'd been saving. The sharp, metallic flavor bit into my tongue. I closed my eyes and savored it. For those few seconds, I was back at the springs, the water holding me, caressing me, knowing all my secrets and fears. An arm grabbed me around the waist. I held my breath, ready to be pulled under.

"What on earth are you doing, Ethel?" Will asked. I snapped my eyes open, found I was still balanced on the stool, the empty jar in my hand.

"Just getting some beans for dinner," I told him, reaching back to the shelf for a jar of string beans. He helped me down off the stool. "You've got to be more careful," he said, touching my enormous belly. He didn't ask about the empty jar in my other hand.

January 1, 1930

Felix took ill again on New Year's Eve. Myrtle ran over without her overcoat or a hat on and arrived at our door half-frozen, with icicles in her hair and in near hysterics. I brought her inside and wrapped her in a heavy wool blanket. "It's going to be all right," I told her. "Will should know what to do." Then I poured her a bit of apple brandy to settle her nerves.

While Will was getting his bag, she moved close and whispered, "Do you have any of the water left? Any at all?" Her eyes were frantic, streaked with red. She explained that all of hers was gone. Felix had drunk the last of it three days ago and began to lose the feeling in his legs almost immediately. But this time the numbness, the paralysis, was spreading up. Now, she said, he could not use his arms. Worse than that, he was having difficulty breathing.

"I need more spring water, but I can't bring my-self to go." She pulled the blanket around her tightly, wringing the edges in her hands. She was still shivering despite the warmth of our kitchen. "I should have gone back before winter set in, but I couldn't bring myself to. I was too afraid. I *am* too afraid." I patted her back, told her everything would be all right. I was wrong to make such promises.

The sad fact is, little could be done. Will had Felix brought to the hospital by ambulance and stayed with them.

Felix was dead by morning. A spinal infection, they said.

Such a ghastly way to start off the new year.

Will came home at dawn to tell me the news. He gets a certain look when he has truly terrible news to deliver: a sadness in his eyes, two little worry lines on his brow. He took me in his arms, kissed my head.

"Honestly, Ethel," he said. "It's a miracle he had so many good years after the war. The amount of shrapnel in that man's body, the damage done—I don't understand how he was up and walking around."

I started to get my coat and hat.

"Where are you going, Ethel?"

"To Myrtle, of course. She shouldn't be alone."

He shook his head, told me Myrtle was in the hospital herself under heavy sedation.

"Then I'll go to her there."

Will took the coat from my arms, hung it back up in the closet. "You'll do no such thing. Myrtle isn't herself. She's in no shape for visitors, and seeing her like this would just upset you."

"But I—"

"You have to think of the baby," he told me, resting his hand on my belly, rubbing gently.

January 8, 1930

Last night I dreamed of the pool again. It was calling my name. The voice was as soothing as a stream flowing over rocks. Singsongy and familiar. *"You said you would give anything,"* it reminded me. *"Anything to have a child."*

"What is it you want from me?" I asked.

The sound of running water turned to laughter that shook me to the bone.

chapter nineteen

June 19, 2019

We stood in the driveway. Ryan had borrowed an outfit from my father's suitcase—a paint-spattered pair of shorts and a Guinness T-shirt. His soaked dress clothes were in a plastic grocery bag in the backseat of his car. His mother was waiting in the passenger seat. She looked exhausted and shaky. "Call if you need anything," he said.

I leaned over and gave him a hug. "Thank you," I said. "If you hadn't been there to pull my father out—"

"It was nothing," he said, looking me in the eye. "Maybe it'll be a lesson to him that alcohol and pools don't mix."

A lesson I very much doubted would sink in.

"Drive safely. I'll stop by the bakery tomorrow."

"Good night." He grabbed the door handle on his car. "Oh, and Jackie? What's with the grid around the pool? The crayon marks?"

Shh. Mum's the word, Jax. I thought of all the secrets I'd kept for Lexie over the years. What harm was there in keeping one more?

"I don't have a clue."

He looked at me, frowning. "Okay," he said. "You've got my number. Call if you need to. I'm five minutes away."

Back inside, I found Ted and Diane in the kitchen at the table with cups of coffee. Diane was stirring hers a little too hard, the spoon clanking against the mug. My father was dry, in shorts and a T-shirt, staring down into his own murky coffee. The guests had all cleared out. Someone had tidied up, stacking glasses and plates in the sink, dumping all the empty cans and bottles into the recycling bin. The food had been put away. I sat down to join them. My head hurt so bad that my teeth were throbbing. I said as much, and Diane rummaged in her purse. "Try this."

I eyed the pill skeptically. "What is it?"

"Tylenol with codeine. They're left over from my last root canal." She handed me the bottle. "Keep them. Sounds like you need them more than I do." She yawned, rubbed at her neck. "I'm exhausted. And I've had way too much to drink."

"Why don't you stay here tonight?"

She flinched. "I haven't spent a night in this house since I was a teenager."

"Well it beats driving drunk. Please, Diane. I'll feel much better if you stay." I gave a concerning look in my father's direction. "I can put clean linens on the bed in Lex—in Gram's old room."

"All right," she said at last. "I don't suppose one night here will kill me."

I turned to the elephant in the room. "How are *you* doing, Ted?" I asked, dry swallowing the pill Diane had given me.

"Fine," he snapped. "I wish to God everyone would stop asking me that." This was followed by an awkward silence.

"Do you want to tell us how you ended up in the

water?" I asked, sounding more like a therapist than I intended.

My father remained silent.

"I think Lily was disappointed that you didn't need mouth-to-mouth resuscitation. Maybe I should try falling in the pool next time," Diane chimed in, giving me a look, trying for levity.

My father said nothing.

Diane's face grew serious. "I think we should have the damn thing filled in. Nothing good has ever come from that pool." Her eyes shifted to the kitchen window, the pool beyond. She looked guilty, a little frightened, like she worried it may have heard her.

"Nothing?" I asked. "What about the people who believe the water has healing powers? All day I had people asking me if they'd be able to go on using the pool, claiming it helped with all kinds of maladies. I think I even saw someone filling a jar with magic, healing water."

I'd gone too far. I hadn't meant to bring it up. It just popped out. Diane wasn't the only one who'd had too much to drink today.

Diane glared at me, jaw clenched.

After a moment, she stood and said, "I'll go change the sheets. I'm going to turn in. I'm exhausted. Good night." She started out of the kitchen, shooting me a *keep an eye on your father* look.

"Diane?" I called. "That paper boat you pulled out of the pool. Was there anything written on it?"

Her body stiffened. "I don't think so," she said, frowning at me the way she'd always looked at Lexie when she had one of her out-there ideas. "It was just a bit of trash, Jackie."

We listened to her pad down the hall and up the stairs.

I went to the fridge and got out two beers, putting one down in front of my father—a peace offering.

"I know you think I'm a crazy drunk who doesn't know what he's talking about," my father said. His shoulders were hunched, and he looked defeated, old. It frightened me to think what might have happened if Ryan hadn't pulled him out of that pool in time.

"That's not what I think at all," I said. But deep down, it really was. And it was what I had always thought. The truth was a corkscrew in my heart to acknowledge. "I think— " I said, choosing my words carefully, "that you've done the best you could."

"That's bullshit therapist talk," he said, shaking his head. "I've been a shitty father. But I've never lied to you. You or Lexie. Jackie, I swear to you, I know what I saw. Yes, I'd been drinking, but it was no hallucination. It was *not* my eyes playing tricks on me!"

"Okay," I said. De-escalate and problem solve. "Let's take it step-by-step, Ted. Tell me exactly what happened."

"I'd been talking with Lily. You know her, from the bed-and-breakfast? Sweet woman. She invited me to come outside with her, said she had a little of Vermont's finest greenery to share."

"Wait. You're saying you and Lily got high?" I couldn't help barking out a laugh. So much for remaining objective.

"No! We didn't, because when I went outside, I couldn't find her. She went out to the garden. I went out to the pool. A simple matter of miscommunication."

I nodded.

"I was looking at the crayon writing around the pool, over by the back corner of the fence. I heard a splash. I thought maybe someone had snuck over and jumped into the pool. I saw ripples, bubbles—"

"The wind?"

He stared at me, his eyes shimmering with the intensity of his story. "I saw a hand reach up! Someone *was in the water*! Drowning!"

"Could it have been a reflection?"

There's nothing in that water but what we bring with us.

I closed my eyes, a glimpse of a memory surfacing. Me, out by the pool, alone at night when I was a little kid.

But I wasn't alone.

There was someone, something, in the water.

I opened my eyes, shaking the memory—if it even was a memory—away.

"I'm positive!" my father said. "I jumped in without thinking about it. I didn't even take my shoes off. I swam for them as hard and fast as I could. But they went under. Then suddenly I was under, too. Someone was pulling on my leg; the swimmer in distress, I figured. They were disoriented, panicked. I've always heard that rescuing a drowning person is incredibly risky, because chances are, they'll take you down with them."

I'd heard that, too, at the swimming lessons Gram made Lexie and me take at the lake each summer. One of the older lifeguards told us.

My father continued. "I struggled, reached the surface." His breathing was coming in short bursts now, like he was still trying to catch his breath. "Then, she had me by the wrist. She was pulling me down. I saw her face, Jackie. It was *Lex*. I know my own daughter!"

"Fear and adrenaline can do crazy things to your body and mind," I said. I wanted to steer us back to solid ground.

He sat up straighter, looked me in the eye. "So you think I just got confused? That I imagined it?"

"That water's so black," I said. "It's hard to see your own hand in front of your face down there."

He shook his head in frustration.

"I believe you saw something," I soothed. "But I also know how easy it is to see shapes in the darkness, to imagine things."

And I did know, didn't I? Hadn't I seen things in that water?

Again, I had a flash of standing by the side of the pool at night, looking out into the dark water.

What had I seen?

I went on, "Lexie died in that pool a few days ago. You want nothing more than to see her again. I know I'd give anything to have her back. So your brain—under the influence of booze, and not working at one-hundred-percent capacity—took confusing, scary stimuli and tried to make sense of it in a split second. It showed you what you *wished* to be true. That's totally normal, Ted."

"Sure. Whatever you say, Jax."

———

When I finally went back up to my room, Lexie was waiting for me on the bed. The painting of her, at least. I'd forgotten all about it and jolted. "Idiot," I mumbled to myself.

Scaredy-cat, Lexie taunted.

I picked the painting up and leaned it against the

wall on top of the dresser. Lexie seemed to be watching me, unblinking. I moved closer and saw that there was something in her eyes, in the dark pupils. A reflection. A reflection of her own reflection—Lexie on land reflected by Lexie in the water.

I settled in on top of the covers, Lexie watching me. Between the drinks and the codeine and my father's unexpected plunge, I was feeling pretty wasted. At least my headache was down to a dull simmer. My cell phone was plugged into the charger, right where I'd left it when we got back from the funeral home. I picked it up and saw two missed calls and voice mails, one from Karen Hurst and one from Barbara. I listened to the voice mails.

"Hi, Jackie, it's Barbara calling you back. I'm free tomorrow between one and three. Give me a call sometime in there if that works. If not, get in touch and we'll find another time."

I listened to the next, from Karen.

"Hey, Jackie, sorry to bother you again, but I was wondering if you'd heard anything from Valerie Shipee? She and Declan never showed up at the hospital yesterday and she hasn't returned my calls. Hoping you have better luck. I'm really concerned. Call me with an update when you get a chance. Thanks."

My phone showed no missed calls from Valerie Shipee. Damn. It was late and I was drunk. I'd try in the morning.

I felt restless and emotionally spent, but not tired enough to sleep. There was the stack of white boxes in the corner of my room, stuffed with Lexie's notes. The lid was still off the top box, dropped on the floor when I'd heard the screams from the pool. I went over, sifted through some of the papers and scraps, wondered how I was ever going to make sense of any of this. But I resolved to try. I picked up the first paper:

> *June 3*
> *I've come to think of the water, the pool, as a living*
> *entity all its own. A creature with its own needs, wants,*
> *desires. Its own . . . hungers.*
>
> *June 6*
>   *G11: 1 p.m.——7.4 meters*
>   *G11: 5 p.m.——15 meters*
>   *G11: 10 p.m.——over 50 meters*

I thought back to her rant into my answering machine. *The measurements don't lie. It's science! The fucking scientific method. Construct a hypothesis. Test your hypothesis.* So many pieces of paper had the same codes—a chronology of Lexie's survey of the depth of the pool? It seemed to change drastically from one time to the next. But how could the depth be one thing at one o'clock, then something totally different later that same night? It couldn't. I heard her voice, the last words she left for me: *She's here, Jax. Oh my God, she's here!* These measurements, they were what Lexie *thought* she saw, what she imagined. I looked at my sister's painting. "What the hell were you doing, Lex?"

I thought of my father, accusing me of always shutting Lexie down; stopping a conversation before it even started.

If I was going to truly try to understand my sister and what was going on with her in her final months and weeks, I'd have to step considerably outside of my comfort zone. I'd have to follow her clues, retrace her steps, no matter how crazy that seemed.

Go see for yourself, Jax. I double-dog dare you.

I turned to the image of Lexie in the painting. "Okay, Lex. Here we go."

———————

I padded down the hall, tiptoeing past the closed door to my grandmother's room where Diane was sleeping. I was a child again, sneaking to raid the refrigerator or meet Ryan for a moonlight adventure. Back then, Lexie always led the way, finger on her lips, shushing me. Making me promise not to make a sound. *Mum's the word, Jax.*

When we were teenagers, we flat out broke Gram's number one rule. Lexie would wake me in the darkest hours of the night, whisper, "Come on, Jax, it's time," and I'd follow her down the stairs, out the kitchen door. I could always tell the times my sister had been skipping her medicine, because these were the times we swam at night. Being in the pool settled her, quieted her mind. So we'd slip out of our warm pajamas and into the frigid water. It felt a little like dying each time. But there was a dreamlike quality, too—Lex and I glowing in the black water, swimming side by side as our limbs grew numb and our hearts pounded, alive. One strange and perfect image I have of Lexie: She is seventeen, lounging naked in the dark, hair slicked back, water dripping off her as she smoked, staring up at the rings that drifted up to meet the black clouds covering the moon.

I could almost hear her whisper, *Come on, Jax, it's time*, as I made my way downstairs and into the kitchen, not turning on any lights. I opened the drawer where we'd put the flashlight I'd found when we were cleaning. I flicked it on to make sure it worked, and the kitchen filled with light. I walked out the front door, opening and closing it as gently as I could so I wouldn't wake my father and aunt. I knew this was crazy and that I was a little drunk and loopy. But I needed to see for myself.

I'd go out, see that the pool measurements were normal, and then I'd go right back to bed and forget that I'd entertained the notion that my sister's notes might have some truth in them. I was the logical one. The one who made my living helping people in crisis. Yet here I was, sneaking around to measure the depth of the swimming pool at midnight, to see if it really was bottomless. Ridiculous.

The flagstone path that led around the side of the house to the gate was still warm under my bare feet, the stones holding the heat from the day. I pushed on the gate latch, and it opened with a loud screech. I made a mental note to give it a squirt of oil in the morning. I tried the switch that turned on the flood-lights my grandmother had installed for early morning swims. But no swimming at night. Not ever.

The lights did not come on. The bulbs were probably missing out here, too, and we hadn't thought to replace them.

So Lexie entered the water in complete darkness that final time. Slipping out of her shorts and T-shirt, leaving them on the edge where Diane and the police and paramedics found them the next day. A thought occurred to me: What if it wasn't Lexie who had removed and broken all the light bulbs? What if she'd woken up in the dark and couldn't turn on any lights? Heard a noise from the pool and come out to investigate? What if she hadn't been alone?

I shook my head. There was no sign of foul play. No sign of an intruder. The police had pronounced it an accidental drowning.

A woman with a long history of mental illness and erratic behavior, including suicidal ideation, enters her pool and is found the next day by a concerned family member. It wasn't such an odd story.

What's your story, Morning Glory? What makes you look so blue?

I switched on the flashlight, cutting through the darkness. I willed myself to move closer to the pool. The sharp mineral smell of the water was mixed with something vaguely unpleasant. Sometimes, like now, the pool smelled dank and sulfurous, more like rotten eggs than the clean, healing water Gram used to promise it was. If we had a cold, the flu, a headache, she claimed a dip in the pool would cure it. I thought of Gladys Bisette asking if Bill could come for a swim to help his old war injury. Of Diane filling a jar for Terri, who probably believed it helped her MS. It was amazing really, the power of the mind. But still . . . what left those scratches on Ryan's leg? Who lured my father in this afternoon?

And what about the time I came down here on my own?

I'd done it on a dare. Lexie said she didn't think I had the guts to go out to the pool on my own in the middle of the night. She'd teased me for days until finally, I was furious enough to prove her wrong. I snuck out of bed close to midnight, crept down the stairs and outside to the pool. It was pitch-dark, and as I waited for my eyes to adjust, I heard a splash in the water. I called out to my sister, sure it was her, trying to spook me. But it wasn't her, was it?

I shook the thoughts away. Being by the pool was freaking me out big-time. The best thing to do would be to go back inside. But not without taking a look. Just checking. "Let's get this over with, then," I said out loud.

I did a sweep with the flashlight beam, saw the empty patio, the still pool. The dark water sucked in the light; became a black hole with its own gravitational force, trying to pull everything around it in. I could not see the hills behind it, but I felt their presence and imagined, for half a second, that they were inching forward.

Keeping my eyes averted from the blackness where I knew the hills to be, I moved to the back side of the pool, where the outlet was, to the corner where we'd stashed Lexie's raft. No way was I going out in that thing in the dark. I'd measure the edges, though. An experiment, I told myself.

Come on, Jax. Try it. Just for shits and giggles.

I shone the light into the raft and found the coil of marked measuring tape with the metal weight hooked on the end. "Here goes nothing," I said, hoping the sound of my own voice would break the nervous fear jolting through me. I carried the unwieldy coil to A1 at the left-hand corner, toward the front gate. Careful of the slippery edge, I lowered the weight. As I fed the measuring tape down, it bounced along the wall of the pool and I found myself holding it fiercely, as if it might get yanked out of my hand. Surely the weight would hit bottom soon—and then it did. Of course it did. Holding the line taut, I crouched down, shining the light on the markings. 6.8 meters. I moved over to A2 and got roughly the same measurement. Moving carefully along the long edge of the pool, stopping every foot, I worked my way all the way down to A45. All spots measured between 6.8 and 7.4 meters, which would be something like 20 to 24 feet. Deep for a swimming pool, but by no means bottomless.

I felt a little disappointed—it seemed a huge letdown to see proof that there was a bottom. Santa Claus and the Easter Bunny weren't real after all. I had a perfect vision of Lexie at ten, blue swimming cap and goggles on, shouting, "I'm going to swim all the way to the other side of the world!"

I opened my eyes, tossed the weight out farther from the edge a couple of times. I couldn't drop the tape down straight, so I couldn't get a precise measurement, but it was also roughly the same depth. I was crouched down, flashlight in hand, looking at the measurements on the rope when I heard a small splash from behind me, near the back end of the pool. Startled, I dropped the flashlight into the pool. I watched it sink, the light illuminating the water for a few seconds until it died.

"Shit," I said, scrambling to my feet, turning around and squinting into the darkness, searching for some sign of movement. "Is someone there?" I pulled the rope up, held on to the last few feet of it, the lead weight swinging. It wasn't much of a weapon, but it would have to do.

I searched the shadows, the dark shapes of chairs, tables, the umbrella, the half-deflated raft. All of it looked ominous in the dark; shadowy monsters watching, waiting, holding their breath to see what I would do next. I heard only the low murmur of the outlet stream at the far end of the pool. I stood up, legs feeling like Jell-O, and walked to where it sounded like the splash had come from. I swung the weight at the end of the rope, thinking I'd aim for the head if anyone was there. I saw no movement. The water was still, unbroken. It was my imagination. I hadn't really heard anything at all.

Denial ain't just a river in Egypt.

"Shut up already," I told her. Told myself. Because Lexie wasn't really talking to me. Just like I didn't really hear a splash.

I imagined it because I was under tremendous stress—grieving, sleep deprived, guilty—just like Ted.

Then, as I stood in the dark looking at the black water, it came back to me. I remembered the girl I'd seen the night Lexie dared me to night swim. She was treading water in the middle of the pool. Younger than me, seven or eight maybe, with hair so pale and blond that it seemed to glow like moonlight. I was sure then, in my ten-year-old brain, that I knew exactly who I was looking at. I'd seen enough drawings of her to know. This was Martha, Rita's imaginary friend. "Come swimming," she'd said. I shook my head. It was against Gram's rules. She giggled, then went under. I waited, holding my breath, counting the seconds. One minute went by. Then two. No air bubbles. No sign of movement. Behind me in the house, the light came on in Lexie's bedroom. I turned and saw her looking out the window, watching me. I ran into the house, and she slapped me on the back, congratulating me for not being a total wimp. I never told her what I'd seen. I never told anyone. Over the years, I convinced myself it had never happened. That it was just something I imagined or dreamed.

From the front end of the pool, a dim glow blinked under the water once, twice, three times, then went out. The flashlight must be short-circuiting in the water.

"Jackie?" I heard the rusty squeak of the gate being opened and turned. Diane came through and saw me standing with the measuring tape and weight swinging from my clenched hand. "What on *earth* are you doing?"

Great question. "I couldn't sleep," I explained, trying to sound matter-of-fact. "So I thought I'd come out and . . . measure the pool."

"I'm sorry, what? You're measuring the pool at midnight? That's totally normal and not in the least bit concerning."

"That's what Lexie was doing," I said. "The notes she left were coordinates and measurements—she was using this tape to measure the depth of the pool at different points. I was curious to know if what she wrote down was accurate—"

"Come on back into the house," Diane ordered, her jocular tone gone. She stood by the gate, holding it open, waiting for me.

"Let me just put this back," I said, and coiled the tape up, brought it back over to the raft.

"We've got to replace the lights out here," she said as she waited. "And maybe get a lock for the gate. We don't want any kids fooling around in here when no one's around. It's not safe. Especially at night."

"Good idea," I called back.

I made my way along the edge of the pool, stopping when I noticed something right by A3. I leaned down to pick it up. "What the—"

"Everything okay, Jackie?" Diane called, taking a few steps toward me. "You're not going to pull a Ted and end up in the water, are you?"

The dazed, removed feeling from the booze and codeine was replaced by a surge of adrenaline. Suddenly

I was very awake and sober and terrified. "Everything's fine," I said, frozen, my heart jackhammering.

Things weren't fine. They weren't fine at all. Because what I was seeing just wasn't possible.

It was the flashlight—the same flashlight that had sunk into the pool not five minutes ago. I picked it up. It was cold and wet. I flicked the switch. It turned on instantly.

There were two possible explanations for this, and standing there, holding the light in my trembling hand, I couldn't decide which one was more terrible: Either I was losing my mind completely, or there was someone down in that water.

chapter twenty

There is nothing quiet, clean, or easy about child-birth. It is like being cracked open like an egg. No one warned me about the pain. I have never known such pain.

Margaret Joy surprised us by coming three weeks early. She was born in our bedroom at seven-nineteen this morning. She is a tiny thing, like a little doll. Five pounds, three ounces.

I am Mrs. Monroe and I am a mother now.

———————

I was home alone yesterday watching the sky grow darker and darker as a storm gathered. The clouds were thick and tinged with orange, and the very air had a weight to it. I spent the day cleaning the house, scrubbing the floors, filled with an odd nervous energy. I was vibrating like a tuning fork. It was the coming storm making me feel that way, I imagined. And then, in the late afternoon, a fog rolled in. I have never seen such a fog before. It crept up from the river and seemed to blanket the whole town. It curled around the windows, seemed to drift in through the cracks, filling the house with damp, making my bones ache. I had a sense, silly I know, that it had come for me; that there was no way I could hide from it.

I stuffed towels in the cracks along windowsills and the threshold of the front and back doors.

I turned up the lamps and was at the kitchen sink washing vegetables for dinner when there was a terrible crash against the window. Then another. I looked to see that birds, lost in the fog, were crashing into the windows of the house. There must have been a flock of them, because one after another smashed against the windowpanes, then fell to the ground. I raced around the house putting out all the lights, thinking that was what was drawing them in. When the birds stopped falling at last, the snow and sleet began.

Will arrived home soaked to find me sitting in the dark, crying over the birds. He'd had to leave the car across town at his office—the roads were impassable already, so he'd walked home.

I didn't eat dinner. Just didn't have an appetite. Around seven my water broke and the contractions began.

"It's too early," I said.

"Babies come when they're ready to come," Will said. "And little Brunhilda is eager to meet us." He smiled and began making preparations to deliver her at home.

"I've delivered many, many babies," he said, kissing my head. "Trust me, darling wife. We're going to be just fine."

After twelve hours of labor, I pushed her out into the world. I was exhausted and delirious when Will put her in my arms.

"She's so delicate," I said to Will. "Like a tiny little

bird." I kissed her damp, downy head. "A sparrow. My little sparrow child."

She is tiny, but perfect. Her skin is porcelain white. Her hair is dark as a raven. And her eyes are like a stormy sea. She has such a serious, almost worried-looking face—so odd to see on such a tiny baby. I see no resemblance to either myself or Will. She is a creature all her own.

Our eyes locked, mine and hers, and it nearly took my breath away. In that look, we each seemed to say: *Here you are, at last.*

chapter twenty-one

June 20, 2019

I woke up to the smell of coffee and bacon.

I'd been dreaming that Lexie came to my room and stood in the corner, dripping and smelling like the pool. We were telling each other riddles. My riddles were old schoolyard things: *What has four legs and a body but can't walk? A table!*

Lexie's were nonsense: *What has gills and pink polka dots? The Brooklyn Bridge!*

But her final riddle stayed with me as I sat up. *Who is cold and dark and smells like rotten eggs?*

And there she was, watching me from the painting propped up on the dresser, gazing at her reflection, her own version of Narcissus.

I glanced into the corner of the room, where she'd stood in my dream. Pig was curled up on the floor there, chin resting on his front paws, yellow eyes watching me.

I got out of bed and made my way down to the kitchen. My head felt thick and heavy, my thinking clouded as I pushed myself to come up with a logical explanation for what happened with the flashlight. Did I actually see it fall? I was distracted, frightened, so maybe I didn't notice that the light hadn't actually fallen into the water. Maybe, I told myself, it had been there on the edge of the pool the whole time. That must have been it.

But the blinking light I saw in the water, did I imagine that?

And the splashing?

"Morning, Jax," my father called. He was standing in front of the stove, flipping bacon on the big cast-iron griddle my grandmother had used to make us pancakes: plain for me, chocolate chip for Lexie. Another large pan full of home fries sizzled next to it.

"Hope you're hungry," my father said. He grabbed two eggs. "Over easy, right?"

Lexie liked her eggs over easy, not me. "Scrambled hard," I said. It wasn't even nine in the morning. The Ted I knew rarely rose before noon. And I doubted he'd ever cooked me breakfast in my life. "I didn't know you could cook," I said.

"Ha!" he said jovially. "Well, then you're in for a treat. Should we wake Diane up?"

"No way," I said, pouring myself a much-needed mug of coffee. "Let's let her sleep. You're up early."

"I had the most amazing dreams," he said. He looked wistful, little-boyish. I sat at the kitchen table and noticed a sketchbook, an assortment of drawing pencils, an eraser, and a sharpener.

"I found your sister's art supplies up in the attic and helped myself," he said, following my gaze.

"The attic? When were you up there?" Growing up, it was off-limits to Lexie and me. When my mother and Aunt Diane were girls, their grandmother lived in the attic. Her brass bed was still up there, covered in a sheet like she might still be sleeping beneath it. The few times I'd been up there it scared me. I'd heard stories from Mom and Aunt Diane about their poor old grandma who'd gone senile and kept her teeth in a jar next to the bed. I was afraid of encountering either her or her teeth up there in the dark.

"I thought . . . I thought I heard something up there. I went up to check it out—must have been a mouse. Anyway, your sister had turned part of the attic into a studio. I started sketching some images from last night's dreams," my father said. "I've gotta tell you, it feels good to be working again. I haven't done any real, honest-to-God authentic artwork in a long time. I started to think maybe the old creativity well was dried up—wrung dry from painting crappy Key West landscapes for tourists. But this may be the best work I've done in years." Eggs hit the pan with a sizzle, and he stirred them with a spatula.

I reached for the sketchbook. I'd loved his drawings and paintings when I was a girl: He worked in broad strokes and used vivid patches of color. His heroes were the German Expressionists: Klee, Kandinsky, Marc.

"Uh-uh," he scolded, wielding his egg-covered spatula. "I'm not ready to show you yet."

"Okay," I said, pulling my hand back. "Were any of Lexie's paintings up there?"

"A few sketches and the beginning of a couple paintings; I had no idea she had such an eye." He dumped the eggs, some bacon, and home fries onto two plates and came to sit down with me.

"What were your dreams about?" I asked.

"I'll tell you all about it when I show you the drawings. Until then, mum's the word."

Mum's the word, Jax. Don't tell a soul.

"Ted, what do you know about Rita's imaginary friend?"

"Martha? Nothing much. Just stories your mother

told. Rita said she lived in the pool, but she came out sometimes. Rita used to make your grandmother set an extra plate for her at the dinner table. Then, when she didn't eat it, Rita would carry the plate out and leave it by the pool."

"And Martha was a little girl, right?"

He nodded. "That's what Rita said. A little girl almost her age."

I nodded, remembering the drawings I'd seen of Martha, the little girl with pale blond hair in a blue dress, like the one inside the box of that old game, Snakes and Ladders.

"Why the sudden interest in Martha?" my father asked.

"Martha?" Diane said, coming into the kitchen and heading straight for the coffeepot. "Who's Martha?" She was wearing old running shorts and a T-shirt of Lexie's. Her hair was a mess, and the dark circles under her eyes were like purple bruises.

"Rita's imaginary friend," my father said. "Jax was just asking about her. But you're really the better person to ask."

Diane poured herself a cup of coffee and looked at me. "There's nothing to tell. Rita had a very active imagination. She was younger than Linda and me, and when we lost patience and wouldn't play with her, she invented her own playmate."

"Did you ever think," I began, "that she might be real?"

My aunt frowned at me. "A real girl who lived at the bottom of the swimming pool, who no one but Rita could see?" She chuffed out a laugh. "Um, no, that possibility never crossed my mind." She took a sip of coffee, rubbed her bloodshot eyes.

"How did you sleep?" Ted asked.

"Not well." She turned back toward me. "And how about you, Jackie? I'm hoping you stayed in bed and didn't make any more middle-of-the-night trips to the swimming pool."

My father looked from her to me. "Middle-of-the-night trips?"

"I couldn't sleep last night so I went down to the pool."

"She was *taking measurements*," Diane said, peering at me over the top of her steaming mug.

"I just started thinking about how Lexie had divided the pool into a grid—you've seen the numbers in crayon out there. She had pages and pages of notes showing the depth of each coordinate—"

"She was checking to see if your grandmother's promises of it being bottomless might be true. Clever girl! And what did you and she discover?" he asked, suddenly looking very excited.

"Well, it's definitely not bottomless—obviously. It's between 6.8 and 7.4 meters deep everywhere I measured."

He looked disappointed.

"But Lexie's notes tell a different story—"

"Oh?" my father said, excited all over again.

"Whoa, whoa, whoa," Diane interrupted. "Lexie once tried to convince us there were bees living in her walls and listening to her. How about the time we found her mapping all the sewer grates because she believed the lizard people were using the drainage tunnels?"

"But I just think—"

"It's been a while since you talked with Lex or had

to deal with her," Diane said to me, eyes suddenly piercing. "You need to keep in mind—"

"I know what I need to keep in mind," I shot back at her. "I realize the fact that I shut Lexie out this past year doesn't give me any right to suggest what might have been going on with her, but—"

"I'm sorry." Aunt Diane looked at me. "It was a shitty thing to say, Jax. I'm tired, hungover, and just wrecked by all this, but that's not an excuse. Let's back up." She took a deep breath. "All I was trying to say is that your sister was obviously not well in the last weeks of her life. Putting stock in anything she said, did, or wrote is, frankly, a fool's errand."

We were all quiet, none of us making eye contact.

"There are home fries and bacon," my father said to Diane at last. He pushed back his chair and stood up. "What kind of eggs do you like?"

"Just coffee's fine for me now," she said. "Sit down and finish eating, Ted, before your food gets cold." My father did as he was told. Diane's phone rang, and she picked up and had a short, terse conversation that involved the word "ineptitude" numerous times.

"I'm afraid I've got to go into the office for a while," Diane announced once she'd hung up. "There's a meltdown with a closing that's supposed to happen. I need to iron things out. I was hoping we could do the trip out to the lake with the ashes—"

"Tomorrow's fine with me," I said.

"Fine by me, too," my father said. "I have a ticket back home on Sunday. If I'm gone any longer, Duncan gets cranky and starts shitting all over the house. Vanessa won't put up with it and will leave him out on the curb."

Duncan was my father's ancient, one-eyed orange cat. To be honest, I was a little surprised he was still alive.

"Vanessa?" Diane repeated.

"Dad's girlfriend," I said.

"Female companion," he corrected.

"What about you, Jackie? How long before you have to go back to Tacoma?"

"My flight back is on Sunday, too."

Diane set down her coffee cup. "This may not be the time to discuss it, but you do realize the house and everything in it is yours now, right? Did Lexie discuss her will with you?"

I shook my head, feeling like it was someone else's body I was moving. "I didn't even know she had a will."

"She did. And she left everything to you. The house, whatever's left of Mother's savings, even the car. You certainly don't have to make any decisions right away."

I remembered how badly I'd wanted these things when they'd read Gram's will. How deeply wounded and furious I'd been when I didn't get a single piece of any of them. And now . . . all I wanted was to have my sister back.

"I work with an excellent property manager who can maintain everything while you decide. We could arrange to rent it if you'd like the extra income. We can put all of your sister's things into storage until you're ready to go through them."

"Do *you* want the house?" I asked. "Gram was your mother. You grew up here. Maybe it should go to you?"

"I most certainly *do not* want the house. And my mother knew it. This house and I, and that damn pool—we're done with each other, and have been for many years now." She paused, looked away. "There's also the trust."

Our grandmother had set up the fund once it became clear that Lexie might never be able to support herself. I didn't know the details but was always relieved to know that it wouldn't be on me and my crappy human services salary to help my sister financially.

"At any rate," Diane went on, "the trust was set up to be passed on to Lexie's children, should she have them. If not, it was to go to you."

"Oh," I said, dumbfounded.

"Michael Knox, the attorney who oversaw it all, will be in touch soon."

"The trust payouts are quarterly; it's a decent chunk of change," my father added. There it was again—the pang of guilt and regret that he knew facts about her life I was clueless about.

"I'm going to run back to my place, get cleaned up, and get to the office," Diane said. "I'll grab us some takeout and wine for dinner and stop by later."

"Perfect," I told her.

"Sounds good," my father said.

"In the meantime," Diane said, throwing us warning glances, "maybe you two should get out of the house for a while today. And stay the hell away from that pool."

———

The stairs leading up to the attic were narrow and dark, and when I reached the top, I smelled dust, mothballs, and things long abandoned.

The floral wallpaper, yellowed with age, was peeling in places. The wide pine plank floors were once painted white but were now worn down to bare, splintery wood.

Immediately to the left of the attic door a rack held old coats. Beneath it, a heavy cedar chest. Opening it, I found it stuffed full of linens—tablecloths, curtains, a wool blanket, and a worn yellow-and-white baby quilt. I closed the trunk and turned to see the brass bed shoved against the wall, still covered with a white sheet. I held my breath as I whipped the sheet off, half expecting . . . what? A fossilized old woman? A jar of chattering teeth?

Of course, there was nothing but a stained old mattress.

Something moved behind me. I turned slowly. The coats were moving, swaying on their hangers. Someone was there behind them.

"Hello?"

Pig jumped out, and I screamed, stumbled backward.

"Damn it, Pig!"

He brushed up against my leg, purring, evidently quite pleased with himself.

Sunlight filtered in through a big half-circle window. I made my way to it, kicking aside stacks of paper and photos. Beneath the window was an old folding table Lexie had been using. Tubes of paint, uncleaned brushes, palettes caked with layers of crusty mixed colors. Abandoned teacups and small plates of crumbs. More joints stubbed out in saucers. And then, three objects I recognized immediately: an old cut-glass doorknob, a tarnished silver fork, and a porcelain faucet handle with the word COLD on it in black. The treasures from the old hotel that Lexie and I found in the woods when we were kids!

The day we found the doorknob, buried in leaf litter, we thought it was a giant diamond. Then Lexie had picked it up. "It's a doorknob!"

"It must be from the old hotel," I said. We looked at it, took turns holding it, wiping the dirt off. "What do you think it was like? The hotel? It must have been pretty fancy, right?"

Lexie looked around the woods, squinting. "Maybe," she'd said with a smile, "maybe it's still here."

"Huh?"

"Maybe somewhere there's a magic door leading to the hotel," she said.

"What, like in another world?"

She nodded. "Like a fairy world, and now we've got the knob, so we're the only ones who can open it," Lexie said. "It's in these woods somewhere, hidden. That's where the peacock comes from!"

I laughed. "Right. A fairy-world peacock? Makes perfect sense, Lex."

Now I picked up the doorknob from Lexie's art table, turning it in my hand, watching the way the cut glass caught the light coming in through the window. I held my breath. The room was utterly still.

No magic door opened.

Pig mewed, looking up at me as if to say, *What did you expect?*

There was a pencil sketch of the doorknob on the table. I set down the knob and stepped toward the wall, where sketches and watercolors were tacked up: the silver fork, the faucet handle, flowers, a view of the garden, a sketch Lexie had done of her own left hand.

I reached up and lightly touched the fingers, tried to imagine it was actually her hand I was touching, not charcoal lines that my fingers left smudges in.

I pulled my fingers away, realizing I was ruining her drawing.

Maybe I shouldn't have come up here at all.

It felt invasive, like I'd found a private corner of Lexie's that I wasn't meant to look at. If she'd wanted me to know about her painting, she would have told me.

I would have told you if you'd picked up the phone.

To the right, an easel was set up with a half-finished painting of a peacock, his body a vivid, almost iridescent blue, his tail feathers spread, the green spots on them terrifying eyes, his beak open in a scream. It was unsettling.

I reached for a beat-up-looking sketchbook and flipped through it. Though my father always said she had the soul of an artist, I never thought of her as one. When had she started drawing and painting? Had she mentioned it to me? Had I forgotten? Or worse, wasn't really listening? How many things were there that had slipped through the cracks because she talked a mile a minute sometimes, while I drifted off, saying, "Uh-huh, uh-huh"?

What else had I missed?

The trouble with you, Jax, is you don't know how to live in the moment. You don't appreciate the here and now.

My sister was right. She lived inside each moment, sucking all she could from it, while I was only half-present, preoccupied with how annoyed I was to be listening to her share some crazy theory when I had other things, *important things*, I needed to be doing. And it was too late to promise to do better.

Her sketchbook was nearly full of pencil and charcoal sketches, some dated, most not. Most seemed to be from earlier in the summer. A drawing of the kitchen sink with a china teacup in it, a used Lipton tea bag wadded up inside. Random scenes from around the house: the dining room chairs, the circle window in the attic, the old claw-foot tub, a dress hanging on the back of a door. Then the flower pictures began, some labeled with dates and the names of the flowers: *forget-me-nots, bearded iris, sweet william*.

I turned the page again and came to a drawing of a woman I didn't recognize. She was in the pool, Sparrow Crest in the background. Her dark hair was cut in a bob, her large dark eyes had a mischievous light. She had a small scar under her left eye. It felt like she'd been teasing my sister, an inside joke that the two of them got, that seconds after the drawing was done, they'd both broken down in fits of giggles. In the lower right corner, my sister had penciled the date: *June 10*.

Who was this woman? I was sure she hadn't come to the memorial service—I would have remembered such a striking face. I flipped ahead. Nasturtiums. Lilacs. Phlox. Roses. Page after page of roses. And another sketch of the dark-haired woman, this time reclining by the pool, naked. It was nighttime—the patio cast in dark shadows, the pool pure darkness behind her. Her skin seemed to glow, to radiate. Lexie had scribbled in the corner: *A nap after night swimming.* I stared at this drawing, at the woman's closed eyes, the dark areolas around her nipples, the soft triangle of pubic hair. It felt voyeuristic. There was a certain intimacy in the drawing, and a sense of longing. Were Lexie and this woman lovers? Had Lexie shown her the drawing? Or had she kept it to herself?

I turned the page again. Here were close-up sketches of the front door and some of the windows on the house. The gate to the pool. The entire house as viewed from the bottom of the driveway. Lord's Hill and Devil's Hill looming behind it. The thick woods where we'd found our treasures from the old hotel and where Lex had insisted she'd seen the peacock.

When we showed Gram what we'd found, she warned us to stay out of the woods.

I turned the page to an odd drawing: There was Sparrow Crest, but underneath it (or perhaps over it?) was a lighter pencil sketch of a much larger building, three stories tall with a wraparound porch. The Brandenburg Springs Hotel. The two buildings seemed intertwined, tangled together—one more solid, the other, a ghost.

At the bottom of the page, she'd written: *The key to understanding the present is to look at the past*. Then, some words she'd scribbled out beyond recognition, followed by a name she'd circled: *Eliza Harding*.

The rest of the book was drawings of the pool, my sister's obsession laid out on paper.

It reminded me of Declan's drawing of the dark swirling water, the monster fish. The swimmer being pulled under. Not just any swimmer, but me.

I closed my eyes, tasted the mineral tang of black water, felt it fill my mouth as I sank.

"Shit!" I said, coming up for air, back to reality. Declan!

I had to deal with his mother, check in with Karen. I'd call as soon as I went back downstairs.

I hurriedly flipped through the rest of Lexie's drawings. She'd captured the pool so well that I could feel the cold water, smell the sharp mineral scent of it. In some of the drawings, I thought I could make out a face in the water, the flash of a pale arm or leg. The dark-haired woman again? Or someone else? In one, I was sure I saw my own face looking up.

I shut the sketchbook, shoved it to the back of the table, rummaged through the stacks of papers on the floor, photocopies and journal entries.

May 17
Gram didn't leave Sparrow Crest, because she
COULDN'T.
She knew it would kill her.
She knew and she went anyway.
She'd never been anywhere. And she wanted to see
the desert.

An old leather album was buried under the papers. I picked the album up and opened it. There were old, yellowed photographs of my great-grandparents in Sunday finery. He looked like a man on the verge of laughing; she looked fragile, and it was impossible to imagine that she would one day become the senile old woman in the attic who terrified my mother and Aunt Diane.

I looked at them on their wedding day. Honeymooning in Europe. I turned several pages and came to an old advertisement pasted into the album:

We invite you to the Brandenburg Springs Hotel and Resort—Vermont's newest elite destination for the most discerning clientele tucked away in the idyllic Green Mountains. Come take the waters and experience the legendary restorative healing powers of our natural springs! Vermont's own Fountain of Youth and Vitality! Our luxury hotel features 35 private rooms, each piped with water from the famous Brandenburg Springs. Dining room with world-class chef, sunroom, tennis courts, immaculate gardens. Open May through November. Do not delay! Book your room today!

The ad showed a drawing of a large white three-story hotel with a wraparound porch—an exact replica of the building in Lexie's drawing. Behind it, a landscape I instantly recognized: Lord's Hill and Devil's Hill.

I'd never seen a picture of the old hotel before. It was all just stories growing up—not even entire stories, only fragments, rumors. But here, in this scrapbook, was solid evidence that once, long ago, a grand hotel had stood right where Sparrow Crest now was. It took my breath away.

"You still up here, Jax?" my father called up the stairs, startling me.

"Yeah," I called down, my eyes still locked on the old advertisement, the picture of the hotel.

The key to understanding the present is to look at the past.

"Come on down. We've got company."

I hurried down the stairs, still clutching the album. "Look what I found. It's the old hotel." I held out the album. "Did you ever see a picture of it?"

"No. Totally wild. Your mom told me there'd been a hotel here once, but I had no idea it was so big."

He flipped the pages to a series of pictures of Sparrow Crest being built, but we saw nothing more about a hotel. He flipped back to the drawing of the hotel.

"Do you know what happened to it?" I asked.

He shook his head. "No. All I really know is that the hotel was one of the many subjects off-limits with your grandmother."

I nodded. Rita. The hotel. Old stories about the pool. All things we were warned not to bring up with her, things she didn't want to discuss.

"Hello?" a voice called from downstairs.

"Oh, I almost forgot!" my father said. "Ryan's here. And he brought us a bunch of goodies."

———————

Ryan was in the kitchen, a white paper box of scones and muffins on the kitchen table. He'd also brought a bag of espresso beans and a glass bottle of milk.

I gave him a hug, happy to feel how real and solid he felt. I looked beyond him, out the window at the pool. In the bright sunshine, it didn't look frightening at all. I thought of telling Ryan and my father the story—*The silliest thing happened last night. I freaked myself out big-time and thought there was something in the pool. I dropped a flashlight and thought it landed in the water. But obviously it must not have because it was right there on the edge. Isn't it funny how the mind can play tricks on you?*

I thought telling the story, making light of it, would make everything better. But I couldn't bring myself to say the words.

"How are you guys doing today?" Ryan asked, looking at my father, a hint of worry in his eyes.

"Just fine, right, Jax? We're right as rain."

The rain in Spain falls mainly on the plains, sang some long-ago version of Lexie. I could see her so clearly, dancing around the house with an umbrella open, me chasing her, telling her it was bad luck, her singing, *Rain in Spain, does rain make a stain, right as rain, hold on to the reins in the rain. Get it, Jax? Reins in the rain!*

I nodded at my father, my head feeling heavy, my neck tight.

"Glad to hear it," Ryan said, still looking at my father, as though waiting for him to say more—to bring up the incident in the pool, to say thank you, maybe. My father shifted back and forth on his feet like a nervous boy, not looking Ryan in the eye.

He grabbed a muffin and took a bite. "Best muffins on the planet, hands down," he said, mouth full. "Now, if we could only figure out how to work Lexie's rocket ship of an espresso machine, we'd be in business."

"I'm on it. What'll it be?" Ryan asked, heading to the big espresso machine on the counter.

"I'll take a cappuccino," my father said.

"Make that two," I said. I set the album down on the table. "Ryan, what do you know about the old hotel that used to be here?"

"Not much," he said, dumping beans into the grinder. "It burned to the ground. The owner was ruined. He took what your great-grandfather offered for the land and ashes and got the hell out. Went back to New York, I think. Or wherever he was from."

"How is it that I never heard this story?" I asked.

He shrugged. "Lexie knew about it. She was really interested in the hotel and what happened to it. She was asking my grandma about it not long ago, actually. My grandmother had a bunch of old photos, and Lexie was so excited to see them."

"Do you think she'd mind showing me?"

He smiled. "Are you kidding? She'd be thrilled! She loves talking about all that old stuff. We can swing by today, if you'd like. She's always up for a visit. Today's

Wednesday—no bingo or music, so we won't be interrupting anything."

I remembered my brief conversation with Shirley
after Lexie's service—the clear signs of dementia—
and doubted she'd be a reliable source of information,
but it couldn't hurt to hear what she had to say.

"Sure," I said, checking my watch. It was nearly
one. "Let's finish our coffee. Then I have to make a
couple of calls."

We drank coffee, stuffed ourselves on muffins, listened to my father tells stories about surviving Hurricane Irma in a high school gymnasium with his
girlfriend and cat. He and Ryan got into a discussion
about how global warming was affecting weather pat-
terns, and the ramifications of living on a changing
coastline. I excused myself to make my calls.

Once upstairs, I checked my phone—no new
messages. I called Declan's mom, again leaving both
my cell number and the landline at Sparrow Crest.
"Please call me back," I said. "It's important that we
talk." Then I called Barbara and filled her in.

"So you're going through your sister's papers, hoping
they'll help you make sense of what's happened? You
know what I'm going to say about that, right, Jackie?"

I blew out a breath. "I know. My sister was sick.
Nothing's really going to help me make sense of what's
happened. I know all that. I just want . . ." What?
What did I want? "Looking through the papers, organizing them, trying to get a sense of what her life was
like these last weeks and months, it's like . . . like I can
hear her voice. Like she's with me again. It's a way to
feel close to her. It's what I need to do right now. And
it gives me something to do. Something to focus on."

"I understand. Just try to watch your expectations. Don't think you're going to find answers."

"I know," I said. "Only a lot more questions. But right now, that's enough."

I didn't tell her about what had happened last night at the pool.

chapter twenty-two

Something is wrong with the baby. We noticed it right away. Margaret spent more time sleeping than she should. And she was not nursing with much enthusiasm. I would put her to my breast and coax her, but she would close her eyes and fall asleep, as if just the act of being awake was too much for her. She seemed to grow smaller and paler. I could see the blue veins through her white skin, watch them pulse.

"Something's wrong," I said, stroking the cool cheeks of my beautiful baby girl. She opened her eyes and looked up at me with that serious expression, my little sparrow. I so wished she could tell me what was wrong, what I needed to do to help her. I've never felt so help-less and inadequate; so thoroughly unprepared.

"She'll come around," Will promised at first. "Keep trying to feed her. It's common for babies to lose weight in the first few days." But I knew this was different.

Even her crying seemed weaker and quieter than it should.

At times, her chest made a funny wheezing sound. I called Will in to listen.

"What's wrong with her?" I asked.

Will did not answer. He examined her, his face tightening with worry, his brow wrinkling.

Will brought us to the Valley hospital. We carried Maggie down the waxed floors and up the elevators to the pediatrics area. The hospital smelled of antiseptic and sickness. I could hear a child crying far off, saying, "Mama, Mama, Mama," over and over.

One of Will's older colleagues, Dr. Hansen, greeted us and brought us back into an examination room. Dr. Hansen spent a good deal of time listening to Margaret's chest with his stethoscope. He tried to give me a reassuring smile, but I could tell something was wrong.

I could hear Dr. Hansen and Will out in the hall, speaking in hushed tones, but could not make out what they were saying. I held Maggie close to my chest, stroking her hair, cooing to her. She looked up at me with her mermaid eyes, gray and stormy. Flecks of black in them caught the light and reminded me of the springs—of their vast depth, the possibility the water held.

"You are my wish come true," I told her. She blinked and sighed.

When Will came into the room as last, his face was cloudy with worry. "It's her heart," he said. "We've got to take her to Boston right away. Dr. Hansen is making calls to specialists there. They'll be expecting us."

He tried to take Maggie from me, but I held tight to her. I put my own ear against her chest, listened to her heart beating, small and far away.

I made myself ask the question: "Will she live?"

"She's a fighter. And she's got the best mother in the world." He gave a weak smile, but his eyes told me the truth. It was as though he'd reached into my chest and squeezed my own heart until it nearly stopped.

I felt as if water had rushed in, surrounding us, filling my mouth and lungs. I could not move or speak. Will helped me up from the chair. Again, he tried to take Maggie, but I would not let go. We hurried home and packed a suitcase for an overnight trip—an extra suit and pajamas for Will, my black wool dress, stockings, and a nightgown. And plenty of diapers and changes of clothes for little Margaret. I layered her up in her warmest things for the car ride, then wrapped her in the quilt my sister had made for her.

The drive to Boston went on forever. I sat beside Will in the car, the swaddled baby on my lap. She slept most of the way, and I kept checking to make sure she was still breathing. There was a blueish cast to her lips and fingertips.

We navigated the maze of city streets, Will white-knuckling the wheel, shaking his head at the traffic, the busyness of the city. The Children's Hospital is quite impressive: a massive stone building next door to the Harvard Medical School on Longwood Avenue. There are four columns at the front and a large copper dome that houses the atrium.

We were immediately greeted by a team of doctors. Margaret was examined by cardiac and pulmonary specialists. The best there are, Will said.

After their examination, they brought us back into a wood-paneled office. A nurse brought us coffee and sandwiches, which neither of us touched.

"Perhaps you'd like to wait outside, Mrs. Monroe?" the tall doctor, the cardiologist, suggested. A nurse with a well-meaning face came and touched my elbow, ready to escort me.

"No," I said. "I want to hear. I want the truth. Tell me what's wrong with my baby girl."

The doctors cast glances at Will. He looked at me, then back at them, and nodded.

The news was bleak. They confirmed that due to her premature birth, her heart and lungs would not grow and develop in a normal way. There was more to it than that, medical jargon about valves and oxygen. The doctors spoke slowly. Will asked questions. They all seemed to be speaking another language. Again, I felt the waters rising, roaring in my ears. I shivered from the cold, felt myself sinking down, down, deep underwater, holding little Maggie in my arms.

Together, we sank.

I am Mrs. Monroe and I am drowning.

There is nothing to be done, the doctors said. No operation or medication that may save her.

She is not expected to live to see her first birthday.

"There must be something we can do," I said, the words little bubbles of air floating up to the surface and bursting.

"Bring her home and love her," the doctors said. "Treasure each moment."

Little Margaret struggled for breath in my arms.

And I clung to her, silently promised to never let her go.

April 3, 1930

Will tells me we must prepare ourselves for what is coming; for the inevitability of losing our child. How does one possibly prepare for such a thing? His words sound practiced and strange. He has become a wooden man, an actor reciting lines he doesn't quite believe. He walks around in wrinkled shirts, hair uncombed, dark circles under his eyes.

"Why?" I demanded. "Why should we have to prepare for such a thing? It isn't fair or right."

"It's God's will," he said.

"Then he is not a God I wish to believe in," I said.

Will opened his mouth to say something more, to argue, to reason, but no words came. He turned and shuffled off like a sleepwalker.

Will sent Reverend Bickford in to see me, thinking surely the dear reverend could offer words of comfort, could quote scripture, give me something to cling to. But I closed my eyes, held the baby to my chest, and asked him, as politely as I could manage, to please leave us alone.

I heard them speaking in the kitchen after. The reverend said, "Even in the most difficult times, we must keep our faith."

And I laughed then. A snarling, spiteful laugh.

I went into the bathroom and pulled down my thick wool tights. My legs had become a garden of scratches and pokes. I was like a grim version of the tattooed lady at the fair. Here was my daughter's name, etched into my skin, surrounded by designs of dots, little constellations forming pictures: a sparrow's egg, a rose, the Brandenburg Springs Hotel, the springs. I pulled out my pin and went over her name again and again, the blood blooming on the surface of my skin.

Margaret
Margaret
Margaret

Yesterday afternoon, I was lying in bed with Margaret on my chest, she and I both drifting in and out of sleep. This is how we spend our time—bound together, drifting. I bury my nose in her hair, stroke her back, run my fingers over her shoulder blades, sure I can feel the beginnings of wings there.

I keep her by my side both day and night, my little sparrow child.

If she is to die, it will be in my arms.

Our bed became a boat and we were floating, tossed on a turbulent sea. There was a knock at the door, and Myrtle calling, "Ethel?"

She's still thinner than she should be, but she's doing much better now. There is color in her cheeks, and she has been so good to me and Will. In truth, I think the tragedy of our situation has given her new purpose. Helping us seems to allow her to forget the loss of her beloved husband. She cooks us dinner. Cleans the house. Comes over every day to check on us. She holds little Margaret so I can eat and bathe without leaving her alone.

"I've been to Brandenburg," she said, voice barely above a whisper.

I sat up, holding the baby tight against my chest.

"I didn't make it to the springs, couldn't find my way, but I went to the General Store and asked the shopkeeper if I could pay someone to go get me some water. It just so happened he had one jar of spring water left." She showed it to me. "So I bought it. I bought the last jar." She unscrewed the lid, dabbed a little of the water on her fingers, and touched Margaret's china-white cheek. "Turn her so I can put some on her lips. A little on her tongue."

"But Will, he'll think me mad—"

"Will doesn't need to know," Myrtle said, voice firm and sure. "It was the water that brought her to you.

Perhaps the water can keep her here. What harm can it do to try, Ethel?"

I lifted the baby from my chest, turned her face out. Her eyes were open. She was looking at Myrtle, eyes wide and expectant.

"There's a good girl," Myrtle said, dipping her fingers in the water once again, bringing them to the baby's lips. "Such a precious girl." Again and again, she dipped in her fingers, parted Margaret's lips, placed drops of water in her mouth. The baby made a contented little cooing sound, like a dove. "It would be easier with a dropper," Myrtle said.

"There's one in the medicine cabinet," I told her.

———————

Myrtle left the jar and dropper for me. I hid them in the drawer of my nightstand. I gave Margaret another dose before Will got home. Then a third later in the evening, when Will was smoking his pipe in the living room.

When I was changing Margaret before bed, I called for Will. He hurried into the bedroom, sure our daughter had stopped breathing, that this was it, we'd reached the end. He saw her wiggling on the table, the soft rise and fall of her chest. Her hands and feet were a healthy shade of pink. In fact, she was pink all over. Her breathing seemed easier. She made a delighted little squeaking sound when he touched her cheek. She nursed for a long time before falling asleep, then slept through the night for the first time.

"I don't understand," Will said, shaking his head, examining and re-examining her, listening to her chest with his stethoscope.

"Perhaps it's not for us to understand," I said. "Perhaps it's a miracle."

"A miracle," Will repeated slowly, as if trying the word out, seeing how it felt.

I nodded, smiling. *I am Mrs. Monroe. I now believe in miracles.*

chapter twenty-three

June 20, 2019

Lexie called this place 'the geezer farm,'" Ryan told me as we pulled up to Edgewood. It was a single-story building tucked up against the woods, sheathed with dark siding so that it blended into the landscape.

I could imagine her using the term, even when she went to see Shirley.

"I don't think she meant it in a mean way; she liked it here. She came once a week to visit my grandmother, and got involved in hot games of hearts or Scrabble. The residents all loved her. One day, when the regular music guy didn't show up, Lexie sat at the piano," Ryan told me. "She had them singing old rock and roll. When I came in, they were doing 'Blueberry Hill.'"

I pictured Lexie holding forth, banging away at the piano, directing the chorus of seniors singing about finding their thrill. Must have been quite a scene. "Now that, I would love to have seen!"

"I've gotta warn you," Ryan said as he pulled into a parking space and turned off the car. "My gran, she's got some strange ideas about things. She's in good shape overall, but she's nearly ninety and she's definitely got a little . . . confusion. Says things that don't make a whole lot of sense. Loses sense of what time period she's in, I think. She talks about her mother, who's been dead for ages, like she's just seen her. So just . . . keep in mind that not everything she says is based in reality."

"Okay," I said. "Thanks for the heads-up."

Ryan and I walked into the building and stopped at the front desk. We signed in, and the receptionist recognized Ryan. "Shirley just finished lunch and is back in her room."

Ryan led the way down the hall, through a big room with a piano, then turned right, down another hall. We passed a small exercise room, a library, then rooms belonging to the residents, most with two names on the door. At last, we got to room 37—only one name on the door: Shirley Dufrense.

"Is that my favorite grandson?" Shirley called out when Ryan walked through the door.

The room was surprisingly homey. The adjustable hospital bed was covered with a pink-and-purple quilt and bright pillows. Another small quilt hung on the wall above the bed. A set of shelves was full of books and photographs. A little desk where Shirley could write. Beside it, an overstuffed chair upholstered in a floral print.

"It sure is," he said, moving in to give her a quick kiss on the cheek. Then he turned and said to me, "I'm actually her only grandson, so don't feel you have to bow down in the presence of greatness."

"Ignore him," Shirley said. "I'm so happy you came, Jackie. Come sit with me." She gestured at the uphol-stered chair, and I came in and took a seat.

"Just look at you," she said, smiling at me. "Your grandmother would be so proud! I so wish she was here now."

I nodded. "I do, too."

But then I imagined the pain she would have felt at losing Lexie. At having her drown in the pool just like poor Rita had—losing a daughter and then a granddaughter in the same terrible way would've been unbearable for her.

"You look like her, you know," she said. "Your grandmother, when she was your age."

I nodded, though I didn't see the resemblance other than our dark hair.

"Ryan, dear," the old woman said. "Why don't you go see if you can sweet-talk Becky into bringing us some tea and cookies."

"Becky? I'm not sure I'll get very far. She's pretty by-the-book—"

"Then go into the kitchen yourself! Good heavens, boy—be resourceful. Go on now!"

He held up his hands in surrender. He flashed me a look, eyebrows raised: *Okay with you?* I nodded. "Yes, ma'am," he said, and headed off.

"Mrs. Dufrense," I began.

"Oh no, dear, please call me Shirley."

She'd been Mrs. Dufrense to me all my life, so it felt more than a little odd, but I gave it a try. "Shirley . . ." I began. "I was wondering if you could help me with something. I was hoping you could tell me about the hotel. The one that was where Sparrow Crest is now."

"Did *they* send you? The ones from the water." She studied my face, waiting.

"Um, no. I—"

"Of course, dear. I don't know much, mind you, but I do have some photographs of it. Pictures my own parents and grandparents took." She rose, went to the shelves, and pulled a large brown scrapbook from the bottom shelf. She set it down on the table and opened it up to a photograph of the hotel with a large group of people posed in front of it: the men in suits, the women in chambermaid outfits. *May 15, 1929*, someone had written below the photo. *Grand Opening of the Brandenburg Springs Hotel and Resort*.

She turned the pages and more photos followed, close-ups of the hotel and grounds. One showed a small stone pool—*The Springs* written beneath it.

"Wait," I said, pointing. "Those are our springs? The springs that feed the pool?"

"Yes. It was much smaller back then. Your great-grandfather had it excavated, made into the huge thing it is today."

On the page next to it was a photograph of the front of the hotel, showing a fountain surrounded by flowers. And there, at the base, were three peacocks. I blinked, not believing what I was seeing. "There were peacocks?"

"Oh yes, they roamed the grounds. Your grandmother and I, when we were girls, would sometimes see their descendants, out in the woods, gone feral. There had to have been a peahen, if they were breeding. I don't know how they survived the winters. Someone must have been feeding them, I suppose. And they must have found shelter—someone's barn, perhaps?"

Lexie's peacock. Was it possible she'd actually seen a descendant of the hotel peacocks? All those years later?

I was sure she'd made up the story, imagined the peacock to life. But what if it was true—what if there actually had been peacocks in the woods? How many other things my sister told me over the years were actually true? Things I'd brushed off as her wild imagination, as mania, as out-and-out hallucinations?

Shirley turned the page to a photograph showing the charred remains of the hotel, a group of men standing around an old cellar hole that was full of water, all of them with grim faces. "The hotel burned to the ground. The fire moved fast. Fifteen of the guests were killed." She closed the book.

"That's so awful."

"Your grandmother didn't like to talk about it much. That place, the springs, they carry a horrible history." She nodded somberly. "When I was a girl, I wasn't allowed to go to the springs, to Sparrow Crest. My family tried to keep me away from your grandmother and her family. They said your grandmother and her family didn't belong there. But I couldn't stay away. I snuck over again and again."

She was quiet a minute, looking down at the closed album. "Sometimes, we'd find things from the hotel. We made a game of it. Seeing who could collect the most treasures. We found old bottles, silverware, bricks, pieces of plates from the dining room. We had a secret little house we built back in the woods, along the stream. It was made from woven saplings and bits of bark. We made it into a museum to house our collection."

"Lexie and I found things, too!" I said. "A doorknob, a faucet handle, a silver fork, pieces of old tile. We showed them to Gram. She told us not to play in the woods. She never wanted to talk about the hotel."

"Your grandmother had her reasons. She was trying to protect you. She knew how much you and your sister loved the house and the pool—she didn't want to taint it with any of the horrible history behind the place."

She stood up, went back over to the shelf, and picked up a small wooden box with intricate flower carvings on the outside. She sat back down and opened it up. "I still have some of the treasures we found." She pulled out the edge of a dinner plate. Then, a silver spoon that matched the pattern of the fork Lexie and I had found. She held each object like it was something sacred.

"This was always my favorite," she said, holding up a delicate, teardrop-shaped piece of cut crystal. "From one of the chandeliers, I believe." She handed it to me, and I held it up, watched the way it caught the light coming in through the window.

"It's beautiful," I said.

"I used to imagine what the chandelier might have looked like hanging up. How the owners of the hotel, the Hardings, must have stood below it, greeting guests, thinking all their dreams had come true. They had no idea then what was to come. The ruin. The loss."

I handed back the cut-crystal teardrop.

"We don't know the terrible things that are coming our way," she said as she looked down at the cut crystal, her eyes teary. "We just see the shiny surface, our own beautiful selves reflected in it. Not the monster lurking beneath."

"I'm sorry, Mrs. Du—Shirley. I didn't mean to upset you."

"Lexie understood. About the water. She didn't at first, but she learned. She was a clever girl, your sister. Have you seen her yet?"

My mouth went dry. I looked at her, unsure of what to say. "I—"

"Tea is served," announced Ryan as he came through

the door carrying a tray with three teacups, cream and sugar, and a plate of cookies. I jumped up, rushed over to help him set it up on the table, relieved to have somewhere to look other than at Shirley.

—————

After our tea, Ryan suggested we go play Scrabble in the day room. Shirley introduced me to some of the other residents, who all had stories to tell about my sister. One of them even asked if I could play the piano and sing like Lexie had. I shook my head. He frowned in obvious disappointment. Another man told me what a fantastic card player she'd been. "No one could beat her at hearts," he said. Then he leaned in, whispered, "Though between you and I, I suspect she may have cheated."

I laughed. "Sounds like my sister," I said.

Ryan and I stayed at Edgewood until dinnertime, walked Shirley down to the dining room. Then Ryan drove us out to a little snack bar on Meadow Road across the street from the beach at the lake. We ate fried clams and crinkle-cut french fries at a picnic table, just like we had when we were kids.

After we'd eaten, we walked around the lake, thinking the six-mile loop would do us good after the fried food. We talked about our memories, of Lexie and the adventures we all had. The rafting trips, the swimming competitions. He reminded me of a "submarine" she'd made from a plastic barrel, and I remembered how fast it had sunk once she got herself inside it.

Ryan laughed and shook his head. "It's a wonder she didn't drown." Then he immediately realized what he'd said. "Oh God, I'm sorry."

We were quiet for a few minutes.

"You had kind of a crush on her, didn't you? Back when we were kids?"

"A crush? Not exactly. It wasn't like that. It was just . . . well, you know how she was, even back then. I just wanted to be around her. Didn't we all? Didn't we all long for that little buzz being around Lexie could bring?"

I nodded, knowing exactly what he meant.

We were quiet a minute, looking out at the lake. The sun was setting, the reflection hitting the water and making it look like it was on fire. We were a little over halfway along our loop around the lake.

"Can I ask you something?" he asked.

"Sure. Anything."

"Has Diane said anything to you about my mom? About the divorce? My mom's just so weird and secretive lately, and I—"

"No," I said. "Sorry. She hasn't told me anything." I picked up a rock and threw it into the water, watching the splash and ripples, but my mind leaped to Diane and Terri kissing by the pool. I sure as hell wasn't about to mention that to Ryan.

He looked at me expectantly, waiting for more. Could he tell I was holding something back?

"Your grandmother freaked me out a little today," I said, changing the subject so he'd quit looking at me like that.

"Let me guess, about the pool?"

"Actually—"

"Did she tell you what Lexie thought?"

"What Lexie thought?"

"Lexie believed there was something going on with the pool. Something with the water."

"What kind of something?"

He didn't answer.

"Ryan, last night, I went out to the pool and I thought—well, I dropped—"

He looked at me questioningly.

"It's not important. It's silly, really. I just got spooked is all."

"Maybe there's good reason to be spooked," he said. He leaned down and rubbed at his ankle, the one that had been scratched all those years ago.

"What do you mean?"

"Forget it," he said, rubbing his eyes. "I'm sorry. I'm just a little tired, and my brain is fried." He smiled apologetically. "How about we get back to the car before it's too dark to see out here? Then I'll take you back to Sparrow Crest."

chapter twenty-four

I watched the spring water in the jar get lower and lower day by day, until at last, we ran out. I gave Maggie the final dropperful last night. She swallowed it down like a hungry bird, dark eyes wide, watching me with complete trust. "It's the last of your medicine, little sparrow," I whispered. "But you're strong and healthy now. Perhaps you don't even need it anymore." She wrapped her fingers around my index finger, squeezed hard as if to say, *Yes, I am strong!*

In the morning, her fingertips and toes were tinged with blue. She was refusing to nurse.

"No! No! No!" I cried, pacing. I got the empty jar, desperately tried to get the final drops that dampened the bottom into the dropper.

Will came home for lunch and found me in an absolute panic, frantic with worry, clutching the baby to my chest. I showed him the empty jar, little Maggie's fingers and toes.

"We've got to go to Brandenburg," I said. I had the suitcases out on the bed and had been stuffing them full in case we had to spend the night there. "I've packed your black wool trousers and boots. Lots of warm things for the baby. I've been looking for the flashlight and can't find it."

"Flashlight?" He looked at me like I'd gone mad. The way he might look at a gin-soaked stranger who asked him for coins on the street.

"It might be dark by the time we get there. Please Will, we've got to hurry." I started talking quickly, trying to explain everything, the words running together like a river overflowing its banks: *Brandenburg, Myrtle, springs, eyedropper, gone, hurry*.

He took my hand. "You've got to slow down, Ethel," he said. "Please. You're not making any sense. Start at the beginning."

Even though my heart was racing and I felt there was little time to waste, I forced myself to speak slowly, rationally, as I told Will about Myrtle's trip to Brandenburg, the jar of water she brought back, and confessed that I'd been giving Maggie the water three times a day since.

Will blinked at me in disbelief. "But the hotel burned down!" he reminded me. "There's nothing left."

"The springs are still there," I told him, waving the empty jar as if it was proof. "And I can't explain it, but I know, *I know* that it works. The water made her well! You saw so yourself!"

He held little Maggie's hand, looked carefully at her blue-tinged fingers.

"She was a healthy, normal baby," I told him. "Just last night, when we gave her her bath, she was fine, right?"

He nodded, his eyes glazed over.

"I gave her the last drop of water just before bed. And look at her now. She needs more! We've got to bring her to the springs."

He looked from me to Maggie, then back to me. He opened his mouth, then closed it. "I . . . I—" he stammered. Maggie twisted in my arms, let out a raspy, wheezing breath, and looked at her father with big eyes.

"All right," he said, kissing her soft dark hair. "Let's finish packing and get on the road."

———————

We left home a little after one. I'd made a thermos full of coffee and packed sandwiches, apples, and cookies in the hamper. After a cold, wet spring, the roads taking us to Brandenburg were in a terrible state—nearly impassable in places due to mud. The going was very slow indeed. I held the baby on my lap while Will navigated our Franklin touring car through the ruts and washboards. The closer we got to Brandenburg, the bleaker things became. Everything seemed brown, muddy, and ugly; we passed a field of filthy, skinny cows having a hard time walking, their hooves sinking with each step. The barn they were headed toward was faded gray and listing to one side. I saw patches of snow still clinging under stone walls. Winter did not want to let go in this valley. It was after six by the time we arrived in Brandenburg. We saw the sawmill was shut down with a big CLOSED sign painted on it. The old signs for the hotel were gone. "Do you remember which road it was?" Will asked.

I shook my head. "Nothing looks the same." I pointed to a little side road, hardly wide enough to get a single car down. "Try that way. That might be it." Will coaxed the car in about two hundred feet, then pronounced the road impassable. "This mud is like goddamn quicksand. We're nearly up to the axles. If I keep going, we'll be stuck here all night." He maneuvered the Franklin's gear shift into reverse, gripped the wooden wheel tightly, turned, and looked over his shoulder as he backed out to the main road.

We stopped at several houses to ask directions. All the locals we encountered insisted that the road to the springs was closed. One careworn old woman sweeping her porch tried to warn us off when we asked her for directions. "You go there and you're inviting terrible things to happen." She peered into the car, saw Margaret on my lap. "If you want to do right by that little baby, you'll turn your fancy car around. Go back where you came from." She went back to sweeping frantically, creating a great storm of dust around her.

"Let's try the store," I said. "Maybe they can help us."

Will navigated down Main Street and found a place to park a little ways down from the store, in front of the post office.

We walked up onto the porch of the general store and saw a CLOSED sign in the window. Will looked at the hours and checked his pocket watch. "They closed over an hour ago."

I peered in the window. "But the lights are on, Will, and I see someone moving around in there." I rapped on the glass, gently at first, then louder.

"Easy, you don't want to break the window," Will warned.

An old man in a plaid wool shirt shuffled toward the door and unlocked it. It was the same shopkeeper who'd tried to sell us the bottled water last year—the one who'd shown us his hand, which had been healed by the water after he'd burned it.

"We're closed," he said, speaking through the crack in the door, which he held only slightly ajar. His face was more gaunt than it had been when we'd seen him last year.

"Please, sir. We just need directions. We can't find our way to the springs," Will said. "We keep getting turned around and end up going in circles."

"Springs are closed up," the shopkeeper said, starting to shut the door on us.

"Wait!" I called.

Then he noticed little Margaret, who shifted in my arms.

"Please," I said. "She's sick. My friend, she was here a month ago, she bought your last jar of water." I showed him the empty jar we'd brought with us. *"This jar!"* I waved it at him. "We gave the water to our baby, little droppers of it, and it made her better. But now we're out and she's sick again. She needs more. Please."

He looked at me, eyes icy blue, then held open the door. We stepped inside. The store was uncomfortably hot. The little cast-iron pot-bellied stove was roaring away in the corner. The moose head stared gloomily at us from the wall, its fur and eyes glazed with a thin layer of dust. A train schedule was nailed to the wall, but the Brandenburg stop had been crossed off, a penciled note next to it read: *Canceled until further notice.* Another sign next to it announced that the Pine Point Inn and Dance Hall on Lake Wilmore were closed for good.

"You're sure this is what you want?" he asked.

"If she was your child, wouldn't you do the same?"

He looked at me for a few seconds, then turned and disappeared into the back of the shop. When he returned a few minutes later, he had a boy of about twelve with him. The boy was wearing patched dungarees and an old gray sweater that was far too large for him. "This here's my grandson, Phillip. For a dollar, he'll take you to the springs."

Phillip shifted nervously from foot to foot.

Will looked at the boy, then at me. I nodded at him. Will pulled out his wallet and paid Phillip. We followed him out of the store, but as we were leaving, the shopkeeper said, "Just this once. You get what you need up there, then you go home and don't come back. And hurry. It'll be dark soon. You don't want to be up there after dark."

The boy got on his bicycle, and we got back in our car and followed him back up the main road to a muddy turnoff; a little ways up, trees were lying across the road. Trees someone had cut down and placed there to block access.

"You gotta walk from here," the boy said.

Will pulled the car over to the side of the road. We hiked in on foot, Phillip leading the way. He stayed a good ways ahead of us and walked quickly. Will offered to carry Margaret, but I clung tight to her. Our shoes were soon caked with thick black mud, and we were sweating and panting despite the cold air. The walking was difficult and tedious, as if the road itself were trying to stop us, trying to suck us down and hold us. We had a hard time keeping up with Phillip and worried that if we lost sight of him, we'd not only never find our way to the springs, but might not be able to find our way back to town.

Trees and brush had overtaken the road, narrowing until it was only a wide path. The branches had knit together to make a thick canopy, shading out what little light there was. It was overcast, twilight. The sun would set soon.

I thought of the shopkeeper's warning: *You don't want to be up there after dark.*

We walked without speaking. Margaret grew heavier

and heavier, and though Will offered to take her again, I still would not let her go. "Almost there, little sparrow," I whispered into her hair.

At last, the trees thinned, and we came to a large clearing. Where the grand hotel once stood was only a vast cellar hole, the broken and burned remnants of timbers, piles of slate roofing. It smelled of ruin.

Gone was all sense of a familiar place, a place I was meant to be.

I walked up to the edge of the hole, which had a small lake of water pooled at the bottom, black and filthy. I could see bent and broken copper pipes sticking out of it. There was a bathtub down there. Part of the crystal chandelier from the lobby. I felt dizzy and swayed slightly. Will grabbed me, pulled me away from the edge.

"Be careful, Ethel," he scolded, not releasing his grip on me.

Broken window glass was everywhere, crunching beneath our feet. The heat must have caused the windows to explode outward, away from the building. I tried to imagine it: the hotel on fire, the people inside. The screaming.

I was sure I could hear it still; some echo trapped forever down in that cellar hole.

"Do they know what caused the fire?" Will asked as he pulled me a safe distance away, the mud sucking at our shoes, trying to trap us.

"Benson Harding," said the boy, the name coming out like a snarl. "He burned it down."

"Why on earth would he do such a thing?"

Phillip shrugged, kicked at the mud with the worn toe of his leather boot. "Folks say he was sick over what happened to his wife. Went crazy, she did." There was a funny gleam in the boy's eyes. "Said she'd seen a monster in the springs." He turned and spat in the dirt.

Will and I looked at each other. Margaret stirred, breath wheezy, against my chest. I looked at Will, said with my eyes: *We have no choice.*

The boy led us to the springs. We stepped around the wreckage and found the old footpath hidden amid the dead, overgrown grass. Off to our right, astonishingly, the rose garden was flourishing: the leaves green, the untrimmed vines overtaking the trellises, the early buds offering unsettling explosions of color. It didn't seem right, to see a lush oasis of green in such a dead place.

We smelled the pool before we saw it: a rotten, sulphurous stench.

The wooden gate that had once been around it was knocked down, a sign still tacked to it: The Pool is CLOSED. Will reopen tomorrow at 9 a.m.

The grass was overgrown. The deep pool lined with stones looked the same as it had when we visited. I wondered what had happened to the peacocks as I looked down into the black water and thought of Eliza Harding drowning there.

I held my breath as I watched the water, half believing that Eliza might surface—that she'd come up from the depths and swim as she had when Myrtle had seen her.

"It's bottomless," the boy said now. "My daddy, he says you shouldn't even touch that water. Poison, he says." He looked around at the water, the sun falling behind the hills, casting us in deep shadows. "Reckon you can find your own way back," he said. Then he scurried off like a frightened rabbit.

I watched him, thinking, *Could we? Could we find our own way back? Or would we be lost here forever?*

I got down on my knees, laid the baby on the ground. She squirmed, her breathing fast and hard like a chugging train.

"Please," I said to the water, to God, to Eliza Harding maybe, to whoever was listening. "Please save my baby girl."

I scooped up some icy black water, dabbed it on her lips, put some in her tiny mouth. She opened her eyes wide, looking at me. I rubbed it into her skin, on her hands and feet.

"Do you think we should bathe her?" I asked.

"The cold will kill her," Will said, eyes steely. He stepped away, studying the burned-out timbers, kicking at the ashes. If I hadn't known better, I would have thought he was frightened.

I gave Margaret a sponge bath with the water, cooing to her, promising that the water would make her well. "This water is magic," I whispered when Will was far enough off not to hear us. "It's the reason you're here. And I think that maybe, it may help keep you with us. You'd like that, wouldn't you, little sparrow? To stay here with us?" She made a sweet cooing sound as if to answer: *Yes, Mama. Yes!*

Then, I wrapped her back up. Before leaving, I filled four large canning jars that I'd brought along in a satchel. We began the long walk back to the trees that blocked the road. Will took out the flashlight to help guide us. I kept thinking I heard something behind us: footsteps, the sucking sound of shoes moving through mud. But when I turned, I saw nothing, only shadows.

"Should we look for a hotel?" I asked once we were back at the car at last.

"I don't think there is one anywhere nearby. Let's drive back."

The drive home was slow and tedious. There were no other cars on the road.

The canning jars full of water clanked together in the backseat. Margaret, breathing easier now, squirmed on my lap, making contented little sounds.

We arrived back in Lanesborough near midnight. I brought Margaret in and undressed her, got her ready for bed. Her hands and feet were pink, her breathing was normal. And she was hungry.

"Good to see she's got her appetite back," Will said.

"It's not just her appetite," I said. "Look at her, Will— she's all better. The water has cured her."

Will tightened his jaw and nodded. And for an instant, it wasn't just wonder or disbelief that clouded his eyes, but the faint glimmer of fear. I was sure I saw it there, flickering like a tiny fire starting to catch hold.

chapter twenty-five

June 20, 2019

Ryan dropped me off at nine thirty. Diane texted to say she was running late but would be by with pizza and wine soon.

I walked through the door to find my father cooking again. The air smelled spicy and sweet. "Ted?" I called, walking back toward the kitchen. All the lights in the house were out.

I heard him say something. He was talking to someone. Diane? But I hadn't seen her car.

"Ted?" I said again as I stepped into the chaos of the kitchen, trying to make out what was happening. I flipped on the lights. The floor was littered with empty grocery bags. There were pots on every burner. The counters were covered with flour, sugar, canned goods, mixing bowls, measuring cups and spoons. The kitchen table held plates and bowls of chocolate chip pancakes, cheeseburgers, grilled cheese sandwiches. The door to the broom closet was open, and the cat was in there, cowered in the shadows, watching.

"What's going on?" I asked my father, who stood in front of the stove flipping bacon. I tried to keep the panic out of my voice, tried to sound calm and matter-of-fact. But this was a Lexie-style mess. I'd never seen my father do anything like this.

He didn't respond. I walked up to him slowly, put a hand on his shoulder. "Ted? You okay?"

"She's hungry," he said, still not looking me, poking frantically at the bacon, then at a pot of creamed corn. "She's hungry, but she won't eat."

"Who's hungry, Ted?"

He turned, looked at me. "Lexie," he said. His pupils looked huge, his face pale and sweaty. I turned off the burners, took his hand. It was cool and clammy.

"She was here," he insisted. "She wanted food! I kept making her things, but she wouldn't eat. She pushed them all away." He looked so miserable, so agonized.

"Come sit down with me." I led him over to the table. He shuffled forward in a daze, like a sleepwalker. We sat at the table, covered with all of Lexie's favorites.

"She was here," he said. "She sat right where you're sitting. Look!" he said, scrambling through the mess, knocking a cheeseburger off the table, pulling a sketchbook out from underneath a plate. He flipped it open, shoved it at me. "Proof!" he said.

I held the sketchbook in my hands. It was a series of quick pencil sketches: Lexie in the kitchen. Lexie sitting in the chair I was sitting in right now. I struggled to keep my breathing even and level. In the drawings, my sister's eyes were wild, and her hair looked wet.

"She said she could come back to stay. That we could help her do that," he said.

"Ted," I said in my calmest social worker voice, "I don't think—"

The front door banged open, and I jumped. My father looked at me, eyes wide and excited. "She's come back," he whispered. "You'll see."

I dropped the sketchbook, tried to stand, but couldn't move, couldn't breathe.

I was underwater, holding my breath, playing the Dead Game with my sister. *You move you lose, Jax.*

"Honey, I'm home!" called Diane from the front hall.

I exhaled with relief; my father's face fell in disappointment. "You can't mention anything about Lexie's visit today to Diane, okay?" I whispered, handing my father his sketchbook.

"But you believe me, right?" He looked so desperate.

Did I? Did I actually believe my sister had found a way back and come to sit in the kitchen?

Impossible.

"Let's talk about it later, when it's just the two of us," I said. "It has to be our secret, okay?"

Mum's the word.

"I'm sorry I'm so late! But I've got pizza and wine. The Riverbend store does a Greek pizza that's to die for, wait until you taste it!" She came into the kitchen dressed in an eggshell-colored linen suit, hair and makeup perfect. She held the boxed pizza in her left hand, the bag with wine in her right. Her eyes widened in alarm. "What in the name of God happened in here?"

"Ted . . . did some cooking," I explained.

She surveyed the wreckage. "Your father and what army of trained chimpanzees?"

I flashed her a *let it be* glance. She looked at my father, took in his ashen face, his clothing splattered with grease and food. I took the pizza from her, scootched some of the mess around on the counter to make room for it.

———

"Is your father all right?" Diane asked once we were finally alone. We'd eaten the better part of the pizza, polished off two bottles of wine, and my father had turned in early, saying it had been a long day and he was exhausted. He seemed anything but exhausted, though. He was revved up, on edge. We could hear him up above us, pacing in his room. Diane and I were cleaning up the kitchen. I was at the sink doing dishes and she was tossing food, wiping down surfaces.

"I think so," I said.

"Do you want to explain what's going on with all this food?" she asked as she dumped an untouched stack of pancakes into the trash. "I'm not an idiot, Jax." She dropped the syrupy plate into the soapy water. "Chocolate chip pancakes? A bacon cheeseburger with ranch dressing and extra onions? Creamed corn? All of Lexie's favorite foods."

I nodded.

"So what was he doing? Trying to conjure up the dead with some home cooking? He must have said something to you."

I shrugged, gave in, knowing it was pointless to lie. "He says he *saw* her. That she was here, in the house, and she was . . . hungry."

"Jesus Christ!" She leaned back against the counter, physically bracing herself. "You've got to be kidding me. First he sees her in the pool and nearly drowns, now she's come into the house looking for a snack?"

"He's exhausted, grieving, and drinking."

Wasn't I in similar shape? Imagining I heard something in the pool, that something had brought my flashlight back up from the murky depths?

"Is he going to start insisting that we leave out plates of food for her like Rita did with Martha?"

I stiffened at the name. Wondered what I'd really seen in the water that long-ago night.

She picked up dishes from the rack and started aggressively swiping at them with a dish towel. "This is concerning, Jackie. Very concerning. Grief is one thing, but full-on hallucinations—that's something else altogether. You, of all people, have to know that!"

"Yes," I agreed. It seemed this was just an extreme form of denial. My father was unable to accept that she was gone, so he imagined seeing her. Hadn't I imagined seeing her since I'd been back? Hadn't I heard her voice, caught myself talking to her, even? Grief is a powerful force. "I think that between the grief and the drinking—"

"You didn't encourage him, did you?"

"Of course not!" I snapped—too quickly, too loud.

She was quiet a minute, thinking, stacking plates in the cabinet. "I think I should spend the night again. I think it's a good idea to have both of us here." She looked up at the ceiling. We couldn't hear my father walking around anymore. "In case he decides to do any late-night cooking. Or take off on a road trip with Lexie. We can get up in the morning and pick up Val's canoe, head out to the lake and have a little ceremony with Lexie's ashes. Maybe doing that will help your father realize she's *gone*. Give him a sense of closure."

Gone.

"Closure," I repeated. I wasn't a big believer in closure. In my experience, both in my life and working with my clients, solid resolutions to conflicts, problems, or grief were elusive. I believed it was more beneficial to recognize emotions and learn to deal with them appropriately; to find ways to live with the loss rather than tie everything up with a neat little bow and pronounce you've had *closure*.

We were quiet for a minute as we finished the dishes.

"Diane, can I ask you something? What do you know about the hotel that used to be here? Before the house was built?"

She narrowed her eyes, squinting like she was looking at me from the other end of a very long tunnel. "Not much. It was open less than a year. It burned down."

"I think it's weird that I never heard about it growing up. I mean, I knew there had been a hotel here once, but I didn't know a thing about it. And I certainly never heard about the fire. All those people dying."

"It's not that weird." Diane sighed and rubbed her forehead wearily. "Because that's what our family does. Pretends that if we don't talk about a thing, it didn't happen. As if we could shape the truth with our stories, or lack thereof."

I opened my mouth to argue, but realized she was right. No one talked about what happened with Rita. And when Lexie first showed signs of being sick, didn't we all put our heads in the sand, refuse to acknowledge that something was wrong?

"But Lexie found out about the hotel," I said. "She was digging around, not just looking into our family history, but the history of this place. I found some pictures and drawings and old deeds in her papers. She wrote down stuff about the hotel and the history of the land in her journal. And she went to see Shirley. Shirley has a photo album with old pictures of the hotel. She showed them to me today, said she'd shown them to Lexie, too."

Diane frowned. "When I saw her at Lexie's service, she seemed a bit . . . off."

"You know what Shirley said to me? She told me Lexie's out there in the pool."

Diane shook her head. "Your father's cooking for her, and Shirley thinks she's gone for a swim." She was quiet a minute, then said, "Do you know what *I* think? I think you should leave your sister's journals and all those papers and albums she found, right in the boxes we put them in. Put some tape around them so you're not tempted to keep digging through them. I don't think it's good for you, for any of us right now. They're a record of your sister's illness. It's too soon, too heartbreaking."

"But they're a record of her life, too. Of who she was."

Diane shook her head, bit her lip. "The best thing to do is seal it all up. Go back home, get away from all of this, and clear your head."

I opened my mouth to argue, to tell Diane that I couldn't do that.

Diane watched me carefully. "Jackie, you shouldn't make any big decisions right now; you're not thinking of *staying*, of moving to Sparrow Crest, are you? Not that I wouldn't love to have you living close by, but I just don't think it's the best idea. I don't think you should be here, in this house."

She seemed almost frightened by the idea.

"Diane, did you ever see anything . . . weird . . . in the pool?"

She clenched her jaw and shook her head. "Of course not. It's just that this is where your sister died. And I know you blame yourself—you shouldn't, but you do, and to tell the truth, I blame myself, too, it's

hard not to—and all this ancient history, these scrib-
blings from poor Lexie at her worst . . ."

"It's the place she lived, too. And for better or worse,
she loved this house and the pool. Gram loved it, too."
I held my head high, defiant. "I don't know what I'll do
with the house yet. I've got to get back home on Sunday, take care of things at work, but I'd like to plan another trip out here soon to really sort through things,
try to make sense of Lexie's papers and notes."

Diane asked, "What is it you're hoping to find?"

"I don't know. I just think—"

She took my hand. "Whatever you find isn't going
to bring her back, Jackie. It isn't going to change anything. You understand that, right?"

"Of course."

But then I heard Shirley's words: *Go out to the pool.
That's where you'll find her.*

———————

Diane and I said our good nights. I grabbed my father's
sketchbook and went up to my room, holding it tightly,
hoping he wouldn't come out and catch me. Although
he'd opened it up for me to look at tonight, taking it
was crossing a line. I closed my bedroom door quietly
and sat on the bed with the unopened sketchbook.
Lexie watched from the dresser. *Curiosity killed the
cat*, she warned.

"Shut up," I told her, opening the sketchbook.

And there she was again, looking up at me from the
page. Lexie in the pool, smiling, one arm up, beckon-
ing: *Come on in. The water's fine.*

My breath caught, stuck in my lungs.

I flipped through the thick pages: Lexie in the attic,
standing beside her drawing table, sitting on the edge

of my father's bed. The last few, the ones from tonight, showed her at the kitchen table, food piled in front her. I studied the pictures, a chill running through my body like a wire. He'd gotten each detail perfect: the slope of her nose, her damp hair, the tiny dimple in her left cheek that appeared when she smirked, the smattering of freckles across her cheeks. And her eyes, my God, her eyes. They stared up at me, sucking me in, daring me not to believe in her, not to believe that she'd found a way to come back. She was naked, legs crossed, elbows resting on the table. Why would Ted draw her naked? And how did he know each detail of her body—each tiny freckle and scar?

I set the sketchbook down on my bed, pulled out my phone. Still no message from Declan's mother.

I typed *Brandenburg Springs Hotel* into the search engine. The first hit I got was from a blog called *Nellie Explores the Haunted Places of New England*. There was a photo of the burned hotel, very similar to the one Shirley had shown me, and a post beneath it.

ARE THE BRANDENBURG SPRINGS CURSED?

The tiny town of Brandenburg, Vermont, is located in the southeast corner of the state, just across the border from New Hampshire. But legends about this particular hamlet abound.

Deep in the heart of the village lay the springs, long rumored to have medicinal properties. For generations, people have flocked to the springs to drink and bathe in their water. The healing water was said to be a cure for gout, rheumatism, consumption, chronic pain of any type, and some stories say a dip in the waters will even cure the pain of heartbreak. The native people who lived in these hills long before white settlers knew the spring to be a sacred place and called it a door between the worlds. They warned that the springs should be left alone, that their powers could bring great misfortune as well as great healing.

Old legends tell of the Lady of the Springs—a woman who appears in the water, luring men and women with promises of good health and riches, then tricking them into the deepest part of the water and drowning them. In some stories, she appears as a beautiful young woman; in others, she is a child, or an old hag with green hair and clawlike hands.

The first man to try to monetize the power of the springs was Nelson DeWitt, back in 1850. He opened a boardinghouse for visitors to the springs, then bottled the water and had it shipped by train to Boston and New York, marketing it as DeWitt's Miracle Elixir: "a sure cure for what ails you." Only five months into his operation, DeWitt drowned in the springs. His employees claimed he'd gone mad—they'd caught him down on his knees talking to the water, pleading with it day after day.

The springs were closed, and eventually DeWitt's heirs sold the land to Benson Harding, who owned several hotels in New York State, including one in Saratoga Springs. Harding did not believe in curses and was sure that his experience with hotels would lead to tremendous success. Construction of the hotel took six years and faced one setback after another. Trains loaded with supplies derailed, work crews quit, the foundation flooded when a pipe burst. At last, the Brandenburg Springs Hotel and Resort opened its doors in the spring of 1929.

But terrible things awaited Harding, his family, and his guests. Perhaps he should have paid heed to the legends that have long warned people away.

The hotel closed briefly when a child drowned shortly after opening. Seven-year-old Martha Woodcock of Claremont, New Hampshire, apparently wandered out to the springs on her own, fell in, and drowned. Benson Harding closed the hotel, installed gates around the springs, put up lifesaving buoys, hired lifeguards, and only allowed guests to visit the springs during daylight hours.

But despite these precautions, in the fall of 1929, Benson Harding's wife, Eliza, drowned in the springs. Two weeks later, the hotel burned to the ground. Fifteen of the twenty-four guests were killed. All that remained of the property was a gaping cellar hole flooded from the pipes that had been installed to route the springs into the hotel. Benson Harding returned to Saratoga a ruined, haunted man. He shot himself later that year.

Are the springs cursed? Look at the history and judge for yourself.

*Please note: The springs are now privately owned. They are not open to the public!

My head spun. I reread the article. The little girl who fell in and drowned—seven years old. I said her name out loud, "Martha."

Martha W.

Rita's imaginary friend.

The little girl who lived in the pool and came out sometimes. The little girl no one but Rita could see.

But I'd seen her once, too. Hadn't I?

I shoved my phone back into my bag, looked down at my father's drawing of Lexie on my bed. She grinned up at me.

"You knew," I said. "You figured it out."

I went back to the boxes, tore through the papers until I found the one I was looking for. The list Lexie had made:

Nelson Dewitt
Martha W.
Eliza Harding
Rita Harkness

They were all people who had drowned in the springs.

I put my finger on the next line, the one under Rita's, thinking I should write Lexie's name in there.

Listen to me, I heard my sister say, clear as could be. I held my breath, listening. I was losing my mind. Lexie's death, being here, back at Sparrow Crest—it was unraveling me.

I made out my father's voice through the propped-open window. "Please," he was saying. I stood up, pulled open the screen, leaned out the window, craning my neck, trying to see the pool. My mother, when she was a child in this very room, wondered who her sister Rita was talking to—if Martha was just imaginary or an actual flesh-and-blood person.

Rita's drawing in the lid of the board game, of the little girl in the blue dress: *Martha W. 7 years old.*

My father said something else I couldn't catch, and then I heard a woman say, "Shh. Mum's the word."

I'd know that voice anywhere.

It was Lexie.

I jerked up and back, slamming my head against the window sash, hitting it hard enough to see stars. "Shit!" I ran out into the hall and straight into Diane, who was wearing Lexie's old Nirvana T-shirt and a pair of her running shorts.

I jumped when I saw her.

Ghosts were everywhere.

"I thought I heard something," Diane said. "Your father's gone. He's not in his room or the bathroom."

"He's down at the pool!" I said, rushing past her.

And Lexie is with him! She's come back!

Diane was right behind me as I took the stairs two at a time, got down to the front hall to find the door open. My feet hit the stone floor and I slid, caught myself on the wall before falling. There were puddles of water everywhere.

Footprints, my brain told me. *Wet footprints.*

Her footprints.

"It's wet, be careful," I called back to Diane, as if my near wipeout wasn't caution enough. I turned to see Pig crouched farther down the hall, eyes on the open door, his back arched and fur raised.

Outside, my father yelled, "Please!"

I ran through the open front door and across the driveway, along the flagstone path to the gate, which also stood open. I could not understand what I was seeing: only my father. No Lexie.

"Ted?" I called, taking care not to slip on the wet stone.

My father was at the far end of the pool, holding

something in his hands. I willed my eyes to adjust, to see what he was struggling with. Trying to open.

"What are you doing, Ted?" Diane yelled, hurrying toward him.

My father was holding the plastic urn that contained Lexie's ashes. He'd gotten the top off, pulled out the plastic bag inside and opened it. Now he was holding it over the pool while he looked down into the dark water as if waiting for a sign.

"No!" Diane cried, flying toward him. "Ted! What are you doing? Stop!"

We watched in horror as my father dumped all that was left of my sister's physical body into the inky black water. No words of goodbye. No sentimental ceremony or talk of how much we loved her. My father's movements were quick and jerky—like watching someone dump the contents of a Dustbuster into the trash.

"No!" Diane wailed.

"It's what she wants," he said. "She told me."

"Jesus!" Diane said. She'd stopped, just a few feet away from him. "Ted! What have you done?" She looked at the empty plastic bag in my father's hands, then down at the water, where there was a thin skim of fine gray ash resting on the top. And she began to cry. She collapsed into a nearby chair, put her head in her hands, and wept harder than I had ever seen her weep.

My father looked at me, eyes widening. "Don't you see," he said, frantic. "This is what she wants. She told me! It'll help her come back. Come back and stay!"

I watched the pale ashes floating, sinking, mixing with the black water.

"Look," my father said, pointing. "There she is! Look!"

I lifted my gaze from the sinking ashes to where he was pointing: the dark heart at the center of the pool.

It couldn't be . . .

I held my breath.

There was movement, a ripple in the still surface of the water.

Squinting, I stepped forward, too close to the edge, teetering dangerously. The water smelled like blood.

I was sure, for a half second, that I *did* see something: a flash of white in darkness.

A pale hand and arm rising up out of the black water.

"Lex?" my mouth made the shape of her name, but no sound came.

I blinked, and she was gone.

chapter twenty-six

We've made two more trips to the springs. When we stop giving Margaret the water, her health declines immediately. As long as she consumes a small amount daily, she does very well. She's got a healthy appetite, is growing, has a lovely complexion, and when Will listens to her heart and lungs, he can detect no abnormalities. Will cannot explain how it is possible that the water helps our girl, but no longer denies that it is indeed the water keeping her alive.

We made both trips in the daylight, on lovely summer days, packing a picnic and rucksacks full of empty jars and bottles.

As we drove along, I told myself, *I am Mrs. Monroe. My husband and I are on an outing on a lovely summer day with our infant daughter. We have packed a picnic. I have made us ham salad sandwiches and a jar of ice-cold lemonade. We have tarts for dessert.*

The springs were waiting for us. Expecting us. That's how it felt. We found our way easily each time and did not have to stop to ask for directions. We've started to recognize all the landmarks along the way: the run-down farmhouses, the fields, the leaning stone walls, the closed-up sawmill.

The grass has grown up, overtaking the paths. And the rose garden, untended, has gone wild; the vines reaching out, escaping the cage of trellises, filling the air with a sweet, heady scent.

Come closer, the garden seems to say. But I can't bring myself to. I'm afraid of what I might see there in the heart of it; of what might be waiting on the bench inside the overgrown gazebo.

On our last visit, Will saw me looking at the garden, suggested I might pick some flowers to bring back home.

"I couldn't possibly," I said, taking a step back.

And wasn't I sure then, that just for an instant, I saw the shadows in the gazebo shift as though someone was hiding in the rosebushes? I turned to Will, wondering if he had seen it, too.

"A shame, really," he said. "All that beauty going to waste."

We filled our containers with water, and all the while I felt as though we were being watched.

And there was indeed something watching us. Just at the edge of the woods, I saw a flash of color. "Look!" I cried. It was one of the peacocks. He gave a screech and retreated back into the trees.

———

Will left us for a few days. He said he needed to go to Saratoga on business. He'd spent days in his study, making columns of numbers, drawing sketches. When I asked him what on earth he was up to, he only said he was playing with an idea.

It was all very mysterious.

Margaret and I went and played bridge, and the ladies cooed and fussed over her, took turns holding her, said she was absolute joy. "And such a beautiful child," Myrtle said. "Like a fairy baby."

I said nothing of my nightmares.

———————

After three days, Will returned in wonderful spirits with gifts: a pair of sturdy leather boots for me and a tiny sweater for Margaret. "For our new lives out in the country," he told me. His face was flushed, and he was all but bouncing with excitement.

"I went to Saratoga to meet with Benson Harding," he said.

"Mr. Harding?" I could scarcely believe it. I felt my throat tighten as I said his name, remembered him and Eliza moving through the dining room at the hotel, greeting each guest, looking so splendid and handsome in their fine clothes.

Will nodded. "The poor man. He's in a terrible state. I told him I was interested in buying the land where the hotel was. The springs. I asked what his price would be, and he suggested we play a game of poker. If I won, the springs would be mine. If I lost, I would walk away and forget all about the springs. 'We shall leave it to Lady Luck,' he said."

"A game of poker?"

"Five-card draw. And Lady Luck did indeed smile upon me, because I was dealt a royal flush. Benson Harding had a pair of twos. The springs and the twenty acres of land around them, they're all ours."

My heart hammered in my ears like crashing waves. "But that can't be legal, can it?"

"It's entirely legal. We went to see a lawyer. I've got the title and deed. The land is ours, Ethel." He reached into his bag, took out the papers, and showed me.

Will looked so pleased with himself, so happy. I tried to mirror his joy, but a knot of fear and apprehension began to grow like a newly kindled fire.

He threw his arms around me and led me in a little dance right there in the kitchen. My legs moved stiffly as I tried to follow along and match his steps.

"I've been drawing sketches for the house we'll have built. A great stone house. Like the castle you dreamed about living in when you were a little girl!"

He reached into his bag once more, pulled out a neatly sketched drawing of a large stone house with big leaded-glass arched windows, a slate roof with high peaks. *Sparrow Crest*, he'd written at the bottom.

"It's lovely," I said, kissing his cheek, giving him the best smile I could muster. Then I excused myself, went into the bathroom, and pricked myself seven times with a pin. Blinking my tears away, I saw that the dots formed the rough shape of a house. I tried to rub them away, but only succeeded in staining the house red.

chapter twenty-seven

June 21, 2019

So, how are you doing, really?" Ryan asked. "The no-bullshit answer, please."

I didn't know who else to tell about Lexie's ashes, so I had gone to Ryan. We were settled into a corner table at the Blue Heron with lattes. Soft rock from the '70s drifted from the speakers, America singing "Tin Man"—the kind of music Ryan's parents had always played. I rubbed my eyes. "Okay. The truth is, I think I'm going crazy." I was unsure where to start. I wasn't ready to tell him about dropping the flashlight in the pool and then finding it on the edge. Or that there was a real girl who drowned who had the same name as Rita's imaginary friend. Martha wasn't such an uncommon name, was it? So I said, "My father is insisting that Lexie is visiting him. He's been sketching her as proof. I've seen pictures he's done of her in the attic, bedroom, and kitchen. The details . . . they're unsettling."

"Where's your father now?" he asked, his voice serious.

"At Sparrow Crest. Diane's there with him. She thinks he's had a total psychotic break."

"And what do you think?" he asked.

That maybe I'm having one, too.

"Last night, after he put her ashes in the pool—*dumped* them in, really—he pointed at the water and said Lexie was there." I paused; here was the tricky part. Did I admit it? And what had I really seen? *The only thing in that water is what we bring in with us.* "I saw something," I admitted. "A flash of white. Like an arm and hand coming up, breaking through the surface. Then it was gone."

He looked at me, then down at the foam on his latte. His face had lost all its color.

At that moment, Terri brought over two raspberry muffins, fresh out of the oven. "So nice to see you, Jackie," she said. "How are you holding up?"

I smiled back at her and lied. "I'm doing okay, thanks."

"And your father?"

"Oh, you know. He's managing."

"How long will you two be in town?"

"We both leave on Sunday."

"Well, if you can manage it, I hope you'll have a chance to see my mother again. I heard you had a lovely visit. I know she'd love to say goodbye before you go."

I nodded. "Absolutely." Terri went back behind the counter. I turned back to Ryan. "Maybe my father's not the only one having a psychotic break." I forced a laugh. "Maybe it's grief. Guilt. Lack of sleep. Or likely all of the above."

"I don't think you're crazy," he said, keeping his voice low so that his mother wouldn't overhear us. Terri went back into the kitchen, leaving the register to a young man with a pierced eyebrow.

Ryan looked at me. "I don't think Lexie was either." He took in a deep breath and let it out. "She told me she believed there was something in that water. Something terrible. Something that had been there a long, long time."

The hairs on the back of my neck felt prickly. "She *told* you that? When?"

"The last time I talked to her—we were sitting right here, actually. But I thought it was just Lexie being Lexie. Or at least, that's what I told myself."

"And now?"

He picked at the muffin on his plate, pulling it apart. "There's something I need to tell you," he said, eyes not meeting mine.

"Okay." But it didn't feel okay. I wasn't sure I wanted to hear this, whatever it was.

"That same day—the last time we talked—Lexie asked me if I remembered what happened to me that afternoon in the pool when we were kids. That day Lexie and I had the contest?" His voice was small and squeaky, as though he was turning back into his twelve-year-old self.

I nodded. "The last time you were in the pool."

"Right. Anyway, she asked if I saw anything down there in the water." He frowned hard, sighed. "I told her I hadn't seen a damn thing. She got really mad. Wouldn't believe me. She sat back, crossed her arms over her chest, and said she wasn't leaving the bakery until I told her the truth. She even did the whole 'Liar, liar, pants on fire' thing."

"Was this what your fight was about?"

He nodded. "I held my ground. Told her it was nothing. I let her think she was crazy for believing otherwise. It was such a shitty thing to do." He looked away, rubbed at his eyes. "She got so mad at me. Said the reason the water had power was because of its secrets. Because no one ever talked about what they'd really seen, things that had really happened there. She stormed out. That was the last time I saw her." He looked down at his ruined muffin, pushed the plate away, looked up at me. "But the thing is . . . I lied to her. I did see something that day. But what I saw, it didn't make any sense. Not then or now. And I guess I thought that by not talking about it, not admitting what I'd seen, that would make it less real."

I nodded, understanding completely. And I steeled myself for whatever he was going to tell me. "What was it?"

There was a long pause.

"A girl," he said at last. "A little girl with dark hair and eyes. She was wearing a white dress or a night-gown? She grabbed my leg. She was pulling me down."

As I listened to Ryan, part of me was floating in the pool with my sister, eyes wide open, terrified of what I might see.

"It sounds crazy, I know, like I made it up, but I swear it was real."

"I don't think it sounds crazy," I said. But then I added the practiced words I'd been telling myself my whole life. "The water down there is so black."

Keep telling yourself that, Jax.

Ryan said, "Later that night, when I was back at home, underneath the three scratches on my ankle, there was a bruise. My ankle turned black and blue from whatever grabbed me in that water."

Something's in the water.

"Do you think I'm nuts?"

I shook my head. "If you are, then I guess I am, too." I blew out a breath. Thought for a few seconds about how carefully guarded I'd become. The only person

I was truly upfront and open with was my therapist, and even then, I didn't tell her everything. I thought of what Diane had said, about how our family was: If we didn't talk about something, it was like it didn't happen. And look where it had gotten us all. I was a social worker. I knew how secrets could fester, bloom into something much bigger, much more powerful and frightening. I knew the importance of facing things, getting them out in the open, talking through them. I knew all of this, yet had been pretty lousy at applying it to my own life.

But it wasn't too late.

"When I was a kid," I began, forcing myself to say the words quickly, before I lost my nerve, "not long after your episode in the pool, I went out there at night, alone. And I saw something. *Someone*. A girl in the pool."

"With dark hair? A white nightgown?" He looked hopeful but frightened.

"No. She had long blond hair and a blue dress. I think . . . I think it was Martha."

"Who's Martha?"

"My aunt Rita's imaginary friend. The little girl who lived at the bottom of the pool but came out sometimes."

"Jesus!" he yelped.

"And the girl you saw." I swallowed, couldn't believe what I was about to say. "I think that was Rita."

He pushed back in his chair, balancing on the two back legs, rocking slightly.

"Martha was a real person once," I said. "At least, I think so. A little girl named Martha Woodcock drowned in the springs back in 1929. Lexie had been doing all this research, learning about the history of the springs. I found a list she'd made of names of people who had drowned in them."

"So the girls we saw both drowned in the springs." Ryan rubbed his face hard. "Now I'm thinking about other things Lexie said. Other stuff that I wrote off—things I wasn't ready to hear because I was too freaked out. She saw someone in the pool, too."

"One of the girls?"

"No. A pale, dark-haired woman."

The woman from Lexie's sketchbook.

"Lexie said she came from the water. She said there were others down there, too. She'd seen them. But she thought maybe they were all one . . . *thing*."

"I don't understand," I said.

"I know. Neither did I. She was talking so fast, one of those famous Lexie tangents. She said for every life it took, it just grew stronger. That's what gave the pool its strength—to heal people and grant wishes and stuff. And the water, it used those people, kept hold of them somehow. Like everyone who drowned became a part of it. It sounded like such crazy nonsense to me at the time." He shook his head.

"Ryan, all this is—" What? Impossible? Just another clear example of Lexie's delusional thinking?

"Your father, when he put Lexie's ashes in, he said she told him to, right?" He was talking fast, like things were clicking in his brain. "What if that's true? But what if what he's seeing isn't Lexie, but some twisted version of her? Acting on behalf of whatever's *really* down in that water?"

How many times had my sister gotten other people to go along on the magic carpet ride of her mania, against their better judgment? Even though she was dead, she was working on me now. Clearly Ryan was caught up in it, too.

He rubbed his face with his hands. "Crazy," he said again, quieter this time. Then, "Jackie, whatever the truth is, it might not be safe for you to keep staying at Sparrow Crest." He looked genuinely worried. Like the young Ryan who'd run away from the pool that day. "You and your dad should pack up and stay at Diane's for the next couple days. Or you can come stay at my place. I've got a spare room. Get out of that house— away from that pool—as soon as possible."

The acidic coffee felt like it was burning a hole in my stomach. I picked at my muffin but couldn't bring myself to eat any. "I leave day after tomorrow. So does my father. I'm sure we'll be all right at Sparrow Crest until then."

When we said our goodbyes, Ryan hugged me extra tight. "Be careful," he whispered. It came out sounding more like a threat than a warning.

"Folie à deux," Barbara said.

I'd called her as soon as I'd left the bakery, and told her everything as I walked back through town and up the hill to Sparrow Crest. "I'm sorry?"

"Or more properly, folie à trois, or, if we include your father, folie à quatre."

"I'm sorry, but my French is limited to *please* and *thank you*."

"It's a shared delusional disorder. Delusional beliefs and even hallucinations are passed on from one person to the next. Technically, I think yours is more a case of folie à familie."

"I'm not feeling very comforted here," I said. "Am I losing my mind or not?"

There was a long pause. Too long for my liking.

"You're grieving, Jackie. You've been gutted by the unexpected loss of your only sister. You're dealing with a lifetime's worth of guilt and regrets and old memories. And you've thrown yourself into this project, this idea that if you go through your sister's papers, you'll be able to make sense of what happened in some way. All of this has made you very open to being caught up in all kinds of shared delusions, conspiracy theories, legends, what have you."

"So what am I supposed to do?"

"Keep your head, Jackie. Keep yourself safe. I think you should box up your sister's papers and deal with them later, when you're out of that house and the grief isn't so raw and fresh. Come home on Sunday, and give yourself time and distance to heal."

"Okay," I said.

"And above all else," she continued, "I think you should stay the hell away from that pool."

———————

I walked back to Sparrow Crest, and when I reached the driveway, I saw not only Diane's car, but a little red Volkswagen Beetle. The gate to the pool was wide open. I steeled myself, thinking of Ryan's and Barbara's advice, and went to latch the door. The pool seemed to be waiting for me, perfectly still, black as onyx, the sun above reflecting off it like a mirror.

Someone was there, at the water's edge. My heart jackhammered.

But no, this wasn't Lexie or little Rita. This was no ghost.

Diane was crouched at the edge of the pool, leaning down, over it. She was talking. Saying something to herself—or to the water? Was she making a wish? I watched as she dipped a jar in. Then she looked up, saw me, and started.

"I didn't know you were back," she said. She was pale. There were dark circles under her eyes.

"What are you doing?" I asked. There were three big glass jars of water beside her. She put the one she'd just filled next to them.

"It's for Terri." Diane blushed a little. "Her symptoms have been better since she started drinking it and swimming in it. More than better, actually. She was in a wheelchair this time last year."

"So you think the water's . . . healing her?"

She thought a minute. "I think she believes it is, and maybe that's enough."

I looked at my aunt. "You and Terri—" I began.

I was so tired of all the secrets. Of everything we'd all been keeping from one another.

"Terri is one of my oldest, closest friends," Diane said.

"If you don't want to tell me, that's fine. I just feel like all of us, this family, we're drowning in secrets. You were absolutely right yesterday when you said that's what our family does."

I thought of what Ryan had said Lexie believed about the pool: that all the secrets were what gave it its power.

Diane was quiet, looking at the jars she'd just filled, then at the house and the shadow it was casting over us.

"Terri was my first love," Diane began, voice low and hesitant. She smiled a bittersweet smile, looked down at her own reflection in the black water.

"We were both teenagers, completely freaked out because we'd fallen in love. It was the seventies, people weren't exactly *accepting*, to put it mildly."

"Did anyone know?" I asked. "Mom? Gram?"

She shook her head. "No. We kept it a secret, which only gave it more weight, but it also made it . . . toxic. We'd end things dramatically, swear each other off, then end up together again a week later. We just couldn't stay away from each other, no matter how hard we tried." Her smile was a sad one, but her eyes lit up, and I caught a glimpse of teenaged Diane, young and madly in love, the secrecy only adding fuel to the fire.

"It was a tumultuous relationship that ultimately ended with both of us running off to the safety of boyfriends. We moved away, went to college, got married. But you know what they say—you never get over your first love? It's absolutely true." She looked back toward the house. "Nothing, no one, compared to what I'd had with Terri. In my dreams, it was her I went back to again and again."

It broke my heart a little to think of my aunt pining after Terri for all those years, trying desperately to make some other life work.

"And now?"

"It's complicated," Diane said, the muscles in her face tightening.

"What isn't?" I asked. I looked at the jars of water, thought of my father dumping Lexie's ashes, of the flash of white I'd seen in the water.

"This pool," she said, looking down into it. "It has a hold over all of us, doesn't it?"

I nodded.

"A while back, before Mother died, I was here visiting. I'd had a lot to drink. I actually came out to the water and made a wish. I wished for the thing I wanted most—the thing I'd longed for my whole life. I wished to have Terri back." She shook her head. "I feel like an idiot admitting to it."

"It's not wrong. I think we all make wishes for things that feel impossible. Some do it through prayer. Some wish on shooting stars. I don't think there's anything wrong with wanting to believe the pool might have the power to grant those wishes."

She shook her head. "The only power it has is whatever power we give it."

"But you got your wish," I said. "You and Terri."

"It's not that simple."

I nodded, imagining she meant Randy and the divorce and all the secrecy.

Diane's jaw tightened. Her eyes seemed to darken. "See, Terri wasn't sick then. Not long after I made the wish, she was diagnosed with MS. Her symptoms progressed so rapidly. Her mother, Shirley, pushed her to try the spring water from the pool. Terri resisted at first, but nothing else was helping, so she started coming to Sparrow Crest. I'd meet her. Help her into and out of the water. The old spark between us was still there, and over time, it grew."

"Wait, are you saying you think your wish made Terri sick? You know that's not really possible, right? You can't blame yourself."

Diane frowned, looked down at the inky water. "No! Of course not!" She kept her eyes on the water, on her own wavering reflection. "But Terri does."

"What?"

"I told her. I told her about the wish I made. And in her mind, she's connected it all."

"So wait, you're saying she blames you for her MS?"

She shook her head in frustration. "I don't know. She's never come right out and said it, but she's hinted at it. 'The pool gives and the pool takes,' she says."

"That's what Gram used to say," I told her.

"Like wishes have a price," Diane said, scowling. She leaned down, tightened the lid on the last jar of water. "Terri's a big believer in the power of the water. She got it from her mother, I think. Terri says that the pool grants wishes, but only if it's the one thing you wish for most."

"Lexie believed that, too," I said. "She told me once."

Diane went on, "But for each wish it grants, it takes something in return. Something to 'balance the scales'— that's how Terri puts it."

I shivered.

"Complete nonsense," she said. "All these people believing this freezing cold water could possibly hold so much power." Diane looked back toward the house. "Terri should be out any minute. She went inside to change into her suit for a quick swim. I don't want her to catch us talking about all this."

I nodded. "And where's Ted?"

"Inside. He was going to do some artwork, then go lie down."

"I think I'll go check on him."

"Jax, don't let on that you know about me and Terri, okay? She's still . . . unsure about our relationship. She was sure enough to ask Randy for a divorce, but that whole thing has been messier and more difficult than she'd hoped. She feels like shit for hurting him. She isn't ready to tell people about us yet. Not even Ryan."

I smiled. "Mum's the word," I said.

I headed inside and upstairs, walked down the carpeted hall to see if Ted was in his room before going up to try the attic. The door to my own room stood open—but I was sure I'd closed it. I slowed my pace. There was someone in there. Someone sitting on the bed. From my vantage point, I could see a pair of bare legs. *Lexie?*

It was Terri.

She was sitting on my bed in shorts and a T-shirt, no sign of a bathing suit, with her back to the open door, going through the boxes of Lexie's papers. She was rummaging quickly, like she was searching for something specific. She pulled out a blue envelope. She opened it up, flipped through the contents, then set it down on the bed on top of a pile of papers and photographs she'd already pulled out. She reached back into the box, pulled out something else, and studied it. Then, as if sensing that she was no longer alone, she turned and saw me standing in the hall.

"Oh!" she said. "You frightened me!"

I'd frightened her? "Is there something you're looking for?" I asked.

"Yes," she said. Her face was red and sweaty. She looked . . . caught. Guilty. She held out the photograph in her hand. "I was looking for this." I stepped into the room and looked down at the photo: Terri and Diane at fourteen or fifteen standing in front of the pool in bathing suits, hair wet, arms around each other, sly expressions on their faces. Two girls with a secret. "Lexie showed it to me not long ago. I was hoping to find it so I could show it to Diane." She glanced down at the photograph. "It seems impossible that we were ever that young. Do you mind if I take it and show her?"

"Not at all," I said.

She slipped the picture into her back pocket, then

gathered up all the other papers and photos she'd pulled out and shoved them into the nearest box. "Lexie found a lot of great stuff," Terri said. "A real treasure trove of family history." She put the lids back on both boxes and stood, reaching for her cane.

"Yes, she did," I said.

I watched her go. Then I went to the window and looked out. Terri was heading for her car—so much for her swim. Diane loaded the jars of water from the pool into the backseat—she seemed flustered. She touched Terri's shoulder, but Terri shrugged her away and got into the car. Diane leaned down, spoke to Terri through the open driver's-side window. Terri shook her head and drove off.

Diane and I made sandwiches for lunch.

"Terri decided against a swim?" I asked.

"She wasn't up for it. She gets tired easily."

I told her about Terri rifling through the papers in my room. She immediately snapped to Terri's defense.

"She was looking for a photo, Jackie," she said, setting down a jar of mustard too hard.

"I know. She showed me."

"So what's the problem?"

"I just think it's odd, don't you? That she'd sneak up there and go through the boxes on her own instead of asking?"

"Jesus, after everything I just told you out by the pool? Terri is not the enemy here." Diane glared at me. "You're sounding a little like your sister, looking for secrets and conspiracies that just aren't there."

Diane turned away from me and sliced her sandwich in half decisively; the conversation was over.

My father came into the kitchen, whistling. Then, sensing the tension, he fell silent too. He made his own sandwich and we had a quiet lunch, no one saying much of anything.

After fifteen uncomfortable moments in which the only words uttered were "Pass the chips, please," Diane cleared her plate and announced she was going into work and then home and she'd see us tomorrow. "I trust you two will be all right here on your own tonight?"

"Of course we will," I said, the words coming out with more of an edge than I'd intended.

chapter twenty-eight

February 11, 1931
Lanesborough, New Hampshire

Our girl is one year old today! I can scarcely believe it! Will made us paper hats, and I baked a vanilla cake with buttercream icing. We danced around the kitchen in our silly hats, the three of us holding hands while the cake cooled, the air thick with vanilla and sugar, all of us deliriously happy. Maggie laughed and laughed. She fell down and laughed. Then Will pretended to fall down and she laughed more. Will made up a silly birthday song about a little girl who was actually a bird who flew all the way up to the moon and did a little dance there, surrounded by stars. She listened, wide-eyed, looked up at the ceiling like she could see through it, all the way up to the stars Will pointed toward as he sang.

Maggie was wearing a new pink dress with white trim that I had sewn myself.

"She looks like a cherub," Will said, kissing both of her rosy little cheeks. "I can't believe you and I created something so perfect."

Sometimes all I can do is stare at her with wonder. I can't believe she's real.

Maggie is very much her own little person. She's always watching us with her huge dark eyes, taking everything in. She can look perfectly serious and pensive one minute, and the next, she's overcome by fits of giggles. Her laugh is infectious—you hear it, you see her so caught up in absolute joy that you have to laugh along, too, even if you don't know the joke.

Myrtle came by with a gift for Maggie—a little white stuffed dog. Maggie loved it at once, clutching it to her chest, saying, "Daawg," over and over. She's nearly walking on her own now—holding herself up on furniture and holding our hands while she takes brave, sure steps. And she's talking up a storm, speaking her own language, which I can understand just fine. And she does speak three clear words of English: *Mama*, *Dadda*, and of course, *Dog*.

We continue to give Maggie a small drink of spring water each day. When we stop, her health declines. But soon, getting water won't be any trouble at all— we'll just walk out the back door of our house! We talk about it every day, how our lives will be once we're there, but still, it does not seem real. It feels like a far-away thing, our future there in a house called Sparrow Crest in Brandenburg. A made-up story.

It's somehow easier to think of it this way. To keep it at a distance.

Will has hired a special crew of quarrymen and stone carvers from Barre to turn the small pool that was behind the hotel into one nearly six times the size. Our new swimming pool will be lined with granite blocks, and we'll build the house right alongside it so that the kitchen door opens onto the patio.

Workmen have already cleared away all the charred timbers and rubble. At my request, they left the rose garden intact. I plan to keep it going, my own tribute to Eliza Harding, to the hotel that once was. I've been studying up on roses, on how best to care for them. I have mail-ordered books and talked with all the best gardeners in town.

In the spring, as soon as the roads become passable and supplies can be delivered, work will begin on the house and pool. Will promises we'll be in by the first snow.

"I will miss you all so much when you move away. You most of all, little sparrow," Myrtle said to Maggie, who giggled when Myrtle tickled her under the chin.

"We won't be that far," I reminded Myrtle. "And you must visit often. You can stay in the guest room. A regular visitor to Sparrow Crest!"

She flinched a little, averted her eyes.

I knew she would never come. Never return to that water.

"And you must write often," she said. "To let me know you're all right."

I wrapped my arms around Maggie protectively.

Will laughed. "Of course we'll be all right. Better than all right. We're moving into the house of our dreams! A castle! Isn't that right, Ethel?"

I smiled and nodded, hoping it was convincing, that the kernel of dread I felt deep in my heart did not show. I knew the water was keeping our girl alive, that what we were doing was for the best, but still, the idea of living beside that pool, of actually being there day after day, night after night—it unsettled me.

I frosted the cake and lit the candle in the center. I held on to the match a second too long, burning my fingers, letting the exquisite pain pull me back into my body, into the reality of the here and now.

I am Mrs. Monroe and I am having a party for my daughter. I have a beautiful, healthy little girl who brings joy to everyone who sees her. She is real and she is

here to stay. I have everything I could ever want. Soon, I
will be moving into the house of my dreams.

We all sang "Happy Birthday," and Maggie cooed
and laughed and clapped her hands with joy. The
kitchen was warm and bright.

As I helped her to blow out the candle, I made a
wish: *May we always be this happy, this safe.*

June 26, 1931

Will returned from Vermont with a load of jars and
bottles of water for Maggie and news of the progress
on the house.

"The main timbers are all up. The house looks like
a great skeleton. They couldn't get trucks up the road
because of the flooded brook and how muddy things
were, so we hired teams of horses to pull the final load
of timbers in. It was something to see, Ethel!" He was
filthy from the worksite, his boots and pants caked
with mud. He looked like he hadn't slept a wink and
had dropped several pounds. I worry that the stress
of supervising the building of Sparrow Crest is too
much for him. It's all-consuming. When he's not there
watching over the construction, he's at home drawing
plans for the workers, making lists, doing sketch after
sketch of little details: the built-in bench in the front
hall, the shape of the hand-carved newel post for the
stairs. He's changed the location of the kitchen windows four or five times already. He wants everything to
be perfect. Sometimes I come down to make breakfast
in the morning and find he's been sitting at the table
working all night. I've never seen him, or anyone else
for that matter, so consumed.

He's having trouble keeping workers at the site.

Men keep leaving without even giving notice. The foreman there, Mr. Galletti, seemed a capable man when Will hired him, but now he's beginning to have his doubts.

"We're weeks behind where we should be," Will says. "I told Galletti to double the size of the crew. And to get some decent, hardworking men in there! I'm sure it won't be any trouble to find them. Mention an opening here and you get a line of applicants around the corner—too many good men out of work."

"Can we afford that? Hiring all those extra men?"

Will nodded. "It'll put us over budget for the house, but we're already over budget." I saw the worry lines in his brow. He noticed me studying his face and smiled. "But it's worth it, to have a home for you and Maggie as soon as we can, darling wife." He clasped my hands in his and kissed them.

August 2, 1931

Will returned home late this evening after being away in Brandenburg for over a week. He looked exhausted, thin and sickly, like a hollowed-out version of himself.

Maggie was in the nursery, sound asleep.

"Will, darling, have you eaten? Have you slept?" I asked as I kissed his scruffy cheek, dusted mud off his good coat. "There's a chicken in the oven—I've been keeping it warm. I wasn't sure when to expect you. You get cleaned up, and we'll sit down to a nice dinner. I'll pour you some brandy."

"That can all wait," he said, taking off his hat. "I have news." He looked nervous, but excited. His fingers worked their way over the band of his hat, fidgeting, plucking. He had dirt under his nails.

"What is it?"

"We're moving to Sparrow Crest."

I nodded, now more worried than ever. "Of course we are," I said. "Before the first snow, right?"

"Next week," he said, a wide, almost frantic-looking smile taking hold of his face.

"But . . ." I stammered. "The house isn't finished."

"No, but it's finished enough to live in. The roof is on, the outside walls are up. I'm having the men finish up our bedroom and bathroom right now. And the stove will arrive tomorrow. There's a lot to be done still, but there's no reason we can't move in. It'll be fun. A great adventure! And I can supervise the final stages of the building more carefully. There will be no more going back and forth. If we're there, the men will work harder; I have no doubt things will progress much more rapidly."

"But . . . next week, Will? Really?"

He nodded. "I've hired some men and trucks to help us move."

"Oh." It was all I could think of to say.

He came, wrapped his arms around me. "Isn't it wonderful, Ethel? We can start packing right away. Tonight!"

chapter twenty-nine

June 21, 2019

My father and I spent the afternoon in the rose garden. He'd gotten it into his head that it should be pruned, so despite the heat, we donned heavy leather gloves and went to work with the pruning shears we found in the garage. We shaped the bushes, deadheaded, and trimmed errant runners. It felt good to have work to do: a physical task to keep us occupied. We took breaks for cold beers and to stand back and admire our progress. "I think Gram would be pleased," I said.

"I wish I could see a picture of what it looked like back in the hotel days," my father said. "My guess is that your great-grandmother and grandmother didn't make many changes. I bet it looks pretty much the same."

"It's strange to think about," I said. "The rose garden and springs being here this whole time. The hotel burned, Sparrow Crest built. Lexie used to say she wished the roses could speak and tell stories."

Ted smiled. He'd found Lexie's stash of pot in an old cigar box up in the attic. He lit up a joint, and together, we smoked it sitting on the old bench in the gazebo. I hadn't smoked pot since college. He asked me, "Do you think you'll keep Dracula's castle?"

"My and Lexie's summers here were such a huge part of growing up. I feel like they shaped the person I turned out to be. This house and I . . . we're bound. I don't feel like I can sell it," I said honestly. "Gram wanted it to stay in the family. I feel like I owe it to her, to me, and Lexie, too, to keep it."

"Will you move out here? Pick up and leave your life in Tacoma? Your practice?"

"I don't know," I said. I looked at him. "What do you think I should do?"

He barked out a laugh. "You're asking *me* for advice?"

I laughed with him, but then said, "Yeah, I guess I am."

It was funny, here was this man I'd spent years trying to change. And now, sitting here with him like this, I realized he was exactly the way he should be. I really didn't want him any other way. I felt like we got each other in the way only family could. I trusted him, felt like I could be vulnerable with him. And, crazy as it seemed, I actually wanted his advice, valued his opinion.

He thought a minute. Rubbed his beard in a philosophical kind of way. "A part of you is always going to be here. You, Lexie, your mother, your grandmother and aunts, great-grandparents—you're all as much a part of this place as this rose garden; as the mortar that holds the stones of that old house together." He looked at me. "Does that make any sense at all?"

I nodded and hugged him.

We went into the house and raided the kitchen, then went into the living room, where I put on one of my sister's old-time records, Fats Domino. I closed my eyes, floating from the pot. *A part of you is always going to be here*. I knew he was right. He was right about Lexie, too. I felt her here—her presence was so strong.

She used to say we were two halves that made a whole, the yin and the yang. For better or for worse, the times that I'd felt most whole, most like myself, I'd been with my sister.

When I went up to my room, I grabbed the binders I'd bought and pulled the boxes over to the bed. I started with the ones Terri had been going through.

She was just looking for a photo, I told myself.

But what if she'd been looking for something else? And the photo was just a cover-up?

Stop it, I told myself. You're being paranoid.

I began pulling things out of the boxes and sorting them: more journal pages, which went into the red binder, sorted by date as best I could. There was one that I found particularly unsettling:

June 2
Something was in the house last night. There was
water on the floor. Wet puddles leading from the open
door and up the stairs.

Had there really been an intruder? If so, who? Or *what*?

Something was in the house last night.

I kept digging through the box and came across the birth certificates of my mother, Rita, and Diane. Obituaries for Rita and my mother, and prayer cards from their funerals. I put each of these into plastic sleeves and into the binder I'd dedicated to family documents.

I opened up an old leather-bound diary with a cracked spine. The pages were wrinkled and mildewed, like the book had gotten wet. The ink was blurred, washed

away in places. I made out a name on the front cover:
Mrs. Ethel O'Shay Monroe. My great-grandmother. I
flipped through it, but could only read bits and pieces:
a trip my great-grandparents took to the Brandenburg
Springs Hotel, a woman named Myrtle with a sick husband, a sick baby, the building of Sparrow Crest. Most
of the diary was illegible.

I set the diary aside, continued digging. At last, I
came to a worn blue envelope—one I was sure Terri
had pulled out and set aside. I opened the envelope
and found several newspaper clippings, the first about
the hotel fire.

> Samuel Claiborne, a bellboy at the hotel, was first to
> see the flames and has stated that he witnessed re-
> cently widowed Mr. Harding in the halls with a can
> of kerosene shortly before. Claiborne broke down
> the door to the Harding suite, and was able to res-
> cue the Hardings' infant daughter.

The Hardings had a daughter! A girl who lived.
Why hadn't Shirley told me about her?

There was another short article clipped from a yellowed newspaper:

> **Flemming family takes out-of-state doctor to
> court in dispute over the Brandenburg Springs
> property**
> Walter Flemming of Lord's Hill is legally contest-
> ing the sale of the Brandenburg Springs property,
> which was the site of the Brandenburg Springs
> Hotel and Resort. The property was apparently
> deeded to Dr. William Monroe of Lanesborough,
> New Hampshire, after winning a poker game with

the former owner of the hotel, Mr. Benson Harding. Flemming, whose daughter Eliza was married to Mr. Harding before her tragic drowning at the hotel, contests that the land should legally belong to the child of Benson and Eliza Harding, Shirley Harding, now just one year old.

"It's all she has left of her parents," Mr. Flemming stated. "The property should stay in the family."

Mr. Benson Harding took his own life shortly after turning over the hotel property to Dr. Monroe.

Shirley Harding is being raised by her grandparents, Walter and Eureka Flemming of Lord's Hill.

The final newspaper clipping was a wedding announcement from June 21, 1951:

Miss Shirley Harding, granddaughter of Mr. Walter Flemming and his wife, Eureka, of Brandenburg, was married to Mr. Christopher Dufrense of Chickopee, Mass., on June 17. The ceremony took place at the Brandenburg Methodist Church and was officiated by Reverend David Thorn. The bride was given away by her grandfather, Mr. Walter Flemming. Best Man was Mr. Stephen Dickerson of Chickopee, Mass., and Maid of Honor was Miss Margaret Monroe of Brandenburg.

My mind whirled. Shirley, Ryan's grandmother, was the *daughter* of Benson and Eliza Harding, the owners of the Brandenburg Springs Hotel. And their family had contested the sale to my great-grandparents.

Shirley must have known who her parents had been and what had happened to them.

Did she also believe the springs and land were

wrongly sold? That Sparrow Crest should be hers? Did she grow up believing that everything my grandmother had should all rightly belong to her? Was *that* why she couldn't stay away from Sparrow Crest, the springs, and my grandmother?

Had Terri come to find these papers, to take them, so that I wouldn't learn the truth?

How much did they all know? What were they trying to cover up?

Fats was singing "I Hear You Knocking" on the turntable downstairs. Over the music, I started to hear knocking, actual knocking on the front door. I wasn't sure it was real, but it was. I went downstairs, wishing I wasn't still so stoned. Whoever was out there was trying to open the door, the knob turning in place.

"Ted?" I yelled up the stairs, hoping for a little backup. But either he couldn't hear me, or he was too caught up in his artwork to tear himself away.

The wall phone in the kitchen began to ring, the alarm-like jangling of the bell startling me. I stood between the ringing phone and the door. Torn, I moved up to the door, peeking out the window. No one was there.

I went for the phone. "Hello?"

There was no answer. But someone was on the line. I could hear them breathing.

"Who's there?" I said. No response. The line crackled and hummed, made strange, underwater noises. Then, a faint whisper: *Sorry, sorry, sorry.*

Again, there was another loud knock at the front door, and I jumped. I slammed the phone on its cradle, made my way back into the hall. Heart pounding, I crept up to the door, and peeked out the window.

Again, no one was there.

I unlatched the door and flung it open. Nothing. But then I looked down. There were wet footprints leading to and from the door, along the path to the pool.

I turned, yelled for my father again, and got no answer. Where the hell was he? No time to wait or go searching upstairs for him. I went to the hall closet and grabbed the speargun from where we'd stashed it behind coats and boots. I grabbed one of the spears and pulled the elastic band to load it as he had shown me, then walked back to the door. I stood there on the threshold, pointing the speargun into the darkness as I searched the driveway and yard for movement.

Had I imagined the knocking? I may have imagined the sound, but I wasn't imagining the wet footprints. Just to be sure, I dropped down to my knees, touching the damp stone on the front step. No. This was real.

No folie à deux.

I stood up, forced myself to move forward, away from the comforting light and noise of the house. With heavy legs, I followed the wet footprints, not at all surprised when they led me right to the gate to the pool.

Back in the house, the phone was ringing again.

Raising the speargun, finger on the trigger, I pushed the gate open, cringing at the loud screech.

"Hello?" I called, stepping through the gate onto the flagstone patio. "Who's there?"

An oddly sweet smell was coming from the pool, all mixed up with the metallic tang of rusted metal, the sulfurous stench of rotting eggs.

At a small splash, I caught a glimpse of movement in the pool out of the corner of my eye. I turned and aimed the speargun at whatever I'd just seen, but there were only ripples now. "Who's there?"

Lexie. Please let it be Lexie.

Let the wish I made come true: Bring her back to me.

I held my breath, waiting. There was nothing. No splash, no movement, only stillness.

The pool pulled me closer, the blackness sucking me in. I went right up to the edge. The lights from the house behind me were enough to cast my shadow, and the water gobbled it up.

I walked carefully to the other side of the pool, hands wrapped tightly around the speargun. I heard the telltale screech of the rusty hinges on the front gate. I spun in time to see a dark figure moving slowly toward me across the pavers beside the pool. I almost called her name. But this was not Lexie. It was someone much taller.

"Stop! Stop right where you are!" I shouted.

"It's me, Jackie! It's Ryan," he said, freezing and raising his hands above his head like a criminal. "Jesus, is that a crossbow?"

"What are you doing here?" I demanded, not lowering the weapon.

"I was worried about you. I came to check to make sure you were okay."

"I didn't hear your car. I didn't see any lights."

"I walked over," he said. "I couldn't stop thinking about our conversation. I was worried."

"So you took a twenty-five minute walk uphill in the dark?"

"Walking helps me think. I thought the air would help clear my head. But seriously, Jackie, why are you pointing a crossbow at me?"

"It's not a crossbow, it's a speargun. Are your feet wet?" I asked him. I moved closer to him, trying to see if he'd left footprints.

His hands were still in the air. "Jackie, you're starting to really freak me out."

I took a step back, realizing I sounded like a crazy person. But I didn't lower the speargun.

"I'm a little freaked out myself."

A serious understatement.

"Can you please lower that thing?" he asked. My eyes had adjusted to the darkness, and I could make out his pale, worried face. His furrowed brow. His feet looked dry.

"Tell me again why you're here. Why you decided to come sneaking around this late at night."

"I came because I was worried! I haven't been able to stop thinking about our talk this morning. That maybe Lexie was right. I stopped by Edgewood and talked to my grandmother about it. I really listened to her for the first time. She says there's something dark down in the pool, something that's been gathering force for a long time. And that the people who die in that water are trapped there forever. I know it sounds crazy, and I'm not saying I understand any of it, but—"

"Oh, I understand."

And I did. Suddenly, it all made sense.

I thought back to all the interactions I'd had with him since returning, the spooky stories he'd told me, how dangerous he said the house and pool were.

"You do?" He looked astonished.

"I know who you are."

"Who *I* am?"

Pathetic, him playing dumb.

"You're the great-grandson of Benson and Eliza Harding, the couple who owned the hotel."

He said nothing. He didn't deny it, but he wasn't ready to admit to it, either. He took a step back, his eyes on the speargun.

"You didn't want me to find out. Your mother came here today to try to make *sure* I didn't, to get rid of any evidence."

But I caught her before she got the chance.

Everything was falling into place. There was no haunted swimming pool here. No ghosts creeping out of the water. Only a family who wanted what they believed was rightly theirs.

"My mother? What?"

"It all makes sense now! God, I was such an idiot. How could I have trusted you?"

He shook his head. "Jax, I don't understand what any of this—"

"You, your mother and grandmother, you think this land, the springs, all of it, should belong to you! That my great-grandfather got it unfairly, which maybe he did, but it doesn't make what you're doing right."

"What I'm doing?" He was acting totally dumbfounded, an innocent wrongly accused. "What exactly are you accusing me of here, Jax?"

"Trying to scare me off like this. That's what you did to Lexie, too, isn't it? Tried to scare her? Fill her head with crazy stories about the pool, about the curse. You probably even got some girl to play the dark-haired woman. Some girl who'd come creeping out of the pool. Was she the one who broke into the house? Came sneaking around when Lexie was in bed? Or maybe that was *you*?"

The chills I'd had being out here alone were replaced by the heat of rage. Sweat formed on my forehead and arms. My hands shook from gripping the speargun so tightly.

"I would never do anything like that! That is crazy, Jax. Stop and listen to yourself. You're not making sense."

Fury burned through me. No way was he going to turn this around, to make me the crazy one!

"I can't believe you messed with Lexie like that! Manipulated her. Used her illness to your advantage. God, were you getting her drunk on vodka, too? Was it you who talked her into going off her meds?"

"No!"

I shook my head. "When we were kids, you were desperate to impress her, you followed her anywhere she asked, gave her those little notes. You were crazy about her, Ryan."

He nodded. "I would never have lied to her, then or now. Lexie meant the world to me. So do you. Please, Jax."

I was crying now, which made me more furious. "I can't believe I listened to those creepy stories you and your grandmother told me, and really started to believe them. I read Lexie's journal entries like they might actually be real."

I'd lost all perspective.

The gate squeaked open again. My father appeared behind Ryan. "What's going on?" he asked, looking from Ryan to me and the speargun. "I heard shouting. You okay, Jax?"

"Fine," I said. "Ryan's just leaving." My hands were shaking, and my body was covered in sweat.

"But I—" Ryan said.

I stepped forward, aiming the speargun right at his chest, "Just fucking go!" I shouted.

Ryan nodded, and slowly backed away, hands in the air. I kept the speargun on him the whole time. He turned once he got to the gate, and scuttled off without another word.

———————

I began to lose some of that ramped-up adrenaline surge once my father and I were at the kitchen table. He'd opened us each a beer. He'd disarmed the speargun and put it on the counter. I'd spent several minutes pacing, furious. At last, I went up to my bedroom to gather up my evidence and bring it down. I showed my father the newspaper articles about the baby rescued from the hotel fire, the contested property sale, and Shirley's wedding announcement. I even showed him Lexie's entry about someone coming into the house and leaving wet footprints behind. Then I laid out my theory.

"I don't get it," he admitted. "Ryan and his grandmother were trying to scare Lexie?"

"Yes! And me! They made up stories about the springs, about this evil spirit who lives inside them and somehow traps all the people who drowned there, uses them. Lexie was vulnerable enough to get completely caught up in it; to live inside this fantasy they were perpetuating. They probably convinced her the pool changed depths, too—that some portal or something opened up down there at random places and times. Maybe that's how the spirits were supposed to come and go? I'm sure they found someone to play the dark-haired woman, made Lexie think she was an ethereal, dangerous creature from the pool. Then they tried to scare me off, too—"

"What dark-haired woman?" he asked. My father

still looked puzzled. Worse, he looked downright concerned.

Realizing how quickly and frantically I'd been speaking, I took a breath. My thoughts were all over the place, rising and jumping like red-hot sparks. *Slow down*, I told myself. *Focus and speak calmly.* "The woman in Lexie's sketchbook. The one who told her she came from—"

"So you're saying Ryan and his family got a woman to pretend to be an evil spirit who came out of the pool?"

I took a good swig of my beer. "Something like that."

I understood how crazy it sounded, how alarming I must have looked holding a speargun on Ryan. I needed to get my thoughts together, lay things out so that he'd understand.

I flashed back to my conversation with Karen the other day, going over the symptoms of psychosis—erratic thoughts and behaviors, delusions, hallucinations—and now here I was looking like the one who'd cracked, exhibiting all the symptoms. My head was pounding. I couldn't keep my thoughts straight.

I needed to call Barbara. But I knew that if she could see me and hear me now, she'd be so worried. I was worried.

The front door opened. "Jackie?" Diane called from the front hall.

"We're in the kitchen," my father called back. Diane stormed into the room. "Do you want to tell me what in the name of God you were doing pointing a speargun at Ryan? It's a wonder he isn't calling the police. You could have killed him!"

"News travels fast around here," I said.

"Terri was with me at my place—"

"Of course she was," I said.

"What's that supposed to mean?" Diane asked. Her eyes were blazing. I said nothing. She continued, "Ryan called her. You terrified him, Jackie! What on earth possessed you?"

"Jax thinks Ryan and his family were messing with Lexie," my father said. "That they filled her head with creepy stories and got an actor to pretend to be a spirit living in the pool."

"Maybe she was just a friend, not an actor," I said.

Diane looked from my father to me. "But *why*?" she asked. "*Why* would they do such a thing?"

"Do you know who they are?" I asked, reaching for the articles I'd showed my father. "Shirley is the daughter of the couple who owned the hotel! After it burned, Benson Harding lost it to your grandfather in a poker game!" I held the articles out to Diane, but she shooed them away.

"I know all of that," she said, waving her arms, her bracelets jangling. "I've known for years. It isn't some big secret. Terri told me about it ages ago, back when we were kids. I still don't understand why you think they hired someone to try to scare your sister." She was looking at me like I'd gone off the deep end.

"So Lexie would sell the property. And they could buy it. Or for cosmic justice because they feel the land and the springs belong to them."

"So you're saying it's about money and Sparrow Crest?" Diane asked.

"Yes! And the springs."

Diane looked at my father, then back at me. She didn't look angry anymore. Her face had softened into pity.

It hit me hard: This was how my sister must have

felt, again and again for years; having no one believe her, everyone giving concerned, pitying looks—poor crazy Lexie and her runaway thoughts.

"Jax," Diane said, her voice low and calm. "I think this is projection. These are the reasons you became estranged from Lexie. The house and money. You felt wronged."

"That has nothing to do with it!"

"Now it's tangled up with the guilt you feel, and you're looking for someone other than yourself to blame," Diane went on.

I glared at her. How dare she take on this pseudo-therapist role with me!

"No!" I turned to my father. "You believe me, don't you, Ted?"

"I want to," he said. Diane glared at him. He looked down at the ground, then back up. "I think you're hurting, Jax. We all are. We're all trying to make sense of why Lexie is gone. Looking for someone or something to blame. Blaming ourselves, too." He dug his palms into his eyes. "Put all of that together, and we're all wrecked and raw and imagining all sorts of crazy shit."

"No! I'm telling you—"

"Here's what's going to happen," Diane said. "We're all going to sit down and have some tea. Then go to bed. Tomorrow, we'll get up and you two will get packed up. We'll have a quiet day, just the three of us. No drinking. No trips to the pool or into town. No spearguns! Then Sunday morning I'll bring you both to the airport. I think the best thing for both of you is to go back home, get a little distance from this place. God knows it's got its hooks in us all. This house, everything that's happened here, it fucks with you. It pulls you in, twists everything all around."

She looked at my father. "Ted, would you please put on the kettle?"

As he did, she pulled out her phone and stepped into the hall. I sank down in my chair, reached for my beer. I heard Diane out in the hall: ". . . under control now. I'll tell you all about it later. I need to stay here tonight and tomorrow. Keep an eye on things." A long pause. "I know. Me too."

I drank my tea like a good girl, then said I was tired.

"May I be excused?" I asked, not attempting to hide the sarcasm. "I'd like to go up to bed now."

"Try to get a good night's sleep, Jackie," Diane said, her voice calm and sweet, but tinged with annoyance. "I'm sure things will look better in the morning," she added.

Up in my room, I continued going through Lexie's journals, putting them in order and into the red binder.

June 9
I have stopped swimming in the pool. Silly, I know.
Me and that pool, we go way back. But lately, lately,
I can't bring myself to get into the water. It just
seems . . . too black. Too deep. Too dark. And the weeds,
they've been bad lately. And the smell seems to grow
worse every day.

> *Then, there are the things I've seen.*
> *But I don't even dare to write them down.*

I dreamed of Lexie. I woke up and there she was, standing by the edge of my bed. Pig was there at her feet.

She was soaking wet; I could hear drips of water falling to the wooden floor as she bent down to pet the cat.

"You're not real," I said, more to remind myself than to piss her off. She was a hallucination. Part of a dream.

"You've gotta stop thinking so hard about what's real and what isn't, Jax. You see me, don't you?"

"Yes."

"Then let that be enough."

chapter thirty

Today I saw it for the first time: Sparrow Crest. Our new home.

Will drove us there, little Margaret on my lap, chatting, pointing at and naming the sights along the way: *house, cow, horse, car, man, lady, dog, tree*. She's such a clever girl and has become quite the talker, knows a dozen words and uses them again and again. Will says she is very advanced for her age.

Everything is such a delight to her! And to Will and me, now that we see the world through her eyes.

She giggled with delight at each cow.

"And what noise does a cow make?" I asked. "Does a cow say *moo*?"

"Moo!" she cried. "Moo, moo, moo!"

Will was nervous, fidgety as a little boy—he so wanted me to be pleased with the house. He wanted it to be everything I'd hoped and dreamed for.

We drove through town, passing the general store, the church, the post office, the little schoolhouse.

I am Mrs. Monroe, and my family and I live here in Brandenburg now, I told myself as I took it all in, trying to make it real, to make it sink in. I imagined us all walking through the doors of the church on Sundays, buying bread at the store, introducing ourselves to our new neighbors, Margaret one day being old enough to go to school.

When we turned up the road to the house, Will told me to close my eyes.

"Keep them closed and no peeking, darling wife," he said. "You too, little sparrow," he added, and Maggie covered her eyes with her hands as I did, giggling. She started counting, the way she did when we all played hide-and-seek. Only she hadn't quite learned to count and just listed the numbers she knew: "One, four, six, one."

He drove another minute, then stopped the car. "Keep them closed," he instructed. He came around and opened our door. I stumbled out, holding Maggie in my arms, Will guiding me.

"Okay, open your eyes."

I gasped. Will, I'm sure, took it as a gasp of awe and delight. But really, it was fear. I sucked air into my chest, which felt as if it was being crushed by a giant fist. I held Maggie tightly in my arms, and we gazed upon Sparrow Crest. It was so much more massive than I had imagined, like a great stone fortress. It truly was like the castle I had dreamed of living in when I was a little girl. The front door was heavy wood with a rounded top. The windows were arched with leaded glass. Two stories high with an attic, the roof had steep peaks and was covered in gray slate shingles. There was a large half-round window in the attic at the very front of the house.

The whole building seemed alive to me; it felt as though it was a part of the landscape, as if it had risen up right out of the rocky soil. It fit the backdrop of trees on the hill behind it perfectly. The windows and door looked like a fierce face under the steeply angled rooftop.

The front door stood open, a mouth waiting to gobble us up.

"Oh, Will," I said, taking a step back away from it, wanting to get back in the car and drive as far away from this place as we could.

But it was too late. We had nowhere else to go. This was our home now.

Will took Maggie from me, swooped her though the air as if she were flying. "And what do you think of your new house, little sparrow?"

She laughed with delight and pointed. "House," she said.

"Your house," he told her. "Sparrow Crest. Shall we go inside?"

I followed him on shaky legs.

A work crew was inside, as well as the movers, who had come ahead of us, trucks loaded with our furniture and all of our belongings in baskets and boxes. All the men scuttled to and fro like ants.

Will introduced me to the foreman, Mr. Galletti. He was a broad-shouldered man with dark hair and a thick, bushy mustache. "A true pleasure to meet you, Mrs. Monroe," he said.

The front hall was magnificent—heavy, dark wood-paneled walls, a stone floor, built-in benches to sit on while we take off boots and coats. Off to the right, a large living room with a stone fireplace. There was a mason pointing the cement between the stones with a tiny trowel. He tipped his hat to me. Beyond the living room, a dining room connected by a hall to the kitchen. Oh, the kitchen! It's enormous.

"You could cook a feast every night!" Will said. There were plenty of deep wooden cupboards and a large pantry. A huge soapstone sink. The newest and fanciest gas stove.

"It's big enough to get lost in," I told him.

"And look," he said, showing me the kitchen door, divided into two halves. "It's called a Dutch door. You can open just the top if you'd like to let the breeze in. Or, latch it together and open the whole thing at once."

He opened the door, stepped aside.

"Go see," he said, but I stood frozen. A breeze blew in through the open door, giving me a chill, making the hairs on my arms stand on end. I rubbed at them.

At last, I willed myself forward and stepped out onto the patio, shuffling my feet like a sleepwalker.

The pool was nothing like what I remembered, and yet so familiar. It was so much larger, a great rectangular pond. The water was as black as ever, perhaps more so. And there was the familiar smell: metallic tinged with rotten egg. The taste got caught in the back of my throat. I tried not to gag on it.

"It's so much bigger," I said. "We could sail a boat in it."

Will laughed. "Not quite large enough for that, but plenty large enough for proper swimming."

I walked around it, maintaining a safe distance between myself and the edge. Neat blocks of granite lined the top; the slate of the patio was laid up in a neat bed of mortar (only half of the patio was finished, the rest a sandbox and stacks of stone). At the far end was a little stone-lined canal that led across the yard, all the way to the stream. I could hear it running.

We stood, looking at the pool. I was mesmerized, watching our reflections in it—the three of us, the house and hills behind us, the clouds overhead. The wind blew, rippling the water, making everything waver as if none of it were real.

Maggie squirmed in Will's arms, and he set her down. She got too close to the edge, and I swooped her up in my arms, kissed her soft dark hair, whispered low, "This is where you came from. Where it all began." *And it's the water keeping you alive*, I thought.

We have to be here, I told myself. I would have to find a way to put my fears in a box and put on my best, brave face. For Maggie. It was all for Maggie. I kissed her again and again. She smelled like sweet apples and warm milk. Like all that was good in the world.

Inside, one of the men hammered. One said something to another, and they laughed.

The water in the stone-lined canal sounded like it was laughing, too.

A mocking little laugh.

"We still have the whole upstairs to tour," Will said. "And there's the attic. That's where I thought we'd put your sewing room."

"You never said anything about a sewing room." I felt my spirits brighten.

"I wanted it to be a surprise! You can set up under that big window at the front of the house." He was bouncing up onto the balls of his feet, so excited.

It was going to be all right, I told myself. *We are going to be happy here.*

I followed him back in through the kitchen door, holding Maggie in my arms. "What do you think, little sparrow? Isn't it magnificent? Shall we go up and see your bedroom? I hear Daddy's had it painted a lovely yellow."

Maggie pointed out the open door, back at the pool. "Lady," she said. My arms tightened around her, my whole body going rigid.

I turned slowly, looked back at the dark surface of the water, glanced around the patio, out at the edges of the yard.

"There's no one there, my love," I said, my throat tight, heart beating so fast and hard I was sure it would burst.

"Lady," she said again, smiling, giggling.

"What's she saying?" Will called from up ahead in the hall.

"Nothing," I called back, my voice high and strange.

"Lady!" Maggie said, the word mixed in with delighted laughter as she pointed at the pool. "Lady! Lady! Lady!"

August 17, 1931

My nerves are a mess. I'm not sleeping. Can hardly eat.

I tell Will it's the construction: the constant banging and yelling and sawing. The men tromping with their big boots, stinking of sweat and cigarettes and last night's rum. The sawdust and plaster dust that seems to cover every surface of the house. The fact that I can't find anything—my favorite shoes, our cast-iron frying pan. Our lives are still packed away in boxes, and we are only taking out what few things we absolutely need until the house is finished. The last thing we want to do is add to the chaos.

But the truth is, living at the building site is not what's put me on edge.

It's the pool. I feel like I spend all my energy each day trying to avoid it, trying not to look. It's a childish game I play: If I can't see you, you're not there. It's foolish, really. What am I afraid of?

"It's a hot day," Will says. "You should swim. I'll watch Maggie."

"Perhaps."

"You haven't been in the pool at all yet."

"I've been so busy with unpacking and setting up house. Not to mention chasing Maggie around and trying to keep her from being underfoot—or crushed by a ladder or scaffolding."

I'm not the only one unsettled by the pool. The workmen avoid it, too. I see them looking at it, speaking to each other in low voices. They all eye the pool like it's full of poison.

When I go into town, I feel the people looking at me, judging me. My clothes are too fine. Our car is too nice. I am an outsider here. They smile and are polite, but I hear them whisper when my back is turned. *That's her. The one from the springs.* Some look at me with fear. Others, with pity. Like I'm a doomed woman.

When I went to church last Sunday, a young woman asked me about the springs. "I heard your husband had a swimming pool built from the springs."

I smiled. "Yes, it's quite lovely. Perfect for these hot summer days."

Her face grew pale, she moved closer to me, whispered, "But don't you know? That water's cursed."

The day before yesterday, a tramp showed up at the front door of Sparrow Crest looking for work and a meal. He was dusty and thin but had a kind face. Will convinced Galletti to try him out. I invited him into the kitchen and made him a sandwich and a cup of coffee. "Can't work on an empty stomach," I said. Blanchard was his name. He was terribly polite.

"Thank you kindly, ma'am. Beautiful house you have here, ma'am." He sat down at the table after I invited him to do so, took off his hat, said grace, and ate. "I do believe that meeting you good people means my luck is turning," he said with a smile. "And you won't be sorry you took a chance on me. I'm a hard worker. I've laid railroad tracks all over New England. Helped build stone houses on the coast of Maine. Built boats down in Connecticut. I'm good with my hands, see." He held up his hands, which were calloused, weathered, his fingers stained yellow from cigarettes.

After lunch, Galletti sent him outside to finish the stonework around the pool—a job none of the other men would take. Blanchard went to work mixing mortar in the wheelbarrow and laying stones. Not twenty minutes later, he was back in the house, pale as could be, telling Galletti that he quit. The foreman was outraged. "These are nice people! They took you in. They fed you. And now you're leaving without even putting in an hour's work? It's a disgrace."

"The pool," Blanchard said.

"What about it?"

"I saw—"

"What?" Galletti barked.

"I can't—I'm sorry." And Blanchard left the house, practically running to the front door. I watched him out the window. He jogged down the driveway, looking back over his shoulder like he expected someone might be chasing him.

August 21, 1931

This evening, after eight o'clock, I was upstairs in Maggie's room. I'd just put her to bed and was sitting in the rocking chair, holding the book I'd been reading her, when I heard the commotion outside. Men yelling out by the pool. The men have been working late each day, and weekends, too. Will's pushing them to get back on schedule, says there will be extra money for all of them if they finish early.

I went downstairs, out the kitchen door.

"What's happened?" I asked Will.

"One of the men fell in," he told me. "Galletti got him out. Everything's fine, Ethel. Go back inside."

I stepped closer, moving through the circle of workmen, saw that it was young Brian Smith, the one they call Smitty, who'd fallen. He was backing away from the water, dripping wet and shivering. Galletti was behind him, also soaked.

"Are you all right? Let me get you some blankets and hot drinks," I offered.

"I did not fall in," Smitty said. "She pulled me. She grabbed my leg and pulled me in."

"Who?" I asked.

"There was a woman."

"A woman . . . in the water?" My heartbeat made a whooshing sound inside my ears.

Smitty nodded. I watched his Adam's apple bob up and down on his thin neck. "She was right there," he said, pointing at the black water.

"I saw her, too," said another man.

"It was her," someone whispered. "The woman in the water."

"The woman in the water?" I asked, my voice trembling.

"She grabbed me," Smitty said. "Pulled me under. She wouldn't let go."

"We've all seen her," said another man, the stonemason. His voice was raised, high and frantic. "Haven't we? Hasn't every man here seen her at least once? Heard her calling?"

"Who?" I said. "Heard who?"

"Please, Ethel," Will said. "Go back inside."

"Yes," I heard men saying. Then whispers, as one by one they each admitted it, each beginning his own tale in a hushed breath. I only caught a few words: *woman; beautiful; she sings to me sometimes; "come swimming," she says.*

"It was Eliza Harding," said Galletti as he stepped farther away, eyes on the dark water of the pool.

"That's impossible," Will said.

"Eliza," I repeated.

"Go inside, Ethel," Will ordered, his voice stern. "Now."

Eliza.

I closed my eyes, heard her voice—the voice of the nightmare Eliza with weeds in her hair, pale green skin, and black eyes: *Don't you understand? She belongs to the springs.*

The world went black as if I was the one who'd fallen into the pool. I felt the dark water rushing up around me as I was pulled farther and farther down.

———

When I opened my eyes, I was on the settee in the living room.

"Maggie," I said.

"She's fine, Ethel. She's upstairs sleeping. You fainted," Will said. He was beside me, holding a glass of brandy. "Here, sip this."

I sat up, took a drink of the brandy. "Are you sure? Have you checked on her?"

"I'm sure. She's sound asleep. How do you feel?"

"I'm fine," I said. "A little woozy, maybe."

My name is Mrs. Monroe, and I am sipping brandy on my couch. Everything is fine.

"How's Smitty? I think he needs the brandy more than I do."

Will frowned. "He's gone."

"Gone?"

"The entire work crew quit." He took a long pull from the glass of brandy. His hand seemed to tremble slightly. "Damned fools."

"All of them?"

He nodded. "Even Galletti. The ridiculous stories they tell! Talk of curses and ghosts. Superstitious fools." He ran his hands through his hair, exasperated.

"What will we do?" I looked around at the walls and ceiling that weren't yet plastered, the pile of trim boards stacked in the corner of the room. "We can't finish it on our own!"

"Of course not." His jaw tensed. "I'm going to interview more men. Men who aren't from Brandenburg, who haven't heard all these crazy stories. I'll go back to New Hampshire if I have to. Or get men all the way from Boston. There are so many good men out of work these days, I'll have a line of candidates a mile long. I'll offer double pay if they can get the work done by fall—half the salary on a weekly basis and the other as a lump sum when they finish. The lure of hard cash should be stronger than ghost stories and folktales."

And I wanted to say that we should leave, too. We should pack up, get in our car, and drive as far away from here, from this house and the pool, as we possibly could. I wanted to beg.

But then I thought of Maggie sleeping upstairs.

And I knew we could not leave.

We and this place, we're bound together.

November 12, 1931

"None of this is right," I say as I drag the settee into yet another location. Two plush chairs are across from it, a low polished maple table in the middle. I've been rearranging the living room furniture all afternoon and evening, and I am exhausted. My back aches. My head feels like it's being split open by a hammer and chisel.

Sparrow Crest is finished at last. Will hired a team of men from New Hampshire who came and camped in big canvas tents while they finished the house. Will paid them an extravagant amount of money and had them each sign a contract stating that any talk of ghosts or curses would mean they'd be instantly let go without pay. The men worked like machines, quiet and determined; obviously eager to finish the job and get out.

I don't know if any of them saw anything in the pool. They did not dare say. But it was obvious to me that they sensed that something was not quite right. Any visitor to Sparrow Crest notices right away.

Not everyone is afraid of the pool. Some still come looking for the springs, hoping for a cure, a miracle. People on crutches, the old and infirm, parents carrying sick children. Will sends them all away. He's put up **PRIVATE PROPERTY NO TRESSPASSING** signs.

Sparrow Crest is so much larger and more grand than the house we left behind in Lanesborough—I think there is no way we will ever fill it. The rooms look sparse. The furniture we have looks out of place—our table is much too small for the dining room; the settee and armchairs all wrong for the living room.

"We'll get new furniture," Will says, coming to wrap his arms around me and kiss my head. "We'll take measurements. We can have things shipped by train from Boston." I relax, feel myself melting into him. "I promise, darling wife, that I will find you the perfect furniture for this room if it's the last thing I do!"

I feel like a little girl playing house. I move from room to room like a shadow. I am always cold, no matter how large a fire we build. I layer on the sweaters and coats until I am nearly lost inside them. I lock myself away in the bathroom and prick myself with a pin.

I am Mrs. Monroe and I am home. I am home. I am home.

I often remember that first night Will and I were at the hotel. How I stood on the balcony, dizzy with this strange sense of familiarity. How I turned and said to Will: *Like we're meant to be here. Like coming home when you've been away a long time.*

Did some part of me know then that we would one day make our home here, become caretakers of the springs, for better or worse?

Maggie loves Sparrow Crest and spends her days thumping along from room to room, sitting by sunny windows and playing, talking nonstop. She has never seemed healthier, more energetic.

Her favorite thing to do is sit by the pool. She has long conversations with it, stringing together a babbling of words I only half-understand.

We eat lunch out there beside the water. It's far too cold to swim now, but we sit at the edge and dip our feet in, me holding tight to Maggie so she won't slip in.

"We must be very careful with Maggie around the water," Will says. "We must keep the kitchen door locked at all times so she can't wander out there on her own. And we must never, ever take our eyes off her when we're out near the pool."

As though I didn't realize the dangers.

"Come on, darling wife," Will says, taking my hand. "Let's go up to bed. You've put in a long day. The furniture conundrum will still be here tomorrow."

"You head up," I tell him. "I'll join you in a minute." I watch him go up the stairs and I walk into the kitchen, slip out through the kitchen door, inhaling the night air, the iron-y scent of the pool.

It is not at all like living in town. The nights here are so dark and quiet; more dark and quiet than anything I have ever known. But oh, the stars! The stars are so much more beautiful. I tilt my head back and look. So many stars! They seem closer, brighter than they ever did in town. As if I could just reach out and touch them. I spend a few minutes looking, head back until my neck aches, inventing constellations: an egg, a girl, a castle. I look down and see their light reflected in the pool, like a black mirror. It's as if the water is its own galaxy full of constellations. I look down at it until I am dizzy, disoriented, then I go back inside, latching all the doors, turning out the lights.

I am Mrs. Monroe, closing up the house for the night.

Slowly, I climb the steps and pad down the hall, look in on Maggie, sleeping peacefully, then join Will in our room.

"I brought you a glass of brandy to help you sleep," he says.

I thank him and dutifully sip it down as I get ready for bed.

"It's getting too cold for your night wanderings," he tells me.

I've been unsettled at night. I toss and turn and have such strange dreams. Sometimes Will wakes up, and I'm not in bed beside him. He comes down to find me in the kitchen with a cup of tea, or out by the pool or in the rose garden.

I make a noncommittal noise, a sort of grunt in response. I'm not agreeing or disagreeing. Only acknowledging that I heard him.

Tonight, despite the calming effects of the brandy, I lay awake listening to the wind against the house. Will is sound asleep, has been since he put his head on the pillow. There it is: the sound of the front door opening.

I slip out of bed, gently, so as not to wake Will. I go down the hall to check on Maggie—sleeping soundly in her crib.

Could have been the wind that blew it open. That's what Will would say. What any sensible person would say.

But I know it wasn't.

chapter thirty-one

June 22, 2019

There was a hand on my arm, rubbing gently.

You've gotta stop thinking so hard about what's real and what isn't, Jax.

I was afraid to open my eyes. Afraid that she'd disappear. Surely, I was dreaming again.

I opened my eyes and found my father looking down at me. "Hey, sleepyhead," he said. "You planning to get up today?"

I blinked at him. "What time is it?"

"Nearly two in the afternoon."

Pig was curled up at the foot of the bed.

I sat up, reached for my phone on the bedside table. He was right, though I had trouble believing it. I *never* slept in.

"Your aunt sent me up to make sure you hadn't escaped out the window or anything. You slept through breakfast." My father smiled. "I brought you coffee."

"Thanks," I said, reaching for the cup, taking a sip. Cream and four sugars—just how Lexie liked it. I preferred mine black. I sipped gratefully anyway.

My father took a seat on the edge of my bed. "Listen," he said. "I'm sorry about last night. Sorry for throwing you under the bus, not believing you."

"It's okay. I know how crazy it sounds."

"No crazier than cooking for your dead daughter," he said. "Maybe Diane's right. Being here isn't good for either one of us right now. The house . . . the pool. They mess with you. It's good that we're both out of here tomorrow."

I nodded, sipped at my overly sweet coffee.

"We've got sandwich stuff downstairs. Or I could make you some eggs if you want."

"A sandwich sounds great. I'll be down in a few minutes."

I went down and had lunch. Diane had a Scrabble board set up at the table. "I thought maybe we could play a game."

I smiled. "Sounds great."

We spent the afternoon playing Scrabble and drinking tea, my aunt watching me like a hawk the whole time. I felt like I was under house arrest.

"What would you like for dinner?" Diane asked, getting up to check the fridge. "We've got ground beef, some vegetables, stuff for salad."

"Doesn't matter," I said, flashing another agreeable smile. "Anything's fine with me." I stood up, stretched. "I think I'll go start packing. And maybe take a shower."

"Sounds good," Diane said. "Your father and I will figure out dinner."

Ted jumped up and started looking in the cabinets. "How about spaghetti? I make a terrific Bolognese sauce."

Upstairs, I looked at the boxes full of my sister's things. I felt unsettled. I couldn't just leave Sparrow Crest without knowing the truth.

I grabbed my purse and my phone from the bedside table. My phone was dead. No time to charge it now.

I went into the bathroom and turned the shower

on full blast, then snuck out of the bathroom, leaving the door closed and the shower running. Pig sat in the hall, washing his chest and giving me a *what are you up to now?* look. I crept down the stairs slowly, avoiding the ones that creaked. I could hear Diane and my father in the kitchen, talking, Ted asking for a grater.

"Some people chop the carrot, celery, and onion," he was saying. "But the key to a really fine sauce is to use a grater."

I slipped right past them and grabbed the keys to Lexie's car from the hook in the front hall. I opened the door as quietly as I could, then ran for the car, started the engine, and took off without looking in my rearview mirror to see if they'd heard me.

Nice getaway, Jax!

"Thanks," I said, turning to look at the passenger seat, but of course there was no one there.

I drove straight to the nursing home. I checked in at the front desk and told them who I was there to visit.

If Ryan wasn't going to confess, I'd try Shirley. How hard could it be to get her to tell me the truth?

"Oh, she's been waiting for you," the woman in scrubs said cheerfully.

"Has she?" My throat went dry. I nearly turned and ran back out to the parking lot.

"Yes, she skipped going down to dinner because she was afraid she might miss you."

I walked down the corridor to Shirley's room feeling like I was moving in slow motion. I had the terrible sense that I was walking right into a trap. But what harm could an old woman in a nursing home possibly do?

The door to her room was open and she was there, waiting at the little table, playing solitaire.

"What took you so long?" she asked when she saw me. She set the cards aside. "Don't just stand there, Jackie. Come in. Come in. Shut the door behind you."

Shirley had the table in her room laid out with cookies and juice, like we were two little girls about to have a tea party. "Sit down," she said.

I remained standing, arms crossed. "I know who you are," I said.

"Oh?" She reached for a sugar cookie and took a bite.

"You're the daughter of Benson Harding and Eliza Flemming." Shirley said nothing. She just kept chewing her cookie. "Your family believes the springs and the land belong to you. That your father hadn't been in his right mind when he lost it to my great-grandfather."

She nodded, set down the cookie, and dabbed at her lips with a napkin. "My father died a ruined man. That hotel and everything that happened there— it destroyed him financially, physically, emotionally. My grandparents felt we'd been wronged, yes. They were outraged."

My head was starting to hurt—a little jab behind my left eye that I knew would soon turn into a full corkscrew twist. Cool sweat began to form on my forehead. The room seemed impossibly bright.

"How far did you go to punish my family?"

"Punish them?"

My mind was whirring. "There was someone with my aunt Rita the night she died. My mother heard *two* voices. Was it you? Did you lure Rita into the water that night?"

"Me?" She looked pained. "Why on earth would I do such a thing?"

"To hurt my family. To get back at them. Did your grandparents put you up to it?"

"No, dear. You've got it all wrong."

The room seemed to waver. I squinted. My left eye was watering.

"What really happened to Lexie?"

Shirley sighed in frustration. "She discovered the truth. But she didn't listen to my warnings. She didn't understand how dangerous the situation was."

This was too much.

"The only *truth* she discovered was the story you carefully fed her."

"The stories I told her were all true. Just like what I've told you."

"I don't believe you." I struggled to keep my voice calm and level. The last thing I wanted was a bunch of nurses and aides busting in. "I think you talked Lexie into getting off her meds. You and Ryan and Terri filled her head with all the stories about the pool. I think you even hired someone to play the dark-haired woman from the pool."

She laughed, throwing back her head. "That sounds like an awful lot of work, dear."

"Was she the one who came sneaking into the house while Lexie was upstairs? Did you lure her out to the pool that last night? I don't want any more crazy stories. I just want the truth."

The old woman looked down at her hands, folded neatly on the table. She sighed, then looked up me.

"We were like sisters, your grandmother and I," she said. She went over to the shelves and pulled out the scrapbook again. "I would never, could never, do anything to harm her or anyone in her family. All I've ever done, ever tried to do, was to protect you all. Come sit," she said, patting the spot next to her, the book on her lap.

She opened it to a photo of a bunch of schoolgirls. "That's your grandmother, there," she said, pointing. "Second row, third to the left."

And there was my grandmother, impossibly young, with dark hair and eyes, smiling into the camera. Shirley had been right: My grandmother and I did look alike.

There were more photos of the two of them: in the pool, on horses, in a canoe on the lake, and Shirley holding a string of fish, my grandmother looking on, holding both their poles. They looked happy and young and reminded me of Lexie and myself adventuring around Sparrow Crest and Brandenburg.

Then Shirley flipped back toward the front of the book and held it open, waiting for me to see. It was the photo she'd shown me of the newly opened Brandenburg Springs Hotel. A small gathering of people stood out front—the employees of the hotel.

"I've already seen this," I told her, not even trying to hide my annoyance. This little trip into the past was getting us nowhere.

"But you're not really looking," she said. Now it was she who seemed impatient with me. "There's little me." She pointed at the baby.

I looked. There, front and center, were the Hardings, no doubt. Mr. Harding in a black tie and jacket, his dark hair slicked back, a tiny, well-groomed mustache, smiling into the camera. Beside him stood his wife, holding an infant, little Shirley. My breath stuck in my lungs, my blood felt cold, and my heart worked to push it through my veins.

"And that's your mother holding you? Eliza Harding?"

"Yes, dear," she said, looking right at me. "Eliza Flemming Harding."

I recognized her face, her eyes, the little scar under her eye. There was no doubt. "It's the same woman Lexie drew. The one who visited her at Sparrow Crest, swam with her in the pool. How can that be?"

"Haven't you figured it out yet?"

I shook my head in disbelief. There had to be a rational explanation. The woman Lexie had drawn was a descendant of the woman in the photograph—a secret sister or cousin of Ryan's? Or had Shirley shown Lexie this photograph, and Lexie simply imagined this woman back to life? That was the mostly likely explanation—she showed Lexie the photo, planting the idea that Eliza was still there, in the water. Found a dark-haired young woman to splash around in the pool, bringing the legend to life, providing proof that everything Shirley and Ryan had told Lexie about the pool was true.

The pain behind my eye intensified, traveled down my jaw, into my teeth, making my fillings ache and buzz.

Shirley spoke. "My mother died in the springs. She drowned. Anyone who dies in the springs, they become a part of the springs. My mother, your aunt Rita, your sister—they're all part of it now."

"Bullshit. I'm not Lexie. I won't be manipulated into believing something that's . . . impossible."

I heard a whooshing sound, my own blood traveling as my heartbeat quickened.

"The water gives and it takes," Shirley said, unmoved. "The springs saved your grandmother. Kept her alive. She was born with a heart defect—did you know that? She shouldn't have lived past her first birthday. But the springs gave her the gift of a long and healthy lifetime, of family. You wouldn't be here if it wasn't for that water."

She looked at me. "But then, she'd had enough. She chose to end her life, to sever her ties with the water once and for all."

I shook my head. Thought of my grandmother dying alone in a hotel room in Arizona. Remembered the postcard I got from her three days after I learned of her death. A Sedona landscape on the front and on the back just one line: *It's more beautiful here than I could have ever imagined.*

"She understood," Shirley went on, "better than anyone perhaps, that the water gives miracles, but it also takes in return. And each time it takes someone, it grows stronger. Do you understand?"

I said nothing. The whooshing sound was like water slapping, waves threatening to overtake me. I had a coppery, metallic taste in my mouth.

"The people who die in that water can come back," Shirley said. "When it's dark, they can come out of the pool, talk to you, walk around, touch you. Leave footprints. They have physical form. I've visited with my own mother many times. She said if I wanted, I could come, swim down, stay with her forever. But I had too much holding me to this world."

"Please," I said, backing away, closing my eyes, wanting to cover my ears. "No more."

Listening to her, it hit me that these weren't just stories Shirley made up to scare me and Lexie. She actually believed all of it. I was sure. The question was, how far did she go to make Lexie believe, too?

"Your sister is down there. You've seen her, haven't you?"

I shook my head, the pain sickening.

"Just be careful of her, Jackie. She's still Lexie, but she's doing the spring's bidding now."

"Enough!" I said, opening my eyes, glaring at her. "You actually expect me to believe that the pool is full of dead people?"

"Lexie believed."

"And look where it got her," I said.

"Lexie made one final wish to the pool. The thing she wanted most. Did she tell you? Do you know what she wished for?"

I turned and walked away, pushing my way through the air, which felt thick and heavy. The smells made my stomach flip—boiled vegetables from the dining hall, bleach, floor wax, the sour smell of old people. "I'm done with the stories," I said over my shoulder.

I hurried away as quickly as I could, nearly knocking over some poor old woman pushing a walker with tennis balls on the front legs. Out in the parking lot, I gulped at the fresh air, willing myself not to throw up. I got into the Mustang, locked the doors, slipped my sister's keys into the ignition, and slammed the car into reverse. My hands clenched the wheel as I navigated my way out of the parking lot, my left eye closed and watering. *Breathe*, I told myself. *She is just trying to scare you. Scare you like she scared Lexie.*

Are you so sure? I could see my sister out of the corner of my eye beside me in the passenger seat.

I turned and she was gone.

chapter thirty-two

Last week, I made a terrible mistake.

I took Maggie by train all the way to Boston, where my youngest sister, Constance, recently moved with her husband. Constance has been pestering me for some time about why we never visit her, how terrible it was that she rarely sees Maggie. "Her cousins barely know her!" she says.

And Maggie was so excited for the trip! She wanted to see the city. Go to the Public Garden and ride the swan boats with her cousins. Eat dinner in a restaurant. We planned to stay for three days. She had never left Brandenburg before. In fact, she rarely leaves Sparrow Crest. Will gives her lessons at home rather than sending her to school. The one-room schoolhouse here is fine, and we tried sending her there at first, but she seemed so tired, so pale, when she was away from home for long. She is excelling in all the subjects Will teaches her—science is her favorite. She plays the piano very well—we have a music teacher, Mrs. Tufts, who comes to give her lessons each Tuesday. Mrs. Tufts says Maggie is her most gifted student and that she should really be taking lessons at a proper music school.

In a strange twist of fate, Maggie has become close

friends with Shirley Harding, the child of Benson and Eliza. Shirley lives with her grandparents on the back side of Lord's Hill. She is a year older than Maggie and the spitting image of her mother. It unsettles me sometimes to see little Shirley playing in the rose garden her mother planted, swimming in the pool. And my Maggie, with her dark hair and eyes, looks so much like her. They could be sisters.

I packed two bottles of spring water for the trip to Boston. On the way there, Maggie was so excited—she'd never ridden a train before. She talked nonstop about all we would do and see. We went down to the dining car and had sandwiches and tea for lunch. "Isn't it funny, Mother, that we're moving so fast, and eating just like we'd eat at home, sitting still in our dining room?"

As soon as we arrived and settled in at my sister's house, Maggie went off with her cousins, to unpack her things in their room. Constance and I were in the kitchen with cups of tea, listening to the girls all laughing together. Not ten minutes later, Constance's girls came running into the kitchen. "Something's wrong with Maggie," they said.

Constance and I hurried in. Maggie's breathing had turned wheezy. Her fingertips began to turn blue.

"Whatever is the matter with her?" Constance asked, her face heavy with worry. "Is it asthma? Should we bring her to the hospital?"

"No," I said. I ran and got one of the bottles of water I'd packed from my suitcase. I had Maggie sip at the water.

"What is that you're giving her?" Constance asked, frowning.

She drank half a jar and her breathing did not improve. Her face grew paler.

"I need to take her home. Right now."

We caught the very next train back to Vermont. Maggie lay against me the whole way home, struggling for breath, shivering and frightened, so frightened. I stroked her hair, sang to her, apologized over and over. "We were wrong to leave Sparrow Crest," I told her. "We should not have traveled so far away." I gave her sips of water the whole ride back.

We arrived in Brandenburg late that evening. Will picked us up from the station, and we brought Maggie home, put her right in the water. "Isn't that better, my sweet girl," I said as I swam beside her, shivering. She is like a fish in the water, my girl. Such a strong swimmer. And the cold does not seem to bother her. She dunked under, took a mouthful of water and swallowed it down. Her breathing eased. The color came back to her fingers and toes. She splashed me, laughing. "Who needs swan boats when we have this," I told her. "The water in Boston Common is so dirty, not like our pool. Aren't we the lucky ones?"

———————

Today, Maggie asked if she might take the train to White River Junction tomorrow with Shirley and her family to visit relatives. "It would just be for the day," she said. "We'd be home by bedtime. Please? The train is such fun! Shirley's aunt and uncle have a farm, and they've got baby pigs and a foal that was just born!"

I stroked her hair. "I don't think so, little sparrow. I don't think leaving home is a good idea at all."

She made a sour face at me.

"You don't want to get sick, do you?"

Her face turned serious, worried. "No, Mama," she said, cuddling up beside me.

"Let's plan a special picnic tomorrow, out in the rose garden, just you and me."

She was a quiet a minute.

"Can we bring the teapot and good china cups?" she asked.

"Of course, my love." I pulled her tight against me, rocked her like I did when she was ever so little.

"We can put on fancy dresses," she said. "And make strawberry tarts."

"I think that sounds like a very good plan indeed," I told her. "We have all we need right here, don't we, my sparrow? Why would we ever want to leave?"

chapter thirty-three

June 22, 2019

Dad?" I called, using my key to open the locked front door to Sparrow Crest. "Diane?"

No answer.

"You here?" I called.

Diane's car wasn't in the driveway; the house was empty. The kitchen smelled amazing—I found a pot of sauce on the stove, still hot. The sink was full of dirty dishes: knives, grater, a cutting board. There were vegetable scraps on the counter.

My headache was firing up again. I opened the fridge, found a bottle of beer, cracked it open, and swallowed another one of Diane's pain pills from my purse. I sipped the beer as I walked from room to room, not sure what to do with myself. Upstairs, the bathroom door was open, the shower turned off. I wandered into my room, said hi to the Lexie painting.

Hi yourself, Jax.

I took my dead phone out of my purse and plugged it into the charger. Then I got my suitcase and started packing.

By the time I finished, my head was pounding, and Diane and Ted weren't back yet. Where were they? I thought of calling them, sending texts, but knew they'd be angry with me for sneaking off. I decided to put off that confrontation for a while longer. I looked over at the boxes, wondered if I should try to bring any of my sister's papers back home with me. I opened the boxes, started rummaging through, sorting. Another pile of photographs, another stack of journal entries. I pulled out the last one, read it.

> *June 14*
> *Weeks of research and still so much I don't know, don't understand. But maybe I'm not meant to. Maybe none of us are.*
>
> *One thing I'm sure of: the power of the pool. The pool gives miracles. Grants wishes, just like Gram always said it did. You just have to be prepared to pay a price.*
>
> *I went out tonight and made a wish. I wished for the thing I want most in this world.*
>
> *I wished to have Jax back.*
> *Back here at Sparrow Crest.*
> *The X girls, always and forever.*

The room got strangely dark, and I saw little lights in the corners of my vision. I worried I might pass out. I closed my eyes, held tight to my sister's journal page, to her words, to her wish.

"You got your wish," I said, my words a low whisper, my mouth tasting coppery and acrid, like the pool.

How cruel wishes can be.

I laid down on my bed, closed my tear-filled eyes, still clinging to my sister's journal entry.

I wished to have Jax back.

———————

I opened my eyes to discover that it was nearly dark. Reaching for my phone to see what time it was, I saw it was still dead.

It wasn't even plugged in anymore.

The house phone was ringing. I sat up, listened, wondering if my father and aunt had come back, waiting for one of them to pick up the phone. It stopped ringing. The house was silent. "Ted?" I called out. "Diane?"

I heard tapping on the other side of the wall.

I tapped back.

Then, realizing that the noise wasn't part of my dream, I bolted upright, raced down the hall to the room next door, Lexie's old room, where my father had been staying. The room was empty of course. Well, not quite empty. Pig was there, curled up in the center of the bed, purring.

"Did you do that, Pig?" A ridiculous question. He stared at me knowingly, eyes glowing in the dim light.

I sat down on the bed and scratched the cat behind his ears. There was the tapping on the wall again, this time from my room. I put my ear against the wall. Heard Lexie's voice come through it, muffled, but still clear.

"Ready or not, here I come."

I went back into my bedroom and I swore I could feel her there. Her image gazed back at me from the painting, taunting: *Catch me if you can*.

I walked out into the hall, listening for more taps, footsteps, anything.

And there *was* something, downstairs.

Someone was at the front door. I heard the knob rattle. The whole house was quiet, seemed to be holding its breath just as I was, waiting, listening. Suddenly, the door clicked open, and I heard footsteps in the entryway.

I shouted, "Lex?" down the stairs.

"Hello?" Aunt Diane called up. "You here, Jackie?"

Light-headed but relieved, I let out the breath I'd been holding. "Up here," I called, making my way down the hallway to the stairs. "Where were you guys?"

"Looking everywhere for you! We were worried sick," Diane said. "You snuck off without saying anything!"

My father added, "We've been all over town!"

"You weren't answering your phone. We were looking for a wrecked yellow car in all the ditches! We heard you went to see Shirley?"

I nodded. "I saw Shirley, then came right back here. My phone battery's been dead. I'm sorry if I worried you."

Diane stared at me. "Well, we're all here now, and I, for one, am starving. Let's go get that pasta on." She was already heading for the kitchen.

My father mumbled, "Good idea," and followed Diane. I joined them, my eyes bleary and my head aching. The codeine made the world seem dull, fuzzy. My father got down a big pot and brought it to the sink to fill with water. Diane flipped the light switch on the kitchen wall. Nothing happened. She tried it again, irritated. Click, click, click. "I thought you replaced all the light bulbs," she said, her tone accusatory.

"I did," I told her, checking the fixture over the sink. The bulbs were gone.

I got on a kitchen chair and checked the ceiling fixture and discovered the same thing. A very bad feeling wormed its way from my head down my spine, settling in my guts.

"They're gone," I said. "All the light bulbs have been taken out."

"Screw the teetotaling," Diane said. "I'm making a drink."

She opened a cabinet, grabbed the cocktail shaker, tequila, and triple sec. "Well, if they're gone, then let's put some new ones in." She was talking to me like I was a child.

My father set the pan on the stove, turned on the burner. The gas came on with a hiss and whoosh of flame.

I went to the closet where we'd stashed the three boxes of extra bulbs. They weren't there. My fingers searched, spider crawling all the way to the very back, but no light bulbs.

"Margarita, Jackie?" Diane asked.

I shook my head, stared dumbly at the empty shelves. "No thanks."

"Come on, Jax," my father said, getting a box of spaghetti down from the cupboard. "Let's all have a drink together."

"Three margaritas coming up," Diane said. "Now if I could just see what I was doing. Have you found the bulbs yet, Jackie?"

"No," I said, doing my best to keep my voice level and calm. "They're not here."

My father was humming a tune I vaguely recognized but couldn't name. I went out into the hall, tried the lights there. Nothing. The same was true in the living room. I went upstairs, discovered that all the light bulbs were missing there, too. The sun was down, and the house was grower darker by the minute.

When it's dark, they can come out of the pool.

I went back down to the kitchen; my aunt was

lighting candles and setting them on the table. She'd poured three margaritas. My father was sitting in a chair looking at his; he seemed agitated. Keyed up. He was still humming, drumming his fingers nervously on the table, casting furtive glances around the room. What was going on with him?

"All the light bulbs in the house are gone," I announced. "Someone must have come in and taken them."

"Who steals light bulbs?" Diane asked.

"I don't know," I said. *The thing in the pool. That's who.* My heart was pounding. Shirley's stories were getting to me.

"Well I know I sure as hell didn't take them," Diane said. "Ted, did you take the light bulbs?"

"Wasn't me," he said.

Diane looked at me. "You were here in the house alone."

"You think *I* took the light bulbs?" My voice came out angrier than I intended. My aunt stared at me, then shook her head. "I have no idea who took the goddamn light bulbs."

"What I *do* know," Diane said, settling in at the table and taking a sip of her drink, "is that we're all here, we're all in one piece, and dinner smells amazing. Come join us, Jackie. It's our last night together. It's a wonder we're not all locked up in the loony bin." She took a sip of her drink, then shook her head, muttered, "This fucking house."

I sat down at the table.

"Do you remember," my father asked, "when your mother and I would pick you up at the end of each summer, and we'd all take a walk, go on one last trip down to the store? The four of us?"

I nodded. "Of course."

"Lex, she was always way ahead of us, she couldn't wait to get there. Most times," he went on, "it was like we were chasing her. We could hardly keep up. The best we could do was to try to keep her in our sights."

He started to hum and drum his fingers on the table again. He was looking out the window above the sink, then at the door that was still bolted closed with metal plates.

Diane finished her drink and poured what was left in the shaker into her glass.

"She'd be off in this whole other realm, and we'd be two steps behind, doing our best to keep up. But we never could, could we?" my father said. "Not any of us."

I was crying, and when I looked at my father, I saw that he was, too. His eyes looked dark, the pupils seeming nearly as black as the irises. They shone in the flickering candlelight like two black pools. He was humming again, and this time I recognized the song. *I hear you knocking*.

The phone rang, impossibly loud. Diane looked at me, expectant. "Are you going to get that?"

I walked on jelly legs over to the big black phone and picked it up. "Hello?"

"I'm sorry," a small voice said. It sounded like my own, only much younger, and I had the strangest idea that my childhood self was calling. Me at ten, having just wished that Lexie wasn't always the special one.

Maybe my wish had come true after all. Maybe I'd put everything in motion that night: Lexie's illness, the way we'd grown apart, even her death.

"I shouldn't have done what I did," the little-me voice on the phone said.

"It's okay," I told her. "Everything's going to be okay."

But really, it wasn't. I wanted to tell my childhood self to hold on to her love for her sister, to not let anything petty screw up the bond they had.

I choked back a sob, felt tears prick my eyes, trickle down my cheeks.

"Who is it?" Diane asked, staring at me. "What's happened?"

I opened my mouth, not sure what I would say. Me?

"But I killed the fish," the voice at the other end said.

The fish.

Declan! I was talking to Declan.

"Declan, I'm so glad you called. How did you get this number?"

"You left it on our voice mail. I've been calling you."

The phone calls had been Declan. Of course. It wasn't messages from the spirit world or from some time-traveling version of my young self.

"I wanted to tell you about the fish. I tried telling the other lady, Karen, but she wouldn't listen."

"Okay," I said. "Tell me about the fish." I could feel my mode switch. I was the professional. I was in control here.

"They weren't who they said they were. They wouldn't stop talking to me. Telling me things. *Showing* me things."

"What kinds of things?"

I listened to the sound of his breathing, the static of the phone. But there was something else there: the sound of crinkling paper, of furious scribbling.

"Things I didn't want to see," he said.

I closed my eyes, trying to imagine what hideous scene he might be drawing: more nightmare fish? Me drowning, being pulled under?

"Who is on the phone, Jackie?" Diane asked, moving closer to me.

I covered the mouthpiece with my hand. "One of my clients," I told her.

She looked at me in disbelief. "How would they get this number?"

"Have you ever seen things you didn't want to see?" Declan asked.

Just then, out the window, I was sure I saw Lexie's face.

Lexie looking in at all of us, smiling.

"I—"

Diane snatched the receiver, put it to her ear. "Who's there?" she demanded. She shook her head. "There's no one there, Jackie. Just a dial tone." Her look said she thought I was crazy.

Maybe I was.

I checked the window again. There was no one there.

Maybe it had just been my own reflection.

I started walking backward. My heart was pounding. Every part of my body was telling me to run. To get out of there.

"Where are you going, Jax?" my father asked, standing up.

"To the Quick Stop. To get more light bulbs," I said. "It's so dark in here."

"It's nice and cozy with the candles." He reached out, wrapped his fingers around my wrist. They were cool, damp, tight as a vise. "Stay with us, Jax." His eyes flashed me a desperate look. *Don't go. Don't leave. Please. Not now.*

"Okay." I lowered myself back down into my seat. My father released my wrist but stayed standing. "To

Lexie," he said, raising his glass. "May we all one day catch up with her again."

Pig had come into the kitchen and was crouched about a foot away from the closed-off door, staring at it, yellow eyes glinting in the candlelight. His ears were back, and he was growling.

Diane put some cheese and crackers on a plate and brought it over to the table. My father walked over to the sink and looked out the window, toward the pool. I could see the reflection of the candlelit room, of my father's frown turning into a wide smile. "She's out there," he said. "I see her."

I knew I should stand, should go and look, but I felt too afraid to move. It's Ryan, my logical mind told me. Ryan or maybe Terri. They're just fucking with us. Trying to scare us.

But then I pictured what I'd just seen: Lexie's face in the widow, smiling in at us.

Why don't you all come out and join me for a swim?

My father turned to us and said, "It's her! She's here! She said she'd come. She promised." He turned, looked right at me. "She came back for you!"

She was my wish.

And I was hers.

I shook my head. It wasn't possible.

He started walking, practically running, out of the kitchen.

"Ted, wait!" Diane jumped up, started following him out of the kitchen at a steady clip. Their footsteps echoed down the hall.

"No," I yelped, getting up to follow them.

"Ted!" Diane called. "Be reasonable."

I heard the dead bolt on the front door click as he

opened it. "You'll see," my father said again. "It's her. She's here. She's here!"

He flung open the door and stepped out. Diane and I followed him into the cool night. The air was still, the sky scattered with clouds that filtered the light from the stars and moon.

The gate gave a loud rusty screech as my father pushed it open, called her name. "Lexie!"

I followed.

The pool smelled dank, rotten.

"There's no one here," Diane said. "Let's go back inside, Ted. Please."

In the dim blue light, I could make out the flat surface of the water, the rough shapes of chairs on the patio like hunched-over figures lying in wait. I looked back into the house, saw the candles flickering through the kitchen windows, casting strange, dancing shadows.

"She's in the water," my father said, looking down longingly. "It's Lexie. Don't you see her? I told you!" He grinned so wide his teeth glowed.

Then he jumped into the water. I saw only ripples as the pool took him.

"Ted!" I screamed, running forward like it was still somehow possible to stop him.

Then he surfaced, gasping, "She's down there. In the water!"

"Get out of there," I said, reaching a hand out. He swam away from me. "You've gotta see this!" he said. "Come into the water, Jax! She wants you to come into the water!"

Then he took a deep breath and dove back under.

"Ted!" I yelled. Only bubbles surfaced.

"We've got to help him," Diane said, moving to the edge, ready to jump in. "He's out of his mind! He'll drown!"

I kicked off my shoes. "I'll get him. You wait here."

I dove in.

The water was as painfully cold as ever. Stung every inch of my skin and made my muscles feel frozen and slow. Moving was difficult.

Open your eyes, Jax.

What had Lexie seen her last time in the water? Who had brought her out to the pool?

Eliza?

Rita?

Martha?

Or was it simply the promise that maybe she'd get her wish? That I'd return to her, return to this place.

I'm here, I thought, water numbing me, washing everything else away. *Lexie, I'm here.*

I struggled to see anything in the dark water.

Just like that I was ten years old again. My fingers grew numb. My heart pounded.

I swam deeper down, reaching, and touched something, an arm or leg—*Ted, please God, let it be Ted.* I grabbed hold and struggled to get back up to the surface. Please let this not be little Rita, face pale and bloated.

"Your sister's down there," Ted said once our heads were above the water. "I saw her!"

There's nothing in that water but what we bring with us.

I dragged Ted to the edge; he was choking.

"Out of the pool," I ordered. He scrambled at the slippery edge. I pushed him as I treaded water. Diane took his hand and, together, we hoisted my father out of the pool. Once out, he crouched along the edge, shivering and coughing.

"It *was* her," he said. "I saw her face!"

I put my hands on the edge, but it was so slick, I couldn't get a good grip.

Something brushed against my leg and I screamed.

Frantic, heart pounding, I got my forearms over the edge, planted my hands, and began to push myself up. Then I felt fingers wrap around my legs like tentacles. I thought of Declan's drawing, had this absurd sense that I'd slipped inside it.

"Ted!" I called, reaching for him, but it was too late. I slid backward into the water, sucking in a deep breath of air before going under.

I was being pulled down to the other side of the world.

My sister looked back at me. Not some imaginary version. Not a re-creation born of denial. My sister.

Somehow, despite the darkness of the water, I could see her clearly and perfectly. I knew my sister's body better than my own. There was her appendectomy scar. Her muscular swimmer's torso. Her long eyelashes, looking longer still when wet. She let go of my leg, reached for my hand. I felt her fingers entwine through my own and suddenly, we were kids again, floating, playing the Dead Game. Gram was in the house watching her programs, and Lex and I were holding our breaths as long as we could.

Open your eyes. The dead have nothing to fear.

Behind us, back on land, I felt the shadow of Sparrow Crest looming, our favorite place on earth, the house we were going to live in together when we grew up.

Jax and Lex. The X girls. Forever.

I'm sorry, I thought, wishing I could say the words out loud, but feeling she heard them anyway. *So, so sorry.*

And I *was* sorry. Sorry I'd made that stupid wish all those years ago. Sorry I'd never been able to really help her, to fix her or save her. Sorry I'd moved across the country to get away from her. Sorry I'd shut her out after Gram died. Sorry I hadn't picked up the phone that last night.

Lexie's fingers wrapped tightly around mine. She was as cold as the water, a girl made of ice.

She pulled me down, deeper, deeper, the water as black as the night sky.

And I made out pinpricks of light—some bright, some dim. They looked like the day Lexie took me to outer space in her cardboard rocket and held the flashlight, created her very own galaxy, making the stars spin across the ceiling, just as the stars were dancing now.

Only these weren't stars—I saw that now as I got closer. The lights were people.

Each person emitted a greenish white glow like they had night-lights inside them, something to keep the darkness away.

Lexie kept her hand clamped around mine and was taking me deeper, toward them.

Isn't this wonderful, Jax? she said. No one could speak underwater. But still, I heard her. It was my sister's voice. *We're actually going to do it! Get to the other side of the world.*

My lungs were screaming for air. I fought the urge to open my mouth, take a desperate gulp of water. My vision narrowed.

It was cold. So cold.

I fought against her, tried to pull away, but it was useless.

Lexie held tight to my hand. Kept pulling me down. Down, down, down.

Who are all these people? I asked her in my mind, looking at the faces we passed.

But I knew the answer. I recognized some of them. There was little Rita, seven years old, our dead little aunt whose books we read, whose games we played.

Nelson DeWitt, who bottled water from the springs. Eliza Harding, Ryan's great-grandmother. Martha Woodcock, the little girl who drowned at the hotel and made friends with Rita. And others I didn't recognize but who must have drowned in the springs. So many people, swirling around us, dancing lights in the darkness. And I knew, as I floated down with them, that what Shirley had said was true, they were the source of the water's strength.

Stay, they seemed to say. *Stay down here with us. Make us stronger.*

I thought of my father, of Diane, of my life in Tacoma, my friends. I thought of Lexie's cat, Pig. I thought of Declan, of all the kids I'd helped and needed to go on helping.

I can't stay. I don't belong here.

I fought harder against Lexie, tried to swim back up, up to the land of the living, but my movements were so slow, so weak. And Lexie was so strong.

I didn't feel cold anymore.

On the contrary, I felt a new warmth radiating from my chest out to my arms and legs. I looked down and saw that I, too, had begun to glow.

Don't you see? Lexie said. *Both of our wishes can come true.*

That's when I felt it. Hands on the back of my shirt, tugging, jerking, trying to pull me up, away from the lights. Away from Lexie.

Lexie held out her hand, pointer finger up. I crossed it with my own.

Me and you, Jax. Jax and Lex. The X girls, always and forever.

I closed my eyes, felt myself being pulled away from her, up out of the water.

I was sorry to go.

"I've got her!" my father shouted as we reached the surface, as he pulled me from the water.

chapter thirty-four

June 26, 1972
Sparrow Crest

Time is a funny thing, moving so fast and so slowly. Will has been gone for so many years; my life with him feels like a dream I had. Sometimes, I look at my life the way I flip through a photograph album. Will and I at the hotel, standing on the balcony, his arm around me. Little Maggie learning to sew, making her first cross-stitch that turned out so well, we hung it in the front hall: *To err is human, to forgive, divine.* Back before she met Stephen—who gave her three healthy girls, each perfect and beautiful. How I love the children! Careening through this house, bringing it to life with their chatter and giggles.

I hear what Maggie and Stephen tell them about me: *She's going senile. Don't listen to Grandma. She doesn't know what she's saying.*

Maybe I am going senile. Maybe I don't know what's real and what isn't anymore. The other afternoon, I was sitting by the pool reading my old diary. I had the strangest idea then that what was contained in those pages wasn't meant to ever be found. That the story of the pool and the springs belonged to the water itself. So I tossed the book into the pool. My oldest granddaughter, Linda, screamed, dove down, and got it as it was sinking. "What'd you do that for?" she asked, holding the waterlogged book up. "Look, now it's all ruined!" She flipped through the pages, saw the running and washed-away ink. "You can't even read it now."

Just as well.

Later, at dinner, there was much talk about how I got confused and threw my book into the pool. They all shook their heads, clucked their tongues. I said nothing. Let them think what they will.

Rita, the youngest, is most like my Maggie. Dark hair and eyes. Otherworldly. She slips up the attic steps into my room and crawls into bed with me at night, asks me to tell her stories, to braid her hair. The stories she loves most are about her mother when she was just a little girl. "I called her 'little sparrow' because when she was born, she looked like a little bird," I tell Rita.

And sometimes, Rita tells me stories. She came to me last week, telling me all about her friend Martha who lives at the bottom of the pool.

"She says she's lonely," Rita told me. "She likes it when I come to play."

"Stay away from her," I said, my voice stern. "Stay away from the pool."

But no one listens to me.

I tried to protect her. I did. I took out the needle I keep hidden in my mattress and scratched a little *R* into my thigh. My skin is so thin, fragile as trace paper. It bled and bled.

———

I heard howling this morning, Maggie's desperate wailing just after dawn. I heard and I knew what had happened. And the knowing split me open inside. I can no longer get down the stairs on my own. So I waited for them to tell me the terrible news, tell me what I already knew.

Maggie came upstairs hours later, after the sirens came and went, after the loud voices and footsteps of strangers left the house. Her dark hair was unkempt. She was still in her robe and nightgown, even though it was afternoon. Her eyes were black and wild.

"It's happened," she said, her voice sharp as a knife, her eyes swollen from crying. "What you warned me about. Accidental drowning, they say. But you and I, we know different, don't we?" Maggie was sobbing, her whole body shaking.

I nodded.

"And do you know who I blame, Mother? Who I feel is truly at fault?"

I opened my mouth to say that we don't know its true name, this thing that we have carefully balanced our lives around. It has many faces, some familiar. But whatever is behind it all, we have never known what to call it. Maybe the power isn't singular, but a thing of many. Maybe the water *is* the spirits in it; a collective being of shared yearnings and hungers.

"You," Maggie said. "You are to blame."

She stared at me then with such loathing, such hatred, I felt my heart seize, shatter in my chest as if it were made of glass.

"If you had never come to this place, if you had let me die when I was an infant . . ." Her voice trailed off, lost to sobs.

I promised my delicate little sparrow the world. And in all the years that followed, I tried to give it to her. I reached for her, my beloved, my angel, the little girl I had wished to life. I touched her face before she flinched, pulled away as if she'd been burned.

"Miracles are not without their price, my darling," I said.

epilogue

June 5, 2020

S orry we're late," Diane said, setting the two bottles of wine she was carrying on the counter. "Terri's appointment ran over."

Ryan was standing in front of the stove in the kitchen sautéing garlic and onions. Jazz played softly from Lexie's old turntable in the living room. Candles glowed and flickered around the room.

Pig was curled up on one of the kitchen chairs, keeping his eye on us, on me in particular.

"How'd it go?" Ryan asked, stepping away from the stove to give his mother a hug and kiss on the cheek.

"Great," Terri said. "He says to keep doing what I'm doing and not change a thing."

"*And* he agrees that a month in Spain is a wonderful idea," Diane added, stepping up behind Terri and wrapping her arms around her. "I think he was a little jealous that we didn't invite him along."

"I'm a little jealous you didn't invite *me* along," Ryan teased.

Diane and Terri looked so happy together. I was thrilled they were going to Spain and loved listening to them plan their itinerary and practice the Spanish they'd been learning. *Viajo a España con mi amada.*

"Smells amazing," Diane said, peering into the pot Ryan was stirring.

Friday dinners at Sparrow Crest had become a tradition over the last few months. Sometimes, when she was up to it, Shirley joined in. My father and Vanessa had come up from Florida to stay a couple of times and planned on a longer trip this fall. They'd gotten married, of all the crazy things, and adopted a one-eyed pug to go with their one-eyed cat.

Ryan got down glasses while Diane opened the wine. She poured everyone a glass, then settled in at the table, leaning in to whisper something that made Terri blush. I glanced out the window, through my own reflection, at the pool. It shimmered there in the darkness, beautiful and waiting.

Dinner, as usual, was perfect. Diane and Terri went upstairs to bed a little after eleven, and Ryan stayed until midnight, cleaning up.

Then I stood in the hallway, watching him pull out of the long driveway.

I always felt a stab of regret when I saw his taillights move down the street, toward town and his well-lit house, his alarm clock waiting to wake him at five to get to the bakery.

I went to my room in the dark, knowing the way by heart. Moonlight filtered in through the windows. I looked at the Lexie painting that hung on the wall above the dresser. The pool and Lexie. Each reflected in each other so perfectly. Together they went on into infinity. I laid down on top of the covers, listening to the house breathe and shift and settle around me.

My great-grandparents built this house to keep their little girl alive. They would have sacrificed anything, gone to any lengths, to keep her with them.

They made a pact with the springs to keep her safe. Gram's whole life revolved around Sparrow Crest and the pool. She was trapped, yes, but she must have been so grateful for all she had. And heartbroken by all that had been taken. Heartbroken enough to walk away knowing it would kill her.

Me, I was too heartbroken to walk away at all.

———————

I tapped on the bedroom wall. *You and me, Jax, we're like twins. Yin and yang. One can't exist without the other.*

She tapped back. Once, twice, three times.

I heard her bedroom door creak open and footsteps in the hall.

I closed my eyes. Listened as my door opened and she walked into my room, stood above my bed. I could hear her breathing. Smell the tang of minerals, the dampness, that green primordial scent. She smelled like wishes. Like birth and death. Like possibility.

"Open your eyes," Lexie said. "The dead have nothing to fear."

But she was wrong. There was a lot I feared. Most of all, these moments, when she'd come to fetch me, to pull me out of the land of the living and back into the pool. I was just an imposter here. I could only come out of the water at night, in the dark. Sometimes they could see me—Shirley always did, though she wouldn't speak to me in front of the others. Diane saw me occasionally, I was sure of it—but always pretended she didn't.

Whether they saw me or not, I always, always pretended I was still one of them.

The night I drowned, I realized that Lexie was right—we both got our wishes.

She wished to have me back. I wished to have her back.

The X girls, always and forever.

I opened my eyes, took her hand.

And together we walked out of my room, down the steps, through the front hall, past the cross-stitch—*To err is human, to forgive, divine*—and out to the pool.

We slipped into the black water.

Two dead girls, side by side.

Alone, but together.

acknowledgments

Huge thanks to my agent, Dan Lazar, who cheers me on and believes in me and my stories, and is always there with helpful feedback and guidance—this book would not exist without him. To Allison McCabe, who helped shape an early draft (and suggested I put a cat in it!). To Sara Baker, who told me a story about haunted springs that thoroughly creeped me out and helped inspire this story. To Kate Dresser and the whole team at Scout Press—I'm so thrilled and grateful to be working with you all! And to Drea and Zella, for riding the book roller coaster with me once more—I love you both!

Turn the page for a sneak peek of
Jennifer McMahon's next novel,

THE CHILDREN ON THE HILL

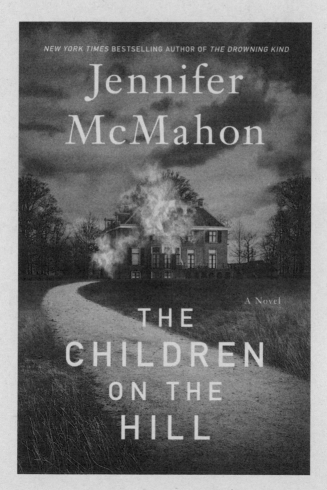

NEW YORK TIMES BESTSELLING AUTHOR OF *THE DROWNING KIND*

Jennifer
McMahon

A Novel

THE
CHILDREN
ON THE
HILL

the monster

August 15, 2019

Her smell sends me tumbling back through time to *before*.

Before I knew the truth.

It's intoxicating, this girl's scent. She smells sweet with just a touch of something tangy and sharp, like a penny held on your tongue.

I can smell the grape slushy she had this afternoon, the cigarettes she's been sneaking, the faint trace of last night's vodka (pilfered from her daddy's secret bottle kept down in the boathouse—I've watched them both sneak out to take sips from it).

She smells dangerous and alive.

And I love her walk—the way each step is a bounce like she's got springs at the bottoms of her feet. Like if she bounces high enough, she'll go all the way up to the moon.

The moon.

Don't look at the moon, full and swollen, big and bright.

Wrong monster. I am no werewolf.

Though I tried to be once.

Not long after my sister and I saw *The Wolf Man* together, we found a book on werewolves with a spell in it for turning into one.

"I think we should do it," my sister said.

"No way," I told her.

"Don't you want to know what it feels like to change?" she asked.

We sneaked out into the woods at midnight, did a spell under the full moon, cut our thumbs, drank a potion, burned a candle, and she was right—it was an exquisite thrill, imagining that we were turning into something so much more than ourselves. We ran naked and howling through the trees, pretending ferns were wolfsbane and eating them up.

We thought we might become the real thing, not like Lon Chaney Jr., with the wigs and rubber snout and yak hair glued to his face (my sister and I read that in a book too—"poor yaks," we said, giggling, guffawing about how bad that hair must have smelled). When nothing happened that night, we were so disappointed. When we didn't sprout fur and fangs or lose our minds at the sight of the moon. When we went back home and swore to never speak of what we'd done as we pulled on our pajamas and crawled into our beds, still human girls.

"Can you guess what I am?" I ask the girl now. I don't mean to. The words just come shooting out like sparks popping up from a fire.

"Uh," she says, looking at me all strange. "I don't know. A ghost? Someone who was once a human bean?" And that's just how she says it. Bean. Like we're all just baked beans in a pot, or maybe bright multicolored jelly beans, each a different flavor.

I'd be licorice. The black ones that get left at the bottom of the bag. The ones no one can stand the taste of.

I shift from one foot to the other, bits of my disguise

clanking, rattling, the hair from the tangled wig I wear falling into my eyes.

I love this girl so much right now. All that she is. All that I will never be. All that I can never have.

And mostly, what I love is knowing what's coming next: knowing that I will change her as I've changed so many others.

I am going to *save* this girl.

"When do I get my wish?" she asks now.

"Soon," I say, smiling.

I am a giver of wishes.

A miracle worker.

I can give this girl what she most desires, but she isn't even aware of her own desires.

I can't wait to show her.

"So, do you want to play a game or something?" she asks.

"Yes," I say, practically shouting. *Yes, oh yes, oh yes!* This is my favorite question, my favorite thing! I know games. I play them well.

"Truth or dare?" she asks.

"If you wish. But I have to warn you, I'll know if you're lying."

She shrugs, tugs at her triple-pierced right earlobe, squints at me through all her layers of black goth makeup; a good girl trying so hard to look bad. "Nah. Let's play tag," she says, and this surprises me. She seems too old for such games. "My house is safety. You're it." She slaps my arm so hard it stings, already running.

I laugh. I can't help it. It's nerves. It's the thrill. There's no way this girl, with her stick-thin legs and cigarette smoke–choked lungs, can outrun me.

I am strong. I am fast. I have trained my whole life for these moments.

I'm running, running, running, chasing this beautiful girl in the black hoodie, her blond hair with bright-purple tips flying out behind her like a flag from a country no one's ever heard of. A girl so full of possibility, and she doesn't even know it. She's running, she's squealing, thinking she's going to make it back to safety, back to the bright lights of her little cabin that are just now coming into view through the trees (only bright because of the low hum of the generator out back, no power lines way out here). Thinking she's actually going to make it home, back to her parents (whom she hates) and her warm bed with the flannel sheets, back to her old dog, Dusty, who growls whenever he catches my scent—he knows what I am.

I have weeds woven into my hair. I am covered in a dress of bones, sticks, cattail stalks, old fishing line and bobbers. I am my own wind chime, rattling as I run. I smell like the lake, like rot and ruin and damp forgotten things.

I can easily overtake this girl. But I let her stay ahead. I let her hold on to the fantasy of returning to her old life. I watch her silhouette bounding through the trees, flying, floating.

And just like that, I'm a kid again, chasing my sister, pretending to be some movie monster (I'm the Wolf Man, I'm Dracula, I'm the Phantom of the motherfucking Opera) but I was never fast enough to catch her.

But I'm going to catch this girl now.

And I'm a real monster now. Not just pretend.

I'm going to catch this girl now because I never could catch my sister.

Here it is, forty years later, and still it's always her I'm chasing.

vi

May 8, 1978

The building was haunted, Vi thought as she ran across the huge expanse of green lawn to the Inn. How could it not be? If she squinted just right, it could be an old mansion or castle, something from a black-and-white movie where Dracula might live. But the Inn was made from dull yellow bricks, not craggy stone. There were no turrets or battlements, no drawbridge. No bats flying out of a belfry. Only the large rectangular building with the old slate roof, the heavy glass windows with black shutters that no one ever actually closed.

Vi stepped into the shadow the building made, could feel it wrap its arms around her, welcome her, as she hopped up the granite steps. Above the front doors was a carved wooden sign made by a long-ago patient: HOPE. Vi whispered the secret password to the monster castle, which was *EPOH*—the word spelled backward.

Vi held tight to the plate in her hands, not a flimsy paper plate but one from their cupboards with the bright sunflower pattern that matched the kitchen curtains and tablecloth. She'd fixed Gran lunch— a liverwurst sandwich on rye bread. Vi thought liverwurst was gross, but it was Gran's favorite. Vi had put on extra mustard because she told herself it wasn't just mustard, it was a special monster-repelling potion, something to keep Gran safe, to keep the werewolves and vampires at bay. She'd centered the sandwich on the plate, put a pickle and some chips on the side, and covered it all up with plastic wrap to stay fresh. She knew Gran would be pleased, would coo about what a thoughtful girl Vi was.

Holding the sandwich in one hand, Vi pushed open the door with the other and entered the reception area, which they called the Common Room, with a tiled floor, throw rugs, a fireplace, and two comfortable couches. The first floor was the heart of the Inn. From the Common Room, hallways jutted to the right and left and the staircase was straight ahead. Down the hallway to the right were staff offices and the Oak Room at the end of the hall, where they held meetings. The left wing held the Day Room, where activities took place and the television was always on; the Quiet Room, full of books and art supplies; and, at the end of the hall, the Dining Room and kitchen. The patients took turns working shifts in the kitchen: mashing potatoes, scrubbing pots and pans, and serving their fellow residents at mealtime.

The second floor was what Gran and the staff referred to as "the suites"—the patient rooms. Divided into two units, 2 East and 2 West, were a total of twenty single rooms, ten on each unit, along with a station in the middle for the nurses and staff.

The door to the basement was just to the left of the main staircase leading to the second floor. Vi had never been in the basement. It was where the boiler and mechanical rooms were. Gran said it was used for storage and not fit for much else.

On the wall to her left hung the latest portrait of all the staff standing in front of the old yellow building, Gran right in the middle, a tiny woman in a blue pantsuit who was the center of it all: the sun in the galaxy that was the Hillside Inn.

The window between the Common Room and the main office slid open.

"Good afternoon, Miss Evelyn," Vi said, chipper and cheerful, her voice a bouncing ball. Children were not allowed in the Inn. Vi and her brother, Eric, were the only occasional exceptions, and only if they could get past Miss Ev.

Evelyn Booker was about six feet tall with the build of a linebacker. She wore a curly auburn wig that was often slightly askew. Vi and Eric called her Miss Evil.

Vi looked at her now, wondered what kind of monster she might be and if the mustard potion would work on her too.

Miss Ev frowned at Vi through the open window, her thickly penciled eyebrows nearly meeting in the middle of her forehead.

Shapeshifter, thought Vi. *Definitely shapeshifter*.

"Dr. Hildreth is dealing with an emergency," she said, as a cloud of cigarette smoke escaped out her window.

"I know," Vi said. It was Saturday, one of Gran's days off, but Dr. Hutchins had called, and Gran had spent several minutes on the phone sounding like she was trying to calm him down. At last she'd said she'd be right over and would handle things herself.

"But she ran out so fast she didn't get a chance to eat breakfast or make herself a lunch. So I thought I'd bring her a sandwich." Vi smiled at Miss Ev. Gran was often so busy she forgot to eat, and Vi worried about her—always putting the Inn first and thinking she could survive all day on stale coffee and cigarettes.

"Leave it here and I'll see that she gets it." Miss Ev eyed the plate with the sandwich suspiciously. Vi tried to shake off the disappointment of not being able to hand Gran the plate herself. She smiled and passed it through the window.

Tom with the wild long hair came sauntering into the Common Room and called out to her, "Violets are blue, how are you?" He was one of the patients on what Gran called the revolving-door policy; he'd been in and out of the Inn for as long as Vi could remember.

"I'm good, Tom," Vi said cheerfully. "How are you doing today?"

"Oh, I'm itchy," he said, starting to rub his arms, to scratch. "So, so itchy." He peeled off his shirt, panting a little as he scratched his skin, which was covered with a thick pelt of black fur.

Werewolf, thought Vi. No question.

Tom threw his shirt to the floor, started unbuckling his pants.

"Whoa, there," said Sal, one of the orderlies, whose neck was as thick as Vi's waist. "Let's keep our clothes on. We don't want to get Miss Ev all excited."

Miss Ev frowned and slammed the little glass window closed.

Vi smiled, said her goodbyes, and headed out of the Inn as Tom continued to yelp about how very itchy he was. She heard Sal telling him that he couldn't have a cookie from the kitchen if he didn't keep his clothes on.

Werewolf or not, Vi liked Tom. Gran had brought him home a few times and he and Vi had played checkers.

"Gran's strays," Vi and Eric called them—the patients Gran brought home. People not quite ready to be released back into the real world. Some deemed lost causes by the other staff at the Inn.

Gran had once brought home a man with scars all around his head who had no short-term memory—you had to keep introducing yourself to him over and over and reminding him that he'd already had breakfast. "Who are you?" he asked with alarm each time he saw Vi. "Still just Violet," she'd said.

Mary D., a woman with curly orange hair, told the children she'd been reincarnated almost a hundred times and had vivid memories of every life and death. (*I was Joan of Arc—can you imagine the pain of being burned at the stake, children?*)

And then there was the silent, disheveled woman with sunken eyes who burst into sobs every time the children spoke to her. Eric and Vi called her simply the Weeping Woman.

Sometimes the visitors came back to the house just for a meal or to spend a night or two. Sometimes they stayed for weeks, sleeping in the guest room, rattling around like ghosts in hospital pajamas, spending hours talking with Gran in the basement, where she tested their memories, their cognitive abilities, and tried to cure them. She poured them tea, played cards with them, sat them down in the wing chairs in the living room and had Vi and Eric bring them plates of cookies and speak to them politely.

How do you do? Very pleased to meet you.

"A hospital, even a fine place like the Inn, it's not exactly a nurturing environment. Sometimes, to get better, people need to feel like they're at home," Gran explained. "They need to be treated like family to get well." Gran was like that; there was nothing she wouldn't do to help her patients get well, to help them feel taken care of.

Vi and her brother were fascinated by the strays. Eric took photographs of each one with his Polaroid camera. He did it secretly, when Gran wasn't around. They kept the photos in a shoebox hidden way at the back of Eric's closet. Paper-clipped to each picture were index cards that Vi had written notes on—a name or nickname, any details they'd picked up. Vi and Eric called the shoebox "the files." The cards said things like:

> *Mary D. has orange hair, which suits her because her favorite thing is toast with marmalade. She says she ate marmalade all the time back when she was Anne Boleyn, married to King Henry. Before her head was chopped off.*

The shoebox also had a little notebook full of details they'd gleaned about Gran's other patients, the ones they never saw but only heard about; things Vi and Eric had overheard Gran discussing on the phone with Dr. Hutchins, the other psychiatrist at the Inn, when he came over to sample Gran's latest batch of gin. When Gran and Dr. Hutchins talked about the patients, they always used initials. Vi liked to flip through the notebook from time to time, to try to figure out if any of Gran's strays were people she'd heard them talking about.

———

Just last week, she had eavesdropped on Gran and Dr. Hutchins while they sat sipping gin and tonics on the little stone patio in their backyard. Vi was crouched down, spying on them around the corner of the house.

"Batch 179," Gran said. "I think the juniper's a bit overpowering, wouldn't you agree?"

"I think it's delicious," Dr. Hutchins said, which was what he said each time he tried a new batch of Gran's homemade gin. Vi guessed that the poor man probably didn't even like gin. More than once, she'd caught him surreptitiously dumping the contents of his glass in the flower beds when Gran wasn't looking.

Dr. Hutchins seemed more nervous than the patients. He had a long thin neck, a small head, and thinning hair that sprang up in funny tufts. Vi thought he looked a little like an ostrich.

They'd talked about the weather, and then about flowers, and then they started discussing the patients. Vi got out her notebook.

"D.M. has had a rough week," Dr. Hutchins said. "She lashed out at Sonny today during group. Took three men to restrain her."

Sonny was one of the social workers. He did art therapy and helped in the clay studio. He was a nice man with a huge mustache and bushy sideburns. He sometimes let Vi and Eric make stuff in the ceramics studio: little pots, mugs, and ashtrays.

Gran rattled the ice in her glass. She poured another gin and tonic from the pitcher on the table between them.

"And there was the episode between her and H.G. on Wednesday," he continued.

"She was provoked," Gran responded, lighting a cigarette with her gold Zippo lighter with the butterfly etching on it. The other side had her initials engraved in flowing script: *HEH*. Vi heard the scratch of the flint, smelled the lighter fluid. Gran said smoking was a bad habit, one Vi should never start, but Vi loved the smell of cigarette smoke and lighter fluid, and most of all she loved Gran's old butterfly lighter that needed to be filled with fluid and to have the flint changed periodically.

"She's dangerous," Dr. Hutchins said. "I know you feel she's making progress, but the staff are starting to question whether the Inn is the best place for her."

"The Inn is the *only* place for her," Gran snapped. She took a drag of her cigarette, watched the smoke rise as she exhaled. "We'll have to increase her Thorazine."

"But if she continues to be a danger to others—"

"Isn't that what we do, Thad? Help those no one else can?"

Yes, Vi thought. *Yes!* Gran was a miracle worker. A genius. She was famous for helping patients others couldn't help.

Dr. Hutchins lit his own cigarette. They were quiet a moment.

"And what about Patient S?" Dr. Hutchins asked. "Things still progressing in a positive way?"

Vi finished up her notes on D.M. and started a new page for Patient S.

"Oh yes," Gran said. "She's doing very well indeed."

"And the medications?" Dr. Hutchins asked.

"I've been drawing back on them a bit."

"Any hallucinations?"

"I don't believe so. None that she'll admit to or is aware of."

"It's amazing, isn't it?" Dr. Hutchins said. "The progress she's made? You should be very proud of yourself. You've given her exactly what she needs. You've saved her."

Gran laughed. "Saved? Perhaps. But I'm starting to think she may never lead a normal life. Not after all she's been through. She'll have to be watched. And if the authorities or the papers ever . . ."

"Do you think she remembers?" he asked. "What she did? Where she came from?"

The hairs on Vi's arms stood up the way they did during a bad storm.

"No," Gran said. "And honestly, I believe that's for the best, don't you?"

They both sipped their drinks, ice cubes rattling. Their cigarette smoke drifted up into the clouds.

Vi listened hard, wrote: *WHAT DID PATIENT S DO? Murder someone???*

She knew the Inn had violent patients, people who had done terrible things not because they were terrible people, but because they were sick. That's what Gran said.

But was an actual murderer there? Someone Gran was protecting, keeping safe?

She scribbled *WHO IS PATIENT S???* in big letters in her notebook.

———————

Vi thought about Patient S now as she walked back across the lawn and drive to their big white house, directly across the road from the Inn. "Who is Patient S?" she asked out loud, then listened for an answer. Sometimes, if she asked the right question at the right time, God would answer.

When God spoke to Vi, it was like a dream. A whispered voice, half-remembered.

When God spoke, he sometimes sounded just like Neil Diamond on Gran's records:

I am, I said.

And Vi pictured him up there, watching her, dressed in his tight beaded denim suit like the one Neil Diamond wore on the live double album Gran loved to play—*Hot August Night*. God's hair was wild as a lion's. His chest hair poked out through the V of his jacket.

There were other gods too. Other voices.

Gods of small things.

Of mice and toasters.

God of tadpoles. Of coffee perkers that whispered a special hello to her each morning in a bright bubbling voice: *Good morning, Starshine. Pour a little cup of me. Take a sip. Gran says you're old enough now. Take a sip of me, and I'll tell you more.*

But today, so far at least, the gods were silent. Vi heard birds and the slow drone of bees gathering nectar from early blossoms.

It was a bright, sunny spring day, and Vi settled in on the porch swing, reading one of Gran's books—*Frankenstein*. Each time she went into Gran's gigantic library or the little brick Fayeville Public Library in town, Vi let the God of Books help her choose what she'd read next. He spoke in a thin, papery voice, as she ran her fingers along the spines of the books until he said, *This one*. And she had to read the whole thing, even if it didn't truly interest her. Because she'd learned that, even in the dullest book, a secret message was inside, written just for her. The trick was learning how to find it. But *Frankenstein* felt like the whole thing had been written just for her. It made her feel all electric and charged up.

She read some passages again and again, even underlined them in pencil so she could copy them out later when she sat down to write her report for Gran, as she did for each book she read: *No one can conceive the variety of feelings which bore me onwards, like a hurricane, in the first enthusiasm of success. Life and death appeared to me ideal bounds, which I should first break through, and pour a torrent of light into our dark world.*

She was swinging and reading, and listening to the porch swing creak, creak, creak until the creaking became a song—*torrent of light, torrent of light, torrent of light*—and she closed her eyes to listen harder.

That's when she heard her name being called. From far away at first, then closer. Louder, more frantic: *Vi, Vi, VI!*

She opened her eyes and saw her brother. He was tearing up the driveway, bare-chested. His red T-shirt was wadded up in his hands, wrapping something he cradled carefully as he sprinted toward her. He was crying, his face streaked with mud and tears. Whenever Vi saw him shirtless, she thought her little brother looked like one of those terrible pictures you saw in *National Geographic* of a starving kid: his head too big for his pale, stick-thin body, his ribs pressed up against his skin so you could count each one like the bars of a xylophone.

Eric's tube socks were pulled up nearly to his knobby knees, yellow stripes at the top. His blue Keds were worn through at the toes, his shorts ragged cutoffs of last year's Toughskins jeans. His crazy tangle of curly brown hair bobbed like a strange nest on top of his head. After the long Vermont winter, he was pale as the inside of a potato.

"What happened?" Vi asked, standing up, setting her book down on the swing.

"It's a baby rabbit," he gasped, holding the filthy bundle to his chest, unwrapping it enough for Vi to see the brown fur of the tiny creature. "It's hurt," Eric said, voice cracking. "I think . . . I think it might be dead."

Eric was always saving animals: stray cats, a woodchuck rescued from the jaws of a dog, countless mice and rats from Gran's experiments in the basement—rodents too old to run the mazes, to be conditioned by treats and little electric jolts. Eric felt bad for the animals in the basement and had even freed one—Big White Rat, who Gran thought had managed to escape on his own and now lived in the walls of their house and made appearances from time to time, but could never be caught.

Eric's bedroom had been turned into a crazy zoo full of aquariums and metal cages. He had a whole city of plastic tubes connecting Habitrail cages full of mice running on wheels, building nests with cardboard and newspaper. His room always smelled like cedar shavings, alfalfa, and pee. Gran not only put up with Eric's bedroom zoo but seemed pleased by it, proud even. "You have a way with animals," she would say, smiling at him. "A gentleness and kindness they pick up on."

He knew everything about animals: their Latin names, how they were all ordered by family, genus, species. His hero was Charles Darwin, and Eric said he wanted to grow up and travel around the world studying animals just like Darwin had.

Vi leaped down off the porch steps. "Let's see," she said.

"Is Gran here?" he asked hopefully. Even though she was a human doctor (not even a regular doctor, a psychiatrist), Gran was a miracle worker with hurt animals. She could mend broken bones, do stitches, even minor surgery. She also knew when an animal couldn't be saved and was quick to put it out of its misery with a tiny injection or a rag soaked in chloroform.

"No. She had to go to the Inn."

Vi lifted the folds of the red shirt, put her hand on the rabbit. It gave a twitch when she touched it. She couldn't tell where the blood on the T-shirt was coming from, but it seemed like a lot for such a tiny body. She looked from the rabbit to her brother's worried face.

"Old Mac killed the mama. Got her with his twenty-two. He shot at this guy too, but then it ran into the bushes, and I grabbed him." He bit his lip, more tears sliding down his cheeks. "Mac's probably on his way here right now to finish the job." He swiveled his head around, looking down the driveway, out across the road, at the massive front lawn and gardens that surrounded the Hillside Inn. And sure enough, Mac was heading their way: a stooped scarecrow of a man in a wide-brimmed hat and tan work pants, carrying a rifle. Why Gran would ever let the caretaker at a lunatic hospital walk around with a loaded gun was beyond Vi, but as Gran was fond of pointing out, the Inn was not like any other hospital anywhere.

"What we're doing here," Gran always said, "is revolutionary." And as Vi watched Old Mac, an ex-patient himself, stalking toward them, she thought, *Revolutionary?* as her heart hammered and all the spit in her mouth dried up.

"Take the rabbit into the kitchen," Vi ordered her brother. "Go!"

"What about Mac?" he asked, swallowing hard, eyes wild.

"I'll take care of Mac. Don't worry."

Eric rewrapped the baby rabbit and ran up the porch steps, flung open the front door, and hurried inside.

Vi stood waiting, hands on her hips, watching Old Mac get closer, adjusting the gun in his hands, his jaw working like he was chewing something tough.

"Help you, Mr. MacDermot, sir?" she said when he was close enough to hear.

"Those rabbits are destroying the entire vegetable garden. No more spinach or lettuce left," he said. He spoke slowly, with a slight slur, like the words were thick and heavy in his mouth. *Medication*, Vi thought. Most of the patients at the Inn were on medication. It could make them move and walk funny, have trouble talking.

Mac was a tall man with a weathered face and icy blue eyes. He licked his lips constantly so they were always chapped and raw-looking. "T-t-tell your brother to bring that animal out here. It don't belong in the house."

He took a step forward. Vi held her ground, standing right in the middle of the flagstone walkway to the house, her own roadblock.

She was thirteen years old, tall for her age, but still not even up to this man's shoulders. Gran was always telling her not to slouch, to stand tall and proud, and that's what she did now.

"Mr. MacDermot, I'm sure if you talk to my grandmother, she'll tell you it's okay for animals to be in the house. My brother brings home plenty, and Gran encourages it."

"Does she now?"

"You go ask her yourself. Or, if you like, I can go in and call over to the Inn and ask her to come home, but

I hear she's real busy so she might not be too happy about that."

He frowned at her, ran his pasty tongue over his dry lips, clenched his hands around the rifle. "She'll hear about this," he said.

"Yes, sir," Vi said, smiling as big as she could, like the silly smiley face on the *Have a Nice Day* mug Gran drank out of sometimes—a gift from one of her patients.

"It ain't right," he said, turning to leave. "Keeping a wild thing captive." Old Mac shuffled back down the driveway, muttering to himself, cradling the gun.

Vi went inside, her bare feet cold against the tiled floor of the front hall. She bolted the door, just in case. She let her eyes adjust to the darkness, took in the walnut-paneled walls, the french doors to the right that led into the parlor and the huge tiled fireplace, the curved staircase to the left. The house smelled of dust, old books, lemon furniture polish.

She heard soft mumbling coming from the kitchen. Sometimes Eric had conversations with his animals, made them talk back in different voices. He was really good at voices. Vi thought that maybe when he grew up he'd go to work doing voices for cartoons or *Sesame Street* or something. He could do a perfect Bugs Bunny: *"What's up, doc?"*

"Eric?" she called. "You in the kitchen?"

"Yeah," he snuffled. Then she heard a squeaky rabbit voice say, "So scared."

Vi hurried down the hall toward the kitchen.

Sunlight streamed through the window over the sink. The Crock-Pot hissed on the counter—they were having sloppy joes for dinner and the kitchen was full of the smell of spicy, meaty tomato sauce. Gran had made Jell-O parfaits for dessert—they were chilling in the fridge.

Eric was still cradling the bunny in his shirt.

Vi cleared everything off the kitchen table, pulled the sunflower tablecloth off, and laid down a clean dish towel. "Put him down here and let's take a look," she said.

"Save him, Vi," Eric said, as he set the rabbit on the table. "Please."

Vi touched the rabbit carefully. She turned it over and gave it a quick exam. It didn't look like the gunshot had hit any organs, just grazed the outside of his left haunch. He was holding very still but breathing very fast. "I think he's in shock," Vi said.

"Is that bad?" Eric asked.

She bit her lip. "Sometimes, when you're in shock, your heart can stop."

"Don't let that happen," Eric whimpered.

"I know what to do," Vi said, spinning away from her bare-chested brother. She ran back down the hall, to the enclosed porch that Gran called the sunroom. It was where they played games and did artwork and stored weird stuff that didn't belong anywhere else. It was also where Gran made her gin.

In the corner of the room, Gran's still was set up on a heavy table: a crazy contraption of copper and glass tubes, flasks, and Bunsen burners. Gran was on a never-ending quest to distill the perfect batch of gin. One of the burners was on, and the still bubbled gently. The air smelled tangy and medicinal.

Vi turned away from it, went to the shelves, and found what she was looking for: the battery-powered camping lantern they used when the power went out. She took it down and opened it up, taking out the blocky six-volt battery. She rummaged around in a basket full of odds and ends on the shelf and pulled out some pieces of wire.

"What are you doing?" Eric asked when she brought the battery and wires back to the kitchen. The little rabbit was holding perfectly still under his hand. Its eyes were closed.

"We have to be ready to restart its heart. Give it a shock."

Eric looked baffled.

"Trust me. A body, it's got its own electrical system, right? Gran's explained that a thousand times—how it's all connected: the brain, the nerves. It's what keeps our hearts beating, right? And you know how on *Emergency!* they use those paddles to bring people back? It's like that."

She licked her lips, then attached two wires to the big six-volt battery from their camping lantern. She thought about all of Gran's lessons on circuits and electricity, how Vi had made a lightbulb glow once with the electricity generated from a potato, nails, and wire.

Gran had once said the human body had enough electricity running through it to power a flashlight.

And yes, Vi thought of *Frankenstein*. Not of the book she'd been reading, but the movie. Of Boris Karloff being brought to life in Dr. Frankenstein's lab.

It was her favorite scene in the movie. The storm raging, Dr. Frankenstein lifting the table with the monster up out of the room, into the sky so lightning could strike it, bring the creature to life with a great jolt. Then lowering him back down, seeing the creature's hand twitch: *It's alive, it's alive, it's alive!*

"I don't think I feel a heartbeat," Eric said.

Vi nodded, carefully placed her hands on the sides of its chest.

"Is he dead?"

"Maybe not forever," Vi said. The rabbit was warm under her hands. She could feel it breathing, twitching a little. But she wanted Eric to believe. To believe that she had the power to save it. "We can bring him back."

"Are you sure? Are you sure he's dead?" Eric asked, rocking back and forth, looking smaller than ever.

"Of course I'm sure," Vi snapped. "Now, stand back."

He bit his lip and started to cry again. She looked at him, guilt washing over her. How could she be so cruel? What kind of sister was she?

She turned back to the rabbit and placed the wires attached to the battery on either side of its chest.

"Wake up," she said. "Come back to us."

As if on cue, the rabbit lifted its head, gave a little hop forward.

"It's alive," Vi said.

Eric gave a squeal of delight and threw his arms around her, hugging her tight. "I knew it," he said. "I knew you could do it."

The front door opened with a creak and a thump.

Then the sound of footsteps in the front hall, coming their way.

"Old Mac," Eric whispered, eyes wide and frantic.

THE HELPING HAND OF GOD:
THE TRUE STORY OF THE HILLSIDE INN
By Julia Tetreault, Dark Passages Press, 1980

In the 1970s, the Hillside Inn was widely considered one of the best private psychiatric institutions in New England.

Located on fifty acres atop a forested hill in the small town of Fayeville, Vermont, it housed no more than twenty patients at a time in an environment more like a country estate than a hospital.

The grounds of the Hillside Inn held five buildings. The director's residence was a white wooden Greek Revival structure with a large front porch supported by carved wooden columns. The stables, which hadn't held horses for fifty years, had been renovated into a large arts and crafts area for the patients, complete with a pottery studio and kiln. Next to the stables was the freshly painted red barn, home to maintenance and groundskeeping equipment, as well as the van the Inn used to transport residents on therapeutic field trips. The carriage house had been converted to an apartment where the office manager lived. And then there was the Inn itself: a hulking two-story building of yellow brick with large shuttered windows and a steeply angled gray slate roof. South of the Inn, a large garden allowed patients to work outside in good weather, helping grow a significant portion of the produce used in the dining room. The staff believed strongly in the curative powers of fresh air, sunshine, and a good day's work.

The Inn was built in 1863 as a hospital for Civil War soldiers being shipped home from field hospitals with missing limbs, infections, typhoid fever. In the early 1900s, it had served as a sanatorium for tuberculosis patients where the afflicted were treated with rest and fresh Vermont air. The grounds were beautifully landscaped. The building itself was on the National Register of Historic Places.

With a holistic, humanistic approach, the Inn helped patients "discover who they truly were, heal all parts of themselves, and realize their true human potential" through a carefully curated program of individual therapy, group therapy, meditation, arts and crafts, exercise, music, and gardening. Patients working in the pottery studio produced pieces (mugs, bowls, plates, and vases) sold in local craft galleries and markets. Pottery bearing the Inn's signature mossy-green glaze and the Hillside Inn stamp at the bottom can be found in homes all over New England and is prized by collectors.

The Inn treated the wealthy, but also took in those who could not pay, as well as patients deemed "lost causes" at other facilities. Its therapeutic approach, thought of as radical at the time, seemed to work. The majority of patients who stayed at the Inn not only improved, but learned skills that helped them thrive in the outside world.

Doctors and directors from other facilities all over the country visited the Hillside Inn to see it for themselves. Articles were written on the Inn's innovative approach and rate of success.

To outsiders, the staff at the Inn were pioneers. It was a place of miracles, giving hope to those who had long ago lost it.

The woman behind these miracles was the Inn's director, Dr. Helen Hildreth. Dr. Hildreth had been at the Inn for nearly thirty years and had been director for fifteen. Short in stature and well past the age of traditional retirement by the late 1970s, she was a true pioneer in the field of psychiatry.

"We must always remember," she wrote in an article for the *American Journal of Psychiatry*, "that we are not treating the illness. We are treating the individual. It is our role, as doctors, to see beyond the symptoms and view our patients holistically. Above all else, we must ask ourselves, 'What is this individual's greatest potential, and how can I help him or her achieve it?' "

lizzy

August 19, 2019

Four a.m. and I sprang up to a sitting position in bed, the sheets damp with sweat, listening to the noises of the swamp. Something had woken me. I'd caught the tail end of a strange sound—a wailing sort of groan—that jerked me away from sleep, foggy-headed and unsure what was real and what was still dream.

I'd had another nightmare. Another dream about *her*.

I looked around, orienting myself and taking slow, calming breaths.

I was in my van, in the bed I slept in every night I was on the road, parked at the edge of the swamp. And I was alone.

I checked to see if my little .38 Special Smith & Wesson revolver was there, in its holster on the shelf beside the bed. I touched it, felt myself relax.

I'd spent yesterday out on a little metal boat exploring the swamp with a local named Cyrus, searching for signs of the Honey Island monster—a creature who, according to legend, stood seven feet tall, walked upright on two legs, and was covered in shaggy fur. The color of the fur varied depending on the storyteller—some said brown, some orange, some gray or silver.

The tracks showed webbed toes. Some said the creature's eyes glowed red in the dark.

I'd been at the swamp for the last three days, recording interviews with locals who'd told me stories about the creature, and I'd gotten some good audio of the swamp's sounds. I'd taken some great pictures of gators, ibis, feral hogs, nutrias, and raccoons. But no sign of the Honey Island monster. Now I was lying awake on the bed in my van, all of the windows open, listening to the calls of night birds, splashes, an odd trilling sound.

The air was heavy, humid and thick in my lungs.

I heard it again, the sound that had woken me: a far-off groan.

Alligator? Hog?

Or could it be the monster? I held still, listening, then reached for my digital recorder, mic, and headphones.

One of the benefits of staying in a van is that everything is within easy reach—you're always only a step or two away from whatever you need. And I kept my recording equipment on a shelf right next to the bed.

I slipped on my headphones, flipped the mic and recorder on, held my breath, listening, hoping to catch the groan again. I pushed back the curtain and peered out the window at the starlit night.

I got out of bed, still holding the recording equipment and grabbing my headlamp and the little gun, just in case. I took the two steps to the side door, sliding it open and letting the moist air hit me. I stepped out into the night, walking toward the water. Cypress trees draped in Spanish moss stood out in the swamp like huge sentries wearing tattered, ghostly clothing. Frogs and crickets sang. Something splashed. The air smelled slightly rotten, primordial, like death and life all mixed up together. As I moved closer, a shadow moved along the edge; I held my breath, flipped on my headlamp, and spotted an alligator slipping into the brackish green water. He went under so that only his eyes were visible, watching me.

Eric would love this, I thought, locking eyes with the gator.

But Eric was halfway across the country.

Eric wasn't even Eric anymore.

"Not Eric," I said out loud without thinking, capturing the sound of my own voice on the recorder.

Idiot.

The alligator sank under and swam away.

We'd changed our names after what had happened. Eric became Charles (after his hero Charles Darwin). He didn't grow up to be a naturalist, a veterinarian, or a zookeeper like we'd always thought he would. Charlie lived in Iowa and owned an auto dealership. He had thinning hair, a paunch, and high blood pressure (too much beer and fast food), a daughter in college and another in high school. His wife was named Cricket (her real name, believe it or not) and they loved each other very much. They lived in a blue ranch house on a dead-end street where they knew all their neighbors and held potlucks and backyard barbecues. It made me uncomfortable to visit him there, as if I were visiting a sitcom set, but after all we'd gone through, my brother deserved safety and happiness. I was glad for Eric—no, Charles . . . I was always doing that, thinking of him by his old name. It suited him much better than Charlie, or even worse, *Chuck,* as Cricket sometimes called him, like he was a pile of ground meat or a furry animal that destroyed gardens.

The name I'd chosen for myself was Lizzy. I'd picked it because Gran's middle name was Elizabeth and I felt I owed her that much, to carry some piece of her with me. I needed a last name too, and I chose Shelley, because, well, because of Mary Shelley, of course.

So I was Lizzy Shelley now. I was fifty-three years old, my hair going gray. And I made my living hunting monsters.

I had a blog and now a popular podcast, named for my long-ago childhood project: *The Book of Monsters*. I'd been a member of the team on last season's series *Monsters Among Us* and featured in the documentary *Shadow People*. I'd given lectures at colleges on the role of the monster in contemporary society. I criss-crossed the country hunting Sasquatches, shapeshifters, lake monsters, cave-dwelling goblins, vampires, werewolves—all manner of cryptids and bogeymen. People posted on the forums on my website every day giving me leads, sending photos, telling their own stories of close encounters, begging me to come investigate. Between advertising, sponsors, affiliate links, the TV gigs, book royalties, and the branded merchandise I sold, I made more than enough to cover my expenses and hit the road as often as I liked, moving on to the next town, the next monster.

My mission was to do everything I could to get the message out loud and clear: *Monsters are real and living among us.*

But the Honey Island monster so far had not provided any proof of that. I worked my way along the edge of the water, listening to the sounds my microphone picked up, the chorus of the swamp: another splash, frogs croaking low, two owls calling plaintively back and forth, crickets rubbing their legs together in shrill song. So many creatures, such an alive place. Again I wished my brother—not the man he'd become, but the little boy he once was—were here to listen with me.

I picked my way along the edge of the swamp, sweeping my headlamp back and forth carefully so as not to surprise a gator, until I got to Cyrus's metal boat, moored at a rickety wooden dock. I climbed aboard, made myself comfortable in the captain's seat, and waited, listening, searching the darkness for shadows. At last the sun started to come up, making the sky glow a fiery orange. The monster hadn't made another sound. But I imagined him out there, watching and waiting. Finally I headed back to the van.

The van was my home away from home and had cost a ridiculous amount of money but had been totally worth it. It was a high-ceilinged Ford Transit that I'd paid a custom-van-build company to turn into the ultimate monster-hunting machine. I had a raised loft bed with lots of storage space underneath for clothing and gear and a small chemical toilet. Along the driver's-side wall was my tiny kitchen: a twelve-volt fridge, a sink with a foot pump that pulled water from a six-gallon water container and drained into a bucket, and a one-burner butane stove for cooking. I carried one coffee mug, one titanium spork, one bowl, one plate, a kitchen knife, a can opener, a corkscrew, and a one-quart saucepan. My meals on the road were simple: instant oatmeal every morning and canned soup, chili, or beans for lunch and dinner. I supplemented with fresh fruit and vegetables and ate peanut butter and jelly sandwiches when I didn't feel up to cooking.

On the passenger side of the van was a work zone,

a small desk set up with my laptop, beneath it a file cabinet and space to store my recording equipment. There were two solar panels on the roof, two more in a suitcase that I set up outside, and a portable power station with a built-in battery and inverter on the right side of the desk. I carried a small Honda generator and gas can to cover me for the days when the sun didn't generate enough power to keep things up and running. With both Wi-Fi and cell phone boosters, I could remain connected and self-sufficient for days, even weeks on end, no matter how far off the beaten path monster hunting took me.

"You live like a woman on the run," Eric (Charlie!) had told me not long ago. "You're never home more than a few days at a time, always on the move." I'd just smiled, bit my lip to keep from saying, *And you, little brother, live like a man stuck in quicksand.*

I set the recording equipment and headlamp on the desk and turned to the stove to heat water for coffee, which I made with instant powder from a jar. Once I'd downed the first gulp of thick, sludgy coffee, I turned around again, pulled out the stool under my desk, and flipped open my laptop. I figured I'd spend a little time getting the eyewitness interviews and swamp sounds imported from the digital recorder onto the laptop and start editing. Then I'd need to record my introduction, talking about the history of the monster, my own experiences in the swamp. I'd tell my audience about the groan that had woken me from sleep, about how I'd gone out to search and startled a gator. I was good at this: telling stories, building suspense.

My computer booted up and I took another sip of coffee, then clicked over to check my email before starting to work on the podcast.

First I heard the blood thrumming in my ears.

All the hairs on my body stood up as if lightning had struck close by.

An alert had come in.

I clicked through and scanned the article.

GREEN MOUNTAIN FREE PRESS
August 18, 2019

GIRL MISSING FROM CHICKERING ISLAND

Police are searching for 13-year-old Lauren Schumacher, who was last seen at her family's summer cottage on Chickering Island on the afternoon of August 15. Her family believes she may have run away. She reportedly told friends she'd met the Island's legendary ghost, Rattling Jane, just before her disappearance.

Schumacher was wearing cutoff denim shorts, a black hooded sweatshirt, and black Converse sneakers. She is 5'3", weighs 100 pounds, and has brown eyes and blond hair with dyed purple tips. Anyone with information is asked to call the Vermont State Police.

I read the article, then reread it. I searched for any other news about the case, but only came up with the same information.

I opened the calendar to double-check.

Yes.

The little tingle at the back of my neck turned into a buzz.

August 15 had been the full moon.

The girls always went missing on a full moon.

How many girls had it been now?

I didn't need to check my notes: nine. Lauren Schumacher from Chickering Island would make ten. Always in a different part of the country. Always on a full moon. Always from a town with its very own monster. And always, just before disappearing, the missing girl had told someone she'd had an encounter with the local legend.

And always, it was a girl who didn't raise big alarms. A girl from a troubled family; a girl who hung out with the wrong crowd; a girl who skipped school and smoked cigarettes; a girl everyone assumed would come to no good; a girl who had every reason to run away.

A coincidence, some would say: the girls, the monsters, the full moons.

But it was no coincidence.

I was sure that this was the work of one very clever, crafty, shapeshifting monster.

The most dangerous monster of all, the one I'd been chasing my whole life, who always managed to elude me. Except in dreams. She always came back in dreams. In real life, I'd gotten close a time or two. But only because the monster had let me. It was a game we played. Cat and mouse. Hide-and-seek. Just like we had when we were kids.

Me and my once-upon-a-time sister.